Fiona Higgins is the author of *The Mothers' Group* (Allen & Unwin, 2012) and *Love in the Age of Drought* (Pan Macmillan, 2009). She lives in Bali with her husband and three children.

www.fionahiggins.com.au
www.facebook.com/fionahigginsauthor

**Also by Fiona Higgins**

*The Mothers' Group*

**Non-fiction**

*Love in the Age of Drought*

FIONA HIGGINS

First published in 2014



Allen & Unwin
83 Alexander Street
Crows Nest NSW 2065
Australia
Phone: (61 2) 8425 0100
Email: info@allenandunwin.com
Web: www.allenandunwin.com

Cataloguing-in-Publication details are available
from the National Library of Australia
www.trove.nla.gov.au

ISBN 978 1 74331 026 7

Text design by Lisa White
Set in 11.5/18 pt Minion Pro by Bookhouse, Sydney
Printed and bound in Australia by Griffin Press

10 9 8 7 6 5 4 3 2 1

The paper in this book is FSC® certified. FSC® promotes environmentally responsible, socially beneficial and economically viable management of the world's forests.

*For Melissa and Amanda,*
*the best of sisters*

*De médico e de louco todo mundo tem um pouco*

Of doctors and madmen we all have a bit

Brazilian proverb

# 1

Blow Queens

Paula squinted at the words on the screen, emblazoned in red font across the top of the Facebook post. Worse still, the image beneath: an erect penis, with multiple lines of lipstick streaked along its shaft, like coloured quoits stacked on a wooden pin.

Then, the shocking caption bearing her daughter's name: *Look what Caitlin McInnes and Amy Robertson got up to last weekend.*

'That's . . . disgusting.' A suffocating heat was rising in her chest and rampaging up her neck.

The school principal turned the computer screen back towards him.

'I wanted you to come in person, Mrs McInnes, for obvious reasons.'

'Who . . . who did this?' she stuttered.

Mr Nelson pressed his lips into a terse line.

'We can't confirm that yet. The post appeared last night on Charlotte Kennedy's Facebook page. Do you know her?'

*Everyone* knew Charlotte Kennedy, a popular Year Eleven student widely predicted to be elected school captain next year.

'The author of the post is James Addams,' the principal continued, 'but we don't have a student of that name here. I've spoken to Charlotte and she's never heard of him. We've lodged a formal complaint with Facebook, requesting the post be removed immediately, but more than a hundred students have already "liked" it. Mostly boys in their senior years, unfortunately.'

'Oh, that's horrible.' Paula felt physically sick.

Mr Nelson studied her for a moment. 'Does Caitlin have a boyfriend, Mrs McInnes?'

She shook her head, incredulous. 'She's *fourteen*. Catie's more interested in soccer than boys.' Her daughter was one of the school's rising sport stars.

Mr Nelson didn't appear persuaded. 'And has Caitlin been herself lately? Has she been fighting with any of her friends?'

Paula's mind spun, trying to recall anything unusual over the past few weeks. 'No . . . she's been her normal, happy self. If something was wrong, I'm sure she would've told me.'

Her words didn't seem to register with the principal.

'We've seen cyber-bullying in senior years before,' he said, 'but never in Year Nine.'

*Cyber-bullying?*

Paula had only ever conceived of this happening to *other* people's children. Not in middle-class suburban Melbourne. Not at Burwood Secondary College. And certainly not in her family.

'But Caitlin doesn't have any enemies.'

'The thing is, Mrs McInnes,' Mr Nelson interrupted, 'we need to get to the bottom of *why* your daughter and Amy Robertson have been targeted. Presumably there's a reason.'

'Have you spoken to Caitlin yet?' she asked, hugging her handbag to her chest. As if it were her teenage daughter, at risk of slipping out of her grasp.

'Yes. She's very upset, understandably.'

'Where is she? I want to see her.'

A protective surge propelled Paula out of her chair; she needed to take Caitlin in her arms and comfort her. The winsome child who'd shadowed her for years, clambering onto her lap and into her bed, tugging at her hands and heartstrings. An extension of Paula's own body, before morphing into a lanky and enigmatic teenager—beautiful, confident and talented—almost overnight. And yet, more vulnerable than ever to all manner of threats that Paula couldn't bear to contemplate. Drugs. Sex. Unwanted pregnancy. The unspeakable risk of so much potential being squandered before her young life had even really begun.

'Caitlin's with the school counsellor now, they'll be finished after lunch.' Mr Nelson stood up, as if to show Paula out. 'You're on canteen duty today, aren't you?'

'Not anymore,' she said quietly. 'Will you please call Caitlin *now*.'

'I see.' Mr Nelson reached for the telephone on his desk. 'Then I'll have to tell Leanne you're not coming.'

*Leanne*. It was almost a threat.

The cantankerous canteen manager at Burwood Secondary College was a person with whom Paula would never ordinarily associate. But she'd endured her every Thursday lunchtime for the past nine months, as an act of goodwill towards the school.

The principal spoke quietly into his telephone, then walked to his office door. 'Take a seat out here, Mrs McInnes,' he said, opening it for her. 'I'll let you know when Caitlin arrives.'

Before she could reply, he'd closed the door after her.

Feeling like a truant schoolgirl, Paula sat down on the green leather sofa.

'Would you like a cup of tea?' a kindly-faced secretary asked, looking up from her work.

'That'd be nice, thanks,' Paula replied, without knowing why. She really didn't feel like anything at all.

'How do you have it?'

'Just white, please.'

The secretary disappeared into a kitchenette, returning promptly with a steaming mug.

'There now,' she said, passing it to Paula. 'Careful, it's hot.'

The secretary took her place behind the desk again and began to engage Paula in benign small talk. The senior toilets had been repainted, the new shade-cloth over the bubblers was working well, and wasn't the kitchen garden coming along nicely? Paula felt barely able to conceal her own turmoil, but tried to nod at appropriate intervals. Her mind was preoccupied by the grotesque Facebook post: how could her daughter be connected to it? With her friend Amy, too?

Could it possibly be *real*?

She screwed her eyes shut at the thought.

During her earlier years of schooling, Caitlin had always been quiet and studious, with 'exceptional athletic potential' according to her teachers. She'd clearly inherited her father's genes in that regard, because Paula herself had never been sporty. Caitlin was a natural at almost any athletic activity: captain of the Under 15s netball team, pitcher on the softball team, striker on the girls' soccer team. And she'd fulfilled all these roles with an endearing modesty, up until three months ago, when she'd fallen in with a new peer group. These were the 'cool' girls, apparently, the popular and pretty ones, some of whom were on Caitlin's netball team.

Since then, Paula had detected a shift in her daughter's attitude; she'd become a little more obstinate, more image-conscious, and more susceptible, somehow, to the influence of others. Her new friends spent entire weekends together at slumber parties, shopping at multi-level malls, or watching teen chick-flicks at the movies. When they weren't together, they sent endless messages and tweets to each other, about banalities that could almost certainly wait until they met again at school.

Paula didn't particularly warm to any of them, except for Amy, the goalie on the soccer team, who seemed far more sensible than the rest. Caitlin and Amy had struck up a close friendship born of their mutual love of soccer, and regularly spent hours in the backyard playing striker and goalie. Amy was polite and down to earth—which only made the Facebook post all the more confounding. She simply wasn't a trouble-maker, unlike some of Caitlin's *other* friends. Always flicking their long hair over their shoulders, glossing their lips and pouting at the older boys.

Was I like that once? Paula sometimes wondered. She couldn't remember much about being fourteen; it was, after all, twenty-five years ago. What she *could* recall was an acute self-consciousness about her maturing body. Breasts and hips and buttocks straining against clothes suddenly grown too small. A stumpy-legged child one year, the object of male attention the next. She'd found the rapid transition confusing, and a little alarming. She wasn't sure she wanted men to look at her that way, their eyes roaming across her body. But girls nowadays were different—or some of Catie's peer group were, at least. Always coveting male attention, in their too-short skirts and long white socks pulled up over bronzed calves. Their ear and navel piercings, sleek manes of hair, fake tans and tattoos. Provocative girl-women, with the trappings of adulthood inscribed on a child's body.

*But they're just being teenage girls*, her husband insisted. *That's what teenage girls do.*

*As if you'd know*, Paula was sometimes tempted to snap at Hamish. *You, who grew up with no sisters and went to an all-boys school. Since when were you an expert on teenage girls?*

Hamish.

Paula looked at the secretary, still nattering away.

'Excuse me,' she said, standing up from the sofa. 'I need to make a call.' Paula slipped out into the corridor and dialled Hamish's number.

It rang out, as it usually did.

Hamish was rarely without his phone, but always too busy to answer it.

It's the middle of his working day, she thought. What was she hoping he'd do? Drop everything, bolt to his car and drive over to the school? He couldn't get to most parent–teacher evenings, let alone an unscheduled meeting at the principal's office.

Paula stuffed her telephone into her handbag and stepped back into the waiting area. The secretary, she was relieved to note, was now busy with a telephone call.

She resumed her seat and began composing a message to Hamish.

*Please call me ASAP. Issue at school.*

It wouldn't necessarily raise him. Hamish was a willing slave to his job at Crossroads Cars, the biggest corporate-fleet rental company in the country. He'd joined as a mechanic more than ten years back, steadily working his way up from the shop floor into management. But his considerable professional success had come at a personal cost.

A long time ago—it felt like forever, now—they'd done things *together.* Reading the weekend newspapers on a Saturday morning over a leisurely café brunch. Going to the cinema on cheap Tuesdays, then debating the critics' ratings on the way home. Rambling along the beach at Brighton on a Sunday, doing fitness sessions on the sand. Hamish playing the personal trainer—tall, broad-shouldered, blond—to her curvy, brunette trainee. Enrolling in a host of adult-education courses at the local community college, just for the hell of it: ballroom dancing, wine appreciation, organic gardening. They'd especially loved the course called Plan Your Own Ultimate Adventure, creating a scrapbook of dream travel goals: hiking in the Andes, a safari in Kenya, a campervan tour around Australia. But they'd collapsed into hysterical laughter during the Yoga for Couples course, prompting the teachers—a long-haired pair who called themselves Yoni and Linga—to question whether they were 'truly ready to trust'.

They'd had *fun* together, before the kids arrived, and for a few years afterwards. And then, incrementally, their interests as a couple had taken a back seat. As the children had grown and changed, they'd demanded more—not less—of Paula's time, while Hamish's work responsibilities had expanded. Gradually their focus had shifted from enjoying life together to dividing and conquering it instead. It made sense for Hamish to prioritise money-making, and for Paula to cultivate their home life. But spontaneity had been sacrificed along the way.

For months, Paula had wanted to talk it over with Hamish. To propose that they reinstate Saturday date nights and once-a-month movies. To suggest taking a community-college course together again or, now that the kids were older, even begin planning a trip to one of their dream destinations. But her best intentions had been derailed—primarily by Hamish's long working hours, which encroached on their weeknights and weekends. Not to mention her sneaking suspicion that Hamish wouldn't be all that receptive anymore. She could anticipate his responses already.

*Other people would kill to have our life.*

*It's just a busy phase.*

*Someone's got to make the money.*

'Mrs McInnes?'

The secretary's voice startled Paula.

'Mr Nelson will see you now,' she said, motioning towards the principal's door. 'Caitlin will be along soon.'

Paula took a seat at the polished teak desk, noticing that Mr Nelson's face was slightly pink.

'Mrs McInnes, this is a very *unfortunate* matter,' he began. 'I've given it some thought and may I suggest that Caitlin takes some time off school? Just while we investigate, at least until Facebook removes the post. All of next week, and probably the week after.'

It wasn't really a suggestion, it was a directive.

Paula blanched. 'So, let me get this clear. Someone—we don't know who—puts a photo of uncertain origin on Facebook with Caitlin's name on it.' Her voice wavered a little. 'And on the basis of that, you're going to suspend my daughter for a fortnight while you *investigate*? That doesn't seem very fair on Caitlin.'

The principal pulled his chair closer to the desk. 'I'm not *suspending* her, Mrs McInnes. I understand you're upset, but I'm trying to make things easier for Caitlin. The image has been circulated through the senior *and* junior years.'

Paula glared at Mr Nelson's poker face. 'But *Caitlin* is the victim here.'

There was a knock at the door—a timid, apologetic sort of tap—and the door opened.

The principal looked relieved. 'Mrs Papadopolous.'

The counsellor's thick hair, grey and wiry at the temples, was pinned in a loose bun on top of her head. She nodded at Paula over tortoiseshell spectacles, then turned to Caitlin, who stood behind her as if cowering.

'Are you alright, dear?' she asked.

Caitlin's eyes were red-rimmed and puffy. She looked at Mr Nelson fearfully, before catching sight of her mother. Instantly she ran across the office, throwing herself into Paula's lap like a much younger child.

'Oh, Caitlin,' Paula whispered, pulling her daughter close. She smoothed Caitlin's long blonde ponytail beneath her fingers. *My beautiful little girl.*

'Sit down please, Caitlin.' Mr Nelson nodded at the empty chair next to Paula.

Caitlin reluctantly moved onto the seat.

'Thank you, Mrs Papadopolous.' He dismissed the counsellor with a nod, before fixing his gaze on Caitlin.

'Was it helpful talking to Mrs Papadopolous?'

Caitlin shrugged.

Mr Nelson waited, then, when it was clear Caitlin had no intention of speaking, prompted, 'Is there anything else you'd like to tell us?'

'No, Mr Nelson.' Tears welled in her blue eyes.

The principal passed Caitlin a box of tissues.

She took one. 'I haven't done . . . *anything* to anyone. Amy hasn't either.'

Mr Nelson leaned back in his chair. 'Caitlin, we've reported the photo to Facebook, but I'm not sure how long it's going to take for them to act.' He turned a pen over in his hands. 'I think you'll probably agree, it's best for you to stay home for a while. I've asked Amy to do the same.'

Caitlin looked up at her mother. 'Yes, it's so *embarrassing*.' She hid her face in her hands.

Paula put an arm around Caitlin's shoulders, feeling outraged and overwhelmed. Who on earth would do this to her daughter?

Mr Nelson stood up. 'Mrs McInnes, I'll contact you when we have more information. In the meantime, you might like to consider some extra counselling for Caitlin. Mrs Papadopolous is available if you need her.'

'Thank you.' Paula helped Caitlin up.

'Do you have all your things, Caitlin?' he asked. 'Nothing left in your locker?'

'No, Mr Nelson.'

'Goodbye for now, then.' The principal ushered them to the door and closed it behind them. Too abruptly, Paula thought. She hovered there for a moment, contemplating the pompous gold lettering on the door. *Mr Geoffrey J. Nelson, Principal.* She wanted to tear it right off.

'Come on, Catie,' she said, nodding at Mr Nelson's secretary as they passed. Paula could feel the woman's eyes following them down the corridor.

They crossed the empty playground in silence, their shoes crunching on the gravel. It was spitting with rain, and the boughs of the majestic oak tree near the main entrance were creaking quietly in the wind. After weeks of welcome spring sunshine, winter coolness had inexplicably returned in the latter half of October.

Caitlin dragged her feet across the playground, weighed down by her school bag, sports kit and art folder.

'Here, let me help you.' Paula reached for the school bag.

'Are you angry with me, Mum?'

'Should I be?'

Caitlin's lower lip trembled.

'Why would someone just post a photo like that out of the blue?' asked Paula. 'It's got your name on it, and Amy's too. What am I *supposed* to think?'

Caitlin began to cry softly.

'Look, I'm sorry. Come here.' Paula put her arms around her daughter. 'Let's go home and regroup. We'll work it out.'

They'd almost reached the school gate when they heard a piercing wolf-whistle. Turning automatically, they saw a group of senior boys milling around the gymnasium.

'Hey, cocksucker!'

Paula flinched. It was difficult to determine who had called out.

*'Caitlin cocksucker!'*

Caitlin looked mortified.

'Let's go.' Paula shepherded her daughter through the gate.

A teacher emerged from the gymnasium and corralled the boys inside.

Caitlin wept all the way home, her slim body shaking. As Paula steered her yellow hatchback through the streets of Glen Waverley, she realised she'd never take the same route without recalling this exact moment. Two o'clock on Friday 19 October—when Facebook's intrusion into their lives skyrocketed beyond daily disagreements about screen time.

As they pulled into their driveway, Paula spotted a small figure hunched at the bottom of the stairs leading up to their double-storey weatherboard home. *Lachie.* She practically leaped out of the car. Caitlin remained slumped in the front seat.

'Lachie, sweetheart, are you alright?' Paula crouched down in front of him. 'How did you get home?'

'I walked.'

'What, the whole way?'

He nodded.

'Someone showed me the Facebook photo at lunchtime. I was so grossed out I came home.'

'Why didn't you *call* me?'

'I did,' he said, in an injured tone. 'You *never* answer your phone.'

'I must have been with Mr Nelson.'

Her son had a point, Paula thought. All too often she temporarily lost her telephone; under the car seat, behind a cushion, or deep in her handbag. And if she silenced it for a meeting—like she'd done with Mr Nelson—she almost always forgot to reactivate it afterwards. It drove her husband mad, but Paula wasn't fazed by being unreachable—unlike Hamish, whose phone was virtually grafted onto his hand. On the odd occasion he misplaced it, Hamish would become tetchy, like an alcoholic deprived of drink.

'I'm sorry, Lachie,' Paula said, patting his knee. 'It's been a tough morning.'

Caitlin emerged from the car, dragging her sports kit behind her.

'I'm going to soccer practice this afternoon,' she announced, lifting her chin defiantly.

'Catie, no.' Paula stood up from the step. 'That's not a good idea.'

'Why not?' Caitlin hurled the kit onto the lawn.

'Because the whole school's calling you a cocksucker,' said Lachie.

'Lachlan!' Paula admonished.

Caitlin stared at her brother.

'Did you do it?' he asked.

'Do *what*?' spat Caitlin. 'I can't *believe* you'd even ask, dipshit.'

She stormed up the stairs to the front door.

'Catie!' Paula followed her and unlocked it.

Pushing past her mother, Caitlin ran down the hallway and slammed the bedroom door.

Paula turned back to her son, unsure what to do. 'Would you . . . like some afternoon tea, Lachie?' She felt mildly ridiculous for resorting to conventional maternal overtures.

'Okay.' Lachlan jogged up the stairs. 'I'm hungry.'

Since he'd turned thirteen, Lachie's appetite had become insatiable. On return from school, he'd often demolish half a loaf of bread or several bowls of breakfast cereal.

Lachie dropped his school bag near the front door, then flopped down onto the lounge-room floor.

In the kitchen, Paula set about preparing a peanut butter sandwich and a glass of milk.

'Come and sit up.'

'Can't I have it in here?' Lachie objected.

He'd already turned on the games console; she could hear its irritating mechanical melody.

'No, you may *not*.' She was tired of this argument, more so this afternoon. 'Just sit up now.'

He sauntered into the kitchen, perched on a bar stool and began to devour the sandwich.

'Do you'—she could feel herself blushing—'want to talk about what's happened?' Hamish had only recently had a 'man-to-man' chat with Lachlan. She'd been too uncomfortable with the idea of discussing sex with her thirteen-year-old son to broach the subject herself.

'Nah.' He chewed and swallowed. 'It's a fake picture, right? Doesn't even look like a real dick to me. More like a dildo.'

'Lachlan!' Paula had no idea the word 'dildo' was part of her son's lexicon.

He sniggered. 'Don't freak out, Mum.'

Swallowing several hunks of sandwich and draining the milk, he pushed back the bar stool.

'No computer games until your homework's done,' she said.

'Don't have any.' He ambled towards the lounge room.

'I find that hard to believe, Lachlan.'

He turned to her, his hands pressed together in the prayer position. 'C'mon, Mum. Just thirty minutes. I'll do my homework after, promise.'

Her resolve wavered. 'Okay. Just make sure it's thirty minutes and no more.'

He grinned, rushing forward to hug her, before almost as quickly pulling away again. But these were the contradictions of a thirteen-year-old boy, she was discovering. One minute craving Mum, the next minute ignoring her.

She watched him stroll into the lounge room, all knobbly knees and pale, ungainly limbs. He was not nearly as physically coordinated as his sister; not yet, anyway. *But that might change*, she often told Hamish, who was baffled by Lachie's preference for cerebral activities like chess, computer games and Lego. The fact that Lachie still loved Lego worried Hamish, despite the fact that his creations were complex and elaborate. They're *kiddy* blocks, Hamish would sniff, having once again failed to entice Lachie outdoors. He might be the next Jørn Utzon, she'd reply.

Paula put the kettle on.

I should check on Caitlin, she thought wearily, but I need a cup of tea first. And a chocolate biscuit or two. Lately it had been three or four, as evidenced by the extra rolls of flesh around her stomach.

'Pauuula!'

Her father had waited the mandatory ten minutes before pouncing.

She walked down the stairs to the laundry and saw him, loitering hopefully at the glass sliding door. Beyond it, three steps led to a steep side path that wound its way up into their large, flat backyard. He was wearing his mandatory gardening uniform: green gumboots, grey tracksuit and a Richmond Tigers football scarf. Tiny flecks of soil had settled in his shaggy white eyebrows and moustache. His blue eyes twinkled and his skin was ruddy from the wind. Like Santa in civvies, Paula thought, smiling. She unbolted the door.

'Hi, Dad.' She couldn't resist planting a kiss on his cheek.

He grinned. 'Time for a cuppa?'

'Sure.'

'Your place or mine?' he asked, as he always did, referring to the caravan parked in the backyard.

'I've just put the kettle on. Come on up.'

'Good-o.' He slipped off his gumboots, then bounded up the stairs two at a time. He was spritely for seventy, more like a man ten years his junior.

'You've got a spring in your step, Dad,' she remarked, following him into the kitchen.

'Picked a trifecta at Moonee Valley this morning.'

He reached into his top pocket and removed a small leather-bound notebook—his 'scribbler', as he called it—and flashed some calculations at Paula. 'If I'd put six dollars on it, I could've won twelve grand. Now *that* would've sorted out those school fees of yours, I reckon.'

Paula laughed. One of her father's interests was horse-racing, but he staunchly refused to place a bet. He claimed to have developed a foolproof formula for picking winners and studied the form daily, but described gambling as 'one of the worst things ever to happen to humanity'. His own father, Paula's grandfather, had gambled away the family's savings not long after the Second World War, and they'd been forced to rely on charity and welfare to survive. As the youngest of five children, her father could still remember the day he'd received his first pair of new shoes: he'd been sixteen years old and about to start work as an apprentice butcher. Before that, he'd been forced to wear the ill-fitting hand-me-downs of siblings and generous neighbours, a fact he credited with causing his bulbous bunions. These days, he got around in the only shoes capable of accommodating his misshapen feet: a pair of thongs in summer, or gumboots in winter.

'What's wrong, sweetie?' he asked, as soon as they sat down.

Paula marvelled at how her father could intuit her mood. Prior to her mother's death a year ago, their relationship had been affectionate but distant. In her youth, he'd always been too busy in the butchery; the blue and white signage above Jones Quality Meats was an enduring image of Paula's childhood. She could still remember the smell of her father as he walked in the door of an evening, the pungent aroma of blood and bone, overlaid with hospital-grade bleach. Not altogether offensive—she never failed to run and throw her arms around him—but pervasive nonetheless. Even now, eight years after he'd sold the business, Paula sometimes fancied she could still smell the odour on certain items of his clothing, despite all the laundering her mother had done to expunge it.

Her mother, Jeanette, had been the dominant partner in the relationship for as long as Paula could remember. The natural anchor of the family, she'd run the household, looked after the children, and done practically *everything* for her husband: choosing his clothes, issuing instructions, even speaking for him. Her mother had been vivacious, charismatic and the life of social gatherings, with an occasionally volcanic temper. By contrast, her father had been soft-spoken, measured and loath to offer an opinion. Paula had always attributed this to a natural passivity on his part, a certain laziness even. It had taken her mother's death for her father to begin to reveal more of himself to Paula: his capacity for engaging conversation, his lively sense of humour, a genuine interest in the world beyond himself.

A month after her mother died, her father had moved into the second-hand caravan parked in their backyard.

'It's just a temporary measure,' she'd explained to Hamish, who'd been using the caravan as an after-hours office. 'Until we're sure Dad can cope by himself.'

Hamish had assented grudgingly. While always respectful of his father-in-law, they seemed to lack the common ground so crucial to male bonding. Sid loved Aussie Rules and cricket; Hamish preferred cycling and boxing. Sid was proud of his four decades as a master butcher; Hamish, by contrast, had eschewed his tradesman roots and manoeuvred his way into senior management as quickly as possible. Sid loved nothing more than a 'cuppa and a chin wag', expansive discussions about current affairs, politics and life in general; Hamish had little time for idle chatter and less for debate, preferring instead a solitary whisky in front of the television before completing his evening's work.

Paula needn't have worried about her father's capacity to cope in the wake of his wife's death, it turned out; Sid embraced his newfound independence with gusto. Not long after moving into the caravan, he joined the Waverley RSL and took trips with their day club to scenic locations such as the Dandenongs, Phillip Island and Ballarat. He maintained his long-standing membership of the Doncaster Rotary Club, which he'd first joined as the local butcher in 1972. And then, six months after her mother's death, he embarked on the complete replanting of their backyard. Referring to a moon calendar he taped to the caravan door, he transformed it into a flourishing patchwork of flowers and vegetables. He rose early for his 'daily constitutional', always stopping to chat with passers-by as he power-walked around the neighbourhood. When finally given the chance to speak, it seemed, her father had plenty to say. It was as if her mother had gagged him for forty years, Paula sometimes reflected.

And so Sid's temporary living arrangement in the caravan had morphed into a permanent one, despite Hamish's occasional hints that her father should return to the retirement village.

*Sid's such a social animal, he'll love it back there.*

*The ratio of men to women is stacked in his favour.*

*Why don't you suggest it and see what he says?*

Paula always deflected such comments; she couldn't countenance the idea of sending her father back to an empty one-bedroom unit at Greenleaves. Besides, she was enjoying getting to know him, at long last.

Sid jiggled the teabags floating in their mugs. 'Paula, I can tell something's wrong.'

'I've had a terrible day with Caitlin, Dad. It's not something you'd understand.'

'Try me.'

She hesitated, then said, 'Okay. A pornographic image has been uploaded to Facebook and it's got Caitlin's name on it.'

He nibbled at the edge of a chocolate biscuit, seemingly processing this information.

She helped herself to another *Tim Tam*, watching him.

'And *is* it a picture of Caitlin?'

'No, it's a picture of . . . well, it's obviously some sort of revolting joke.'

Her father stirred milk into his tea and pushed Paula's mug towards her. 'Who's the idiot responsible?'

'The school's investigating. They've got no idea, as far as I can tell.'

He blew on his tea. 'Well, I guess they'll find out soon enough. And then there'll be consequences.'

'There already *are* consequences,' she said, her voice quivering. 'The whole school's calling Caitlin names. The kids have shared the photo again and again.'

'It's gone virus then?'

She almost smiled. 'Viral, Dad. Yes.'

'Hmmm. That's the problem with the internet, isn't it? It's like the genie in a bottle. Once it's popped out, you can't stuff it back in.' He reached across and squeezed Paula's hand.

She noticed the dirt under his fingernails; it was a hygiene habit that riled Hamish, whose own nails were clean half-moons. She was sometimes tempted to taunt Hamish: *You used to be a tradie, but now you can't stand dirty fingernails?* Yet he still insisted on driving a dual-cab ute as some kind of testament to his blue-collar roots. Hamish was contrary, she'd concluded, often saying and doing things that were irreconcilable. In the early years of their relationship, she'd called him spontaneous, innovative, entrepreneurial. Now she just called it for what it was: inconsistency.

'You're a good mother, Paula,' her father said. 'You do a terrific job with the kids. *You'll* know what's best.'

She sipped at her tea, unconvinced. How *could* she know what was best, as the product of a different generation? The late-twentieth-century childhood *she'd* enjoyed, some thirty years earlier, had seemed much simpler. An environment uninterrupted by the demands of social media, with far fewer distractions competing with parental influence. The power of the peer group had always been substantial, but nowhere near as potent as in her children's world of Facebook, Twitter, Instagram and Kik. Nowadays, it seemed to Paula, there were a thousand potential channels for young people to chat and post, pose and expose, name and shame—all of it enabled by the ubiquitous presence of the smartphone.

In the early days of her children's social-media usage, Paula had tried to find a balance, embracing the zeitgeist while setting parameters. 'Friending' Caitlin on Facebook, for example, then monitoring her posts. But Paula soon found that there were only so many hours in a day to scroll through the idle chitchat of teenagers online. And on some fundamental level, the technology felt intricate and inaccessible; a time-consuming tool of which Paula tired, inevitably, before reverting to more traditional methods of communication.

*You can't beat face-to-face catch-ups or phone calls,* she heard herself repeating to her children. All the while recognising that for *their* generation, social media was no longer a *tool*: it was the global lingua franca. The world was changing and, on some level, Paula was being locked out of her children's lives.

Luckily, Hamish was far less of a social media Luddite.

She swirled the tea in her mug, then looked up at her father.

'I'm not really sure what to do, Dad,' she said. 'But Hamish will know.'

Later that evening, Hamish leaned over her shoulder in the lounge-room, peering at her laptop. He'd gone to the gym directly from work, then onto his usual Friday night beers with his best friend Doggo. The fetid smell of sweat still hung about him, overlaid with alcohol. Paula could remember a time, earlier in their marriage, when his body odour had smelled masculine to her. Enticing, even; part of the Iron Man persona that had attracted her in the first place. His supreme confidence in his body, his charisma and persuasiveness, it had all seemed so seductive. But more often than not these days, when he walked in all sweaty and looking for sex, she just wanted to hand him a towel and point to the shower.

Dinner was long over, not that Caitlin had eaten anything. She'd pushed a baked potato around her plate before disappearing into her bedroom, rebuffing Lachie's invitation to watch *Teen Survivor*, their favourite 'reality' program.

'Well, some boy's involved in this, for sure,' said Hamish finally, still inspecting the Facebook post. 'Everyone who *knows* Caitlin will guess that. I mean, she's hot, right? It's probably just some teenage boy who's pissed off he can't have her.'

Paula disliked the adjective 'hot' being applied to their daughter.

'It could have been worse,' Hamish added, standing up. 'There's no picture of Catie, it's obviously a doctored image. And there's only two hundred likes.'

'But that's *double* the number from this morning.'

Hamish walked to the drinks cabinet and poured himself a whisky. 'Want one?'

He *knew* she never drank whisky. Red wine, yes. Sometimes too much of it as she sliced and diced her way through dinner preparation. But never hard spirits.

Paula shook her head.

He lowered himself onto the lounge again. 'My quads are smashed,' he said, kneading his thighs with his knuckles. 'There's a new instructor at the gym, made us do fifty squats without a break. Bloody torture.'

Paula tried to remain calm. 'We haven't finished talking about this, have we?'

Hamish coughed behind his hand—the wheeze of neat whiskies—then said, 'Look, Paula, I know it's a shocker. But it's almost November, it'll be summer holidays soon and everyone will forget about it. It's the nature of the beast with social media. A scandal one week, until the next big thing comes along.' He shook the ice in his glass. 'Do you think maybe Caitlin's been fooling around with boys? Enough to make someone jealous?'

This line of questioning was almost identical to Mr Nelson's.

'*No*, Hamish. Caitlin just wants to kick a soccer ball around, you know that. She's not into boys yet.'

'You reckon?' He quaffed his whisky. 'Heaps of boys are into *her*. Like that soccer coach, Cooper. Gets a stupid look on his face every time he sees her. And kids these days experiment a lot younger than we did. The world's a different place now.'

Hamish was right about that, Paula had to admit. She'd only recently discovered that some of Caitlin's friends had smuggled alcohol into their last slumber party; bottles of rum and gin purchased for them by obliging older siblings. Paula had been horrified—*she* hadn't touched alcohol until just before her eighteenth birthday—but was relieved to hear that Caitlin and Amy hadn't joined in the drinking, because both had soccer training the next morning.

Paula was struck by a sudden thought. Could the Facebook post somehow be connected to that party? Had the noticeable abstinence of Caitlin and Amy infuriated their friends, so they'd posted a vulgar image about them, out of spite? She resolved to call Mr Nelson in the morning and mention it.

'Come here,' said Hamish, patting the sofa next to him. 'You're thinking too much again, I can tell.' His smile told her he was seeking something more than conversation.

Paula looked in the direction of the TV room, where Lachie was lounging on his beanbag. Why did Hamish always want to make love when the children were still *up*?

She gestured at the mountain of washing in front of her. 'I'm busy folding this.'

It had been weeks since they'd made love—almost two months, in fact. Their sex life had contracted in recent years, whittled away by the demands of domestic life. Her sex drive hadn't been snuffed out completely; it was just missing in action, Paula sometimes thought, trapped outside her body somewhere. Jammed beneath the garden hoses at Bunnings, tucked under junk mail in the letterbox, stuffed between the toothpaste and the tampons in the bathroom cabinet. Initially, when the children were young, she'd explained her loss of libido as *just a phase*. Who could feel sexy, she reasoned, after a chaotic fourteen hours of running after a toddler and pre-schooler? She'd rationalised it to Hamish as a short-term loss: *I'm sure I'll feel like making love more when they go to school.*

But it hadn't happened that way at all. Nowadays she was still busy, and just as tired. Dealing with the daily grind of school lunches, homework, after-school activities. Catie's soccer training, Lachie's guitar lessons, the washing and hanging, ironing and folding, grocery shopping, cooking and cleaning. The unpaid bills, the barrage of birthdays, the medical appointments, the weekend sporting regimen, the never-ending gardening and maintenance jobs. The ceaseless rotation of school term and holidays, Christmas and Easter.

It was just a typical life in the suburbs, Paula understood, but at the end of most days, she had nothing left to give. She knew she had to make more of an effort—to mount a sexual search party of sorts, and invite Hamish along for the ride, so to speak. But the last thing she felt like doing late at night was watching a dirty video, or whatever else the glossy women's magazines claimed would 'reignite the spark' in their marriage. Sex had somehow become just another chore in her domestic routine, to be deferred until unavoidable.

Hamish had found solace in his work. Slogging away at all hours, relishing the responsibility and reputation he'd acquired for himself over a decade. Not to mention the training opportunities, the bonuses, the regular team-building junkets to popular destinations around the country. Even during the toughest period of his professional life—when he'd been forced to lay off more than twenty staff members—Hamish's passion for work never waned.

By contrast, Paula's career held few prospects for advancement. As a part-time social worker at a local aged-care facility, she couldn't say she *enjoyed* her work, exactly: her shifts usually involved liaising with distressed relatives of the elderly residents, flagging their illnesses and issues, or offering bereavement counselling. But she'd made a choice to accept that job when Lachie turned ten, mostly because of its flexible working hours. The pay was paltry, but in the past three years she'd never once been asked to work outside of school hours. It was a job of convenience, enabling her to use her skills in social work, while always being there for the kids.

More than once, however, Paula had toyed with the idea of retraining as a midwife. Her own birthing experiences had been supported by outstanding midwives; she could still remember their voices of quiet authority, their calmness under pressure, their comforting presence through one of life's most miraculous processes. She'd been inspired by the idea of helping other women in the same way and, after researching her study options, she'd raised the idea with Hamish.

'You don't *have* to work,' he'd objected. 'My role covers us financially. If you don't like your job at Bella Vista, reduce your hours.'

'But I *want* to do something different, Hamish,' she'd insisted. '*You* do training all the time. It keeps your brain fit.'

'And I have the big salary to go with it,' he'd replied. 'If you train to become a midwife, what will we see for it at the end of five years of study? Not a six-figure salary, that's for sure. If you want to stay fit mentally, pick something with a decent reward-for-effort ratio.'

From a purely monetary perspective, he was right. Retraining would involve plenty of outlay—of money, time and energy—for intangible returns like *job satisfaction*.

Meanwhile, there was nothing really wrong with her life, Paula had to concede. Many women would envy her the luxury of not *having* to work at all. Women like her sister, Jamie, who was trapped on a treadmill of mortgage repayments. So Paula had decided not to pursue the midwifery idea. Maybe when the kids left home, she told herself.

Paula sighed, folding another pair of Hamish's sports socks. Family life was the ultimate contraceptive; there was *nothing* sexy about socks.

Hamish reached for the remote and turned on the television, flicking through the channels until he found what he was seeking: a mixed-martial-arts program. Men with crooked noses and bloodied eyes, fighting like cocks in a cage.

'Hamish, about Caitlin . . .'

They hadn't really concluded that conversation.

He dragged his gaze away from the television. 'It sounds to me like the headmaster has it all under control.' His eyes strayed to his mobile. 'I've got some emails to answer.'

Of course, Paula thought. Work was always more important. All that typing and swiping, clicking and flicking. People online at all hours, acting as though they were indispensable.

'Do you want me to talk to Caitlin?' he asked, still focused on his phone.

She couldn't suppress her irritation any longer. 'Yes, Hamish, I do. Caitlin needs our support right now, and you're sitting on the couch drinking whisky and reading your emails as if it's no big deal.'

'Okay, okay,' Hamish said, hauling himself off the couch and walking into the kitchen. He plugged his phone into a recharger, then turned back to Paula. 'I *know* it's a big deal, I'm not pretending it isn't. But there's no point getting worked up about it, when we don't have all the information yet.'

Paula relented a little. 'I think I'll call Charlotte Kennedy's mum tomorrow. Maybe she knows something.'

'Good idea.' Hamish walked over and put his hands on her shoulders, massaging them gently. 'I'll go have a father–daughter chat with Catie now.'

'Thanks.' She watched him move down the hallway towards the bedrooms. 'She's a bit delicate,' she called after him. 'Be careful with her.'

He nodded and tapped at Caitlin's door.

# 2

*Fuck that hurts.*

Knives in his knee, blades twisting up his left leg.

'Are you alright, Mr McInnes?'

Hamish looked at the nurse through half-closed eyes.

'Can I offer you some pain relief?'

She smiled at him, in a nursey kind of way. Efficient and caring, with an *I'm-about-to-go-now* edge. 'I'll do your obs first.'

He strained to return her smile. It was difficult to achieve with nasal prongs jammed up his nostrils.

Hamish watched as she wrapped a blood-pressure monitor around his bicep and pumped with her smooth, hairless arms. Caramel skin, hair the colour of ink—the type only Asian girls had—with a tantalising swelling beneath the buttons of her tunic. Manicured hands with neat oval nails. She was probably handy at a lot of things, he decided, imagining those soft hands touching *him*.

'You're doing fine,' she said after a minute or two, releasing the velcro band.

Nice teeth. Lips like a pretty pink bow.

*Ohhh.*

The pain caught him off-guard, slicing through his knee and thigh. A monitor sounded nearby, just another bloody noise in this hellhole of a hospital.

The nurse walked around the bed and checked his drip. 'The bag's finished. I need to ask the doctor what antibiotics we're giving you now.' She smiled down at him again. 'I'll be back soon.'

Hamish watched her leave, her petite arse swaying under her tunic. He'd like to lift that skirt up and . . .

'Daddy!'

Hamish winced as his daughter threw herself against him. She locked her arms around his neck and wriggled in next to him, nuzzling against his shoulder.

'Oh, poor Daddy.' Caitlin was using her baby voice, the one he couldn't resist. 'This is *all* my fault.'

He inhaled the familiar smell of her freshly-washed hair. An impossibly blonde mane, the colour of platinum. Teamed with her olive skin, Caitlin always managed to look like a Scandinavian goddess.

He wound his arm around her waist.

'It's not your fault, honey. It's mine. I shouldn't have said what I did last night.'

One minute he'd been sitting on the end of Caitlin's bed, asking her about the Facebook post. The next moment, he'd posed his own theory that it was all connected to Cooper Johnson, her soccer coach from Year Eleven. He'd seen the way she acted around him; all giggly and flirty behind her fringe.

'You honestly think that's *Cooper's penis*?' Catie's face had turned white with rage before she'd bolted out of her bedroom. Along the hallway, past Paula, down the stairs and out through the laundry.

A moment later, in the backyard, Hamish had watched helplessly as Caitlin cycled down the driveway at breakneck speed in the dark.

Then, realising how badly he'd screwed up—and how ropeable Paula would be—he'd jumped onto his own bike and taken off after her.

He'd been cycling less than a minute when he turned onto Blackburn Road and hit a pothole—crashing arse over head into a parked car. He'd lain motionless on the road, his left kneecap shattered, until a waiter rushed out of a nearby restaurant and dragged him onto the kerb.

Next thing Hamish knew, he'd wound up in hospital. Doped up on painkillers, his left leg puffy like a balloon, awaiting the assessment of an orthopaedic surgeon.

Hamish looked over Catie's head at Lachie, loitering next to his grandfather. His son had drawn the short straw in the genetic lottery, inheriting his mother's height and freckled skin.

A wave of exasperation washed over Hamish. Where *was* Paula? She'd visited him earlier that morning, in the silent hours after midnight, when they'd first brought him in by ambulance. She'd sat by his side, holding his hand, promising to return with the kids in the morning. So why the hell had she sent her old man instead?

'Hello, Hamish.' Old Sid looked worried. 'Bad luck, mate. I'm really sorry.'

'Not sorrier than me, Sid.'

At his grandfather's prompting, Lachie sidled around the bed and gave Hamish a stiff hug, careful to avoid Caitlin, who was still curled up next to him.

Hamish ruffled his son's greasy hair. 'How's it going, mate?'

Lachie grunted, as he often did these days. Around his thirteenth birthday—almost to the day—he'd sprouted body hair and blackheads, while seemingly losing all function of his vocal cords.

'That good, eh?' Hamish winked at Sid over his son's head.

Lachie pulled back and slunk away from the bed. It disappointed Hamish a little, but it didn't surprise him. He'd concluded a long time ago that he and his son were cut from different cloth; Hamish was sporty, while Lachie was turning into a bit of a *nerd*. Hamish tried not to take it personally, but he sometimes wondered if Lachie might end up batting for the other team.

Hamish nodded at the suitcase his son had placed on the floor. 'What's in there, mate?'

Caitlin climbed off the bed. 'I'll unpack it for you, Daddy.'

She unzipped it and began stacking the items into a chest of drawers next to his bed. A toilet bag for the bathroom—that was so Paula. He *hated* toilet bags. Useless pieces of junk, right up there with popcorn-makers and antimacassars. He only knew what an antimacassar was due to Paula's hygiene obsession, when she'd covered their new lounge suite in crisp white squares of linen. *There's no need to protect a sofa*, he'd objected. *It's designed to be sat on, dirtied a bit. We could even dirty it together . . .*

She'd ignored him, as she usually did.

Caitlin continued unpacking. Some old magazines, an alarm clock—what the hell would he do with that in *here*? Paula's favourite muesli bars—the healthy ones that looked like dog turds—and a packet of disinfecting wipes. This is a *hospital*, he thought, they keep things clean in here. But Paula always insisted on carrying those wipes everywhere. Just like she kept her spices alphabetised in the pantry, changed the bath towels thrice weekly and liked to colour-code her Tupperware. She was the sort of woman who climbed out of bed and straight into the shower after lovemaking, to eradicate all signs of human contact. But Hamish was different: he'd happily lie in the wet patch, relishing the post-coital stickiness. Inhaling the lingering sweet and sour odour that told him he was *alive*.

'That's it.' Caitlin held up the empty bag. 'Do you need anything else, Daddy?'

Hamish tried to hoist himself up onto one elbow. Pain ricocheted through his left knee and the room swayed before his eyes. He heard himself moaning; a dull, distant sound, like a patient in another ward.

'You okay, Dad?' It was Lachie's voice, deeper now than it used to be.

'Yes, mate,' he said. 'Did you bring my phone?'

Lachlan and Caitlin looked at one another.

'Mum said she'd bring it later,' said Caitlin.

'What about my laptop?'

'That too,' said Lachie. 'She said you need to rest.'

Treating me like a third child, Hamish thought. No respect for *my* wishes.

Hamish stared at the television suspended above his bed, a screen too small to watch.

'I brought you a newspaper.' Old Sid placed a copy of the *Herald Sun* on his tray table. 'Mind if I keep this?' He was holding the six-page racing guide.

'Be my guest.' Horses held no interest for Hamish. 'You ever actually going to have a flutter, Sid?' he asked. 'It's un-Australian not to.'

'The fun's in the picking,' said Sid. 'I got a trifecta at Caulfield yesterday.'

Hamish closed his eyes, suddenly tired again.

*Bugger this accident*, he thought. *I can't afford any down time.*

'Excuse me.' He opened his eyes to find the Asian nurse next to his bed, looking at his family.

'I'm sorry,' she said. 'Visiting hours don't start until eleven o'clock. You're going to have to come back later.'

*My saviour*, Hamish thought. He'd had enough, even of his kids.

He rolled his eyes at Sid, pretending to give a shit. Then he yawned, causing an oxygen prong to pop out of his nose.

The nurse fussed over him, inserting the prong back into his nostril. As she did, he caught a glimpse of white lace through the buttons of her navy tunic. His dick moved involuntarily under his hospital gown.

*Thank God for that*, Hamish thought. *My knee's trashed, but my vitals are still working.*

'Daddy's tired,' said Caitlin, patting his arm. 'We'll come back later.'

'Okay, honey,' he said. He lifted a hand at Sid and Lachie, then blew a kiss at Catie.

They shut the door behind them.

Hamish let his eyes close again.

Why had he interrogated Caitlin over a stupid Facebook post? He'd hurt her—and himself—in the process.

Paula had nagged him into it, for sure, but he'd also jumped to his own rash conclusions.

At her core, he knew, Caitlin was a good girl.

Right from the beginning, she'd always been his angel.

*

He could still remember Caitlin's birth, just like it was yesterday. He could barely remember the day or the month and, much to Paula's chagrin, sometimes not even the year. But other tiny details were etched in his memory. Like the enormous clock on the hospital wall, its hands circling like a windmill, marking the hours and minutes of Paula's protracted labour. The dulcet tones of pan flutes, punctuated by Paula's animal-like grunting. Beanbags and cushions and lukewarm labour baths. Midwives with sympathetic expressions floating in and out of the room, talking to Paula in hushed tones. Pastels everywhere. Peachy pinks, lavender, powder blue.

And then the angry red blood, flooding everywhere.

The crown of the baby's head pushing down through the walls of his wife's pelvis. Paula, on all fours, her face purple, veins bulging in her neck, straining to look between her own legs. Huffing and heaving and crying ecstatically as a face appeared. Touching the baby with the fingers of her right hand, even as blood gushed between them. Hamish stumbling backwards, simultaneously repelled and elated. The baby slipping quietly into the hands of a waiting midwife, its umbilical cord trailing out of Paula.

'It's a girl,' the midwife said, turning to him and smiling in a knowing kind of way. As if they'd shared something now, the two of them, having watched his wife's vulva explode.

'Want to cut the cord?' she'd asked, just before he'd fainted on the bloodied floor.

He'd been helped onto a nearby sofa by one of the midwives. As the nursing staff buzzed around Paula, he'd closed his eyes, still feeling queasy.

When he awoke, Paula's eyes were trained on the baby nuzzling at her breast, her lips curled in a whimsical smile. Hamish had to cough to attract her attention.

'Isn't she perfect?' she said, without looking up. Paula's lips brushed the baby's forehead. 'Our beautiful Caitlin.'

It was a name they'd chosen together beforehand, in honour of his maternal grandmother; the only grandparent he could remember, with soft wrinkles and kind eyes, who'd plied him with sugar-coated shortbread whenever he visited.

'Can I hold her?' he whispered, desperate to touch his daughter. Wanting to see her face again, stroke those tiny fingers poking out of the bunny rug.

'She's feeding now.' Paula eyed the empty glass on the tray table nearby. 'Can you get me some water?'

Without so much as a 'please', Hamish thought, but he let it go. She'd been through hellish contractions, eighteen hours of labour, a pain he'd never truly understand.

He went to fetch water for Paula.

And that was the beginning of the rot, by his account; the unspoken malaise that had slowly infected their marriage. Paula's first demand as a new mother was only the beginning of a barrage of further demands that he, as father and husband, was apparently required to accept. As if maternity had somehow conferred on Paula the God-given authority to wear the pants in the family.

Her nagging began with the little things, whenever he tried to help with Caitlin. They laughed, initially, when he got things wrong—the nappy he put on backwards, the expressed breast milk he boiled in the microwave. But after several weeks, Paula stopped seeing the funny side. On the night he soothed Caitlin's cries by dipping her dummy in honey, Paula whisked the baby out of his arms.

'You don't give an infant sugar,' she snapped, throwing the dummy into the sink.

'But my mum did,' he replied, raising his voice over the bawling that ensued. 'She swore by it for all of us.'

'Well, your mother was *wrong*,' Paula snarled, stomping off to bed with Caitlin.

He'd slept on the sofa that night.

There was so much he didn't know, it turned out. He'd attended all the antenatal classes religiously, but most had focused on the birth itself, not the weeks and months afterwards. He'd received no training in baby-rearing, possessed no life skills in that department. Sure, he'd been an uncle before becoming a father: his eldest brother had four children, ranging in ages from two to nine years. But Hamish always found their visits from Canberra insufferable: one of the kids was always crying, getting stuck in a tree, whining for food or regurgitating it. He tired of them within hours of their arrival, and was always relieved when they went home.

*Maybe I just wasn't cut out to be a father*, he sometimes thought, in the early weeks after Caitlin's birth. He even said as much to Doggo, who'd been quick to reassure him that it would all settle down soon enough. And Doggo knew his stuff, with five children of his own.

Three months after Caitlin's arrival, Hamish figured out the best way to keep the peace with Paula: by restricting himself to 'blue jobs', bloke-only tasks like assembling cots, fitting car seats and lifting prams. Paula was rarely direct in her criticism, but Hamish could sense her scrutinising his every move. Scanning their surrounds for potential pitfalls, hidden or overt, as if *she* alone could gauge environmental danger. Hamish kept telling himself that it was a biological imperative; that Paula, like every other mother in the animal kingdom, was genetically programmed to defend her offspring. But he still took it personally. He wasn't a bumbling fool and he was, after all, Caitlin's father. *You didn't make the baby by yourself*, he sometimes felt like pointing out. *Why doesn't* my *opinion matter as much as yours?*

By the time Caitlin was six months old, Paula was the undisputed expert on all things parental. Was it nature or nurture? Hamish couldn't be sure. His wife could certainly anticipate Caitlin's every need, like a lifeguard discerning the ocean's currents. But he'd *allowed* that to happen, too, in the interests of marital harmony. He didn't always agree with Paula's decisions, but she clearly wasn't in the mood for amicable dissent. In almost every other domain Paula was easy-going, kind-hearted and generous; all the qualities he'd found attractive in a prospective life partner. But when it came to parenting, her demeanour altered. Suddenly, she didn't suffer fools gladly, and all too often *he* was the village idiot.

It wasn't a recipe for marital passion. He'd always had a healthy sexual appetite and, prior to having children, Paula had matched him. While she wasn't very experienced in the bedroom, she'd always been prepared to try new things. But after Caitlin's arrival, her focus shifted. She went on maternity leave from work *and* life, it seemed to Hamish, and never really came back. The baby consumed her; Caitlin was a night-waker and often unsettled during the day. As the weeks turned to months, Paula became plumper and more resentful, worn down by the ceaseless twenty-four-hour cycle. In the place of sleep, she ate. Their bedroom was no longer a place for adult play; instead, it became an unlit tomb where Paula could be found at any hour, pale and bloated, catching a brief moment of rest before Caitlin woke again.

By the end of the first year of Catie's life, Hamish could count on one hand how many times Paula had been interested in sex. And to be fair, he hadn't really been looking for it either. Every time he saw her naked, his mind flashed back to the birth; the growling animal sounds she'd made as her vulva had split open. And she hadn't exactly bounced back like a Hollywood celebrity, either.

It was all perfectly natural, of course; everything Paula's body had done, or was doing, was thoroughly normal. But *knowing* that didn't help his sex drive. Sometimes he would watch Paula change into her pyjamas at night, willing his dick to do something, anything. But just one word came to mind as he watched her pull on her voluminous pyjama pants and breastfeeding singlet top: *mumsy.* She was a mother now, and she looked it.

*The mother of my beautiful daughter,* he would remind himself, willing his cock to twitch.

But his dick never lied.

It was a surprise to them both, then, when Paula fell pregnant with Lachie. Caitlin was just thirteen months old and, as Hamish later joked with Doggo, it was virtually an immaculate conception. Paula had made a special effort for their anniversary, in honour of their three years of marriage, seducing him as soon as he walked in from work. On the couch in the lounge room, a rare moment of sexual liberty. But, as luck would have it, he'd knocked her up; so much for the supposed contraceptive benefits of breastfeeding. He'd only just started to enjoy baby Caitlin, too, who was crawling around after him like a smitten puppy. Being a dad had suddenly become a whole lot more fun, so Paula's news of a second pregnancy scared the bejesus out of him. Wouldn't having another one so soon just fuck everything up again?

And sure enough, it did.

Baby Lachlan turned out to be a better sleeper than Caitlin, but Paula's fatigue levels soared. Having 'two under two', as she described it—as if it was a badge of honour—was a hell of a lot harder than one. She was short-tempered, forgetful and utterly uninterested in sex.

*I just want a cuddle*, she'd say, whenever he attempted to arouse her.

It was the cruel irony of maternity, he often thought; the one time in her life that Paula's breasts were massive, but they were off-limits. He knew her tetchiness was temporary, but he just wanted his old wife back. The woman who'd laugh at his humour, who'd sit up at night sometimes and watch *Ultimate Fight Club* with him—not because she enjoyed it, but because she knew *he* did. The woman who'd pay attention when he arrived home from the office; kissing him, asking him how his day was, eating with him. Not leaving his dinner luke-warm and cling-wrapped on the kitchen counter, or boycotting cooking altogether. The woman with interests other than babies; who'd wiggled her hips against his in a Latin dance class, who'd burst into laughter during a 'yoga for couples' course. Who'd wanted to travel the country with him in a campervan, before conquering the world. Who'd made love to him more than once a month, and who'd enjoyed it when they did.

Where exactly had that woman gone?

More than a decade later, the question remained unanswered. Deferred, and then eclipsed, by competing demands. Hamish had done well at Crossroads Cars, growing the business more than tenfold in the same number of years. He'd become a poster boy for new recruits within the company, the staffer who'd progressed from faceless underling to executive general manager, operations. Boss of hundreds and second to none; except to the CEO, who'd empowered Hamish to run the business exactly as he wished. His bonuses alone had funded their family holidays to Fiji and New Zealand. Not exactly one of the destinations in their 'adventure scrapbook', but a decent consolation prize nonetheless.

Work was the first thing Hamish thought about in the morning, and the last thing on his mind at night. And in his diminishing hours of leisure time, he spent them mostly with the kids. Hours of soccer practice or Sunday cycling with Catie, chess and Wii tournaments with Lachie, punctuated by fleeting moments of connection with Paula.

By the time Lachie and Caitlin were in high school, Hamish's life had settled into an inexorable routine. Work, always work. Beers with Doggo on a Friday night, mowing the lawns every second Saturday, sex with Paula whenever she let him, but always on their anniversary. There'd been fifteen of those at least, but somewhere along the way, Hamish had lost the urge to count.

He had no doubt that he loved his kids. He could feel it in his body when he caught sight of them sometimes: Caitlin sprawled over her biology textbook at the kitchen bench, her mouth working in concentration; Lachie fretting about his next chess move, rocking on his spindly frame. And he could still remember, aeons, ago, holding their hands and dancing around the apricot tree in the backyard. Chanting 'Oranges and Lemons' as the kids squealed with laughter and their bare feet slipped across the ripe fallen fruit. Watching their eyes widen as he bent down and sang in a deep, menacing tone: *When will you pay me? Say the bells of Old Bailey.* Caitlin's half-terrified, half-excited shrieks as Hamish walked towards her, his legs spread wide, pretending to be the huge prison bell.

He'd invested days and weeks and months and years, rearing these two beautiful children. And he'd done it all with the permanent fixture in his life, Paula, who tried so hard to be a good mother and wife.

*But is this it?* Hamish sometimes wondered, tiptoeing about before dawn on a Sunday morning. Pulling on his cleated cycling shoes and pedalling out into the sleeping suburbs, crouching low over the handlebars.

*Is* this *as good as it gets?*

*

In the week Hamish turned forty, he decided to talk to Doggo.

They'd been observing their weekly ritual of Friday-night beers ever since finishing high school, only ever skipping it on public holidays. Doggo wasn't much of a conversationalist, but there was something reassuring about his rough chippy's hands wrapped tightly around the base of a schooner; something that told Hamish that the planets were in their orbits, and all was right with the world.

'How's Paula?' Doggo asked, sinking his second beer.

'Busy,' Hamish replied. 'Does heaps for the kids. You know how it is.'

'Yep.' Doggo swilled the beer around his schooner glass.

Doggo was one of seven siblings from a Catholic family. He'd finished his carpentry apprenticeship at nineteen, then married Tina, his high-school sweetheart. They'd pumped out five kids in the same number of years before deciding to stop doing God's work in the bedroom; the oldest was now eighteen, the youngest twelve. Hamish hadn't suspected how much Doggo's life must have changed with all those ankle-biters until, a few years later, he'd had a couple of his own.

Hamish looked up at Doggo. 'Things are a bit, I dunno, with Paula. The kids are her life. We don't . . .' He scrounged around for the words. 'Do you and Tina . . . ?'

'Nah, mate.'

Hamish wondered what question Doggo thought he'd answered.

Doggo stood up and fished his wallet out of his back pocket. 'Anothery?'

'Ta, buddy.'

Doggo walked to the bar and waited to be served. A buxom brunette stood behind the taps, pulling beers like a milkmaid. Her cleavage rippled up and down, up and down, as she worked the taps. Smiling through voluptuous scarlet lips, flicking her long plaits behind tanned shoulders, fluttering her thick eyelashes at the blokes drooling all over the counter.

Hamish's cock moved, thinking of her working *him* like a beer tap. Up down, up down, *whoosh*. It wouldn't take more than a few minutes, for sure. And after the hand job, he'd find out if her other lips looked anything like the ones framing her teeth. He'd stick his fingers up her tidy little slit and work her over. Up down, up down, until she bucked her hips and screamed for him to finish her off. He'd do that with his tongue, until he felt her contract around his fingers. In out, in out. *All done, hon.*

Doggo brought their schooners to the table.

Hamish shifted on the bar stool, his cock pressing against his jeans. 'Thanks, mate.' He nodded towards the bar. 'How's that chick, eh?'

'Hot as.'

'She'd be up for it, I reckon.'

'Yep.'

Hamish paused, unsure how to venture further. It was one thing to talk about some random bar wench, but quite another to talk about your wife.

*Ah, bugger it. I've known Doggo for donkey's years.*

'I'm not getting much, mate.'

Doggo looked up from his beer, but said nothing.

*Come on, Doggo, help me out here.*

'Paula's shattered all the time. Doesn't let me touch her with a barge pole. And even when she does . . .' He faltered. 'It's different now. We're older, I guess. And ever since she had the kids, you know, it was rough on her body. It's not as . . .'

He couldn't bring himself to finish the sentence. It was only Doggo he was talking to, but he couldn't spit it out.

'She got a smashed box, mate?'

Hamish couldn't help but laugh. Beer squirted out of his nose and mouth. Doggo slapped him on the back and they guffawed together until even the barmaid looked over at them and smiled.

When they finally stopped laughing, Doggo downed half his beer.

'I know what that's like, mate,' he said eventually. 'After five kids, believe me, I understand. No traction, no action.'

This set them both howling again.

*If we weren't laughing, we'd be crying.*

'Just part of having kids, I guess,' said Hamish.

'Yeah.' Doggo stretched his arms behind his head and belched, letting the air hiss out of the corner of his mouth. 'But a bloke's got needs, y'know.'

'Too right. Can't just keep floggin' the log.'

Doggo shrugged. 'Me and Tina do it every Friday night.'

Hamish looked at Doggo with newfound admiration. Paula refused to touch Hamish when he'd been to the pub; she wasn't a fan of the drunken fuck.

'Mate, that's good,' he said. 'Real good.'

Doggo glanced at the girl behind the bar. 'The eye candy helps. A bit of Friday-night inspiration, y'know? I mean, Tina and I have been together for twenty-five years now.'

Hamish would be thinking about that barmaid, too, the next time he jacked off in the shower. Maybe even the next time he made love to Paula, whenever that would be.

'A few years back, I thought about hiring a hooker,' Doggo continued, as if he was talking about a second-storey addition or a holiday to Hawaii. 'I did the research, found an agency with decent girls, not skanks. But in the end, I couldn't do it. Tina wouldn't forgive me if she ever found out. It just wasn't right.' Doggo absently watched the large plasma screen on the wall behind Hamish, a field of racehorses whipping around a wet track. 'Plenty of girls on the internet, though.'

'Porn, you mean?'

Doggo shook his head, his lips curling into a sly smile. The look on his face transported Hamish back to high-school, when they'd hidden behind the girls' toilets and perved through the cracks in the brickwork. 'Nah, mate. We're talking real girls who want to get off in front of you. I've got a lady friend in the Ukraine now, Nataliya. Bored housewife with some wanker of a husband. We *communicate* when Tina's in bed. She's got the prettiest tits you've ever seen, mate. Brown nipples, as big as dinner plates.' He splayed his fingers for emphasis. 'You can see *everything* with a webcam. And it's not like it's cheating or anything.'

Hamish gawped at his friend, practically salivating.

Doggo smirked at him. 'She's *gagging* for it, buddy.'

*Doggo, you dog.*

'How'd you find her?' Hamish was almost croaking.

'Online forum.' Doggo swigged the last of his beer and planted the schooner on the table with a flourish. 'Horny housewives dot com. Chicks wanting an audience. Suits me just fine, takes the pressure off Tina. That's what you call a win-win-win.'

'Fuck, mate.'

Hamish had watched his fair share of internet porn over the years, but it was too staged for his liking. Drug-stunned bimbos with fake tits pretending to cum while some hung-like-a-horse bloke boned them senseless. Hamish got off when he watched it, of course—all blokes did—but he craved the real thing. Maybe Doggo was on to something.

Hamish left the pub that Friday night determined to learn more. Here he was, at forty years of age, with a successful career, two kids and a problem he'd been repressing for years.

*I still want sex: just not with my wife.*

*Not always, anyway.*

*I need something more.*

As luck would have it, Paula was still soaking in the bath when Hamish arrived home; it was her weekly ritual. Every Friday night she locked herself in the bathroom to battle the passage of time: waging war against cellulite, stray grey hairs in her brown bob, the curly wayward pubes poking out beneath her panty line. He admired her persistence with all that plucking and preening, and her dogged conviction that she could somehow halt the inevitable decline. He could hear her rinsing her hair, filling and refilling a stainless-steel jug, tipping the water over her head.

Hamish looked towards the children's rooms—both were unlit—then booted up his laptop in the dining room. He could escape to the caravan, his personal refuge for the past three months, but there was no real need; Paula took forever in the bathroom.

He paused, fingers hovering above the keyboard, trying to recall the name of the website Doggo had mentioned. Their fifth beer had addled his brain.

He keyed some random words into the search engine.

*Real girls webcam sex.*

Then he added *online forum.*

A results catalogue of more than eleven million pages appeared. He clicked on the fourth item in the list, a website called Hotties at Home. Was that the site Doggo had suggested?

He scanned the thumbnail images that appeared on the homepage. They were young, mostly. Big hair, big eyes, bigger tits. But real, not Barbie look-alikes. Girls that probably had dimples on their arses, one tit smaller than the other, an inverted nipple maybe. Imperfections he could work with.

He clicked on a thumbnail, and was immediately prompted to register as a new user. He used his Gmail address and paid the annual membership fee with a credit card he kept for emergencies. Then he created a log-in he often used, *Hamo95*, and keyed in *1995*, his universal password. Some uptight IT geek from work had once told him never to use the same username and password across multiple accounts, but Hamish couldn't be arsed trying to remember different profiles.

On the form, he filled in his nationality and city, Skype handle and interests.

*Cycling, boxing, hanging out.*

Then he listed his physical attributes.

*Tanned and sporty six-footer, blue eyes, blond hair.*

He was about to complete his profile—zodiac sign, age and sexual preference—when the bathroom door opened and Paula stepped into the hallway.

He snapped his laptop shut and forced a smile.

'Hi.' She sounded peevish. 'I thought you'd never come home.'

She didn't usually wait up for him.

'Doggo had . . . something happen at work this week. We stayed for a few more beers.' Did he look guilty?

'Oh.' Her expression changed to one of concern. 'Is he okay?'

'Fine,' Hamish lied. 'Just a problem with a dodgy contractor.'

'Well, it was good of you to talk it through with him.'

She padded across the dining room bare foot. Damp skin and chin-length brown hair; the long, glossy mane of her twenties had been clipped shorter and shorter over the years, until it became the sensible length for super-mums. Her bathrobe gaped at the chest. Hamish's eyes drifted downwards, and there they were. The same tits he'd been groping for years; soft, warm, sagging a little now.

He smiled and reached out, pulling her playfully onto his lap.

'Hamish . . .' she objected.

He nuzzled her neck and inched his hand inside her bathrobe. Picturing a pair of massive brown nipples, swaying and bobbing above him like firm, round saucers. Nataliya from the Ukraine pounding up and down on his hard-as-a-rock cock.

Paula batted his hand away.

'I'm tired,' she said. 'And *you've* had too much to drink.'

She stood up and, without another word, stalked off in the direction of their bedroom.

Hamish watched her leave, his fury building.

That arse of hers moving beneath her pink terry-towelling bathrobe. He *hated* that bathrobe; the fabric, its feel, how she looked in it. Whenever he suggested she try something more flattering—sexier, even—she always banged on about how damn comfortable it was.

*Comfortable. That's what we are. Middle-aged and too bloody comfortable.*

He reached for the remote and sprawled out on the couch. The effect of the beers soon numbed him to sleep.

*

When Hamish opened his eyes again, he was still in hospital.

It was only ten-thirty, according to the clock on the bedside table—Sid and the kids had visited barely two hours ago.

*Assuming it's still the same day,* Hamish thought suddenly. He squinted at the clock again, with its helpful date indicator: *20 Oct.*

Yes, still the same day.

The day after the bike accident.

But it felt as if he'd been floating in and out of a half-drugged state for weeks. What painkillers did they have him on, anyway?

Hamish craned his neck to read the bag hanging on the IV pedestal, but couldn't read the writing for buggery.

The Asian nurse swept past the doorway to his room, pushing a trolley.

'Hey,' he called out.

She popped her head around the door. 'Yes?'

'Is my phone here?'

The nurse smiled, as a vet might at a castrated dog. 'Your wife will bring it later. Just rest for now, Mr McInnes.'

She whirled away.

He sank back against his pillows, remembering Lachie's words—*Mum said you need to rest.*

It might be *days* before he got online again.

If only he could be back in the caravan, alone with his laptop, the way it had been before old Sid moved in.

# 3

He'd bought the caravan on eBay for a bargain price, just before the winter school holidays. Thinking that Lachie and Catie would use it for hanging out, by themselves or with friends. Hoping that maybe, by getting the kids in the backyard on weekends, Paula might be interested in a bit of daylight sex again. But the kids weren't having a bar of it, preferring their bedrooms or the TV room. And Paula wasn't amused by his 'hide-the-salami-in-the-caravan' jokes, either.

*Bugger it*, he thought, a month or so later. *I'll use the caravan myself.*

He'd started taking his laptop over to the caravan at night, to do some extra work.

Until Doggo's tip-off about Nataliya from the Ukraine prompted him to try it for *other* nocturnal purposes.

'We've got eighteen new clients this month,' he said to Paula, the night after he'd registered on the Hotties at Home site. 'I'll go finish some stuff in the caravan.'

'Really? It's a Saturday night.' Paula looked put out.

'Sorry,' he said. 'It won't happen every week.'

'Alright,' she replied, with a snide little *told-you-so* smile. 'You might as well *use* the caravan.' She'd been unimpressed by his 'teen den' idea from the outset.

'Mate, help your mother with the dishes, please,' he called out to Lachie, who was lying prostrate in front of the television. Lachie grumbled a little before propelling himself off the couch.

'What about *her*?' Lachie pointed at Caitlin, who was sitting at the island bench, thumbing through a textbook.

'Caitlin's two years above you at school and she's got more homework,' Hamish replied. 'Just help your mother.'

'That's not fair,' Lachie objected.

'Life's not fair, mate.'

Paula turned and looked in her daughter's direction.

'Catie, come and help too, please,' she called.

Hamish watched, irritated, as Caitlin closed the textbook and joined her mother at the sink. Paula was *always* cutting across his authority; it did his head in. Lachie was smirking, the little shit, as he dried a saucepan with a dishcloth. Hamish hovered for a moment, tempted to pull Paula aside and say something.

*Don't override me in front of the kids.*

*You're always talking down to me.*

*My authority counts too.*

But there was no point pursuing it, not after so many years. He was never going to change her; all he'd get was some sermon about favouritism and chores.

*You spoil Caitlin, Hamish.*

*You're too hard on Lachie.*

*Everyone has to pitch in.*

He took his laptop satchel from the bench and headed down the rear stairs, stepping out into the night. He knew his way up the steep side path and across the backyard without a torch, even avoiding the extension cord supplying electricity to the caravan. It was cool for November, more like an evening in June. He looked up at the sky, at all the faded miniscule stars millions of light years away. They were up there when he was born, and they'd be up there when he died. None of them aware of the tiny cosmic burp named Hamish McInnes.

*What the hell is it all for?* he wondered. *The whole world spinning in space, everyone too busy eating and shitting and working and sleeping to see that we're dying all the time.*

His head tilted so far back it hurt.

The thick silver handle of the caravan door was reassuring in its solidity.

Inside, it was pitch-black and musty-smelling. An old-man smell, with traces of talc and turpentine. The caravan's elderly owner had been fastidious in maintaining it over the ten years of its life before it wound up in their backyard. In fact, when Hamish had gone to collect it, he'd asked why it was being sold at all.

'Lost the wife a few months back,' the old man had replied, his eyes watery. 'She was my travelling companion. Drove all around Australia in this van, we did. Married for fifty years, before the cancer took her.'

Hamish hadn't known how to respond.

'My mother-in-law's got breast cancer,' he'd blurted, before paying his money and leaving quickly, towing the caravan behind his ute.

He hadn't thought of the old man since. But tonight, as he inhaled the caravan's fusty odour and fumbled around for the light switch, the old man came to mind again. The look in his eyes when he spoke about his wife, even after fifty years of marriage. Or *because* of those fifty years, perhaps.

*What will I be saying about Paula in thirty years' time?*

Hamish found the light switch and closed the caravan door behind him, pushing the lock into place.

He removed his laptop from its case and booted up.

Opening the bar-sized fridge, he took out a beer and flicked off its lid with the bottle opener conveniently affixed to the bench. That old guy had thought of everything, Hamish mused, sucking back the stubby. And it would've been some trip around Australia, too. He and Paula had planned a holiday like that, once upon a time.

He sat down on the seat in the kitchenette, with its thick furry cushions covered in shit-coloured fabric. You wouldn't want to get naked on those cushions, he thought, you'd get rug rash on your balls.

The website took a while to load. Hamish didn't mind; he was still getting used to the idea that some Hottie at Home might take off her clothes and touch herself, just for him. Leaning back against the curtained window, he felt his dick pulsate at the prospect.

A moment later, he keyed in his username and password.

A map of the world appeared. There were 46,753 hotties online, it said, and more than 30,000 of them were women. He rolled his mouse over the map, watching the numbers change with the geography. There were 3953 hotties online just in the former Soviet Union.

Holy shit, he whispered, scrolling through dozens of thumbnails of Russian women. Some of them were dog ugly, some of them were too old. But most of them were hot as fuck.

He scanned his options: pre-recorded video, private viewing or online chat.

Pre-recorded videos he could watch any time. A private viewing was what Doggo had described.

Selecting this tab narrowed his options to just over eight hundred women. He saw the one he wanted immediately, in the first set of thumbnails: blonde hair, blue eyes, a voluptuous mouth. A Russian Claudia Schiffer. Her username was *Valeria87.* If the numerals referred to her birth year, that made her twenty-five. Perfect.

He clicked on the 'request private viewing' icon and waited.

An image of a clock appeared, its hands whirring around its face.

He swigged on his beer and leaned forward, scrutinising the thumbnail. Valeria wore too much blue eye shadow, but she was a natural beauty. *Should've visited Russia when we backpacked through Europe twenty years ago.* He'd been a second-year mechanic, and Doggo a carpentry apprentice. They'd flown direct to Rome with enough cash to cover them for four weeks of annual leave. They'd spent three of them in Italy, France and Germany, then tossed up between crossing the border into Austria or taking a discount flight to Russia. Doggo had been keen on Vienna—something about his pianist grandmother—and Hamish hadn't objected. So they'd ended up doing a Mozart by Night tour, when they could have been doing girls like Valeria. What the *hell* were they thinking?

Several minutes passed, and the clock icon remained static.

*Come on*, Hamish muttered.

He clicked on his emails and scanned the inbox. Nothing interesting there. Four emails from bloody Nick-the-Dick Bridge, the junior operations officer in the national office, trying to curry Hamish's favour by systematising things that didn't need it. He had a policy for everything, that bloke. Since his arrival two years ago, he'd created eight new operational policies, with trendy titles like Values-Based

Supplier Selection and Ethical Communication. Hamish was too busy getting the real work done to bother with any of them.

*Come on*, he urged again.

A noise from the house made him spring up.

'Daddy?'

It was Caitlin, at the caravan door.

'Yes, angel?' He tried to sound composed.

'Are we riding tomorrow?'

Sunday morning, he remembered suddenly, watching Caitlin's jeans through the slats at the base of the door.

'Sure.'

His laptop made a pinging sound.

*Oh shit*, he thought, *I'm connected.*

'Wake me up, okay, Dad?' Caitlin called.

'Okay, angel.'

He listened to her retreating footsteps, waited for the sound of the back door closing.

A bead of sweat trickled down his neck.

He sat down and looked at the screen. Nothing had changed, but his Skype icon was now flashing. *1 new message.*

Disappointed, he clicked on the icon.

*Lisel17 wants to share contact details with you.*

He clicked 'allow'. The username was unfamiliar, but Skype was in common use between the interstate offices at Crossroads.

Seconds later, an instant message appeared.

*Hi Hamo95, I'm Lisel. U sound cute*

Who was she?

*U should put ur profile picture up*

He hesitated, then typed a reply.

*Where?*

The response was immediate.

*On Hotties . . . just saw ur profile there. Tried 2 chat but site 2 slow. Found u on Skype instead, but no pic here either . . .*

Hamish suddenly understood. His unfinished profile summary had appeared in the 'recently registered' section of the Hotties homepage, then she'd searched for him on Skype.

Another message popped onto his screen.

*Maybe u dont look like u say u do?*

That riled him.

*About to upload pic to Skype*, he typed. *What do you look like Lisel?*

*Check me out on Hotties*, came the reply.

He clicked back into his browser; the Hotties website was still loading his 'private viewing' with Valeria.

Screw that.

He clicked the 'cancel' icon and returned to the Hotties homepage. He found the search bar and typed *Lisel17.* An image appeared that made his jaw drop.

A leggy redhead, sitting by a swimming pool in a pink and white polka-dot bikini. Her head was thrown back, auburn hair falling behind her shoulders. Green eyes, ivory skin, pert breasts. A perfectly flat stomach leading down to the bikini bottom, tied at the hips with sexy little bows. In her twenties, by the look of her.

*Location: Western Australia.*

*Star Sign: Scorpio (with a sting in my tail!).*

*Interests: Skinny-dipping, naked chess, Brazilian waxes.*

He'd tried to get Paula to have a Brazilian wax once. She'd refused, accusing him of *infantilising* her, whatever the hell that meant.

University-speak, the clever words she sometimes used to make him feel stupid.

*No way will this chick be interested in me*, Hamish thought.

*Do u like me Hamo?* a Skype instant message asked.

His mind whirled.

*Like is an understatement*, he typed.

*LOL*, she replied. *Show me u.*

What the hell was he going to do?

He clicked on his photos folder and scanned through family photos, work photos, a passport-sized headshot.

*I wanna c u*, she wrote.

*Okay.* He typed back. *Hold on.*

He needed a photo that would make him look youthful, while also being acceptable for work colleagues using Skype. A tall bloody order, he thought.

He flicked through the shots taken at last year's Christmas party, the cruise on the Yarra. Lots of group shots, mostly blurry. But there was one short-range shot of Hamish with his arm around Nick Bridge. He didn't like Nick—a young, self-righteous upstart—but he'd managed to suspend his enmity for the Christmas party. And so they'd ended up holding their beers like microphones, bellowing out Aretha Franklin's 'Respect', both of them completely hammered. The photo was taken late in the evening; Nick was wearing a blue Bonds singlet and a goofy reindeer cap complete with antlers, his unruly surfer's hair poking out at crazy angles. Hamish stood a full head taller than him, his blond hair cropped close to his head, a tight white t-shirt stretched across an even summer tan.

The photo made Hamish look thirtyish, he guessed.

He clicked the 'account' tab in Skype, then 'update profile photo'. Selecting the image on his hard drive, he waited for it to upload.

The delay was excruciating.

And then her instant message arrived.

*U r not cute.*

*U r hot.*

He began to smile.

*Nice hat, Rudolf.*

Hamish blinked. *Oh, fuck. She thinks I'm Nick Bridge.*

He heard the ping of another instant message.

*Hotties website 2 slow . . . I like Skype better anyway.*

*Wanna get to know u.*

*What r u wearing?*

The question caught him by surprise. He couldn't possibly tell her the truth: threadbare navy trousers and an old grey t-shirt.

*Boardies*, he typed.

He waited for her to reply.

When she didn't, he lifted his fingers to the keyboard.

*What are you wearing Lisel?* Feeling a little self-conscious, he scanned her previous messages, then backtracked in his. Abbreviating the words exactly as she did.

*What r u wearing Lisel?*

He hit the return button and waited.

He clicked on her profile photo, zeroing in on the crotch of her bikini. Man, her thighs were smooth, like Snow fucking White.

*My silk robe.*

*Ice blue with pink cherry blossoms.*

*Makes me feel like a Japanese princess.*

*Bet u r a princess*, he replied.

*Im opening up my robe now.*

Hamish swallowed, following the words on the screen.

*Undoing the tie.*

*Letting the robe drop.*

*Its on the floor now.*

*In my G-string n nothing else.*

Hamish leaned forward.

*What colour?* he typed.

*Black.*

*Smooth as silk.*

*U could rub ur dick against it.*

*Wld feel so nice 4 me.*

Hamish exhaled.

*I'm rubbing my dick against it,* he typed. *Boardies on the floor. My cock is hard Lisel.*

Hamish stood up from the bench and unbuttoned his trousers, shaking them to his ankles. His dick was standing to full attention, and he began to move his hand up and down its shaft.

Several minutes passed without another message, long enough to suggest that Lisel was touching herself. This only revved Hamish up even more: to have that pretty package of pussy tweaking herself over him.

And then, a message.

*Ohhh . . . that feels so good Hamo.*

*Rub my clit harder with ur cock.*

*U r making me so wet.*

It had been a long time since a woman had said anything like that to him.

When he made love to Paula, she rarely talked about how her body felt or gave him any direction.

But this chick, Lisel, she knew what she wanted. It wouldn't take more than two minutes before he'd blow, for sure. His cock felt like reinforced steel.

*Now I want u inside me.*

*Put it in Hamo.*

It was difficult to type with his left hand.

*I'm putting it in.*

*Your cunt is so hot*, he added, then decided to delete it. Some women didn't like the c-word. Paula was one of them.

He shut his eyes against the fleeting image of his wife. When he opened them again, Lisel's message flashed at him.

*Ur cock has filled my cunt right up.*

Lisel clearly didn't object to it.

*I want it faster Hamo.*

*Faster n harder.*

*Oooh my cunt is . . .*

*U r gonna make me cum Hamo.*

Her words set him off; he could feel himself spiralling towards orgasm. His hand moved faster and faster.

*O God Hamo ur cock is so good. My cunt is wet.*

He gasped aloud, his frenzied hand tugging like a piston.

*I'm cuming Hamo I'm cuming.*

He arched his back and exploded, hissing with ecstasy.

Then he fell forward across the laminex table, catching his load in a tea-towel.

He could hear the ping-pinging of more instant messages, but he didn't move.

When he finally stood up again, he looked at the computer screen.

*OMG Hamo.*

*Biggest orgasm I eva had.*

*No kidding.*

*U r amazing.*

*U still there?*

He smiled.

*Yes.*

*Was it good 4 u 2?* she asked.

*The load I dropped would stop traffic.*

She replied with a smiley-face emoticon.

He wiped his dick with a handful of tissues, then placed them in a small plastic bag. Better to throw the evidence into the backyard bin straightaway.

He pulled up his trousers.

*Now what?* her next message asked.

He hadn't thought about anything beyond the happy cock feeling.

*Can we meet again like this?* she asked.

He smiled with relief.

*Of course.*

*Guess u have other girls on Hotties tho?* she asked.

*No, u r my first.*

*They all say that*, she typed.

He wondered how many men *she'd* had on Hotties. With a face and body like that, he probably didn't want to know.

*How about u?* he asked, hoping it seemed casual.

*A few*, she replied. *But after a fuck like that, Im all urs if u want me.*

His face flushed.

*Good*, he typed, feeling like a warrior.

*How old r u Hamo?*

The question smashed him back down to earth. He closed his eyes, thinking hard. How old was Nick Bridge? Thirty at most.

*28*, he replied.

A safe number, he supposed. If Lisel was in her early twenties, it wasn't too old. If she was closer to thirty, they'd be equal enough.

*How old r u?* he asked.

*Sweet 17.*

His mouth fell open.

'Oh fuck,' he whispered, running his fingers through his hair.

*11 yrs apart is not 2 much*, she typed, with another smiley emoticon.

Try twenty-three years, he thought.

*I just want u 4 e-sex*, she added.

*But no webcam ok coz mum won't let me lock my bedroom door . . . ROFL.*

He had no idea what the acronym meant.

And her *mother* was lurking nearby?

He paced around the caravan, trying to think.

He'd just told a seventeen-year-old girl that he was twenty-eight.

*Jesus*, he thought suddenly. *She'll see I'm older if we ever use a webcam . . . Thank God she's not allowed.*

Another instant message sprang onto his screen.

*Let's just have fun Hamo. Age doesnt count.*

*Hamo . . .*

*. . . Hamo?*

He sat there vascillating.

*She's right*, he thought finally. *This is not a courtship. We're not having a relationship. We're not even having real sex. We're doing it virtually, getting ourselves off. No strings, no consequences. Doesn't matter how old she is, as long as she's over the age of consent.*

*Ok.* He typed. *Sleep tight.*

She replied with a lascivious-looking emoticon, its little tongue dipping in and out of its squiggly mouth. It could have meant *I'm thirsty*, or even *Euw, that's gross*. But Lisel made sure he knew exactly what she meant.

*Next time I want you to lick me out Hamo.*

He read the words several times over, noticing his cock shift in response. How could she arouse him again so soon after orgasm? It hadn't happened since his twenties.

He closed the browser and shut down his laptop.

Work would have to wait tonight.

He locked the caravan door and crept back across the yard, down the side path and into the house.

All was in darkness: no sign of Paula. He pattered to their bedroom like a cat burglar and found her motionless on the bed. Stripping down to his boxers, he climbed between the sheets, careful not to disturb her. The silhouette that he'd been lying next to for seventeen years. He lay on his back with his eyes closed, suddenly shamed by the realisation: their marriage was as old as Lisel.

Looking again at the lump that was Paula, Hamish felt the guilt growing. It wasn't the first time he'd wanted other women; he'd wanked over the idea again and again. Picturing his cute gym instructor, the hot mother of one of Catie's school friends, a secretary at work. But he'd never *done* anything to betray Paula's trust; he'd never, ever touched.

And I haven't this time, either, he thought suddenly.

*Have I?* Hamish remembered Doggo's words in the pub: *it's not like it's cheating or anything.*

There was nothing *real* about what he'd done with Lisel, Hamish reasoned. It was simply a modern-day form of masturbation. When he was young, he'd used porn mags. Nowadays, there was the internet. No care, no responsibility. Just a pretty little profile picture and words across a screen.

There could be nothing *really* wrong with that, could there?

*

*I'm going crazy in here.*

Hamish squinted against the fluorescent hospital lighting; the bedside clock confirmed that he was still trapped, yet again, in *20 Oct.*

He tried to stretch out his left leg a little.

*Fuckety fuck.*

The pain pummelled the left side of his body. Little orange sparks shot out from behind his eyelids. His fingers reached for the call button, but clawed instead at the blanket.

*Oh shit, I'm going to puke.*

Warm bile gushed into his mouth and down his chin. Some of it ran back down his throat, making him gag. The coughing made it worse; he tried to sit up, but couldn't.

And then he saw her: Paula, perched on a chair next to his bed.

She waved the console at him. 'I've called the nurse.'

'Thanks.' He coughed again, unable to shift the burning acid in his throat. 'Water . . .' He looked at the tray table with the glass on it, then at Paula.

'Let's wait for the nurse,' she said, pressing the call bell again.

'Give me the water, Paula.'

A grey-haired nurse bustled into the room.

'Sorry for the delay, we're run off our feet,' she said cheerily. 'Oh dear, having a little cough, are we?'

She began pumping at a foot pedal beneath the bed, then adjusted the gradient of the mattress. Once Hamish was propped forward, the bile ran back down his throat. He sucked in the air through the oxygen prongs still planted in his nose. She offered him some water, then wiped his mouth and chin with a paper towel.

'We can take these out for a while,' said the nurse, plucking out the prongs. 'So you can talk to your better half.' She turned to Paula. 'Would you like a cup of tea? You've been waiting a while for Sleeping Beauty to wake up.'

Paula pointed to a plastic cup on the floor. 'I had one earlier, thanks.'

'Alright, then. Let me know if you need anything else.'

The nurse pulled the blue curtain behind her despite the fact there was no one in the bed opposite.

'Hi.' Hamish smiled at Paula, glad for some human company. 'How long have you been here?'

'It's almost four o'clock. I got here at twelve-thirty, but I've been catching up on emails. The morphine's knocked you around, I guess. The doctor came while I was here, which was good timing.'

In her lap, he noticed, was his iPhone.

'What did he say?'

'That you were lucky to escape a head injury. You've fractured your kneecap in three places, he'll operate on Monday when the swelling's gone down a bit. He'll have to wire the patella back together.'

'Surgery?'

Hamish had never been under the knife before.

'They'll keep you in hospital on antibiotics for a few days afterwards. You won't be able to bend your knee for six weeks, until the bone fragments grow back together. You'll need to wear a splint too.'

'Oh.' He closed his eyes, daunted by the prospect. In an operational role like his, working from home just wasn't an option. But neither was hobbling around the office like a cripple.

'I called Gary,' she added, as if reading his mind. 'He wants you to focus on getting better. He's putting Nick Bridge in your role for now.'

Paula's voice sounded odd, strained somehow. Probably anticipating how he'd feel about Nick-the-Dick Bridge. That sleazy little brown-noser, he'd lick the CEO's balls if he could. Now, care of Hamish's accident, Nick-the-Dick's career dream had just come true.

'Well.' Paula stood up from the chair and slipped his telephone back into her handbag. 'I'd better get home and start on the tuna pie.'

Just the mention of it turned Hamish's stomach; it wasn't one of his dinner favourites. Paula's patchy success in the kitchen, despite her many recipe books and several cooking courses, had become the target of family taunts.

'Paula,' he said, motioning to her handbag. 'Can I have my phone please?'

'What for?'

*What do you bloody think?*

They locked eyes.

'I don't think you'll be needing it,' she said, her voice low and calm.

'Look, Paula, I know you want me to rest, but I—'

'I've been messaging Lisel.'

He froze, registering her words.

The room upended itself; windows, curtains and bed linen spinning in a vortex. Everything whirling and turning, all except Paula, who stood erect in front of him. A tranquil face with merciless eyes, like a Valkyrie poised to escort him to his fate.

'She was really concerned about you.'

No air in his lungs.

'So I told her not to worry. I told her your *wife and children* would look after you.'

She lowered her face in front of his.

He felt his bladder emptying into his catheter.

'At first I didn't know which was worse,' she said. 'A middle-aged wannabe pretending he's twenty-eight to seduce a seventeen-year-old—or a teenage girl, barely older than Caitlin, behaving like a prize whore.' Her eyes flashed. 'After I told Lisel how old you *really* are, I asked her what her *parents* think of what she's been up to. Funnily enough, she didn't answer.'

Paula stood up and stalked to the door, then wheeled around again. 'Of course, the biggest fool in all of this is me. For believing in *us*.' Tears began to trickle down her face. 'Almost a *year* of deceit.'

*Not every day*, he thought, silenced by her twisted face. *Not even every week. Once a fortnight, tops. It was* never *a relationship.*

'Paula, it wasn't—' He couldn't get the words out quickly enough.

'Lisel could be our *daughter*, Hamish.' She spun around and thrust the blue curtain aside.

'Paula . . .'

She didn't look back.

*

Hamish's eyes followed the thin gossamer web floating in the corner of the ceiling. Everything else was sterile, but somehow that spider had escaped the reach of the hospital's cleaners. He'd been watching the web drift since Monday afternoon, when he'd woken up groggy and aching after the surgery.

It was now Thursday and Paula hadn't returned. Not since her revelation that she knew about Lisel, and had even made contact with her.

After three days of enforced contemplation, Hamish now felt he had a better understanding of Paula's surprise and, to some extent, her anger. But damn it, he'd also found himself thinking, had *she* ever tried to understand *his* needs? Or recognised the devastating impact of the sexual rationing she'd been meting out for years?

Hamish closed his eyes, engulfed by a wave of loneliness.

There was no point trying to justify it.

In his mind, Lisel had been a defensible way of managing sexual boredom in a monogamous relationship. But Paula clearly didn't agree, and the five days in hospital since her visit now felt like five years.

The kids had called by on Monday night after the surgery. He'd held Caitlin's hand and tried to smile at Lachie, but he'd been so furry-mouthed with painkillers he couldn't even speak.

Since then, his only regular visitor was a morose-faced orthopaedic surgeon who'd told Hamish that a post-operative wound infection had set in.

'We'll need to keep you in hospital longer,' he'd explained, 'maybe another four or five days. But once the incision's healed properly, we'll put you in a splint, get you some physiotherapy and discharge you. With a walking stick, I'm afraid. I'm sure you can't wait to get home.' The doctor was trying to sound jovial, but his facial expression didn't convince.

*I'll be lucky if Paula lets me in the front door*, Hamish thought.

Without his mobile phone, Hamish couldn't call anyone. He cursed his dependency on technology—having an electronic address book meant he hadn't memorised anyone's number. Except Paula's, of course, but that was redundant—she simply refused to pick up. He could only remember the first five digits of Doggo's, the first four of his older brother's. He wondered whether Paula had contacted his mother, who'd retired to Mallacoota ten years back. He hoped not, on some level: he didn't want his mother hearing about his misdemeanours from his wife. His father had passed away three years earlier, so he'd never know about any of it, thankfully. His dad had adored Paula, loving her like the daughter he'd never had. *Look after her, son*, he'd always said, *a good woman is hard to find.*

*Dad would crucify me for this*, Hamish thought, watching the cobweb on the ceiling again. *He was a true gentleman.*

It wasn't the first time Hamish had compared himself to his father and found himself wanting. His father had been effortlessly chivalrous, or so it had seemed to Hamish. Women had fawned over him, yet there wasn't a skerrick of lasciviousness about him. This confounded Hamish, whose dick almost always interfered in his relations with women. Fortunately for his professional life, there weren't many female employees at Crossroads.

'Mr McInnes?'

It was Jan, the grey-haired nurse, whose brief appearances at his bedside had become a welcome distraction.

'I found that number you asked for. Only a few people in Melbourne have "Dogger" as a surname. It's quite unfortunate, isn't it?' She chuckled. 'Here it is—*T.G. Dogger*, Springvale.' She waved a small piece of paper at him. 'He's the one, I take it?'

Hamish's eyes brimmed with gratitude. He looked over at the telephone perched on the chest of drawers near his bed, his private line in hospital. It hadn't rung once since his arrival.

'Would you like me to dial the number for you?' asked Jan.

He nodded mutely.

'Oh, darling, you're in the wars, aren't you?'

Her sympathy made him want to lean into her chest and cry like a baby.

She pushed her spectacles back onto the bridge of her nose, picked up the telephone and dialled.

'There you are.' She passed the handset to him and walked to the door. 'If you need to hang up, just press the call bell.'

'Thanks, Jan.'

He lifted the receiver to his ear.

Tina answered.

'Hamo!' she squealed, as she always did.

'Is Doggo there, Tina?'

'He's just helping Mitch with his homework, hang on.'

The alarm clock on the bedside table told Hamish it was now six o'clock, exactly the worst time of day to telephone a family of seven.

'Haaamo.' Doggo sounded his usual chipper self. 'How are ya, mate?'

'I can't get to drinks tomorrow, I had an accident.'

Doggo said nothing for a moment.

'You okay? What happened?'

For the second time in two minutes, Hamish found he couldn't speak. He tried to swallow it down, keep a lid on it. Didn't want to bawl like a girl down the phone to Doggo.

'Fell off the bike. Smashed my knee bad.'

'Where are you, mate?'

'Box Hill Hospital. Orthopaedic ward. They had to operate.'

'Jesus.' Doggo paused. 'I'll come and see you after dinner, mate, around eight-thirty. Unless Paula or the kids will be there?'

Hamish tightened his fist around the edge of the bed sheet.

'Eight-thirty's good.'

'Righto.' Doggo hung up.

Hamish let the receiver drop out of his hand and rebound towards the chest of drawers, swinging by its spiral cord.

*

'Hamo.'

Ants were crawling all over him. Bloody tiny itchy ants, boring their way under his skin and into his ears and up his nose. He couldn't move to flick them off.

'Hamo.'

It was Paula. She was there again, he could smell her. That perfume she'd been wearing since she was twenty-three, the citrus one. Oranges and lemons on a summer's day. He smiled, but couldn't prise his eyelids apart.

'Hamo. You awake?'

His eyes snapped open.

Doggo's face hovered above him.

'Shit, mate. What happened?'

Hamish blurted out the whole story.

How he'd argued with Caitlin about the Facebook scandal and she'd flounced off on her bike. How he'd followed her and crashed on Blackburn Road, shattering his knee in three places. The surgery, the wound infection, the time off work he'd be forced to take. And somewhere in that shit-storm, how Paula had discovered his online liaisons with Lisel.

'Oh, fuck.' Doggo looked genuinely scared.

'It's not good, Doggo.' Hamish noticed that his own voice sounded wispy; a bit like an old man's.

'How much does Paula know?'

'Enough, mate. Everything, probably. She's been in touch with Lisel herself.'

'Jesus H. Christ.' Doggo sat bug-eyed, biting at the edge of his right thumbnail, a nervous habit of his since high school. 'What are you going to do?'

'No idea. Paula hasn't come to see me since the day I was admitted.' His chin trembled. 'Even after the surgery.'

*Don't you cry, you weak-as-piss pussy.*

'Do you want me to . . . to go round to your house and see her?'

Hamish looked at Doggo, his mate of almost thirty years. They'd met as twelve-year-olds at high school and since then, they'd seen and done it all together. Girls, clubs, drugs, porn, hangovers, surfing, Europe, marriage, kids, chicks on the internet. Doggo was a bloke of few words, but he knew Hamish better than anyone else.

Hamish didn't trust himself to speak; he could only nod at Doggo.

'Righto.' Doggo looked relieved to have a plan. 'I've got to finish a big job tomorrow, but I'll go over Saturday.'

'Thanks, Doggo.' Hamish felt like hugging him.

'When will they let you out of here?' Doggo asked.

'Doctor reckons early next week. The infection's fucked me over. But after it's cleared, I'm good to go.'

'Do you need anything from home?' Doggo stood up from his chair.

'Not unless you can get my phone off Paula.'

Doggo chewed his thumb again. 'It'll take a helluva lot to dig yourself out of this one, Hamo.' He reached for Hamish's hand, as if to shake it. But their timing was off, and Doggo's connected with the IV drip.

They laughed at their clumsiness.

'At least we can still laugh, eh?' said Doggo, clapping him on the shoulder.

Hamish choked up. 'Thanks, mate.'

Doggo flicked both thumbs up, his trademark farewell, before heading down the corridor.

# 4

'Mum, what are you *doing*?'

Paula jumped at the sound of Caitlin's voice.

She looked up at her daughter, standing in the bedroom doorway, her blonde hair mussed by sleep, long tanned limbs protruding out of a skimpy pink nightie. The one they'd argued about, a birthday gift from Amy, with a plunging neckline and Playboy bunny insignias plastered all over it.

*It's slutty and it sexualises her*, she'd told Hamish.

*But she's only wearing it at home*, he'd pointed out. *No blokes will* see *her in it.*

*But* I *can*, she'd replied.

*Pick your battles*, he'd said. *It's not a big a deal.*

So Paula had let it go, but it wound her up whenever she saw Caitlin wearing it.

'It's past midnight, Catie,' she said. 'Did something wake you?'

'No.' Caitlin wandered across the room and sat down on the end of Paula's bed. 'I just can't sleep.'

'Me neither.'

Paula placed another pile of folded clothing into the suitcase that lay open on the floor.

'What's this?' Caitlin gestured at the items spread across the bed.

Paula stalled. 'Well, I was going to tell you tomorrow.'

She sat down next to her daughter. 'We're going away.'

'Where to?'

*As far as possible from your father.*

'Around Australia in the caravan. You, me and Lachie. And Gramps, too.'

Paula opened the cover of the adventure scrapbook she'd created with Hamish years ago, with its map of Australia glued across two pages.

Caitlin looked dismayed. 'But . . . I've got school.'

'No you don't. Mr Nelson hasn't given you the all-clear, remember?'

'But he will.' Caitlin pouted. 'Amy said so. As soon as Facebook takes the photo down, he'll let us both back. And Mr Nelson's given everyone three days to unlike the post, or he's going to—'

'I know.' Paula had heard as much from the principal himself, in a brusque voicemail message. But the Facebook post remained active for all to see, and Lachie still hadn't returned to school either.

Paula's world had been turned upside down in less than a week: first, by the Facebook incident with Caitlin, then by Hamish's accident, and finally, her discovery of his online indiscretions. After so many unremarkable years, three disastrous events had occurred within twenty-four hours.

*Bad things always happen in threes*, her mother used to say.

'It's only six weeks until the end of school.' Paula tried to look upbeat. 'We've got nothing else planned for the summer holidays. It'll be a big adventure.' *The one we always said we'd go on, your father and me.*

'I don't want to go.'

'We'll only be away three months. It's not forever.'

'Three *months*? What about Dad? Where will *he* be?'

'Here, at home. I'm sure he'll agree it's the right decision.' Paula didn't quite believe her own propaganda. 'Look, Catie, I don't want to hurt anyone, but I'm in a situation I never imagined I'd be in.'

Caitlin glowered at her.

'The truth is, Dad and I . . . need to have a break. I love your dad, and I love you and Lachie. But I don't think I can stay in this house with your father for a while.'

Paula looked at the pillows on their bed. The idea of lying there next to Hamish made her feel sick.

'Why? What did Dad *do*?'

'I think I'll let Dad explain.'

'You always tell us honesty is the best policy.'

'It is.' Paula couldn't believe how difficult this was. 'But let's talk about it in the morning.'

'No.' Caitlin scowled. 'I won't go anywhere until you tell me what Dad did.'

Paula paused, deliberating. It was one o'clock on a Tuesday morning and here she was, physically and emotionally exhausted by the events of the last five days. And now she was being drawn into a conversation with her daughter that she really wasn't ready to have.

*But how will I be better prepared tomorrow?* she asked herself. *Or any other day, for that matter? It's going to be a difficult discussion at any time.*

Caitlin's eyes drilled into her.

'Alright, Catie. Your dad's been having an affair on the internet. I found out the morning after his accident.'

Paula picked at a stray thread from the quilted doona they sat on. Only last week she'd made a diary note to buy a new doona cover at the January sales. She'd kept everything orderly for years, fulfilling the countless duties of a devoted wife—never imagining for a moment that her husband might be cyber-screwing a seventeen-year-old.

The thread blurred in Paula's fingers as she remembered the appalling discovery. How she'd found Hamish's phone recharging on the kitchen bench the morning after the accident. Her initial relief at finding it, one of the only times he'd ever *not* taken his phone with him. She'd have to call Hamish's workaholic boss, Gary, she decided.

'Lachie,' she said, turning to her son, 'do you happen to know the passcode for Dad's phone?'

Lachlan looked up from his Weet-bix and smirked. '*Duh*, Mum, I've seen it a million times. It's 1995.'

Of course: their wedding year.

'Go and get dressed, kids,' she urged. 'Let's go up to the hospital.'

Paula turned Hamish's phone over in her hands and keyed in the numbers.

A second later, she was looking at a Skype browser already open on the screen.

A tab jiggled at the bottom: *26 unread messages.* That seemed an unusually high number for one night's absence from work.

Paula scanned the list, most of which were from a user named *Lisel17.* Then she clicked on a random entry.

*What r u up 2?*

The informality was odd, she thought.

*Im home alone.*

*Wish u lived closer.*

*Then maybe we could meet.*

Paula frowned.

*Horny alone is no fun. Well let me try . . .*

*Ive got my hands where urs should b.*

*U turn me on Hamo.*

*I'm pressing my pussy with ur big fat cock.*

She gasped.

*Pleeease fuck me.*

*U r pushing in2 me now.*

*Ohhh that feels good.*

*Ive got my hands all over my pussy baby.*

*Im so slippery now.*

*U turn me over and fuck me from behind.*

*Harder Hamo harder*

*In n out in n out in n out.*

*Im about 2 cum.*

*Begging u 4 more.*

*Im cuming Hamo Im cuming.*

Paula dropped the phone, her heart hammering in her ears. She sagged against the pantry, then onto the cold blue tiles below.

She looked around, disbelieving, at the icons of her domestic life. The Suncoaster blender, a wedding gift from Aunty Dinah. The expensive knife block she'd bought on special from Hardy's Knives. The Tupperware canisters of macaroni, rice, sugar and flour, standing tallest to shortest in the pantry like sturdy domestic soldiers. The jaffle-maker, a staple of their weekend routine, perfect for soccer lunches and easy snacks. Her chalkboard shopping list, prompting her to buy mayonnaise, pickles and juices for the school lunches. All of her endless planning and management, oiling the wheels of family life.

Trembling, Paula stood up again and got herself a glass of water.

*Maybe it's not what it seems*, she told herself, gulping down mouthfuls. *Maybe it's some sort of sex spam.*

She seized the phone again. Keyed in 1995.

Scrolling through the messages, she searched for signs of Hamish's innocence.

*Did u get what I sent?*

*Noticed the number . . . PO Box 69 . . . specially for me? :)*

*Ur turn 2 send me something now.*

*12/9 James Street Mandurah WA 6210.*

*Send me something hot ok.*

Paula dry-retched into the sink.

It wasn't spam. Lisel17 knew their postbox number, presumably because Hamish had given it to her. And that looked like a real address, albeit on the other side of Australia.

'Mum, are you okay?'

She turned and saw her daughter, still perched on the end of the bed that Paula and Hamish had shared for seventeen years.

Caitlin suddenly leaned forward, pushing her lithe body against Paula's stout one. In earlier years, Hamish had described Paula's figure as 'womanly', or even 'cuddly'. Now, he said nothing. But she noticed his expression whenever she had an extra helping of lasagne, a second slice of birthday cake, one more row of chocolate. The disapproving set of his mouth that said: *You don't need that, fatty.*

Paula looked into Caitlin's face, which was ashen now.

'Who . . . um . . .' Caitlin looked embarrassed. 'Who did Dad . . . have the affair with?'

'I don't know exactly.' Paula was determined not to reveal anything about Lisel, especially her age. 'Someone he met in a chat forum, I think.'

Caitlin crumpled sideways onto the bed and began to sob, her face buried in the doona.

'Shhh, it's okay.' Paula began stroking Catie's back. It was quite enough to manage her own emotions, let alone have to deal with someone else's. Her open wardrobe, half-empty now, looked exactly like she felt.

'Catie, I'm not saying it's *over* with Dad.' Paula guessed this was the reason Caitlin was crying. 'I just need some time to think.' She continued rubbing her daughter's back. 'We could all do with a break, Catie. You've worked so hard this year, it won't be long until school finishes. And after the holidays, we'll come back fresh for a new school year. Gosh, you'll be in Year Ten next year. So grown up, I can't believe it. I can still remember when I could fit you in here.' Paula pointed at the crook of her arm and smiled, remembering the tiny, gurgling bundle her daughter had once been. 'You were such a gorgeous baby, Catie. People used to stop me in the street and tell me how perfect you were. You still are.'

Caitlin pulled herself up and sat cross-legged, fingering the edge of her nightie.

'You mean, we'd be home by the end of summer?'

Paula nodded. 'And we'd see some amazing parts of Australia on the way.'

Caitlin's bottom lip began to quiver. 'But it won't be the same without Dad.'

'I know, honey.' Paula's voice broke. 'But you and Lachie can stay in touch with him the whole time.'

Paula and Hamish had often talked about taking leave from work and doing the ultimate Aussie road trip with the kids. Just the four of them in a comfortable campervan, toasting marshmallows over campfires, swimming in outback billabongs. But the time had never been quite right.

Until now.

Paula dabbed at the edges of her eyes with a crumpled tissue.

'You don't have to come if you don't want to, Catie. You can stay here with Dad, I won't be cross. But *I* need to get away for a few months.' The more Paula talked, the more resolute she felt. 'Lachie can decide for himself too. I won't be forcing anyone along.'

Paula watched as Caitlin lifted a head torch from the bed, clicking its bluish light on and off. It was old, but with the new battery Paula had purchased, it was still in good working order. It hadn't been used since their first year of marriage, when Paula and Hamish had taken a trip to Jervis Bay. Paula could still recall that magical week over Easter, camping in a pristine national park by the ocean. The dolphins, rosellas and kangaroos at dawn, the rubbish-raiding possums at night. They'd had sandy sex and gone swimming afterwards, drunk too much red wine and cooked every meal over the campfire.

Paula reached for her equipment list.

*Spare batteries for head torch*, she wrote.

'When are we leaving?' asked Caitlin.

Paula smiled at the 'we'.

'Thursday.' Paula knew it was ridiculous, reckless even, to leave in just two days' time. But she also knew that if she waited until Hamish returned from hospital, she'd probably change her mind. In all their years of marriage, she'd rarely resisted Hamish's persuasions.

'Okay.' Caitlin said softly. 'But can we visit Dad again before we go? I mean, it's disgusting what he's done.' She looked conflicted. 'But I still want to see him, you know?'

'I understand, honey,' said Paula. 'Gramps can take you first thing tomorrow.'

Caitlin stood up from the bed and took a few steps towards the door, before turning and launching herself at Paula.

'I'm sorry, Mum.' She hugged Paula to her. 'I hate what Dad's done.'

Paula took Caitlin's face in her hands and smiled, unable to speak.

As she watched her daughter padding down the hallway, Paula's stomach clenched with fear.

*It's real now*, she thought. *I've just made it real.*

*

The following evening, her sister Jamie sat opposite Paula in the kitchen. '*This* Thursday? You're not serious, are you?'

Catie and Lachie weaved around them, carrying equipment in and out of the lounge room. Catie was sorting through the linen, including the sleeping bags. Lachie, having appointed himself providore, was busy selecting non-perishable items for the caravan's pantry.

'Does it look like I'm kidding?' Paula asked, nodding at her children.

Jamie peered at the half-packed crates littered across the floor.

'But surely you can't just pull the kids out of school and run away?'

She'd had a similar reaction from the two friends she'd told about her plan. Shocked silence, followed by random protests.

*It's madness to go in summer—you'll go troppo up north.*

*The flies will be shocking. And what about the snakes?*

*You can't escape your troubles, Paula.*

'Why not?' asked Paula, studying Jamie's face.

'It just seems like . . . an overreaction.' Jamie lowered her voice. 'I mean, Hamish's behaviour was more than bad, maybe unforgivable. But if you uproot Catie and Lachie when they're vulnerable like this, it could destabilise them even further.' Jamie's words carried all the weight of her professional authority as a school teacher. 'I know you're hurt, Paula, and I really feel for you—but you've *got* to put the kids first.'

While she'd hoped for her sister's unconditional support, Paula had anticipated this lukewarm reception. Jamie had always been the quintessential first child: the sensible, mature, responsible one.

'Not this time,' said Paula. 'Catie and Lachie will be fine *without* their social networks. It's bloody social networking that's got us into so much trouble lately.'

Jamie opened her mouth, then closed it again.

'Well . . . what about Dad?' Her tone was more subdued now. 'Who's going to take care of him while you're gone?' Jamie and her family lived a thirty-minute drive west of Glen Waverley.

'He's coming with us.'

'But he doesn't travel! He's never been out of Victoria before.'

'Well, he *loves* the caravan. He even wanted to take it for a spin to Canberra a few weekends back, to see the Impressionists exhibition.'

Jamie looked bewildered.

There was a shuffling sound from the kitchen doorway. 'Ah, my two favourite girls. I *thought* my ears were burning.'

Sid walked over to his eldest daughter and kissed her cheek. 'How are you, sweetheart? Want to come with us?'

Jamie let out an uncomfortable laugh. 'Some of us have to *work*, unfortunately, Dad.'

Paula detected the barb. Jamie's financial situation was precarious, particularly now with three teenage children. As a teacher married to a teacher, and both committed to public education, Jamie and Rick had never been able to afford much beyond the bare necessities. By contrast, Hamish's career success had allowed Paula a level of flexibility that Jamie had never enjoyed. While Jamie returned to work within three months of each of her children's births, Paula had stopped work completely after Caitlin was born, only choosing to resume a part-time career almost a decade later.

'Oh, well,' said Sid, patting Jamie on the shoulder. 'Maybe you and Rick and the kids could meet us somewhere along the road?'

Jamie looked bemused. 'Are you sure you're up to it, Dad?'

'Absolutely. Never felt better.' He winked at her. 'Always wanted to see the Nullarbor Plain, ever since I was a little fella.' His grin faded. 'And if I stay here with Hamish, I might kill the bastard.'

They fell silent for a moment.

Her father looked as disappointed as Paula had ever seen him. She could tell from Jamie's expression, too, that she was torn: Hamish had been part of the family for more than seventeen years.

Lachie lumbered into the kitchen, carrying a camp stove.

'Put it here, big fella.' Her father waved his right hand in front of Lachie, forcing him to put down the stove and return his high-five. 'This is going to be the trip of a lifetime, matey.'

Lachie nodded half-heartedly.

Her son hadn't reacted well to Paula's news of his father's indiscretion and their impending departure. He'd gone all quiet and retreated to his room. When Paula had followed him, trying to explain herself, he'd simply said, 'Whatever, Mum.' Which usually meant he was angry. Feeling rather slighted, Paula had to keep telling herself *he's a thirteen-year-old boy. An enigma wrapped in a riddle.*

Later that same day, when he'd emerged for lunch, she'd offered Lachie the option of staying at home with his father instead.

'What, for the whole summer?' Lachie had asked. 'I hate *Ultimate Fight Club.*'

Paula had nodded in recognition. Hamish's recovery was sure to involve a lot of television, mostly sports programs that held little or no interest for Lachie.

'Looks like the lesser of two evils, then, Lachie,' she'd said.

'Guess so,' he'd replied, before heading back to his bedroom.

She hadn't followed him, sensing his need for space.

Once they were on the road, she reasoned, he'd come around.

'Come on, buddy.' Her father now beckoned to Lachie. 'Help me get the last stuff out of the garage.' As they walked down the stairs, Sid punched his grandson's shoulder playfully. 'You know the Nullarbor Plain? We'll catch a dingo out there. I've got a trap downstairs that's a set of real steel jaws.'

Paula and Jamie exchanged a wry smile; the dingo trap had been a rustic retirement gift from one of their father's rural lamb suppliers. They'd never imagined he might actually find cause to *use* it.

'A butcher on the road.' Jamie chuckled. 'This might be one hell of a trip.'

Paula laughed too, detecting a hint of envy in Jamie's voice.

She rested her chin on her hand and looked at her sister across the bench. With only two years separating them, they'd been close as children and practically inseparable as teenagers. They'd adored each other's company; whiling away weekends together with cycling or hiking in the national park, playing board games, dressing up and styling each other's hair, or singing and gyrating to the season's top hits. It had been a natural extension of their childhood closeness, then, when they'd flatted together at university.

But things had changed after they'd met their husbands-to-be; Jamie first, falling for the handsome Rick and promptly moving to a teaching post in the Riverina. During the course of that posting,

Paula had met Hamish, marrying him within a year. Jamie had been Paula's only bridesmaid and, less than six months later, their roles had been reversed at Jamie's wedding. Paula had always assumed that her sister would be her closest friend for life, but to her quiet dismay, they'd drifted apart after marriage. A function of circumstance rather than choice, Paula reflected now. The complexities of adulthood—of spouses and finances and careers and children—complicating the natural sisterly bond.

Not to mention the reality that their husbands, while cordial enough at family gatherings, would probably never *choose* to be friends. Rick was a science teacher; an introverted, sensitive, cerebral character to whom Hamish had trouble relating. By contrast, Hamish's untrammelled blokey-ness—his sportiness and material ambitions for money, cars and home renovations—seemed to grate on Rick. Her brother-in-law often fell silent in Hamish's presence, which was discomfiting for everyone. While Paula couldn't begrudge Rick his feelings—Hamish was, after all, larger than life—she lamented the invisible wedge it drove between herself and Jamie.

'Do you want me to look in on Hamish while you're away, take him a few meals?' asked Jamie. 'Since I can't seem to talk you out of going.'

Paula nodded. 'Thanks, but I'll leave some supplies for him. Don't go to too much trouble.'

Part of her wanted Hamish to flounder on his own for a while.

'Is Hamish, you know, *okay* with all of you going away?' Jamie looked uncertain.

'I haven't mentioned it, the kids did.' Paula evaded Jamie's eyes, feeling more than guilty. She should have told Hamish to his face in hospital.

Their father suddenly popped his head up from the stairwell. 'I took the kids to see Hamish today,' he said. 'Catie told him about the trip, but he didn't say much at all. He *knows* what he's done to this family.'

No one said anything for a moment, then Lachie emerged carrying another box of camping gear. Sid helped him carry it to the lounge room.

'Three months away is a long time. How will you pay for it?' Jamie asked. Money was always one of her chief concerns.

Paula shrugged. 'I've withdrawn enough to keep us going.'

*Try ten thousand dollars.* She could only imagine how livid Hamish would be when he discovered *that*. But what else was the alternative? She didn't want to leave a tell-tale trail of ATM withdrawals across Australia on the bank statement of their joint account. So she'd walked into the bank earlier that day and signed for the biggest wad of cash she'd ever handled in her life. Burdened by its weight in her bag, she'd sequestered most of it inside the broken freezer compartment of the caravan's fridge.

Paula looked at Jamie again. 'On second thoughts, it *would* be good if you could check on Hamish. He's never really fended for himself. And he's injured too.'

*Am I doing the right thing?*

Jamie suddenly reached across the bench and placed a hand over Paula's. 'I get it,' she said. 'It's a bit rash, but I totally understand why you need to get away. If Rick had done that to me, with a girl of that age . . .' She wrinkled her nose. 'But come back soon, okay?'

Tears pricked Paula's eyes as she gripped Jamie's hand.

Life had taken them in different directions, but her sister still knew her best.

Jamie's mobile beeped.

She checked her phone and rolled her eyes. 'Rick's sent an SOS. The kids are going berserk. Nothing that some baked beans on toast wouldn't fix, I imagine, but I'd better get home. You know how it is.'

'Sure do.' Paula smiled. 'Thanks for coming over. Sorry to drop a bombshell like this.'

'That's okay.' Jamie's expression softened. 'I'm just sad it's happened at all. You deserve so much better.'

She stood up and walked around the bench, pulling Paula into a hug.

Paula leaned into her taller, slimmer older sister. Wiser too, in all probability, she thought.

'It'll be alright,' Jamie said quietly. 'I don't know why I say that, but it will be. I've always just *felt* your life would work out, in here.' She tapped her chest. 'There's a sort of aura around you, protecting my little sister.'

'Really?' Paula smiled. 'Thanks, Jamie.'

Jamie picked up her handbag from the bench.

Paula didn't want her sister to leave. 'Why don't you think about Dad's idea?' she asked. 'You could meet us somewhere like Margaret River. Maybe even leave the kids with Rick and have a few days to yourself? We could do girls' stuff, like old times.'

Jamie smiled wistfully. 'Sounds nice, but we're driving up to Coffs Harbour to visit Rick's mum these holidays. She's sick, you know.'

Paula nodded sympathetically.

'Promise you'll take care of Dad?' Jamie looked unsteady for a moment. 'He's . . . all we've got left.'

So Jamie felt it too. Grateful for the unexpected gift delivered by their mother's death, in the form of their father.

Paula pulled Jamie into a final hug.

'It's only for the summer,' she murmured. 'We'll be back before you know it.'

*

In the next thirty-six hours, Paula somehow managed to finalise everything for their departure.

She called Burwood Secondary College on Wednesday morning and informed Mr Nelson that the children wouldn't be returning for the rest of the term. He was clearly taken aback; she filled the ensuing silence by requesting that he cancel her canteen roster.

'Mrs McInnes . . .' The principal scrambled to keep her on the line. 'There's no need to take such *drastic* action. We might get some news from Facebook sooner than we expect.'

'We just need some family time now,' she explained. 'We'll see you first term next year, Mr Nelson.'

Her next phone call, to Bella Vista Aged Care, was more difficult. Paula dialled the number, hoping the gossipy administration manager, Janelle, wouldn't answer.

'Good morning, Bella Vista. Janelle speaking.'

Paula attempted to sound chirpy. 'Hi Janelle, it's Paula. I need to cancel my shifts, sorry.'

'Oh.' Janelle made some tut-tutting noises. 'Are you sick?'

'Hamish and I are . . .' Paula's voice began to wobble. 'We're going through a difficult patch.'

'Oh.' Janelle was listening intently now.

'I need some time off work. I'm taking a break with the kids for . . . a couple of months.'

'Oh, Paula. I'm so sorry.'

'I just hope my job's still here when I get back.'

'Of course.' Janelle made more sympathetic sounds. 'We'll work something out. Are you alright, Paula?'

Paula screwed her eyes shut against the rising sadness. 'I'm fine, Janelle.'

She replaced the receiver and cried into her hands. Telling someone beyond her closest circle was harder than she'd imagined. In addition to her private pain—the revolving door of anger and grief—the public telling triggered another emotion: shame. The indignity of perceptions:

*You couldn't keep your husband happy.*

*You failed your marriage.*

*It'll screw up your kids.*

As an antidote to sadness, Paula threw herself into logistical overdrive. Cleaning out the freezer and stocking the fridge, packing and repacking, crossing off items from multiple lists: First-aid kit, spare tyre and car jack. Tarpaulin, tent, sleeping bags. Insect repellent, fly zapper, mosquito nets. Solar-powered lamp, matches, picnic set. Bicycles, helmets, beach towels.

Just before midnight on Wednesday, eight hours before they were due to depart, her father poked his head around the lounge-room door. 'Is this the last of it?' He nodded at two milk crates of equipment.

'I think so. I'm sure I've forgotten something.'

'Don't worry.' He grinned. 'We can still buy things on the road, you know. This is Australia, not darkest Peru.'

She smiled at the reference to *Paddington Bear*, one of her favourite children's books. Decades ago, he'd read it to her as a bedtime story.

'Go to bed, Paula.' Her father's face was earnest now.

'I will, Dad. I've just got one more thing to do.' She picked up her notebook from the coffee table.

'Don't stay up too long.'

He disappeared down the stairs.

Paula walked to the sideboard, where she stored their best dinnerware. Her grandmother's Royal Doulton tea set, her mother's favourite Wedgewood pieces, the Sheffield cutlery. She opened the bottom drawer and found the 1940s set of splayds they hardly ever used.

Slipping her gold wedding band and sapphire engagement ring off her finger, she placed them inside the velour-lined box and snapped it shut.

Then she tore a sheet from the centre of her notebook.

*Dear Hamish . . .*

*

Pelting rain greeted them early the next morning. Sid reversed the ute up the drive and parked it in front of the caravan, before donning his raincoat and gumboots to load the final items. Paula held a red-and-white-striped golf umbrella over him as he attempted, with Lachie's help, to hitch the caravan to the ute's towbar.

They huffed and heaved until, finally, the knob slipped into place.

'That's tough work for an old bugger,' her father said. 'Thanks, Lachie.'

Lachlan joined his sister in the ute.

'Better pack this brolly,' Sid said, taking the umbrella from Paula and folding it up. He opened the ute's rear tray and skewered it between two bags, just beneath the canopy. 'How about I drive first, love? Might be a bit slippery out there.'

'No thanks, Dad,' said Paula. 'I'll do it.'

This was a moment she wanted to savour; defying her own doubts to set off for an adventure *without* Hamish.

'Right you are.'

He peeled off his raincoat and climbed into the front passenger seat. Paula walked around to the driver's side and took her place behind the wheel. Her stomach fluttered, as though she was poised to strut out on stage.

*This is it.*

'Couldn't have asked for a wetter day, could we?' Her father wiped his face with the edge of his t-shirt.

'It's an omen,' said Lachie, a small voice from the rear of the ute. 'It's pissing on your plan, Mum.'

'Lachlan McInnes!' Paula spun around. He'd never spoken to her like that before.

Her son squirmed, clearly aware he was out of line.

Paula drew herself up as tall as she could in her seat.

'Let's get a few things straight before we leave, kids.' Her voice was steely. 'If either of you don't want to come on this trip, *now* is the time to say so. You can stay with Aunty Jamie until Dad comes home from hospital.' She looked between her children. 'Any takers?'

They shook their heads.

'Right. Well, here's the first rule of this trip: if *anyone* swears or speaks rudely, there'll be consequences.' She eyeballed Lachie. 'For every rude word spoken, you'll *run* ahead of the car for fifty metres. Understand?'

They all nodded in unison, even her father.

'Not you, Dad.'

'Rules are rules,' he said.

Paula turned the key in the ignition and adjusted the rear-view mirror. The caravan obscured everything behind her; she'd have to rely on the side mirrors.

She looked once more at their family home, the centre of her life over the past fifteen years. They'd bought it at auction just before Catie was born, an unusual sloping block with a steep driveway rising up to a large, flat backyard. Double garage, laundry and under-house storage on the ground floor. Three bedrooms upstairs, a bathroom, a kitchen, dining and lounge room opening up to a rear balcony, plus a funny little nook they'd christened the 'TV room' for the kids. Nothing fancy, they'd renovated it not long after Lachie's arrival. After almost a year's worth of labour and laughter and petty bickering about fittings and finishes, they'd finally brought it to fruition *together.* Every tile, recess and floorboard now represented some piece of shared history.

Paula's eyes stung.

'And another thing, Lachie,' she added, putting the ute into first gear. 'I don't believe in omens.'

Their driveway was steep at the best of times, never mind while towing a caravan in slippery conditions. Paula had never towed anything larger than a box trailer filled with garden clippings bound for the tip.

She tentatively released the brake.

'Sure you don't want me to drive, m'girl?' her father asked brightly. 'A few cars parked in tricky spots down there. It's going to be a tight turn.' He nodded at the road beyond the driveway.

'No thanks.' She inched the caravan forward.

'You're doing well. Want me to get out and wave you down?'

'Okay.'

He climbed out of the car and stood at the bottom of the driveway, gesticulating in the rain. She wound down her window so she could hear him.

She'd just moved past the letterbox when her father pointed at a van parked flush against their driveway.

'Watch that van, Paula. Take the ute right out onto the road and do a big wide loop.'

She'd crossed one lane and nosed out into the next, when she realised she might not clear a red sedan parked on the other side.

'Whoa,' called her father, waving his hands. 'You're running out of turning room.'

She braked hard. And then, panicking at obstructing both lanes, she thrust the ute into reverse.

'No, Paula—'

A crunching sound stopped her.

'Oh, shit.' She peered out her window at the angle she'd reversed the ute into, almost ninety degrees to the caravan, then thumped her hands against the wheel. 'That was *so* bloody stupid.'

'You've jackknifed it, Mum,' said Lachie.

Her father inspected the L-shaped position of the caravan and ute. 'It's a beauty too, with the gradient on the road. We'll have to call for help.'

'Oh, God. I'm sorry.' Paula felt like crying. 'Out of the car, kids.'

They stood huddled on the nature strip, sheltering under the golf umbrella, their vehicle blocking the entire road.

She opened the passenger-side door and found her phone in the glove box. She'd only packed it in case of emergency, and hadn't expected to use it so quickly. She scrolled through her contact list, her hands shaking, until she found the number for roadside assistance.

'Want me to talk to them?' her father asked.

She nodded, passing him the telephone.

'Don't worry,' he said. 'There's a silver lining for every cloud. It's seven o'clock in the morning, not quite peak hour yet. They'll be here in no time.'

She sent the children back inside to wait.

*What a prize idiot*, she thought as she stood beneath the umbrella. *Jackknifing the caravan before we've even left our street.* She watched the water gushing past in the gutter. *Maybe Lachie's right, this trip might just be jinxed from the beginning.*

As her father had predicted, a bright yellow assistance truck appeared within thirty minutes, its hazard lights flashing.

'That's a doozy, mate,' called the driver to her father, assessing the caravan through his open window.

'It was me.' Paula called back.

'Ah.' The driver smirked. *Sheilas*, she could almost hear him thinking.

'Well, let's disconnect you, eh? You'll need a new brake light, too.'

Paula looked towards the house, where the children were standing at the lounge-room window.

'Uh, do you need me to help?' she asked the man.

'The standard call-out fee's a hundred bucks, love. If you try to help, it's two hundred.' He chuckled at his own gag.

'Can you stay here, Dad?'

'Sure, love.'

No skerrick of *I told you so*. She should have accepted *his* offer of assistance in the first place.

Paula could only imagine what Hamish would have said if *he'd* witnessed the debacle. But it was a moot point, she realised: he never would have let her get behind the wheel in the first place.

She joined the children at the lounge-room window and watched as the ute and caravan were manoeuvred back into position, the right brake bulb replaced, the crack in the covering taped. Then she marshalled the children out of the house, relocked the front door and placed the spare keys under the potted cactus.

'Okay, take two,' she said as they walked down the driveway. 'I'm really sorry about that.'

She sat down behind the steering wheel and turned the key in the ignition.

'Excuse me, Mum,' Lachie piped up from the rear. 'You've got a hundred metres of running to do.'

'What?' She checked the side mirrors, then pulled slowly away from the kerb.

'First rule of the trip. For every rude word spoken, you'll *run* ahead of the car for fifty metres. You said "shit" and "bloody" before, Mum.'

Paula noticed her father had covered his mouth and was gazing out of the window. She had a strong suspicion he was laughing behind his hand.

'I heard it too, Mum,' Caitlin volunteered. '*And* you said "God". Does that count?'

'Let's leave God out of it.' She pulled over in a deserted bus stop a little further down the road. 'Okay, Dad, you drive. Lachie, give me my raincoat, you little bugger.'

'That's a hundred and fifty metres,' he said. 'Meet you at Woolies, Mum.'

He pointed at the near-empty car park of a supermarket ahead.

She slammed the car door shut and slipped on her hooded raincoat. Then she began to jog, bending her head against the rain.

Her breathing became irregular within moments; how long had it been since she'd gone for a jog? Ten years at least. Her calves felt gelatinous, incapable of carrying her to the big green W ahead.

*It's not even a couple of hundred metres. Just keep going.*

Her father beeped the horn as he edged the ute and caravan past her. Lachie pressed his face to the window and puffed out his cheeks like a blowfish, while Caitlin waved from behind.

The rain suddenly intensified; splinters became sheets. She picked up her pace, bolting through the deluge, hardly able to see and hearing only herself panting. In the end, she almost ran past the ute and caravan; her father had to sound the horn again to attract her attention.

Paula wrenched open the passenger door, puffing.

'Right, Lachie, I've paid my debt. I just need to change.'

The children sniggered; her jeans and sneakers were soaked.

As she towelled off in the caravan, Paula caught sight of herself in the small square mirror fixed to the pantry cupboard. Skin pink from the exertion, fringe dripping, more fresh-faced than usual.

But still resolutely almost-forty, she thought.

'You keep driving, Dad,' she said, collapsing into the passenger seat. 'I'm buggered already.'

'That's another fifty metres, Mum,' said Lachie.

'Zip it, mister,' she said. 'Now for goodness' sake, let's get out of Glen Waverley.'

Her father saluted and drove on.

# 5

'Hillary needs some petrol. We're almost empty.'

They were barrelling down the M1 on the southern side of Werribee, en route to Geelong.

'Hillary?' Paula repeated.

'Hillary the Hi-Lux. Our trusty chariot's name.'

'You're such a bogan, Gramps,' said Lachie.

Paula turned to reprimand him, but stopped short. Lachie was smiling affectionately at his grandfather from the rear seat. She hadn't heard the word 'bogan' used as a term of endearment before; she still had a lot to learn about teenagers. Too much, she reflected; the Facebook scandal had taught her that.

'Why Hillary, Gramps?' Caitlin asked.

'Well, she's resilient,' Sid replied. 'She's got loads of energy, and she's easy on the eye. She's a fuel hybrid, taking both petrol and gas, so she's all about smart power. Just like the former US Secretary of State.'

Paula laughed. 'You're a fan of Hillary Clinton?'

Her father nodded.

'Well, that's something else I didn't know about you.'

'Didn't know it myself, either.' Her father chuckled. 'Picked up a second-hand copy of a book called *Hillary's Choice* about six months ago. Been a fan of hers ever since. Did you know she sent a letter to NASA as a kid asking how to become an astronaut, and you know what they wrote back? *Girls can't be astronauts.* The silly buggers. She really stuck it to them, didn't she?'

'You're quite the feminist, Dad.'

'Call me whatever you like.' He eased on the brakes, preparing for a turn-off to a petrol station. 'I just don't think genitals influence talent.'

Lachie snickered in the back. They rolled to a stop next to a diesel bowser.

'Come on, Mr Thirteen,' said Paula. 'Let's buy some lollies while Gramps fills up, er . . . Hillary.'

'I'm coming too,' said Caitlin. 'Or Lachie will buy those feral spearmint leaves.'

'Too right,' Sid called from behind the pump. 'Get us some Chicos instead, Catie. And a bottle of water, please.'

'Can't we have a Coke, Mum?' Lachie asked, tugging at her arm.

'No, Lachie. Water will do.'

'Aw, Mum, we want bubbles,' complained Catie.

'Get soda water, then.'

Paula smiled to herself as they trooped into the convenience store and began perusing the sweets aisle. She had the same feeling now that she'd had as a child on Boxing Day, when her family of four would pile into the car and set off on their annual road trip to Albury, the home of their farming cousins. On those summertime trips, Paula had never tired of the road and its secrets: the petrol stations manned by friendly country folk, the sugary treasures hidden in milk bars, the deserted public toilets attached to grassy picnic areas in quiet, shady gullies. Meat pies and cream buns, Big Ms and barley sugar. Her father's tuneless whistling accompanying Bing Crosby cassettes, the relaxed look on her mother's face, Jamie's endless backseat tournaments of I-Spy, Twenty Questions and Thumb Wars. The back aches, the bursting bladders, the bush wees. The exquisite limbo of transit, the mysteries of dirt roads in indeterminate locations. The feelings of optimism and anticipation on departure, rivalled only by the tedium of the return trip. All those long-gone pleasures of childhood when she was still Paula Jones, daughter and sister. Not yet Paula McInnes, wife and mother.

She paid for the lollies and went to find the toilet; a foul-smelling unisex cubicle tucked in a rear corner of the store.

*What is it about blokes and toilets*, she wondered, *that makes them smell this bad?* From the fluid across the seat and on the floor, she could hazard a guess: they didn't aim straight. Which indicated, in her view, either a gross malfunction of motor skills—*why can't healthy adult males just urinate into a bowl?*—or gross thoughtlessness on their part. A kind of egomania that prevented them from imagining as far as the next female user, having to sit down on a wet, rancid seat. Paula pinched her nose between her fingers as she hovered over the toilet. Her thighs cried out for help before she'd finished, but she managed to hold the position long enough to relieve herself.

On her way back to the ute, she remembered to pick up a newspaper for her father. The sports section was dominated by Melbourne Cup coverage already, carrying detailed descriptions of horses and jockeys, despite the fact that the race was more than a week away. They'd be somewhere in South Australia by Cup Day, Paula guessed.

As she approached the ute, she noticed Lachie and Catie seated in the rear cab, chewing lollies and listening to their iPods.

She opened Caitlin's door and stood looking at them.

'What?' Caitlin yelled, overly loud.

Paula leaned over and pulled out their earbuds.

'Mum . . .' Lachie whined.

'Okay, you two, here's the second rule of the trip,' she said. '*No private technology.* If you want to listen to music, we can listen to it all together, as a family.'

Caitlin and Lachie groaned.

Paula turned to her father for support. 'Remember those Bing Crosby cassettes you used to play on our trips to Albury, Dad? They were great.'

Her father chuckled. 'That's not what you said at the time, Paula.'

'Well, anyway.' She turned back to the children. 'You two sort out whose music gets played first. I don't care. But we're *not* going to bury ourselves in our own electronic cocoons. Got it?'

Caitlin looked miffed. 'I hate his music.'

Lachie grinned. 'C'mon, you like some of it. Let's flip a coin and see who goes first. Your call, Catie.' He pulled a dollar coin out of his pocket and flipped it.

'Heads,' said Caitlin.

They watched the coin spin in the air.

Lachie caught it, then showed her the back of his hand, victorious. 'Tails. Pass me that cable, Gramps.'

Lachie began fiddling around with the iPod connection on the dashboard.

Paula laid a hand on her father's shoulder. 'Is it my turn to drive? I won't jackknife us again, I promise.'

Her father chortled and shimmied across to the passenger seat.

Lachie passed his iPod to his grandfather. 'Press play, Gramps.'

Paula took the wheel and they set off from the petrol station, back on the M1.

'Chico?' Her father waved an open packet under Paula's nose.

'Thanks.'

She had just wiggled her fingers into the packet, when music blared out of the speakers.

'Shit.' The Chicos spilled everywhere.

'You're up to one hundred metres of jogging, Mum,' said Lachie.

Paula wondered if it was too late to retract rule number one.

So far, she was the biggest offender of the trip.

*

They'd been on the road for less than three hours when they arrived at the seaside town of Lorne. Where are all these people travelling to on a Thursday? Paula wondered, as they puttered around the civic centre. It was just before eleven o'clock, and the township was already bustling with visitors in cars and buses. Groups of them congregated on the foreshore, spilling out of cafés and across picnic rugs.

Scanning both sides of the road for a parking spot, Paula snapped off Lachie's music—an American R&B song with flagrant lyrics about drugs and sex and, Paula was appalled to note, suggestions of rape. She looked into the rear-view mirror, eyeing Caitlin anxiously.

*Dirty hos who want it nasty?* How can kids develop a healthy sexual identity when they're listening to songs like that?

'Hey,' objected Lachie. 'Why'd you kill it?'

'I'm not sure that can be classified as music,' Paula chided. 'I had no idea you had that on your iPod, Lachie.'

What *else* didn't she know about Lachie?

'But some of *your* favourite songs are like that, Mum,' Caitlin piped up. 'Madonna's "Like a Virgin" and that Elton John song, "Rocket Man". That's totally about drugs.'

Paula shook her head. 'When "Rocket Man" came out, the world was fascinated by the idea of man walking on the moon. My mum used to sing it to me while we made cardboard rockets.' She wondered if her father remembered that too. 'It may *well* be about drugs, but it's not overt. Why are lyrics so *vulgar* these days? You can't compare what we just heard with "Like a Virgin", either. Did you *hear* that song, Dad?'

'Not really, love,' he said, opening his window. 'I'm too busy trying to find a park that won't end with a jackknife.'

'You didn't hear the reference to *dirty hos*?'

He chuckled. 'The only dirty hoes I know are the ones I use in the garden.' He craned his neck to see down a side street. 'In a small town like this, it's a helluva lot harder trying to park Hillary and Clinton.'

'And *Clinton*?' Paula raised an eyebrow.

'Yep. Hillary the Hi-Lux and Clinton the caravan.'

'Aw, Gramps . . .' said Lachie.

'You're such a bogan,' said Caitlin.

'I'll take that as a compliment,' her father sniffed. 'Let's check out the Lorne caravan park, shall we?'

A large green sign with an arrow pointed down a nearby street.

Paula turned right and soon they found themselves outside the Lorne Bay Caravan Park, in a prime position on the Erskine River and overlooking the glittering ocean.

'No doubt about it,' murmured her father. 'Caravan parks and Catholic churches always get the best real estate.'

They pulled into a waiting bay and climbed out of the ute, grateful to stretch their limbs. Paula walked a short distance to a demountable bungalow, the park's administration building. She paused at the doormat—woven with the faded word *Welcome*—and peered through the flyscreen door.

'Hello?' she called.

There was no response, bar a Billy Joel tune warbling out of a radio somewhere. Now *those* were the days of quality music, Paula thought. Musicians with real instruments—baby grand pianos, brass sections and woodwinds—singing heartfelt tunes about human emotion. Not misogynist garbage made with the help of song-making software.

'Well,' she said, joining the others, 'nobody's here. But there's plenty of room to park.' She gestured to a large turning circle further down the driveway, bordered by bushland. 'How about I make us some lunch, then we can push on later this afternoon?'

'I don't want any lunch,' groaned Caitlin, clutching her stomach.

'That's because you and Gramps stuffed yourselves silly with Chicos,' said Paula. 'Honestly, you two.'

'No it's not,' Caitlin objected. 'It's because your cooking *sucks*, Mum. You can't even make a sandwich properly.'

'Yeah, Mum.' Lachie sneered.

Paula had heard it so many times, it didn't really wound her anymore.

'That's enough.' Her father looked hard at the children, before turning back to Paula. 'Do we really *have* to push on, love? I mean, look where we are.' He opened his arms wide and gestured at the bay, sparkling like a turquoise gem in a white arc of sand. 'Not every caravan park has a view like this. We're bang on the Great Ocean Road. Why don't we just camp here tonight and have a lazy afternoon in Lorne? I mean, where else do we have to be?'

Paula was so used to *scheduling* her family's activities: meal time, study time, homework time, work time, exercise time, sleep time. Rarely ever *free time*. She was shocked to realise there was nowhere else they had to be.

'Okay, let's make camp.'

'Right you are.' Sid sauntered over to the administration cabin and rang the counter bell three times, until a female voice hailed him.

Several minutes later, he emerged carrying two keys attached to oversized plastic key rings: one pink, one blue. A round-faced woman in a purple terry-towelling tracksuit trotted after him.

'Paula, this is Brenda.' Sid grinned at the woman. 'She's the most important lady in Lorne. Any question you've got, she'll answer it for you. And she's got the keys to the loo, too.'

The woman giggled. 'Your dad's a funny one, isn't he?'

'*And* she's given us the best caravan site in the park, site 1A, in exchange for a beer later tonight. Right, Brenda?'

'Oh, I don't want to impose.' Brenda looked embarrassed.

'A rose can *never* impose,' said Sid, plucking a flower from a garden bed and presenting it to Brenda.

'Oh.' The woman's face turned a shade of red.

Paula saw that her father was *flirting*. And he was *good* at it.

'How about I drive the caravan down to the site?' Paula said. 'Come on, kids. You can help me.'

'Help with what?' Caitlin said.

'Just *come*.'

*

Site 1A lived up to its promise. A flat green expanse sloping gently down to the beach, in the shade of sprawling eucalyptus trees.

'Direct beach access,' said Paula, pulling into the site. 'How about that, kids?'

Caitlin pushed open the door. 'I'm going in.'

'Not yet,' said Paula, climbing out of the ute. 'Rule number three of the trip: *make camp while the sun shines.* First thing we do when we arrive anywhere is set up, okay?'

'Come *on*, Mum,' grumbled Lachie, flopping down onto the grass. 'I'm tired.'

'We've only been on the road three hours. The sooner we pitch camp, the quicker you'll get down to the beach.'

Paula helped her son to his feet.

'You unpack the ute, Lachie, and I'll let Aunty Jamie know we've arrived safely.' She bent into the car, found her telephone in the glove box, then typed a brief message to her sister.

She turned to her daughter. 'Okay, Catie, come and help me with this tent, please.'

Erecting the tent was harder than Paula remembered; there were more stakes and poles and guy ropes than she could intuit a use for. After almost thirty minutes of fumbling, they finally got it up. It was larger than Paula recalled, too—a three-man tent at least—more than sufficient for her father.

'Thanks, Catie.' Paula laughed, admiring the khaki dome. 'Girl power, hey?'

Much to her relief, Catie smiled back. Paula had been monitoring her daughter's mood since the Facebook incident, but Catie had remained even-tempered. She was handling it with remarkable maturity, in fact. *It's not the end of the world, Mum*, she'd even said, more than once. It was Paula who continued to ruminate about the repulsive image.

Caitlin scooped up two extra pickets and tossed them into the tent bag, lingering over it a moment.

'Uh, Mum . . . what's this?' Catie pulled out a folded square of green plastic.

Paula studied it for a moment.

'The groundsheet,' called Lachie, as he climbed out of the caravan.

'Oh, shit.' Paula slapped a hand against her forehead. 'Bloody, bloody shit.'

'That's another two hundred metres, Mum.' Lachie grinned. 'Three hundred in total.'

Paula paid no attention. 'We're going to have to take this thing down again and put the groundsheet under it. Can you help, please Lachie?'

He set down an inflatable mattress and walked over.

They managed to deconstruct and reconstruct the tent in just under fifteen minutes.

'Well, at least we're getting faster at it,' said Paula.

'*Now* can we go for a swim?' Caitlin asked, pushing in a final picket.

'Sure, get your bathers on.' Paula wiped her forehead with the back of her sleeve. 'It'll be chilly in there, though.'

The children disappeared into the caravan with their bags, then Caitlin emerged carrying her bathers and a towel. Holding the oversized pink key Brenda had given them earlier, she jogged off in the direction of the ladies' change rooms.

The kids had packed remarkably lightly, Paula thought, as had her father. It was she who'd been unable to resist the temptation of packing things she *might* need. Like a poncho for cool nights in the desert, gumboots for wet season in the north, and travel hair curlers just in case they went to dinner somewhere swanky.

*Travel hair curlers? What was I thinking?*

She walked to the ute and heaved her large canvas suitcase out of the rear tray.

'You right with that, Mum?' Lachie asked, strolling past her in a pair of navy blue board shorts.

'Yes, hon,' she answered. 'You go for a swim.'

As she zipped open the suitcase, Caitlin streaked past in a pair of pink Speedos, racing after Lachie. She looked leonine, white-blonde hair billowing as she ran across the sand. She slapped Lachie's bottom as she passed and he gave chase immediately, his white skin and gangly legs so different from his sister's sporty flawlessness. Caitlin turned and pulled a face at him, before plunging into the ocean. Then Lachie was in too, and they were splashing and whooping and pushing each other.

Paula smiled. It had been a while since they'd had such unselfconscious fun, behaving like little kids again. Hamish would've loved seeing it, she thought.

She chewed the inside of her lip, imagining Hamish lying alone and injured in his hospital bed.

*Enough*, she muttered to herself, *you don't have to feel sorry for him.*

She seized a garbage bag from the rear of the ute, then returned to her suitcase and began riffling through its contents.

Enough of all this *stuff*.

Her red woollen jumper with pilling around the neckline. Some shapeless grey tracksuit pants. An ugly pair of orange women's board shorts—a Christmas gift from Hamish last year—that hugged her in all the wrong places. Three sets of thongs—in-the-shower, casual and dressy. *How many pairs does one woman need?* A maroon skivvy that emphasised her small breasts, a flowing skirt better suited to a taller woman, several ill-fitting booster bras. Two pairs of too-tight jeans, still waiting for her to lose weight. The lime-green wedge heels she'd never really loved, despite what the fashion magazines declared. Several old t-shirts that made her feel like a desperate housewife, *not* of the television variety.

Enough of feeling like *this.*

*From now on, I'm only going to wear clothes that make me feel good. Or at least, not so bad.*

The pile of clothes on the ground amounted to more than half the contents of her suitcase.

*And there's something else I'm throwing out, too.*

She hurried into the caravan. The children's bunks were positioned on either side, adjacent to her double bed at the rear. Each had a storage area underneath and could function as seats when not being slept in.

Paula immediately spotted Caitlin's bag under her bunk.

She rummaged around inside it until she found the item: the Playboy nightie.

*I should have done this months ago. Why didn't I stand up to Hamish? Or to my daughter, even?*

She took the nightie outside and stuffed it into the garbage bag with the rest of her own clothes, ready for deposit in the next charity clothing bin along their route.

Suddenly she spied the box of travel curlers, tucked in a side pocket of her suitcase. She pulled them out, took aim at a nearby rubbish bin and lobbed them in.

'Good throw!' Her father appeared at her side. 'Something wrong with them?'

'Something wrong with *me*, I think, Dad.'

Her father put a comforting arm around her shoulders. She noticed the warmth of his tanned skin, how his arms were covered in wiry grey hairs. They stood like that for several minutes, Paula leaning into his chest, watching the children cavorting at the water's edge.

Eventually, her father broke the silence. 'There's *nothing* wrong with you, Paula,' he said. 'Just remember that.' He nudged her in the ribs with his elbow. 'Nothing a few beers won't fix tonight, anyway. How about I go get some stubbies in town and a bag of ice for the esky?' He waved his wallet at her.

She pulled a face. 'Sounds like enlightened self-interest to me. Since you've got a hot date with Belinda later tonight.'

'Her name is *Brenda*.' He poked his tongue out at her. 'Just fraternising with the locals, love. It pays to do that, you know.'

Paula laughed and waved him off.

*

They sat on an ancient log at the edge of the beach, eating fish and chips and watching the sky turn fiery red in the west. Her father plied her with beers, accompanied by endless cheery salutations to her health, to the road, to Hillary and Clinton. The children drank soda water from cans, trying to do the loudest burp, everyone laughing hysterically at their outlandish belches.

When Brenda arrived in a cloud of perfume and hairspray, Sid rigged up the caravan's stereo system so that its speakers faced out the window, sending his music floating over the sand. Paula found herself accepting more beers than she needed or even wanted, because Simon and Garfunkel's 'Homeward Bound' reminded her of everything she'd ever lost or missed. Definitely Hamish, and especially her mother.

As the moon rose over Louttit Bay, Paula left the children playing cards in the caravan and her father dancing with Brenda, the pair of them swirling and dipping around each other like birds in a mating ritual. She picked her way down to the ocean's edge, where the corridor of silvery moonlight stretched from the horizon to the shore. Remembering how she used to tell a younger Caitlin and Lachie, *that's where the mermaids dance*. Remembering, too, the moonlit nights of her honeymoon; how Hamish had held her gently, reverently, like a delicate gift he feared might shatter. Imagining what Hamish had done with a teenage girl online, while Paula had lain in their bed alone.

She craved Jamie's comforting voice, but Paula's phone was still in the glove box, relegated there for emergency use.

*Stuff my own rules.*

Paula walked forward until the waves lapped her knees, scooping up the salty water and splashing her face. Then she took several more steps, until her shorts clung wet to her thighs. For a moment, she imagined walking further still; wading into the indigo depths until the sand dropped away beneath her feet. Then, suddenly frightened by the thought, she propelled herself back out of the water and up the beach.

Finding no sign of her father or Brenda where she'd left them, she rapped on the caravan door.

'Little pigs, little pigs, let me come in.'

Lachie appeared at the flyscreen, a puzzled expression on his face. He opened the door and Paula tripped up the steps past him, falling onto her knees on the yellow lino. Caitlin rushed to help her up.

'Whatcha doing?' Paula asked, pointing at the maps spread across the small table in the kitchenette.

'Plotting our route,' Lachie replied.

'Where to?' she demanded.

Without waiting for an answer, she staggered to the rear of the van and fell onto her double bed. The children followed her.

'Are you alright, Mum?' said Catie.

'Yeshhh,' she slurred. 'I'm just off my nut.'

Paula laughed. The decorative pink bunting suspended over her bed looked like a giant sparkling sea anemone.

'Ooh, flashy,' she said. 'Careful it doesn't sting you, kids.'

Their faces floated above hers, anxious and exquisite, before she closed her eyes.

*

Birdsong.

Clear, crisp notes, rising and falling in the silence. Pristine, like a piccolo on the wind.

Paula opened her eyes. Voluminous pink fabric hung overhead, buffeted by a breeze.

*Where am I?*

She sat up, confused by the proximity of her pillow to a window.

*Oh yes*, she remembered suddenly. *Yesterday I turned my life upside down.*

She rolled off the bed. The garish yellow tessellations on the caravan's floor made her feel a little queasy; she held a hand over her mouth.

She burped quietly, and smelled beer on her breath.

*Oh God, that's right.* The night before came flooding back to her.

Her eyelids felt sticky now, caked with sea salt and sleep. Paula shuffled to the sink and poured herself a glass of water, gulping it down with two ibuprofen tablets from the first-aid kit. She'd forgotten how bad it felt to be hung-over: how it was almost *never* worth it.

The children's bunks were empty. She checked her watch and saw to her surprise that it was almost eight o'clock. At home she was always up by six-thirty, making breakfast and the school lunches.

She pushed open the caravan door.

There it was, the new day, in all its beauty and possibility. Seagulls drifted above the ocean, tiny white dots hovering against an endless blue. Her children were romping on the sun-drenched shore, throwing sand bombs at each other from behind stinking seaweed barricades. The breeze rustled through the fragrant gum leaves, high above the camp site. And then she heard a contented, off-key whistle, a sound that had framed all the other elemental noises of her childhood. The Sunday-morning mower, the buzzing of the kitchen timer, the Barbara Streisand albums, her mother's incessant nattering, the metallic swishing of butcher's knives being sharpened out the back; her father's whistle had accompanied them all.

Paula stepped out of the caravan and looked around.

He rounded the van wearing blue-striped boxer shorts and thongs, a threadbare green bath towel draped around his neck. He carried his toothbrush, a disposable razor and a bottle of Aramis, his signature cologne. A soap-on-a-rope dangled from his wrist. She didn't think those things existed anymore.

'Good morning, m'girl. Had a sleep-in, then?' He was perkiness personified.

She grimaced. 'You could call it that.'

'Bit hair of the dog, are we? Have some Tabasco in tomato juice, it works a treat.'

'I've taken something for it.' She looked at the tent. 'How did you sleep last night?'

'Well, I didn't—' her father coughed—'sleep in the tent.'

'Where did you . . . ?' Then it registered. *Brenda.*

'Of course,' she said. 'You were *fraternising* with the locals.'

Her father looked sheepish.

'I'm a bit rusty.' He laughed. 'It's been a long time.'

Paula wanted to ask him how long it had been. Whether he'd romanced her mother like that, with sunset drinks and dancing and laughter. Whether they'd been happy together right to the end, or whether the gloss had worn off decades earlier. Whether either of them had ever been 'indiscreet', like Hamish, and what it had meant for their relationship.

Caitlin and Lachie raced up the beach towards them, all smiles and sandy limbs.

'Hello, beach monsters,' Paula said. 'Want some Weet-bix?'

'I bet *you* don't,' said Caitlin, almost crowing.

'Alright, alright,' said Paula, trying to salvage some skerrick of parental authority. 'I drank too much last night. But it was our first night on the road, I don't do it all the time.'

'It was *my* bad influence, kids,' said Sid. 'I kept giving beers to your mum. She couldn't refuse.'

Lachie smirked. 'Neither could Brenda.' He spun around on one heel, hacking at an imaginary guitar. 'You busted some smooth moves last night, Gramps.'

Paula stifled a laugh. 'Okay, kids, go wash off first, then come and have some breakfast.'

Caitlin and Lachie bolted towards the outdoor showers attached to the toilet block.

'Good to see them looking so chipper,' her father said, watching them go. 'All that Facebook hoopla doesn't seem to be bothering them much anymore.'

'Doesn't look like it,' Paula agreed. 'And we're not arguing about screen time either, which is nice for a change.'

'Nothing like good old-fashioned fresh air and exercise.' Her father smiled with satisfaction. 'Want me to cook some bacon and eggs? They'll be hungry.'

'No thanks.' Paula climbed back into the caravan and opened the pantry door. She found the Weet-bix, a can of two-fruits and a carton of long-life milk. 'I've got to keep *something* normal on this trip.'

'Why?' he asked, unfolding several portable chairs. 'We're on holidays, love. And "normal" is just a cycle on the washing machine.'

Paula smiled; she'd heard that quote somewhere before. She took some plastic bowls, cutlery and four mugs from a drawer, then began laying them on the card table outside. The table was wobbling on uneven ground; she scouted around for something to wedge under it. Spying Lachie's *Chess World* magazine, she jammed it beneath a table leg.

'Jamie told me I shouldn't destabilise the kids too much,' Paula explained. 'I need to keep some sort of routine on this trip, and a healthy breakfast is a good start.'

Her father's silence spoke volumes. He began piling Weet-bix bricks into a bowl.

The children returned dripping from their showers, and Catie was now carrying Paula's phone.

'We want to call Dad,' she said, wrapping herself in a towel.

'Oh. Of course.'

It was an obvious exception to Paula's 'no private technology' rule.

Caitlin held the phone to her ear for a minute.

'He's not answering,' she said, her expression flat.

Lachie took the phone from her hand. 'I'll email him. Can I send him the itinerary, please Mum? We typed it up on Brenda's computer this morning and sent it to your email address.'

Paula could hardly say no.

She watched her son's fingers move across her phone; the deft movements of a digital native. None of the clunky backtracks she was always making.

'Sent,' said Lachie, handing it back to Paula. He eyed the Weet-bix box. 'Six please, Gramps.'

'Six?' Her father pulled a shocked face. 'Are you a man or a machine?'

They sat down to eat. It wasn't like their vast island bench at home, at which everyone sat at a distance. Outside of the car, this was the closest their bodies had been for a long time. It reminded Paula of when the kids were younger, invading her physical space for seemingly endless kisses and cuddles.

Only it *had* ended, and their cuddles were so rare now she was enjoying nudging knees with them.

'Nothing like eating al fresco, is there?' said her father, yawning. 'I need a nanna nap. But I guess we've got to break camp.'

Paula nodded and began clearing the plates. 'Why don't you two do some homework while Gramps and I pack the car?'

Caitlin and Lachie looked aghast.

'Homework?' said Caitlin. 'But . . . we've got none.'

'I brought some for you,' Paula said, retrieving a large paper bag of workbooks from the caravan. 'English, maths and social science. You don't want to fall behind.' She placed the books on the table. 'You can start with maths. You'd normally be at school at this hour.'

'Hogwash,' said her father.

'Pardon?'

'You're talking hogwash.'

Paula tried to appear unflustered. 'How so?'

Her father clasped his hands behind his head and stretched back in his chair. 'Look, I'm just an old fella . . . I only finished third form in high school.' He leaned back further, balancing on one chair leg, which unnerved Paula no end. 'But if I learned anything as a butcher's apprentice and a small business owner, it's this: the things that help you most in life are the things you learn *outside* the classroom.' He swung forward again, much to Paula's relief.

'Like what?' asked Lachie, slathering honey on another dry Weet-bix.

'Like the value of a job well done, mate. Like valuing money and what it can do for you, and knowing what it *can't* buy . . . like respect and integrity and a decent night's sleep. I studied *people*, Lachie. Butchers know the community like the back of their hands.' He held up his for emphasis, scarred with countless nicks of the butcher's trade. 'Most of what happens in life is about *relationships*, not talent or hard work. It's about who knows who, and whether they like each other or not.'

Paula didn't disagree. 'Sure, Dad. But there's a role for formal education too, you drummed that into us.' Her father had worked hard to put her and Jamie through university.

'Yes, Paula, but *look* at these kids.' Her father thumped the table with his palms, causing his spoon to flip out of his empty bowl and onto the ground. 'They're bright, they're inquisitive; they're *not* going to fall behind in a month off school. You've got to *relax* a bit. And if you want 'em to learn on this trip, you can chuck that homework away.' He wrenched the study aids off the table, then pitched them into the rubbish bin, right on top of her travel curlers.

'Shot, Gramps,' said Lachie.

'Give the kids to *me* instead,' he said, slapping his chest with gorilla-like vehemence. 'I'll give 'em some life lessons they'll *never* forget.'

Paula hesitated. It wasn't the reaction she'd been expecting. Throughout *her* upbringing, he'd always prioritised the value of a solid education, primarily because he'd missed out on one himself. But something she'd noticed about older people was their tendency to behave differently as grandparents, compared to when they were parents. Disciplinarians mellowed, the exclusive became more inclusive, the rigid became less controlling. It was as if they'd spent their parenthood learning the lessons they needed most, only to be applied at their next point of contact with children—as grandparents.

'Go on, Mum,' Lachie urged. 'Let's do Gramps's homework instead.'

Caitlin was sitting at the table like the Mona Lisa, her expression unreadable.

It *would* be nice for the kids to spend some quality time with their grandfather, Paula thought. He won't be around forever.

Her eyes smarted at the memory of her mother's untimely death from breast cancer. The grief had knocked Paula sideways for months afterwards; she couldn't contemplate the gym or lovemaking or almost any activity beyond her basic household routine. Eventually, the initial, searing agony became a dull ache in her chest, but even now, more than a year on, Paula sometimes caught herself thinking, *I must tell Mum about . . .* only to remember, *Mum's not here.*

Paula looked at her father, then at her children. *Stuff the rules.*

'Alright,' she said. 'Let's bin the homework. You two can take life lessons with Gramps.' She smiled at them. 'But you've got to show me that you really are learning something, okay?'

'Oh, don't you worry about that.' Her father grinned. 'It'll be as plain as the nose on your face.'

*

Later that morning on arrival in Apollo Bay, Sid set the children's first challenge.

'How much will we spend on groceries this week, Paula?' he asked, parking the caravan in a wide bay adjacent to the main road.

'No more than two hundred and fifty dollars,' she replied. She'd done the sums prior to their departure and their budget was tight. Her father wasn't in a position to contribute, either; he was a pensioner, with most of his money tied up in his unit at Greenleaves Retirement Village.

'Okay, hand it over.'

She stared at him.

'You heard me,' he said, extending his hand. 'Gramps's first life lesson coming up.'

She took out her purse and counted out five fifty-dollar notes.

Sid passed them immediately to Caitlin.

'Back in Lorne you said your mother's cooking "sucks", Catie. Well, there's the supermarket. Go buy what *you'd* like to eat.' He nodded at a shopfront across the road, barely a glorified corner store. 'Kids, it's your job to buy our supplies for the coming week *and* to prepare the meals. You can get whatever you want, but it's *got* to last us a week.' He pointed to the notes in Caitlin's hand. 'Because there's no more dough.'

It took all of Paula's self-control not to slip the children a hastily written list.

Instead, she watched them disappear into the supermarket and emerge thirty minutes later with enough junk food to host a five-year-old's birthday party. Had none of her healthy eating messages ever sunk in? She didn't expect much of Lachie—he didn't give a hoot what he put into his body—but Caitlin was the athlete of the family. Paula couldn't conceal her disappointment.

Later that night, in a caravan park in Port Campbell, the children prepared an unsavoury meal of hot dogs with tomato sauce, wrapped in white-flour tortillas.

'I'm still hungry,' whined Lachie after demolishing his allocation for the evening.

'I'm sure you are, matey,' said his grandfather cheerily. 'So next time, choose a different cut of meat.'

'One with more nutritional value than sawdust,' added Paula, swallowing the last of her hot dog.

Lachie and Caitlin looked at each other.

'We've got jelly for dessert,' Caitlin ventured.

'Hallelujah,' said Paula. 'Now *that* will keep us going.'

They stayed another two nights at the Port Campbell Paradise Park, with an unobstructed view of the famed Twelve Apostles, limestone towers jutting skyward from the sea. Their first improvised meal of hot dog wraps was followed by an unappetising plate of sausage rolls on the second night, and pre-packaged pizza on the third.

*Who exactly is this lesson for?* Paula wondered, glaring at her father as she inspected the pizza's paper-thin crust. She was sure she'd lost some weight without even trying.

Sensing her frustration, Sid waved a bottle of alcoholic cider in her direction.

'Drinkypoos, Paula?' he asked.

Her father had instituted 'Drinkypoos' as a nightly ritual. Everyone was required to congregate outside the caravan at six o'clock sharp. Then, with all the solemnity of a priest dispensing the Eucharist, her father opened his small blue esky and doled out drinks. The children consumed soda water and, much to Paula's chagrin, cans of Coke they'd purchased at the Apollo Bay supermarket. Paula usually had an alcoholic cider, which her father lampooned as 'lolly water'. He preferred a few beers at these sessions, which quickly became public events, on account of her father's unflagging sociability. Watching her father interact with complete strangers in caravan parks, Paula suddenly understood why he'd been agitating for weekend trips away.

Their first night of Drinkypoos at Port Campbell attracted five fellow travellers to their caravan, most of whom her father had met while walking to and from the toilets. A good chunk of the conviviality revolved around counting the limestone stacks after everyone had drunk too much; and to Paula's great mortification, her father insisted he could only see *eight* apostles. She'd deemed this preposterous, ridiculing him as he swayed back and forth in his thongs, only to have Lachie verify the next morning that his grandfather had actually been right. She was forced to eat her words that breakfast, alongside her Weet-bix.

When even the Weet-bix ran out on the fourth day of her father's challenge—with Lachie tipping the box upside down in disgust—the children began to complain.

'Can't we buy some more food?' asked Catie, sitting outside the caravan clutching her stomach. 'I've been hungry since breakfast.'

They'd spent the day meandering along the coast of western Victoria, admiring its lighthouses and shipwrecks, bays and piers, old sandstone buildings flanked by futuristic wind farms. All novel enough to distract the children from their rumbling stomachs, if only temporarily.

'I have a headache,' complained Lachie.

'And I'm all bunged up, kids,' said her father. 'Your dietary choices aren't keeping me regular. And frankly, it sucks.'

'Gross.' Lachie covered his nose with his hand.

'Way too much information, Gramps,' said Caitlin.

'Or maybe not enough?' Sid asked. 'I mean, don't you two *know* what keeps bodies and minds healthy?'

He seized a long stick and drew a triangle shape in the dirt, close enough to the caravan for light.

'This is the healthy-eating pyramid, see? Fruit and vegies at the bottom, then unrefined carbohydrates like bread and pasta and rice. Protein and dairy next, then fats.' He waved his stick in the air. 'Where are the lollies on this pyramid? The pizzas? The soft drinks? The expensive junk that can never satisfy you?'

Catie rolled her eyes. 'We *know* all this, Gramps.'

'Then why didn't you shop responsibly when you took your mother's money into that supermarket in Apollo Bay and spent it all?'

Caitlin and Lachie looked uncomfortable.

'*I'll* tell you why, kids. It's not because you don't *know* the facts. No, siree. It's because you've spent your whole life with your mother running around after you, making good choices *for* you. Deciding what you eat, what you drink, what you wear, how you should behave.'

Paula began to feel uncomfortable too; she'd spent the best part of the last fifteen years doing just that.

'And *that's* why you've got to take some responsibility and start making some decisions for yourself,' Sid continued. 'Because one day your mum won't be there to help you.'

Lachie and Caitlin gaped at their grandfather—as if they were actually listening.

'What are you, a pair of stunned mullets?' he demanded, pointing at the caravan door. 'Go to bed, that'll help with the hunger.'

And to Paula's astonishment, they did.

*

The following night in Warrnambool, their dinner menu took a turn for the worse. In the absence of anything else in the pantry, the children raided the canned supplies packed specifically for the Nullarbor Plain.

'Yumbo, I'll eat *those*,' Sid said, pointing at a one-kilo can of baked beans that Caitlin had found. 'But I can't be held responsible for what happens tomorrow.'

'Huh?' Lachie was riffling through a drawer, looking for a can opener.

'He means he's going to fart,' said Caitlin, pulling a face.

'I prefer the word "fluff". Much more genteel,' said Sid.

Baked beans in Warrnambool were followed by corned beef in Portland and tinned tuna in Dartmoor. They'd run out of milk and other fresh dairy entirely, so had tea and toast for breakfast. Lunch wasn't much better: an unusual mezze of onion-flavoured rice crackers, cheese slabs and generous smears of Vegemite. As Sid had anticipated, this curious cocktail created a perfect storm in his bowels. The fumes were noxious, making Paula's eyes water and the children gag. But her father seemed to be enjoying himself immensely, chortling away as the children hung their heads out of Hillary, gasping for air.

'All part of the lesson,' he said, winking at Paula. 'They'll *never* buy that crap again.'

By the week's end, the children were pleading for fruit and vegetables like they were rare treats.

'I've had it, Gramps,' said Lachie, en route to Mount Gambier. 'You've gassed me out. I surrender.'

He threw an unopened bag of jellybeans into his grandfather's lap from the rear seat. '*Please* can we have some real food tonight?'

'Sure.' Paula looked at her son in the rear-view mirror. 'There's a big supermarket in Mount Gambier. We can buy a roast chook.'

'Oooh, yes,' said Caitlin. 'And can you make, like, peas and broccoli?'

'*You* can,' Sid replied. 'As part of my next life lesson, you're going to show us what you've learned this week. You can go shopping for groceries in Mount Gambier, then cook for us all until Adelaide, maybe even the whole way around Australia. It'll be like *MasterChef*.'

'In a caravan?' Caitlin sounded outraged.

Lachie groaned. 'But I can't cook, Gramps.'

Sid turned back to Paula. 'Would you mind pulling over, please?'

She parked across a gravel driveway adjacent to a gated paddock.

Her father looked sternly at the children. 'So, neither of you are very clever in the kitchen, eh?'

The children shook their heads.

'Well, *none* of us are. But we *all* have to learn how to cook ourselves a proper meal, and maybe even share it with ungrateful family members.' There was a flint-like edge to his voice. 'Now, I've heard both of you complaining about your mother's efforts in the kitchen, so that's where you'll be. You can learn what it takes to whip up a decent meal. Balanced food, not like the past week.'

Sid looked at Paula. 'When your mother died, I couldn't even scramble an egg. I suppose she thought she was doing me a favour, mollycoddling me all those years.' He gave a wry chuckle. 'But after she'd gone, I had to find out how to make myself simple, healthy meals. In the caravan, too.' He turned back to the children. 'It's no fun learning to cook when you're an old fogey. So you'd better start *now.* When you're thirteen and almost fifteen years old, you should be able to look after yourselves. Understand?'

'Yes, Gramps,' they said in unison.

'And Caitlin,' he added, lowering his voice, 'if I ever hear you use the word "suck" again, *especially* in relation to your mother, there'll be trouble. You can hop out of Hillary and run the next kilometre for that.'

Paula could barely recall what Caitlin had said or when, but it had obviously made an impression on her father.

Caitlin looked chastened. She climbed out of the ute and, without another word, began running in the road's narrow shoulder. As they watched her disappear over a small crest, her father grinned at Paula, victorious. 'South Australia, here we come.'

# 6

'Nice lobster,' said Lachie, eyeing a gargantuan orange sculpture in the grounds of the Kingston visitor centre.

They'd broken camp that morning after whiling away five lazy days in a picturesque caravan park in Mount Gambier. Paula felt so relaxed now, she hardly recognised herself.

'Here,' said Sid, handing her a coffee and pushing a box of sticky buns at the children. 'Let's sit near Larry.'

'Larry?' Lachie looked wary.

'The Big Lobster, mate. Didn't you read the sign?'

They sat cross-legged on the grass, in the shade of the sculpture.

'So,' said Sid, sipping at a takeaway cappuccino, 'you've been cooking up a storm with life lesson number two. And the grub's not bad, is it, Paula? The kids are doing a bonza job. Might be getting a bit easy for them, in fact.'

Paula smiled at her children, proud of their efforts. They'd been preparing hearty meals with fresh, local ingredients, using recipes taken from Sid's scribbler. A five-vegie omelette, stir-fried chicken and broccoli, beef skewers, cheesy frittata, corn on the cob. Every evening they'd rolled up their sleeves without complaining, even seeming to *enjoy* the job, from all the hollering and jibing that went on.

It was an unusual feeling for Paula to sit outside the caravan, wineglass in hand, while her children prattled and chopped their way through the dinner preparation. And she had her father to thank for it.

'So, we're starting our third life lesson today,' her father said. 'You still have to keep up the cooking, that's an ongoing challenge. But I've got a new one for you.' He grinned at his grandchildren. 'What did your mum always teach you about strangers?'

Lachlan and Caitlin looked at each other.

'Um, not to talk to them,' intoned Caitlin.

'Bingo.' Sid slapped Caitlin on the back. 'And that's good advice, when you're little. Don't hop in strangers' cars, don't accept lollies from them, that sort of thing. But you're not kids anymore, are you? You're teenagers.' He grinned at them. 'That means you're going to be adults soon enough, and adults talk to people they don't know all the time. It's one of the best skills you can learn. And I don't mean "talk" on the computer.'

Paula gulped down the last of her coffee, wondering what her father was plotting.

'So, this challenge is going to stretch over the rest of the trip too. And *all* of us are going to do it. Even your mum.'

*Uh-oh*, Paula thought.

'Here.' Sid pulled his scribbler from his top pocket and unfolded four sheets of paper, passing one to each of them.

Paula read the headings in the top margin: *Date*, *Place*, *Person*, *Points of interest*.

'Your challenge is to talk to someone you don't know *every day*, for at least ten minutes. After you've had a conversation, write down something interesting about them and share it with us at Drinkypoos. Righto?'

The children made noises of agreement.

For Paula, it sounded like a lot of hard work. She usually avoided the communal areas in caravan parks, and often went for long, solitary walks. She didn't really want to engage with strangers, fearful they might ask her probing questions like, *Where's your husband?*

'You in, Paula?'

'Sure.'

Her father looked up at the garish spines of the giant crustacean above them. 'Let's give Larry the big flick, eh? Adelaide awaits.'

'Hang on, Gramps,' said Caitlin. 'Can you take a photo of me in front of Larry? Amy will think it's hysterical.' She removed an iPod from her pocket and passed it to her grandfather.

'It takes photos, too?' said Sid, inspecting the device.

'It's an iPod Touch,' Caitlin replied, as if that explained everything. 'Amy gave it to me for the trip.'

'Whoa,' said Paula, intercepting them. '*No private technology*, remember?' She swooped down on the iPod and glared at Caitlin. 'You didn't tell me Amy gave you this. Are you sure it's okay for you to borrow it?'

Caitlin reddened. 'Yes.'

'And have you been using my phone, too? You're only supposed to use it for calling Dad.'

'I've sent a few messages to Amy, that's all.'

'A few messages to Amy?' Paula's voice shook. 'I know you've been posting some photos on Facebook again.'

Paula had been undecided about raising the matter with Caitlin at all. Since leaving Melbourne, she'd monitored the 'Blow Queens' post daily, as well as Caitlin's own Facebook page. Much to her relief, traffic to both pages was low. But then Caitlin started uploading travel shots to Instagram and sharing them on Facebook, presumably by sneaking Paula's phone out of the glove box. The people who 'liked' her posts were all the usual suspects—Amy and other school friends, her Aunty Jamie and her cousins—but it was the *principle* of the matter, Paula reasoned.

Caitlin looked guilty. 'I'm just showing people what I'm up to, Mum. It's not dangerous or anything.'

'But you know that phones and computers have caused us a lot of trouble lately, Caitlin. I banned them on this trip for a reason.' Paula glared at her daughter. 'We *can* survive a few months Facebook-free, you know. And if you feel you can't, maybe you should go home.'

Somehow the pain of Hamish's betrayal felt new again.

'But I *have* to stay in touch with Amy. She's my BFF.' Caitlin's shoulders slumped, even as her grandfather put an arm around them.

'What's a BFF?' Paula asked, irked.

'Best Friend Forever,' Sid explained.

Paula didn't pause to ask how *he* knew that. 'We haven't even been away for a fortnight yet, Catie. You don't have to be in touch with Amy *all* the time.'

'But *you're* in touch with Aunty Jamie every day,' said Caitlin, her eyes accusing Paula of hypocrisy. 'How come?'

'Aunty Jamie needs to know that Gramps is safe,' said Paula, knowing that wasn't quite the whole truth of it. She texted her sister several times a day, simply because she wanted to. 'And Aunty Jamie's a member of our family, so it's a bit different.'

*Is it really?* Paula could almost hear Jamie challenging her. *Don't deprive Catie of her social networks.*

'But Amy's been updating me on the Facebook stuff. She's been allowed to go back to school now, you know,' said Caitlin.

'And is she alright?' asked Sid.

Caitlin nodded.

Paula watched her daughter blush again. *Perhaps Caitlin's not as 'together' as I thought. I need to talk to Jamie about it.* As a teacher of teenagers, her sister was far better placed to understand Catie's responses. *I'll call her later and workshop it.*

The redness slowly receded from Catie's cheeks.

'Did you and Amy ever, you know—' Paula cleared her throat—'go out with older boys or anything?'

Caitlin rolled her eyes. 'Not this again. You're as bad as Dad. Can I have the iPod back please, just to take photos?'

Paula turned the device over in her hands, deliberating. *Something's not right here, I can feel it.*

'No.' Paula slipped it back into her handbag. 'You've breached a rule of our trip. But I'll cut you a deal: if you miss Amy so much, write her a letter. Then you can use my phone every Sunday to contact her and do your Facebook posting.'

'A letter?' Caitlin repeated, incredulous.

'Yes, you know—one of those things you write on a piece of paper? You'll need a pen and an envelope too. It's, like, *so* yesterday.'

It was immature to parrot her daughter's speech, Paula knew.

Caitlin looked appalled. 'But it'll take *forever* to get there. And how will Amy write back?'

'Well . . .' Paula found her copy of the itinerary in her handbag. 'You've already plotted our route and the dates we'll arrive in each town.' She traced her index finger along the red line. 'You can use something called Poste Restante, Caitlin. Amy can send a letter to you care of any post office, and they'll keep it for you there.'

Caitlin shook her head. 'Mum, you don't understand. Amy will *hate me* for not contacting her more than once a week.'

'Well, she's not your BFF then, is she?'

'This isn't *fair*,' said Caitlin, her eyes flashing. 'Are *you* going to write letters to Aunty Jamie? You're just punishing me for what Dad did. It's not my fault Dad's been a dickhead.'

'Watch your language,' said Paula, noticing a group of Japanese tourists walking around the base of the lobster. 'And this has got *nothing* to do with your father.'

'You're a liar,' snapped Caitlin. 'Or in denial, Mum.'

She stomped over to the ute and climbed into the back seat, slamming the door behind her.

Paula sighed. *Am I lying or denying?* She glanced at the others, a little self-consciously.

Lachie was kicking at a stone on the ground, avoiding her gaze.

Her father said nothing.

'Where's *your* iPod, Lachie?' Paula asked.

'In the glove box.'

Paula nodded, grateful for his compliance. She knew she wouldn't have the same trouble with Lachie. Male friendships simply weren't so all-consuming.

'So's mine,' added her father.

She raised an eyebrow. 'Your iPod?'

'No, my iPhone.'

Paula stared at him. '*You* have an iPhone too?'

'Yep.'

'Since when?'

'Since about a month before we left. I went to Fonezone and bought one.'

She couldn't believe it. 'Aren't you anti-technology?'

'Thought it might come in handy for my Melbourne Cup research,' he explained. 'And there's just so much good *stuff* on it, Paula.' His eyes danced. 'There's a Great Ocean Road app, and even a natty little sheila *inside* the phone who fetches information for me. I can say to her, "What's the weather in Adelaide tomorrow?" and she'll come back with an answer right away.'

'It's called *Siri*, Gramps,' said Lachie, rolling his eyes.

'Well, it's marvellous. And come to think of it, maybe we could use it for taking photos.' Sid looked at Paula. 'And the kids could use it to contact Hamish, too?'

It was a reasonable suggestion; Paula wasn't thrilled that the children kept using her phone to stay in touch with their father. Or trying to—he'd been offline for more than a week now. After initially accepting some groceries from Jamie on release from hospital, he hadn't answered the front door since. The children couldn't reach him on the landline, either, which made Paula suspect he was staying at Doggo's.

'But if you don't want to, no worries, I respect all your rules on this trip,' her father continued. '*No private technology.* It's only there for an emergency.'

'I'll think about it,' said Paula, still attempting to digest the fact that her seventy-year-old father, formerly a technophobe, was now an avid iPhone user.

'Come on,' she said, conscious of Caitlin waiting in the ute. 'Let's get to Adelaide before the big race.'

'Yee-ha,' said her father, whinnying and tossing his head, before trotting off towards the car park.

It was the first Tuesday in November, the day of the Melbourne Cup, and they were due to meet an old friend of Sid's who'd retired to North Adelaide some years back. The timing was going to be tight: it was already nine-fifteen and they had at least four hundred kilometres to cover.

They travelled on through Salt Creek and into the Coorong, speeding past its deserted saltpans. Flocks of birds—cranes, galahs, pelicans and others they'd never seen before—rose in flocks from the lagoons, shimmering in the air like silver clouds, momentarily blotting out the sun. Paula wanted to stop the car and run beneath them, her arms outstretched, swooping across the sand flats in the searing glare.

Instead, they pressed on through Murray Bridge and Hahndorf without stopping. Finally, some four hours later, they found themselves in the Walkerville sub-branch of the Adelaide RSL with Barry and Shirl Gillespie. Sid and Barry had been Rotary friends and fishing mates in Doncaster for decades, before the Gillespies had moved to Walkerville five years earlier to be closer to their grandchildren. Sid had arranged to park the caravan in the Gillespie's front yard for the coming week. From there, the two men were planning to catch up on five years' worth of fishing, while Paula, Caitlin and Lachie explored Adelaide.

Paula was mindful of her father's new challenge—*talk to strangers*—as she tried to make conversation with the elderly couple. But it was an uphill battle. Barry was deaf, responding to most of Paula's questions by cupping his hand behind his right ear and bellowing, 'Can't 'ear ya.' Shirl was unanimated, mostly, except when recounting an incident involving her ageing Rottweiler, Robbie.

'It happened a fortnight back, chicken-wire injury to the groin. They had to cut off one of his testicles,' she said gravely. 'His personality's been a bit different since.'

*I should think so*, Paula thought wryly. *It could be an option for Hamish.*

If someone had told Paula only a month ago that she'd be sitting at the Walkerville RSL on Melbourne Cup day discussing the state of a Rottweiler's privates, she would've called them crazy. Looking around at the lunchtime crowd—mostly aged pensioners wearing fascinators and top hats—Paula's resolve began to waver for the first time since leaving home. *What exactly am I doing here?*

The club's food was stodgy, the lights low, Paula's morale lower. She watched Lachie flicking beer nuts across the table at Caitlin, who was making a valiant attempt to consume a half-frozen slice of Black Forest cake. They were all wearing hats, at the request of her father, who'd borrowed an old bowler from Barry. Lachie had decorated his beanie with pictures of horses clipped out of the Adelaide *Advertiser*, while Caitlin had found a plastic Viking helmet in a two-dollar shop in Mt Gambier. It made her look Teutonic, with all that blonde hair cascading down her back. Paula had wrapped a red silk scarf around her favourite straw hat, but she doubted it would pass at Flemington. She couldn't get too excited about a horse race, even for the 'race that stops the nation', as the club compere kept bellowing into his microphone.

Paula sighed. There was still half an hour until the race started. She wondered, for a moment, where Hamish would be watching it. Probably at Doggo's, with Tina fussing over him.

'You alright, Paula?'

Her father's knowing gaze. She nodded, not wanting to talk about it.

'Look, Paula . . .' Sid leaned towards her. 'Can I get my iPhone out of Hillary, just this once? Shirl's been looking after Robbie, her dog—'

'I've heard *all* about it,' said Paula.

'Well, she likes to have a flutter at Cup time,' Sid continued. 'Can I help her place a bet on the internet?'

'I thought you were anti-gambling?'

'There are exceptions to every rule. The Melbourne Cup's a bit of harmless fun and Shirl's been feeling down lately.'

Paula relented. 'Sure, Dad.'

'Great.' He nudged his friend. 'Come for a walk, Bazza?'

As they made their way to the door, Paula turned to Shirl.

'So, what'll you spend the money on, if you pick the Melbourne Cup winner?'

The old woman laughed. 'Oh, I'm not serious about betting, I never put more than two dollars on a horse. But if I won Lotto . . .' She looked thoughtful. 'I'd buy a new roof for the animal shelter. Barry and I volunteer there. Seen some awful things too, these past five years.' Her pale blue eyes became misty. 'People who abandon their pets when they go on holiday. Folks who change their minds about the Christmas kitten before January's even over. Poor little things can't speak for themselves, you know?'

Paula nodded.

'The shelter leaks when it rains, but the repair work's been quoted at fifteen thousand. Someone reckons there's asbestos up there too. Our Rotary club's raised two thousand, but we're all pensioners. How are we supposed to find the rest?'

Paula noticed how quickly Surly Shirley had transformed into a passionate animal advocate. She'd enjoy describing this at Drinkypoos later.

'Well, I hope you find the funds somehow,' Paula said, suddenly aware that Lachie and Caitlin had moved away from their table.

She spotted Lachie nearby, sitting next to a war veteran on a vinyl lounge. The elderly man was relishing an audience, fingering his medals and leaning so close to Lachie that his trembling lips were almost touching the boy's ear.

Caitlin had moved further afield, and was standing next to the bar talking to an athletic-looking young man. Late twenties or early thirties, Paula guessed. He was slightly shorter than Caitlin, with dark cropped hair. Even at a distance, Paula could see a razor-wire tattoo spiralling down his tanned arm, beneath a fitted white t-shirt. His jeans were faded and he wore flat grey sneakers. Attractive in a compact sort of way, Paula thought, wondering if perhaps he was a club security guard.

The man seemed respectful, a little guarded even, as he listened to Caitlin talk—what *was* she saying to him?

Paula decided to go over and make her maternal presence felt; he was clearly much older than Caitlin.

As she stood up, her father appeared at her side, with Barry puffing behind him.

'Look at this, love.' Sid brandished his telephone. 'That nice young fellow over there helped me . . .' He waved at an attendant in a tartan waistcoat. 'I opened up an account myself first and did a dummy run, placed a few bets with my own money. They make it so *easy*. Then I opened an account for Shirl.' He patted Shirl's arm. 'You've got ten bucks to blow now. That's the minimum for opening an account, but there's no minimum bet.'

Shirl looked as if Sid was speaking Spanish.

Paula noticed that Caitlin was still chatting to the man at the bar.

'So, which horse do you fancy, Shirl?' Sid prompted. 'They're calling for last bets.'

'But I haven't even *looked* at the form,' Shirl objected. 'You just take a punt for me, Sid. Barry's told me you've got some sort of magic formula.'

'Alrighty, at your own risk.' Sid began moving his fingers across the screen. Paula smiled to watch him; there was something utterly incongruous about it, yet he was quite adept already.

A minute later, her father looked up. 'Okay, you've spent just over three bucks, Shirl. That's about your usual budget, isn't it? You can blow the rest on next year's Cup.'

'Which horse?' Barry asked.

'*Horses*,' corrected Sid. 'I picked a few for you. Three single bets and ten cents on a first four, just for fun.'

'And you did all that with that little *whatsit*?' Barry peered over Sid's shoulder at the iPhone, impressed.

'Yep.'

'Maybe we should get one, Shirl?' Barry nodded at his wife, who didn't appear to object to the suggestion.

It wasn't long until a murmur rippled through the crowd; the race was about to commence.

Paula called Lachie over. She waved at Caitlin, who turned to the man beside her and pointed out Paula in the crowd.

The man's gaze met Paula's and he smiled.

For a moment, the sounds and sights of the club fell away.

Eyes like melted chocolate, toffee-smooth skin, an infectious grin.

The effect was breathtaking.

He began moving towards her, following Caitlin through the crowd, stepping between chairs and tables.

Paula fought the urge to run and hide in the ladies' room. After seventeen years of marriage, she wasn't confident she could still converse with *this* kind of stranger.

And then the starter bell rang and the room was suddenly swaying with jostlers, shriekers and clappers. People shouted out the names of horses as if they had personal relationships with them. One portly bar attendant yelled '*Carn*, Dunaden!' so loudly, a woman dropped her glass of champagne. It smashed to smithereens and she stood over the pieces, cackling and hitching up her dress.

Caitlin and her new friend appeared at the table.

'Mum, this is Marcelo,' Caitlin yelled over the din. 'He's from *Brazil*.'

Her daughter smiled like she'd just found a fifty-dollar note on the pavement.

'Hello,' said Paula, reaching out to shake his hand. 'I'm Caitlin's mum.'

His handshake was warm and firm. 'Caitlin's mum? You don't have another name?'

She laughed. 'Of course. It's Paula.'

'Hello, *Pow-la*.' His accent rocketed her somewhere warm and smoky.

The crowd surged forward as the horses turned into the final straight. Barry helped Shirl to her feet so that she could see the screen beyond the sea of heads and hats moving up and down.

As the winner crossed the line, the crowd cheered.

Second, third, fourth . . . twenty-third, twenty-fourth. It was all over in a matter seconds.

The din receded, but a lucky few were still dancing, yelling and hugging their friends. Meanwhile, the losers in the room tore up their sweep tickets or shook their heads philosophically.

'Win anything for Shirl, Dad?' asked Paula.

He nodded, his eyes still fixed on the big screen.

'How much, Gramps?' asked Lachie.

'Well, I . . .' Sid began scrolling on his iPhone with some urgency. 'I, uh, backed the first four.'

'The first *four*?' Barry heard the words perfectly this time; he was obviously selectively deaf. 'You mean . . . Green Moon, Fiorente, Jakkalberry and Kelinni? *All* of them?'

Sid nodded. 'I put a ten-cent bet on them for you.'

'Oh.' Lachie looked disappointed. 'That won't be much.'

'But it says here . . .' Sid motioned to his telephone. 'Shirl, Bazza, I . . .'

Barry couldn't wait any longer. He grabbed the phone from Sid and squinted at the display.

'Mother Mary!' he yelled, seizing Shirl by the shoulders and shaking her. 'We've just won seventy-seven grand!'

Paula gasped.

'You're pulling my leg . . .' objected Shirl.

'I'm not, darl,' said Barry, his voice shaking. 'We're rich.'

Shirl looked around the room for a moment, as if she'd lost something. Then suddenly she swooned forward, like a bird shot in the forest.

Paula tried to grab her as she fainted, but she wasn't fast enough.

A dark blur lunged in front of Paula, catching Shirl just inches from the floor.

Marcelo lay on the beer-stained carpet, his chest heaving, cradling the old woman in his arms.

Paula stared down at him, open-mouthed. He'd just saved Shirl from a nasty fall.

Supporting her neck, Marcelo deftly rolled Shirl onto her side in the recovery position.

'Water,' he said to Barry, who was dithering nearby. 'Get her some water.'

Seconds later, Shirl opened her eyes, blinking in confusion.

'It's okay,' said Marcelo.

Barry brought a glass of water and crouched down, holding it to Shirl's lips.

A small crowd of onlookers had gathered around them.

Sid was the first to speak. 'Where in Hades did you learn *that* little trick, mate?' He looked at Marcelo. 'I've never seen anyone move that fast.'

The Brazilian laughed. 'In Porto Alegre, southern Brazil. You have to move fast in the *favela*.'

Paula had no idea what a *favela* was, but she hoped Marcelo might stick around long enough to explain.

'You feelin' alright, Shirl?' Sid crouched down next to her.

'Did you really win us all that money?' The old woman was still pale.

'Yes, ma'am.'

'Oh, Barry.' Shirl began to smile. 'Now we can fix the roof at the animal shelter.'

'I know, love.' Barry patted her hand. 'I know.'

Suddenly Sid stood up, climbed onto a chair and cupped his hands around his mouth.

'Cooee!' he called. 'Lady Luck's on my side today, friends. Drinks are on me!'

A loud cheer rose up from the crowd.

'Champion, Gramps!' yelled Lachie, grabbing one of his grandfather's hands. Marcelo stood too, then suddenly hoisted Sid up onto his right shoulder in a single, effortless sweep.

People thumped Sid on the back as Marcelo paraded him around the club, Lachie jumping around them like an excited puppy.

Balanced precariously on a stranger's shoulder, laughing and high-fiving his grandson, Paula had never seen her father look so alive.

*

That evening, Marcelo joined them in Barry and Shirl's backyard for a celebratory barbecue. Shirl reclined on a deckchair with a shandy in her hand, still stunned by the windfall, while Barry and Sid pushed several dozen sausages around a hotplate with metal spatulas.

'This is an Australian barbecue?' Marcelo asked, lifting a scorched sausage with a pair of tongs. 'You have tortured the meat.'

Paula laughed aloud.

'C'mon, mate, it's just a bit of charcoal,' said Sid. 'How do you do it in Brazil?'

Marcelo beamed. 'We are famous for our *churrasco.* Skewered meat over an open fire. *That* is a real barbecue.'

Paula watched Sid and Barry considering this. Australian men were proud of their barbecues, perhaps no more so than Brazilian men.

'I was a butcher for forty-odd years,' said Sid, puffing out his chest. 'And Bazza here, he's cooked more Rotary barbecues than you've had hot dinners. We *do* know what we're doing.'

Marcelo clapped her father on the back. 'A butcher? Then you are welcome in my family.' He dropped the sausage back onto the barbecue. 'We are cowboys from Rio Grande do Sul in the south of Brazil. Cattle workers, all of us, so we know how to butcher a steer. It's been our way of life for eighty years.'

Paula sipped her champagne, watching him. And she'd thought gorgeous intriguing cowboys only existed in movies.

Sid's face lit up. 'Cattlemen, eh?' He passed Marcelo another beer; Paula could tell he was impressed. 'How big's your landholding?'

'Oh, we don't own the land ourselves.' Marcelo looked a little self-conscious. 'We work for a big cattle family, one of the oldest in Brazil. My great-grandfather first worked for them eighty years ago.'

Sid nodded. 'Well, if your family's been barbecuing for eight decades, mate, we're happy to learn from you. Ain't that right, Bazza?'

Barry nodded amiably; he'd had a permanent smile on his face since the Melbourne Cup win.

Sid turned back to Marcelo. 'We've got some interesting cuts of meat in Oz. Kangaroo, emu, crocodile. Great seafood, too—squid, prawns, crayfish. Can't barbecue a dingo though.'

Lachie groaned. 'Aw, Gramps, don't start on the dingos again.'

'What is a *dongo*?'

Lachie and Caitlin giggled.

'A dingo,' corrected Caitlin. 'It's a wild dog.'

Marcelo looked dismayed. 'You eat dogs in Australia?'

'Nah, mate,' Sid began laying out plates, placing buttered slices of bread on them. 'But I've always wanted to hunt one. And I'm going to, on the Nullarbor Plain.' He tilted his head in a westerly direction.

'So you're going there too?' Marcelo lifted a thick travel guide—*Lonely Planet Australia*—out of his small blue backpack and began flipping through the pages. 'It says here you can see *millions* of stars crossing the Nullarbor Plain at night. I want to see that beauty.'

'Bloody oath, mate,' said Sid. 'It'll be a highlight of our trip, I reckon.'

'Marcelo's travelling along our route,' Caitlin interjected, her face alight with excitement. 'He's backpacking to Darwin, right?' She looked at the Brazilian for confirmation.

Marcelo nodded. 'Yes, I have family connections there.'

'Well, now.' Sid glanced at Paula. 'We're going to be in those parts in a month or so, aren't we?'

Paula sensed where this might be going, and wasn't sure it was a good idea.

'So, Marcelo,' she said, 'you've only been in Australia for three days. Do you know someone in Adelaide?'

'All of *you* now.' Marcelo grinned.

Paula couldn't help but notice his perfectly white teeth. Somewhere in Brazil, a dentist was dreaming about that smile.

'But really, I only came to Adelaide because it was the cheapest ticket,' he said. 'I left from Rio de Janeiro, then flew to London and Hong Kong. A very long flight, thirty-one hours and two stops. I was sick every takeoff, I've never travelled by air before. I *much* prefer horses.'

Paula could just picture him in a pair of tight jeans, riding boots and a broad-brimmed hat. The Brazilian Marlboro Man, driving cattle across the lonely, womanless plains of Rio Grande do Wherever-it-was.

'When I boarded the plane, I looked at the map in here—' he pointed to his guidebook—'and only then I realised how far Adelaide is from Darwin.'

'Bloody hell, mate,' Barry said, laughing. 'You stuffed that up, didn't you? Could've flown straight to Darwin. Would've been much easier.'

Marcelo nodded. 'Yes, it was my brother Lucas who booked the flight. He is *um idiota*.' His expression darkened for a moment. 'But

Adelaide is a nice city. South Australian people are very friendly, like all of you!'

'Cheers to that, mate,' said Barry, raising his glass.

Paula resisted the urge to point out that all of their group came from Victoria.

'I think I will see more of Australia this way, by going to Darwin by road,' Marcelo added.

Barry chortled behind his beer. 'Not much to see between here and Darwin, up through the red centre. Not unless you call desert and anthills countryside.'

Marcelo looked deflated.

'Where are you staying in Adelaide?' Paula asked, feeling rather like a private investigator.

'In a youth hostel,' said Marcelo. 'I was planning to catch a bus to Perth, but then someone told me about the Melbourne Cup. It stops the nation, they said.'

Paula refrained from rolling her eyes.

'I was curious and asked, where can I see it? They said, go to any pub tomorrow and you will find out. So after lunch today I left the hostel and caught a taxi. I said to the driver, take me somewhere I can see the Melbourne Cup.' Marcelo grinned. 'And he dropped me at the Walkerville RSL.'

'You were just lucky then, eh?' Sid smiled.

'Welcome to Walkerville,' said Barry, scraping fried onion rings onto a plate.

'And to Australia,' added Sid, leaning forward to clink his bottle against Marcelo's. 'Cheers.'

'*Saúde!*' said Marcelo, standing to reciprocate.

He proceeded to walk around the group, bending down and touching his stubbie against everyone's drink, repeating the word '*saúde!*'. When he finally reached Paula, he pretended to be fatigued. Then, putting a hand on her shoulder, he leaned down and winked at her, touching his bottle to her glass.

That wink, his touch, made Paula blush. She bowed her head and pretended to hunt for something in her handbag, eventually retrieving a pocket-sized packet of tissues.

She went through the motions of blowing her nose.

*Grow up*, she scolded herself.

When she looked up again, Marcelo had returned to his seat, but was still watching her, from behind his beer. He smiled at her, as if they were sharing a private joke.

'So . . .' Paula attempted to regain her composure. 'How long are you planning to stay in Darwin?'

'It depends,' said Marcelo. 'If I like the Northern Territory, then I will try to find some work on one of the big cattle properties up there, maybe learn something new that I can take back to my family in Brazil.' He looked reflective for a moment. 'But really, I haven't come to work. I want to see Australia, to understand it more. My mother was born in Darwin, you see. She met my father when she was a backpacker herself, travelling with a friend through Latin America.'

Paula smiled. 'How did they meet?'

'In Porto Alegre, on my father's day off. He saw her on the street and tried to speak to her. He'd learned a few English phrases on the job, taking the cattle boss's visitors out riding. Apparently he said to her, "Do you like horses? Come and see my horses." And against her friend's advice, she did.'

He laughed.

'After a few days on the farm, she knew he was the man she wanted to marry. She worked in the kitchen with my grandmother at first, but then my father taught her to ride. After a while, she worked the cattle too. I used to ride around the property with her when I was little.'

Paula suddenly understood how a southern Brazilian cattle rancher could speak almost-perfect English. Albeit with an endearing Portuguese accent.

Marcelo drained the last of his beer, his eyes distant.

'And since I was very small, my mother told me about her country. She had no close family left here, but she wanted to bring me and my brothers to Australia when we were old enough.' Marcelo's face softened. 'But she died when I was a teenager.'

'Oh, I'm sorry,' Paula said. Thinking, *my mum died last year too.*

'*Que saudade!*' he replied, his tone earnest. 'There is no English translation for that. In Brazil we say it when we yearn for something so much, our heart aches.'

The others looked uncomfortable.

Marcelo stared moodily at the flames licking the barbecue. 'My family changed after my mother died. My older brother Lucas, he went a bit crazy. He was living in the *favela* with the wrong people, we lost contact with him for more than a year. Me and my younger brother stayed on the farm, but it wasn't the same anymore. It never was, without her.' His eyes met Paula's.

'You will understand this, I am sure, *Pow-la*. Mothers are the foundation of the home. When the mother is alright, the family is alright too. I have come to Australia to understand the culture of my mother, my core. I don't mean the geography, the tourist places. But to discover it in *here*.' He lay a hand over his heart. 'It will be an important lesson for me, you know?'

'I know, mate,' Sid said. 'We're learning a few life lessons ourselves on this trip. Aren't we, kids?'

'Are we ever,' said Caitlin.

Barry moved the sausages around on the hotplate with his tongs. 'Righto, grub's up,' he announced. 'Guests first.'

Barry passed Marcelo a plate piled high with bread, onion rings and several sausages.

'Tomato sauce?' Sid asked, waving a bottle in Marcelo's direction.

'Tell me about this,' said Marcelo, peering at the plate. 'There is some bread here. And . . .?' He pointed at the charred onion rings.

'That's onion. You've got yourself a true-blue sausage sanger there, matey.'

Barry passed Sid a plate.

Marcelo looked around. 'How do you eat it?'

'You just pick it up.' Sid lifted his own sandwich, wrapped the bread around the sausage and bit into it. Tomato sauce squirted out the other end, spattering Lachie's forehead.

'Gramps!' Lachie wiped his face.

'I know, I'm a bogan.' Sid laughed and passed his grandson another serviette.

Marcelo looked puzzled. 'What is a *bo-gun*?' He held his hand up in the shape of a revolver.

Everyone laughed.

Sid slapped Marcelo on the back. 'Stick with us, Marcelo, and you'll learn a lot about Australian English. Otherwise known as *Strine*, right? Bogan means *um idiota*.'

Paula was impressed by her father's recall of Portuguese.

'Can Marcelo come with us, Mum?' Caitlin pleaded, unable to

contain herself any longer. 'There's room in the ute. He could teach us a bit about Brazil, too. It could be part of Gramps's third life lesson.'

That was *talk* to strangers, Paula thought, not *travel* with them.

She watched Barry dole out more sausage sandwiches.

'C'mon, Paula.' Her father smiled at her. 'It'll be good to have another bloke around. He can help me hitch Clinton to Hillary of a morning.'

Paula bit the inside of her lip, thinking. Not long after her mother's death, Sid had been diagnosed with arrhythmia during a routine cardiovascular examination. Now she watched him struggle to hitch the caravan to the ute's tow bar and she worried about the strain it placed on him. There was only so much help she and the kids could offer.

'It'll be good to have some company up north, too,' Sid added. 'Lots of nutters in the Northern Territory, you know.'

*But Marcelo could be one of them.*

'We're going to Darwin the long way,' she objected. 'It might be easier if Marcelo just caught a bus straight there.'

No one said anything.

She looked around the group, feeling defensive.

'Well, okay, what happens if he comes along and it *doesn't work*?' Paula turned to the Brazilian. 'I'm sorry, Marcelo, but the mother in me has to ask. What if we're not getting on? You mightn't enjoy being stuck in the back of a ute. Or you might hate our food, our music . . . You mightn't like *us*. I mean, you don't *know* us. And we don't know *you*.'

She knew exactly how she sounded. The anxious mother. The fun-killer.

When she ventured to look at Marcelo, he was nodding at her. 'You are wise, *Pow-la*. A good mother.'

He turned to Catie and Lachie. 'What do you think we should do, if something isn't working? If you hate my guitar-playing and singing and you say, "Stop, Marcelo! Your voice is hurting our eardrums," but I don't stop. What then?'

Catie giggled. 'Maybe we could try and talk about it?'

'Good,' said Marcelo. 'And I would listen to you carefully, because that is how to solve problems. But what if I *didn't* listen, and your mother or your grandfather said, "*The Brazilian has to go!*" What then?' He didn't wait for an answer. 'Then Marcelo would *go*, right?'

They nodded again.

'Your mama makes all the decisions.'

The children looked dubious.

'Well . . .' Caitlin pushed her hair back over her shoulder.

'No.' Marcelo waggled a finger at Caitlin. 'That is not good.' He tossed his head and flicked a hand at imaginary tresses. Paula stifled a laugh. 'We do not question your mother's judgment. She is the centre of the family.'

If this kind of philosophy was common among the children of Brazil, Paula thought, it might warrant a new entry in her adventure scrapbook.

'Go on, Mum,' said Lachie, adding his voice to the lobbying.

Marcelo turned back to her. 'What do *you* think, *Pow-la*?'

'Alright,' she said, finally. 'We can give it a week and see how it goes. We're leaving Adelaide next Tuesday, though. That mightn't be soon enough for you, Marcelo.'

Her father and Barry had already created a timetable of fishing trips for the coming week that simply couldn't be cancelled.

Marcelo shook his head. 'I am in no hurry, I don't want to see Australia from a bus. I will stay at the youth hostel and come back next Tuesday.' He paused. 'Do you have room for a guitar and a surfboard?'

*A cowboy, a musician and a surfer too?*

'The ute's got roof racks, mate,' said Sid. 'You can have 'em.'

'And you don't have to stay in the youth hostel,' added Barry. 'You're welcome to stay here in the spare room, ain't he, Shirl?'

Shirl smiled indulgently, a grin born of her third shandy.

'This is too much to ask,' objected Marcelo, obviously touched by their generosity.

'My arse it's too much,' said Barry, lifting his beer glass again.

'Well, *saúde* to that,' said Paula, waving her champagne flute at Sid, angling for a refill. She'd had three already, but heck, it was Melbourne Cup Day. *And* they'd just invited a handsome stranger to travel to Darwin with them.

Marcelo flashed her a winning smile. 'Thank you, *Pow-la*. You're the boss, we follow your orders.'

# 7

'Told you, mate.' Doggo looked apologetic, scuffing his work boots on the front doormat. 'No one's home, like when I came round Saturday.'

Hamish hauled himself up using the banister, leaning heavily on his good leg, trying not to trip over the walking stick.

*Where the hell is my phone?* he wondered. Paula had disappeared with it in her handbag after her last visit to the hospital, ten days earlier. Before the operation, before the infection had taken hold.

He needed to call her now.

'Could be some keys under there.' Hamish pointed at a potted cactus near the front door.

He closed his eyes, trying to remember Catie's exact words when she'd visited him with Lachie and Sid the week before. Had it been Tuesday or Wednesday? He couldn't be sure, he'd been in a post-operative haze. Old Sid had nicked off to the hospital cafeteria as soon as they'd arrived, on the pretext of finding Hamish a newspaper. But Hamish could tell from the set of his face that Sid now knew about Lisel too.

What had Catie said, again?

*Mum's ropeable, we're going away.*

*Where to?* Hamish had asked idly.

*Around the country in the caravan*, Catie had said.

That old chestnut, Hamish thought. The fantasy Paula had been trotting out for years, whenever she felt bored or upset. Whenever she wanted to run from her life. Which wasn't all that bad, as he kept trying to remind her.

Catie had climbed up onto the bed and tucked herself next to Hamish, while Lachie stood shuffling from foot to foot, like he'd rather be somewhere else.

*Really*, Hamish had replied.

He'd patted Catie's back, figuring Paula couldn't possibly be serious. It was the middle of the school term, for starters, and she'd *never* let the kids take that much time off school. She wouldn't evict her father from the caravan, either. And he was fairly confident that, despite what had happened with Lisel, Paula would ultimately forgive him. Because he hadn't *actually* done the dirty on her; there *was* a difference between virtual masturbation and real-world adultery. She'd be pissed off, for sure, probably stonewall him for a month, maybe longer. But beyond that, it was all bluster. Paula was so embedded in her domestic routine, there'd be no way she'd set off around Australia by herself. Hamish knew her too well.

So what the *hell* was going on?

Doggo groped under the cactus pot and found the spare key.

Hamish hobbled to the front door and unlocked it.

The door swung open to unnatural silence.

Doggo tried to take some of Hamish's weight as he struggled through the doorway. Even so, a sharp pain blasted through Hamish's knee, making him moan. The splint he was wearing, secured from calf to groin with six velcro straps, was designed to prevent him from bending his knee. But the pain was so acute he felt like lying down right there in the vestibule. Instead, he limped up the hallway, grimacing.

Everything looked exactly as it always did, minus his family.

He headed to the kitchen, the heart of their home, and stared at the bare benches. Everything was in order, as usual; spotlessly clean, free of clutter.

And then he saw the crisp white square, propped up against an empty ceramic vase. His name penned in Paula's neat cursive writing. Doggo hung back, looking increasingly morose, as Hamish unfolded the note.

*Dear Hamish,*

*I can't be in the same house as you for a while.*

*I'm taking the kids on a road trip for the summer.*

*I thought about leaving them here with you, but I guess it'll be hard enough recovering from the surgery. We won't be away longer than three months. I still love you, Hamish. But I'm absolutely furious with you.*

*You may not understand, but I need some time to think.*

*Don't try to contact me. The kids will be in touch and Jamie will pop in too, in case you need anything.*

*Paula*

*PS: Your computer is in the bedroom, your phone is in the bathroom.*

Hamish crushed the note in his fist. 'I didn't think she'd have the balls.'

'Maaate.'

Hamish felt a callused hand on his arm.

'She'll be back in February.'

'That's rough.'

Hamish brushed Doggo's hand away. He wanted to be alone.

'I'll make tracks,' said Doggo. 'I'll call you tomorrow, mate. Oh, and here . . .'

Doggo slipped the wristwatch off his left hand. 'Yours was smashed in the accident. I've got another one at home.'

Hamish looked down at the timepiece. Nothing fancy, but exactly what he needed. 'Thanks, Doggo.'

'No worries.'

Doggo flicked two thumbs up at Hamish, then disappeared down the hallway.

The front door closed behind him.

*Now what the hell do I do?*

Hamish took a two-litre carton of long-life milk from the fridge, prising open the lid and guzzling half its contents. He scanned the supplies on the shelves: packaged pasta, soup, risotto, a ready-made pizza, several tubs of yoghurt, a packet of mint slices.

He slammed the fridge door shut. The silence in the house was unnerving. Was this what life would feel like without Paula? Without the kids, too?

Closing his eyes, Hamish sucked in the air through flared nostrils. His gut felt queasy, like he was trapped on a tinny in high seas.

He pushed his small brown suitcase on its rollers across the kitchen floor, then tried to lift it into the hall. Even with the walking stick, it was too difficult. So he shunted it instead with his right leg, bit by bit, down the carpeted hallway.

By the time he reached the bedroom, he was sweating. He limped a few paces further before falling sideways onto the bed. When the pain receded, he rolled onto his back and grabbed a pillow to prop under his left knee. As he lifted the pillow, he caught sight of something metallic: the shiny silver lid of his laptop.

*At least I can do some work now,* he thought.

He wanted to stay across the business at Crossroads, even if Nick-the-Dick was making the decisions for the time being.

He wedged the pillow under his knee and, grunting with exertion, reached for the laptop.

The lid lifted easily in his hand. He turned it over and stared, stupefied, at its underside. The keyboard was completely missing: he was holding half a laptop.

The screen had been severed with a sharp instrument; there were indentations along the attachment points that suggested a hacksaw or metal file.

Hamish sat up, shocked.

Then, warily, he lifted the other pillow.

And there it was: the keyboard, cleaved from its screen like a headless chook.

He held the two halves of his laptop, just junk now. Paula had completely flipped her lid. How would he explain this to Gary? How could he explain it to himself?

Doggo's wristwatch told him it was only three-forty on a Tuesday afternoon.

*Who bloody cares?* Hamish needed a drink.

He hauled himself off the bed and staggered down the hallway, dragging his left foot. In the dining room, he opened the drinks cabinet and reached for the whisky bottle, but found nothing in it.

He shook the tequila bottle: empty too. Picking up the limited-edition cognac he reserved for special occasions, Hamish tested its weight in his hands. Then he peered down its neck, just to be sure. His hands moved across the vodka, the sherry, the gin, the brandy. All of them had been drained. Hundreds of dollars, if not thousands, down the gurgler.

Rage surged through his body. He grabbed two bottles and, growling, hurled them against the wall. He stood gazing at the glass strewn across the carpet, his chest heaving. Touching a hand to his jaw, he found blood on his fingers; he'd been nicked by a flying shard.

He limped to the kitchen and paused at the top of the staircase leading down to the laundry. A box of cleanskins, a good South Australian red, was stored in the cupboard downstairs. With a bit of luck, Paula might have forgotten about it. Holding on to the banister, he half lurched, half slid down the stairs. He tripped at the bottom and almost fell, his knee throbbing. But, beneath the laundry tubs, he struck gold: two dozen unopened bottles, still in the box. He could only carry two bottles at a time, and practically had to crawl back up the stairs. By the time he reached the lounge room again, his left leg was leaden.

He fell across Lachie's purple beanbag, panting.

Pulling himself up onto his elbows, he fumbled around in the pocket of his shorts for the extra-strength paracetamol Jan had given him on discharge. Unscrewing the top of one of the wine bottles, he popped several pills into his mouth and washed them down with a swig of cabernet sauvignon.

Thank God corks weren't common anymore.

He looked at the drinks cabinet, judging the effort required to haul himself up to fetch a wineglass.

*Bugger it*, he thought. *No one's looking.*

He drank again, direct from the bottle.

The remote was on the top of the television: also too far away.

He lay back across the beanbag, bottle in hand, staring at three framed photos above the mantelpiece. One of them was of Hamish and Paula on their wedding day, laughing together at their reception, Paula's smile as wide and white as he'd ever seen it. In the second shot, Sid and his wife Jeanette—a posher, broader-hipped version of Paula—stood in front of a Christmas tree with Caitlin and Lachie, back when they still believed in Santa Claus. Finally, there was a snap of Paula nursing baby Caitlin in her bunny rug, her maternal beam glowing through her exhaustion.

The faces of his family blurred before his eyes.

'I love you,' he murmured aloud.

They stared back at him as if from another lifetime.

*

When he woke, he desperately needed a piss.

He heaved himself upright, then felt along the wall for the light switch. Flicking it on, he saw two empty wine bottles and an unholy red stain in the middle of the ivory shagpile.

'Paula will be pissed,' he muttered.

*But Paula's not here. Should've put a big antimacassar across the lounge-room floor, hon.*

He reeled down the hallway to the bathroom, noticing the relaxed feeling in his limbs. While he wasn't exactly balanced, at least he wasn't in pain anymore.

The landline began to ring, all the way from the kitchen.

*Could be the kids*, he thought. But the need to urinate was overwhelming. Ignoring the telephone, Hamish lifted the toilet seat and groaned as he relieved himself. By the time he was done, the phone had stopped ringing.

Leaning forward to flush, he detected a glint of silver in the toilet.

He crouched as low as his knee would allow. Something was definitely in there, but it was difficult to see in the semi-darkness. He lurched towards the door, clicked on the bathroom light, then turned back to inspect the bowl.

His iPhone lay at the bottom, submerged in his own rank piss.

He stared, horrified, remembering Paula's note.

*PS: Your computer is in the bedroom, your phone is in the bathroom.*

Who *was* this banshee, hell-bent on vengeance?

He leaned heavily against the wall, feeling suddenly nauseous.

In hospital, he'd somehow convinced himself that it was all going to be okay, but he'd clearly underestimated how badly he'd hurt Paula. Now the realisation slammed into him: things might *not* be okay. And he only had himself to blame.

His left leg buckled beneath him and he slumped onto the cold tiles.

The phone began ringing again in the kitchen, but he wasn't sure he could stand up.

Leaning against the S-bend, Hamish couldn't hold it back any longer. The tears just hammered down.

*

The banging had been going on for hours.

*What is this, a building site?*

Hamish pulled the pillow over his head, where Paula's scent still lingered.

'Hamo?'

A voice he knew, close by.

He pushed himself up onto his elbows and forced his eyes open. The room was visible, so it couldn't be night-time. But everything was fuzzy and churning, enough to make him puke.

He closed his eyes against the rising nausea.

'I know you're in there, Hamo. Open up, mate.'

Doggo's voice.

Hamish looked around the room. The sound was coming from the direction of the window.

He untangled himself from the doona and lurched out of bed. Then he hobbled over to the window and pulled up the blind.

Doggo's anxious face was pressed up against the glass.

It took Hamish several seconds to register that this was unusual; the bedroom *was* on the first floor.

'What the fuck are you doing?' Hamish opened the window and gawked at Doggo, clinging to a garden trellis and straddling a drainpipe.

'What the fuck am *I* doing? Rescuing *you*, ya dumb fuck.' Doggo sounded genuinely offended. 'Give me a hand.'

Hamish leaned out and grabbed Doggo under his left shoulder, helping him through the window. Doggo landed on his hands and knees on the carpet.

'What died in here?' Doggo asked, standing up. 'What've you been *doing* the last ten days, mate?'

'Ten days?'

Doggo looked him up and down. 'Your mobile's disconnected. You never pick up the landline, you don't answer the door. There's a bunch of groceries stacked up on your doorstep with a note from your sister-in-law. You didn't even surface for Melbourne Cup. Tina thought you'd topped y'self, dead set. Kept tellin' me to ring the coppers. I kept telling her to settle down. But when it got to ten days, mate, *I* got antsy too.'

Hamish watched Doggo as he paced around the room, kicking at the items strewn across the floor. Wine bottles, dirty washing, muesli-bar wrappers, and countless silver pill packets.

'Ten days?' Hamish repeated. He'd been on a bender for three, max.

Doggo walked over and stood in front of him. 'Mate, you stink like a pig's arse. You haven't had a shower, have you?'

Hamish's last memory of showering was in hospital, being sponge-bathed by the pretty Asian nurse. It could have been erotic if he hadn't been hurting so badly.

'What did you have for lunch, mate?'

Hamish scowled. 'Is this the Spanish Inquisition?'

'Right, that's it.' Doggo looked resolute. 'You're coming home with me. Can't be trusted to look after yourself.'

'I'm fine, Doggo.'

'Tina told me not to leave without you.'

They stood there, eyeballing each other.

After a minute, Hamish looked away. He didn't have the energy to take on Doggo. Or Tina, for that matter, who was like a bitch with a bone at the best of times.

'Okay,' he said. 'But you'll have to pack my suitcase, Mum.'

*

He'd been at Doggo's for less than a week when he began plotting his escape.

Tina was infinitely hospitable, bustling about in her matronly way; feeding Hamish hearty home cooking, administering his painkillers, even shuttling him to medical appointments. More than three weeks had passed since the bike accident; the swelling had settled down, the pain was more manageable, and the X-ray showed that his knee was healing nicely. The splint had helped his stability and he'd stopped using the walking stick. Good riddance, too: it made him feel like Quasi-fucking-modo.

Doggo hung out with Hamish whenever he could; watching late-night DVDs, playing poker, or just having a beer together on the veranda. But Doggo still worked twelve-hour days, even on Saturdays, and Hamish quickly tired of being a spectator in his friend's home. The noisy routine of his five kids, and Tina's endless scurrying about after them, only served to highlight what Hamish had lost.

*Paula.*

His curvy, intelligent, committed wife.

The only girl with a university degree who'd ever agreed to go out with him; all the others chicks had been too stuck-up. Watching them across the room every Thursday night at the trendy pub near the university, Doggo and Hamish had called them the 'Fig Jam' girls. An acronym for their attitude—*Fuck I'm Good, Just Ask Me.* Skinny girls with chambray shirts and plums in their mouths, studying law, science, medicine. But Paula had been a standout; her big, open smile, her infectious laughter, a not-so-serious degree. And no tickets on herself, either. *She* hadn't thought twice about going out with him.

They'd got together, got married, had two great kids. He'd made the money and she'd run their home.

Except now she wasn't there, for the first time in seventeen years.

*Temporarily, mate*, Doggo assured him. *Give Paula a few months and she'll be back for sure.*

Hamish wasn't so certain.

Paula's destruction of his laptop and telephone had revealed a side of his wife he'd never encountered; it just didn't gel with the warm and cuddly woman he knew. And now she'd taken off with the kids, too—a low act for someone so obsessed with *fairness.*

*But was it fair to me,* he could almost hear his wife saying, *what you did with that girl online?*

*And she'd be right,* Hamish thought to himself. *What the hell was I thinking, risking everything good in my life—my wife, my kids, my home—to have cyber-sex with a girl young enough to be my daughter?*

Whenever he thought about it in those terms, Hamish was in no doubt of his own culpability.

Helped by Tina, he'd organised a new iPhone and sent several conciliatory texts to Paula, but she hadn't replied. According to the itinerary Lachie had emailed, they were heading around Australia in a clockwise direction.

Hamish had paid for a replacement laptop and had his access to the work server reinstated, but monitoring Nick-the-Dick Bridge just didn't hold much interest anymore. In fact, when Gary called around to Doggo's with a 'Get Well Soon' card, then casually asked Hamish when he might return to work, Hamish had baulked at an answer. Then, without pausing to think about it, he'd asked his boss about taking the long-service leave due to him after a decade at Crossroads.

*To completely recover, Gary.*

*To take a break, mate.*

*Things are a bit rocky with Paula.*

Gary had been more than accommodating, agreeing immediately to ten weeks of paid long-service leave.

Knowing he had wages coming in until February made a huge difference to Hamish, reinforcing in his mind the obvious course of action. He had to get the hell out of Doggo's life, and put things right in his own.

*

At his last appointment, the orthopaedic surgeon had cautioned Hamish against driving with a knee splint.

'It's not illegal,' the doctor had conceded. 'But I'd rather you didn't.'

But what else was he supposed to do, hire a chauffeur?

Hamish lowered himself into the driver's seat and eased his left leg into the footwell beside the brake. Then he pushed the seat back to accommodate his height; Paula was usually the one to drive the hatchback, it wasn't designed for a six-foot male. He'd bought it for her a few years back, when she'd returned to part-time work. But now that she'd helped herself to his ute to tow their caravan around Australia, Hamish had no other option.

'Are you sure you should be doing this, mate?' Doggo looked furtive, as if he expected Tina to come charging out of the house.

Hamish had set his alarm for five o'clock on a Sunday morning, an hour before sunrise, to avoid a confrontation with Tina. Doggo had collected the hatchback from Hamish's house the night before, then parked it out of view on the street. They'd packed it under the cover of darkness, with Hamish's duffel bag, a small rucksack and an old swag of Doggo's, in case he needed to sleep out. Plus an esky of food, a bag of ice and a few sneaky beers.

'It can't be safe,' fretted Doggo, peering at Hamish's splint through the driver's window.

'Don't worry, Mum, I won't be arrested,' said Hamish. 'Lucky I didn't smash my *right* knee.'

He wouldn't have been able to use the accelerator or the brake.

'Lucky you didn't smash your right *hand*, ya tosser.' Doggo grinned.

Hamish turned on the engine, cringing at its little purr. Barely a whisper compared to the throaty roar of his ute.

'Hey, take this,' said Doggo, pushing a packet through the window.

Hamish stared at the children's toy, still in its plastic packaging. 'What the hell will I need a toy pistol for?'

'Look, it's a big country out there, Hamo. Lots of lonely roads. Tina keeps one of those in her glove box.'

'Tina's mad as a cut snake, mate.'

'It might buy you some time if you get into trouble.'

Hamish laughed aloud; Doggo shushed him like an old woman.

'Whatever you reckon, mate.' Hamish sniggered. 'I tell you, Doggo, you're pussy-whipped.'

His friend looked wounded.

'But thanks, mate, I appreciate it.' Hamish reached through the open window and shook Doggo's hand. With a slap, a slide and a knuckle bump, just as they'd done since they were twelve years old.

'Don't try anything stupid out there, Hamo. And call me, okay? Or send me a text. Stick to the plan, right?'

'The plan, Stan,' Hamish intoned. He waved a hand towards the house, where Tina and the kids slept. 'You've all been really good to me. Too good, mate.'

Doggo loitered at the driver's window. 'Tina's gonna have my balls for letting you go,' he whispered. 'She'll skewer 'em, fry 'em and eat 'em up for breakfast. So make sure you come back with Paula and the kids.' He straightened up and rapped his hand on the car roof.

Flicking one thumb up at Doggo, Hamish accelerated away.

*

He followed the inland route via Ballarat and Horsham, paying no heed to the natural beauty or historic significance of the towns he passed through. His attention was squarely focused on getting to Adelaide as quickly as possible. He couldn't anticipate how fast Paula was travelling, or whether they were doing any side trips, but he knew they had a good three weeks on him. Using Lachie's rough itinerary, he'd calculated that they must be somewhere between Adelaide and Perth by now. Which was a bloody long stretch of the country to cover.

It took Hamish most of the day to reach Adelaide, stopping once at Bordertown to take a piss and have a bite to eat. The tasteless egg and lettuce sandwich he selected made him fart all afternoon. Only one hundred kilometres short of Adelaide, Hamish felt his eyes begin to droop; so he pulled over for a kip by the side of the highway. When he finally drove into Adelaide's central business district, the roads were practically deserted. Realising he didn't have any accommodation lined up for the night, Hamish did several slow circuits of the city before spotting a sign for a youth hostel. A two-storey building, painted a tasteless yellow.

*Cheap and cheerful, just what I need.*

He parked the car beneath a streetlamp, its neon light flickering as the sun set in the west.

*Damn I need a beer.*

As he reached for the esky on the floor of the hatchback, his phone beeped.

It was a message from Caitlin, at last, using a number he didn't recognise. At least his daughter still acknowledged his existence.

*So good 2 hear from u Dad! We tried u heaps on your old number and the landline. Why do u have a new phone number? Catie xx*

His fingers hovered over the pad; Paula clearly hadn't told the children about her nasty little bout of vandalism.

*Because your mum went bonkers*, he wanted to type.

*Time for a change*, he typed instead. *There's lots I want 2 change. Give your brother and Mum a hug from me, ok? BTW, where r u?*

*Somewhere in SA*, came the reply. *Gramps has a phone!*

Where exactly in SA? he wanted to ask. But he didn't probe any further, not wishing to appear too interested. Like he might be *following* them, or anything; he didn't need Catie alerting Paula to his plan.

The good news was, they couldn't be that far away.

He opened the esky and retrieved a six-pack of stubbies, before climbing out of the car.

He groaned aloud, doubling over. His whole body was as stiff as buggery. He limped around to the boot and stuffed the stubbies into his bag. Then he dragged it out and shuffled onto the footpath.

It'd been almost twenty years since he'd stayed in a youth hostel; the last time had been in Italy with Doggo. He smirked, remembering the Estonian twins they'd met playing table tennis there, all tanned and svelte, with blonde braids and titanic tits. Neither Hamish nor Doggo had known where Estonia was, exactly, but it hadn't been important. The taller twin with the cute little mole above her lip—was it Anna or Johanna?—who'd gone down on Hamish in the dorm one night. The sounds of sleep all around them—the breathing, the turning, the sighing—and Anna-or-Johanna sucking him off like a girl scout with an icy pole. The silent orgasm he'd had within minutes—rampaging out of nowhere like a tsunami—and the way she'd swallowed it all. Wiping the sides of her mouth with the tips of her fingers and smiling up at him, a perfect set of white teeth gleaming in the shadows.

The automatic doors opened and Hamish pondered, for a moment, if he was even eligible to stay in a youth hostel anymore. Would the receptionist behind the desk redirect him to the nearest Country Comfort Inn, or other lodgings more appropriate for a middle-aged invalid?

'Hi,' said the young receptionist. Her name was 'Delaney', according to the tag clipped to her shirt. Whatever possessed some parents to use surnames for their children? She looked like a *Janey* not a *Delaney*, Hamish thought.

'Hi,' he replied. 'I'd like a room, please.'

'Are you a member?' She pushed a form towards him, as if anticipating the answer.

He filled it out and paid the annual fee.

'We've only got a four-share room left. It's thirty-five dollars a night. All the cheaper beds are gone, sorry.'

'Sure,' he replied. 'Anyone else in the room with me?'

Delaney scanned her computer. 'Just one so far. Um . . . Sasha. Here, I'll show you around.'

Hamish nodded. A *fräulein* named Sasha sounded promising.

Delaney escorted him through the kitchen and dining room, the games room, the shared bathrooms and WI-FI zone.

'It's a pity you didn't arrive yesterday,' she said, flicking her mousy ponytail over her shoulder. 'We have free pancakes on a Saturday.'

'Oh.' He feigned disappointment. He'd forgotten how it felt to be a student on a budget, actually caring about the free pancakes.

'And here's your dorm, the pin number is 1234. Pretty easy to remember.' She keyed the digits into an electronic pad on the wall and pushed open the door. 'Sasha, this is Hamish.'

A hulking great bloke with chin-length, greasy hair stood up from a bed on the far side of the room and walked towards Hamish, his hand extended.

'Sasha,' he said, in a thick accent.

Definitely German, Hamish thought, but the wrong bloody gender. Filthy, too.

Sasha's eyes looked everywhere except directly at Hamish. Two firm white beads of spittle adhered to either side of his mouth. As they shook hands, Hamish became aware of a sour stench of body odour.

'Okay, you two,' said Delaney amiably, backing towards the door. 'Let me know if there's anything else I can help you with.'

*Don't leave me here, Delaney.*

The door closed behind her.

'So,' Hamish turned back to Sasha, attempting to be courteous. 'Are you from Germany?'

'Brussels.'

Hamish tried to locate Brussels on the map of Europe in his mind. Austria? Holland? Lichtenstein, maybe—that obscure little tax haven he'd read about, with more shelf companies than citizens.

Sasha took a step towards him. 'You know where Brussels is, my friend?'

Hamish swallowed, looking up at the man. There was something distinctly odd about him; all oily hair and fervent eyes.

Hamish shook his head.

'Belgium,' Sasha held up a finger in front of his nose. 'You Australians need geography lessons, just like the Americans.'

Hamish didn't feel confident enough to reply.

The evening didn't improve. Sasha was fidgety and talkative, with strongly held views on European politics, the world's religions and whacky conspiracy theories. He talked ceaselessly, even following Hamish to the kitchen as he prepared some two-minute noodles.

In the dining room, Hamish sat down at a table and leaned over the steaming bowl, hoping Sasha would leave him alone to eat. Instead, Sasha pulled up a chair and earbashed him about the connection between crop circles and the CIA.

It wasn't until Sasha pursued him into the bathroom after dinner that Hamish decided he'd had enough. He wheeled around from the washbasin.

'Listen, mate.' Hamish looked up into Sasha's zealous face. 'I need to take a shower. Can you leave me in peace to do that?'

Sasha held up both hands. 'No need to be rude, my friend.'

'I'm *not* your friend,' said Hamish, surprising even himself.

'Suit yourself, *klootzak,*' said Sasha, scowling as he stormed out.

Hamish could only assume the word was as uncomplimentary as it sounded. He'd forgotten how full of crazies youth hostels could be; a Country Comfort inn now seemed *very* attractive.

Removing his splint, Hamish stood under the shower for ten minutes, letting the heat and the steam soothe his aching limbs.

As he limped back down the hall with a bath towel wrapped around his waist, a young woman emerged from a nearby dorm.

'What happened to you?' she asked, pointing at Hamish's splint. Her accent was American, or Canadian maybe; Hamish could never distinguish between the two.

She was wearing gym gear—tight blue shorts, a fitted running singlet and sneakers—and her cropped brown hair fell in attractive wisps around hazel eyes.

'Smashed my knee.'

'How'd you do it?'

'Skiing,' he lied.

'Too bad,' she said, wide-eyed. 'I *love* skiing.'

He caught sight of a white gob of chewing gum rolling over a silver tongue ring.

'Where's your room?' she asked. 'Let me help you to it.'

She stepped in close to him; he could smell her perfume. A no-nonsense sporty scent, but feminine nonetheless. He grasped her wiry arm and leaned heavily against it.

'Woops,' she said, putting her other arm around him for support.

He could feel her hand on his bare skin, the point of her shoulder beneath his armpit. He caught sight of her cleavage. Lightly-freckled skin over smooth, firm mounds.

The woman looked up at him. 'Where did you say your room was?'

He lifted his gaze. 'Uh, just over there.'

She helped him across the corridor, then disentangled herself.

'My name's Hamish,' he said, holding out his hand.

'Marie,' she replied, not taking it. 'I hope you feel better soon.' She turned on her heel and jogged off, her compact arse jiggling all the way down the corridor.

'Shit,' he muttered, laying his head against the wall for a moment. He closed his eyes, feeling the cool brick beneath his forehead.

*What the hell am I doing ogling younger women? I'm on the road trying to find my wife, the mother of my children.*

Almost a month had passed since he'd last seen Paula. He missed her warm body nestled against his in the groggy minutes before the alarm went off, her dishevelled hair and soft smile that somehow, within an hour of waking, she transformed into her neat-as-a-pin super-mum style. They'd made memories together; years of fun and laughter and sex before the children arrived, years of hard work and renovations afterwards. They'd *built* things together, literally and figuratively, and they were a good team. As parents, partners and yes, even lovers, when they finally got around to *doing* it. So why would he jeopardise all that on a whim? Distracted by a Lisel, a Marie, or another passing Polly?

Hamish shook his head, still leaning against the wall.

Why were there so *many* alluring women in the world?

It was one of life's great injustices, as far as he was concerned: a commitment to monogamy in marriage, when there was so much eye candy walking around.

He rubbed his forehead across the brickwork again, his nose chasing a final waft of Marie's perfume. *It's a biological urge*, he'd said to Paula, on more than one occasion. *Men are* different *to women. It's Mars and Venus, babe.*

He sighed, confounded by his own conflicting desires.

He keyed in the pin number and the door opened.

'You're back,' said Sasha, lolling on his bed.

The stench in the room was worse, like sport socks soaked in piss.

Hamish couldn't handle it any longer.

Without a word, he dropped his towel and pulled on a pair of boxers and a t-shirt. He struggled with a fresh pair of trousers over his splint.

'Need some help?' asked Sasha, standing up from the bed.

Hamish fixed him with a steely glare.

Abandoning the trousers, Hamish opted for the same pair of shorts he'd worn earlier that day, still smelling of ten hours on the road.

Grabbing his bag from under the bed, Hamish dragged it towards the door. With his gammy leg, it felt much heavier than it was, but the six-pack inside it didn't help. He hadn't even managed to crack one open because of Sasha tailing him around the hostel.

'What's so heavy?' Sasha nodded at Hamish's bag. 'You got a dead body in there or something?'

Hamish didn't deign to respond.

'Where are you going?' Sasha persisted.

'West.' Hamish chocked the door open so he could push the bag out of the room.

'Why leave now? You only just checked in.'

'I've got to . . .' Hamish paused, irritated. He didn't owe an explanation to Sasha. Or to anyone, for that matter. He resumed pushing his bag into the corridor.

'I think I'll tell the police about you,' Sasha called, his voice almost sing-song. 'You're acting very strangely, my friend.'

*As if* you're *an impartial assessor of strange*, Hamish thought.

'Oh.' Delaney stood up at the front desk as he passed, eyeing his bag. 'You're not leaving are you?'

Hamish nodded.

'Is there a problem with the room?'

Hamish was sick of questions. 'I've got some business to attend to,' he snapped.

He didn't stop walking until he reached the hatchback, parked some fifty metres away on the other side of the street.

After loading the boot, he sank into the driver's seat and reclined as far as it would go. He didn't have the energy to find another place to stay, not at this hour.

Locking the doors, Hamish closed his eyes.

Even behind his eyelids, he could still sense the neon streetlight flickering above him.

# 8

The evening before they left Adelaide, the Brazilian arrived from the youth hostel carrying a surfboard, a guitar, an enormous backpack and a daypack.

*I'm not the only one who can't travel lightly,* Paula thought.

He spent the night in the Gillespie's spare room, then joined Paula and her family in the ute.

'Goodbye, love,' said Shirl, pressing a tissue to the corner of her eyes.

'Nice to meet you, son,' added Barry. 'Enjoy your trip Downunder.'

Paula smiled at how attached to Marcelo the old couple seemed, despite having only just met him.

'Thanks for everything,' said Sid, shaking Barry's hand through the ute's window. 'I might come back for an encore next Melbourne Cup.'

'Please do.' Shirl laughed. 'We'll be ringing you for tips at any rate.'

Their first day on the road together was uneventful, with Marcelo sitting quietly beside Lachie in the ute. Drumming his fingers on his knees in time with the music—Caitlin's, this time—and asking the occasional question about the passing landscape. It all felt surprisingly natural, Paula reflected, relieved to have her initial concerns allayed.

On arrival in the tiny village of Denial Bay, eight hours west of Adelaide, they were delighted to discover the area's oyster-growing reputation. Wandering along the main street, they ordered three dozen oysters straight from a grower, before stacking some beers and ice into the esky. Sid struck up a conversation with a craggy-faced fisherman in the general store and, intrigued by the idea of catching one of the region's blue swimmer crabs, bought some bait and a net too.

They carried the gear down to the long wooden jetty protruding over the bay. Her father set up the crab rig as best he could, then stood up to perform his 'lucky dance', as he termed it.

'Watch this, mate,' he said to Marcelo. 'Guarantees a bite every time.'

He executed the dance—a silent hybrid of the chicken dance and the Macarena—with a straight face. Caitlin and Lachie fell about laughing as their grandfather squatted, slapped and swayed his way over the creaking jetty.

Paula wondered what Marcelo might make of it all. Wonderfully, he began mimicking her father.

Marcelo's version included grunting and quacking, which only made the children laugh more. When her father concluded his dance by casting the line, Marcelo turned and, with a loud war cry, pushed the watching children off the other side of the jetty. They squealed with indignation, then climbed out of the water to reciprocate. They all splashed and rumbled like this for at least half an hour, pushing each other into the water with theatrical shrieks, until Marcelo called a truce.

Then he padded up the jetty to sit next to Paula in the late-afternoon light, water dripping off his tanned skin. She tried not to look at the lean muscles moving beneath his torso, the soft fuzz around his navel, his sinewy shoulders. But she noticed the small tattoo above his left nipple, a name inscribed in cursive blue ink.

*Lili.*

Lucky Lili, Paula thought, averting her eyes.

She suddenly felt a dull pang in the pit of her stomach; a wistful yearning for all the things in life she could have done, but hadn't. Travel after study. A proper career before children. Learning a second language. Tattooed Brazilian lovers. Wild nights, lazy days. More travel. The sorts of things enjoyed by twenty-year-olds, maybe thirty-year-olds. But almost never forty-somethings.

She looked out across the pristine blue water of Denial Bay, crisp and flat and still. The sky was streaked hazy orange as the sun moved lower in its western arc.

*I wonder why it's called Denial Bay? What have I been denying, all these years?*

The deepening light was softening the edges of everything: the lines on the gnarled jetty boards; the creases on her father's t-shirt; the sharp triangular sails of a solitary white yacht bobbing out at sea. Hopefully even softening the lines on my forehead, Paula thought.

Her eyes lingered on the smooth skin on the back of Marcelo's hands.

*He's so striking and I'm so . . . freckly.*

Caitlin and Lachie were still jumping off the jetty into the high tide below, pulling martial arts poses mid-air before plunging into the blue depths.

A month ago, Paula thought, I wouldn't have let them do that. I would have argued them down with maternal reasoning.

*We've never swum here before.*

*It mightn't be as deep as it looks.*

*This is great white shark territory, you know.*

But somehow *she* had mellowed in the weeks since leaving home; made malleable, perhaps, by the light, the landscape, the hours of enforced reflection in the car. Somehow her objections and precautions, her endless circumvention of risk, all seemed redundant now.

'Do you know what oysters are good for?'

Marcelo's voice, deliciously close, diverted her thoughts. Paula repressed a smile.

A natural aphrodisiac, of course.

She could still remember the wedding anniversary—was it their seventh?—in which she'd ordered Tasmanian rock oysters as a surprise for Hamish, paired with expensive French champagne. How Hamish had compared the shape of the oysters to her vulva and how she'd forced a laugh, while dying inside.

She turned to look at Marcelo.

Holding her gaze, he sucked an oyster out of its shell. He balanced it on the tip of his tongue, then swallowed it, sighing in mock ecstasy. For one wild moment she imagined Marcelo eating oysters off her bare stomach. Slippery discs of the sea marching across her abdomen and Marcelo, lying next to her, admiring them. Admiring *her*.

'Where are you, *Pow-la*?'

'Oh.' She smiled. 'Well, they say oysters can help with . . . Casanova used to have fifty for breakfast.'

Marcelo's expression was blank. 'Who is Casanova?'

'You don't know?' She was squirming. 'He was famous for his sexual prowess.'

Marcelo looked puzzled. 'What is "prowess"?'

She giggled, unable to explain any further. In fact, she could hardly breathe.

Marcelo was leaning towards her, the tip of his shoulder touching hers. As he placed the box of oysters back on the jetty, his hand accidentally brushed the side of her thigh.

She couldn't look at him, too conscious of the points of contact of their bodies.

'Zinc,' he said eventually, his voice a little husky. 'Oysters have more zinc than any other food. Excellent for healing wounds.'

'Oh.' She laughed, a combination of relief and disappointment. 'I'll keep that in mind.'

She shifted her weight slightly, so that their bodies were no longer touching.

'Hey!' her father suddenly hollered. 'I've got one!'

They turned to see Sid pulling the crab line up, hand over hand.

Marcelo stood up and peered over the jetty. 'It's big, Sid.'

'Yeah?' Lachie clambered out of the water, followed by Caitlin.

A nearby fisherman joined them too, but seemed more interested in Caitlin than in Sid's catch.

'Whoa, Gramps!' yelled Lachie, seizing his sister's arm in excitement. 'That's a blue crab!'

With help from Marcelo, Sid hauled the line up onto the jetty. An enormous, spiny blue creature waved its pincers beneath the net.

'Jeez, mate.' The fisherman tipped up his cap. 'That's one of the biggest blueys I've ever seen. Whatcha use for bait?'

'Just the gear I bought from the general store.'

'Well you're a lucky bugger, aren't you? She's a monster.'

'Have a beer?' Sid snapped open the esky, relishing the attention.

The fisherman introduced himself as Stan, and began acting as if Sid was an old mate.

'Photo time.' Sid pulled his mobile out from beneath a towel.

*That's supposed to be in the glove box*, thought Paula. *Even Dad is breaching my rules.*

Lachie took the phone from his grandfather and prepared to take a snap. 'This can go on your Facebook page, Gramps.'

'Your *what*?' Paula gaped at him.

'Look, I'm not sure yet. Lachie seems to think it's a good idea.'

'Why would *anyone* in this family think Facebook is a good idea? *Especially* after what happened to Catie?' It was insensitive of Lachie to suggest it at all, Paula thought, glaring at him.

'But it can help Gramps stay in touch with his mates, Mum,' said Lachie. 'From Rotary, right, Gramps? And Greenleaves. And Glen Waverley.'

'I can't imagine *any* of your friends are on Facebook, Dad,' Paula objected.

'Brenda from Lorne is,' her father replied.

'*Who?*'

She suddenly remembered the woman her father had courted on their first night on the road.

'I am too,' volunteered Stan the fisherman.

Sid held up his hands as if vindicated. 'See? It's the new world order, love.'

Paula stood speechless.

'How about I take the photo?' Stan suggested, reaching for Sid's phone. 'Get in there, Sid. Hold up the crab.'

Her father motioned to Marcelo. 'Come here, mate. You did the "lucky dance" with me.'

They laughed together, crouching down on the jetty and holding the crab by its claws.

Lachie and Caitlin edged into the frame next to them, giggling.

'Come on, Mum, you too.' The fisherman nodded at Paula.

She stood behind them, resting her hands on Marcelo's shoulders.

'Good. Now hold it . . .' Stan began to fumble about with the phone.

Marcelo moved his right hand up onto his shoulder, and laid it over Paula's. Patting it in a friendly way, a natural extension of the camaraderie of the moment.

And then, slowly, his thumb slid over the soft pad of flesh between her thumb and forefinger.

It was an unmistakably intimate touch.

Paula's mouth went dry.

'Okay, gang.' Stan crouched low before the group. 'Here we go. One . . . two . . . three . . . smile!'

Paula didn't need any prompting.

*

After overnighters at Denial Bay and Ceduna, they headed to Cactus Beach, pitching camp in the dunes alongside a semi-permanent community of surfers. Men and women and winsome tanned children, buzzing about in bare feet adorned with hand-woven anklets. Tribes of friends with long, matted hair, greasy at the crown and wild blond streaks, the work of Nature's hairdresser. The ever-present scent of coconut oil in the morning, corned beef at lunch, pungent smoky weed at night.

Paula spent most of her time lying in a low hammock that her father had strung between the caravan's demountable veranda posts, reading novels and occasionally texting Jamie.

*We picked up a Brazilian backpacker in Adders.*

*Seven years younger than me, but super cute.*

She laughed at Jamie's immediate response: *Careful, cougar.*

Closing her eyes at regular intervals, Paula inhaled the salty sea air. Listening to the wind blowing across the dunes, sometimes punctuated by garrulous laughter or an expletive. Wondering why they hadn't taken a family holiday like this *years* ago. And every now and then, she'd glance up to see Marcelo running through the scrub, board under his arm. Wet and beaming with the rush of surfing the Cactus left break, the Castles right break, Point Sinclair's Witzigs, Backdoors and Cunns.

'So, you're good on a horse *and* a board.' She smiled at Marcelo on their first night at Cactus, as Sid passed them mugs of a homemade brew he'd christened 'Surfin' Sangria'. Combining a Barossa red with brandy, Sid had popped several cinnamon sticks in the concoction for good measure. She'd feared it might taste like rocket fuel, but the effect was more subtle. She sat sipping her drink, lowering her eyes beneath the rim of her glass, watching Marcelo.

'In Rio Grande do Sul, my home state, the surf breaks are not consistent,' he said. 'But I was lucky growing up, my father's older brother lives near Ilha dos Lobos, a small island on the Torres coast. My brothers and I went there every school holidays.'

He paused, swallowing a mouthful of Sid's Surfin' Sangria.

'My uncle taught me how to surf there. It's wild, tow-in surfing with massive waves. I had to learn quickly, because the conditions are so challenging.' He smiled. 'My uncle was very good to me; he had no children of his own. After my mother died, I kept getting into fights on the farm, bad ones. So my uncle taught me Brazilian jiu-jitsu.'

'Je-what?' asked Lachie.

'We call it the gentle art,' Marcelo replied. 'It's a martial art, where you learn to defend yourself against a bigger person by using leverage and technique, but mostly this.' He tapped his temple. 'It helped me to channel my anger. I think it saved me after my mother died.'

Lachie's eyes widened.

'Show us,' said Sid.

'Yeah, go on.' Lachie stood up and began dancing on his toes like a boxer.

'I don't think . . .' Paula objected.

Marcelo raised a hand. 'This is the *gentle* art, *Pow-la*, I will not hurt anyone.' He beckoned to Lachie. 'Come to me.'

'Slowly now, Lachie,' urged Sid.

'Go, bro!' called Catie.

Lachie punched the air, as if warming up. Marcelo simply stood watching, his face a mask of calm.

Suddenly Lachie lunged forward and swung his right arm at Marcelo.

It was hard for Paula to determine exactly what happened next.

Marcelo blocked Lachie's arm, but not with any overt force; it was as if he simply caught it, cushioning the blow with his hands. Then he pulled Lachie into a tight embrace, one arm around his shoulders and neck, before sweeping him down onto the sand.

'Jiu-jitsu takes the fight to the ground, where ninety-five per cent of all fights end up,' said Marcelo in a matter-of-fact way, as though he was gardening, not wrestling. 'On the ground, everyone is equal. It doesn't matter how tall you are, how heavy you are. What matters is your strategy.'

'Hang on,' said Sid, watching as Lachie squirmed beneath Marcelo's weight. 'What're you doing there?'

'This is called *montada*, or "mount". Using only my hips, I am in control,' said Marcelo.

Catie giggled and took a snap of her brother struggling in the sand, using Sid's phone.

'For Facebook?' asked Paula.

'Yes,' replied Caitlin. 'For posting on *Sunday*.'

Paula nodded, tiring of her own vigilance. There was nothing unusual about Caitlin's online activities, or indeed her mood. Whenever she quizzed her daughter about the Facebook scandal now, Caitlin simply offered up some philosophical gem: *Stuff happens, Mum. It's the twenty-first century. It's the world we live in.*

It's the world *you* live in, Paula was tempted to say.

'I can't get up,' Lachie called, still squirming beneath Marcelo.

'You must tap out now, Lachie,' said Marcelo.

'What's that?' Lachie croaked.

'Admit defeat. You tap your opponent's leg, or whatever body part you can reach.'

Lachie winced. 'But I can't reach any part of you.'

Marcelo laughed. 'Here.' He shifted his weight to allow Lachie to tap him.

Lachie rolled away, panting.

'Are you okay?' Paula asked, concerned.

Lachie looked embarrassed. 'Yeah, Mum.'

'Officially cactus at Cactus, I reckon,' said Sid, reaching out to help Lachie up.

They resumed their places by the campfire.

'How long've you been doing that Brazilian jitsa for?' asked Sid.

'Jiu-jitsu,' Caitlin corrected him.

Marcelo poked at the coals with a long twig. 'Since my mother died when I was fourteen.'

Paula sucked in a breath.

Tiny burning embers rose above the flames.

'What happened to her?' Caitlin asked quietly.

It was the question Paula had been wanting to ask since their first night with Marcelo, at Barry and Shirl's barbecue in Walkerville.

He sat back on his heels. 'She was robbed in the *favela* in Porto Alegre, the slum where my older brother Lucas lives. He was fifteen when he left to get better-paid work in the city, *idiota*. He fell in with the wrong people and started taking drugs, then selling them too.'

Marcelo's face was tight. 'On the day she died, my mother was taking money to Lucas. He was always asking for money. My mother couldn't say no, so I went with her. I was right next to her when it happened, I didn't even see the knife. Three men surrounded us and they . . . stabbed her for her handbag. She would've *given* it to them if they'd asked.' His voice broke. 'It happened so fast, there was nothing I could do.'

He held a hand over his eyes, trying to compose himself.

Eventually, he looked up again.

'My father was working that day, it was the middle of calving season. I will never forget his face when I told him. Even now, my father still says, "Marcelo, why didn't you make *me* go with her?" He thinks he could've stopped it somehow. But people who are addicts will do anything. I was lucky they didn't kill me too.'

Paula shook her head, unable to comprehend what it would be like to witness the murder of a family member, let alone your *mother*.

Lachie and Caitlin looked shocked.

'I was only a teenager. I found out there are very bad people in the world.' Marcelo wiped his face with the back of his hand. 'I wanted to learn how to protect the people I love. My uncle suggested jiu-jitsu. He taught me himself for five years, then took me to train with Professor

Julio Mattos. I was very lucky, he is famous in southern Brazil. I trained with him until I was given my black belt, at twenty-three.'

Paula smiled. 'Your mother would have been very proud.'

'Yes.' Marcelo's eyes turned bleak again. 'God took her away too early, she was only thirty-nine.'

Paula blanched. *My age now.*

For a moment, she imagined Marcelo's mother, lying frightened and bleeding in a Brazilian slum. Knowing she was dying, reaching for her son.

She looked at Lachie and Caitlin. How would they fare, if *she* wasn't around? Tears sprang to Paula's eyes. She could only hope that life would spare her children such grief before they were truly ready to cope with it.

'She meant everything to my family,' Marcelo said, suddenly lifting his t-shirt.

Paula stared at his caramel chest, his ferociously fit torso.

'When I received my black belt, I put my mother here, over my heart.'

Marcelo pointed to the tattoo: *Lili.*

'She used to tell me, "One day, I will take you to my birthplace." But she died before she could.' His mouth worked silently for a moment. 'So I made a vow to her: *Mãe, I will go to where you were born. I will take you back to Darwin.* I am carrying her ashes in there.' He pointed to his backpack. 'So now you know the full story.'

Paula could barely breathe; no one else stirred either.

In the silence, Marcelo reached for his guitar.

Gently, he began plucking, gazing up at the night sky.

Then his voice, warm and rich, accompanying a folk melody.

Paula attempted to grasp the sentiment of the song, if not its meaning.

Marcelo smiled at her, strumming the final bars. 'This song is well-known in Brazil, by one of our greatest artists, Caetano Veloso. *Each of us knows the pain and the delight of being who we are.* This is very true. There is good and evil in everyone, and so much beauty in that imperfection.'

He rested his guitar against a rock, then sat back on his heels once more.

The group was silent, each with their own thoughts.

Sid was the first to speak.

'We are honoured you are with us, Marcelo. What you just told us, it must've been a lot for one young man to handle. My wife died a year ago after more than forty years of marriage.' His voice caught in his throat. 'But to lose your mother as a teenager, it must . . .'

'Change you,' said Marcelo, nodding at Sid in the flickering light. 'It changes you forever.' He threw the stick he was holding into the flames. 'When you lose someone, you suddenly understand what you have left. Family is *everything*. There is no time to waste, because at any moment, it might disappear.' He snapped his fingers.

'Well, to recover from that and get a black belt in jiu-jitsu . . .' Sid pronounced it correctly this time. 'It's outstanding.'

Marcelo shrugged—with modesty or embarrassment, Paula couldn't tell.

'Could you teach *me*?' Lachie's voice was timid.

Paula hadn't anticipated this question, given that her son was usually uninterested in sport. He'd flatly rejected every overture his father had ever made in regard to boxing.

Marcelo seemed to relax. He stood up and extended his hand to Lachie, helping him to his feet.

'Yes,' he said. 'I will teach you some of what I know. Not everything, because we don't have the equipment we need, like the rolling mats and the *gi*, the robe we wear for training. So we will have to . . .'

'Improvise?' Paula suggested.

'Exactly.' He grinned at Paula. Her body basked in its glow.

'We will try a few things,' continued Marcelo, turning back to Lachie. 'And then maybe you can find a training school in Melbourne if you like it. We can start tomorrow before breakfast.'

'But tomorrow Gramps was going to . . .'

'Don't you worry about *my* lessons, matey.' Sid smiled at Lachie indulgently. 'Having Marcelo here is a whole life lesson in itself.' Sid turned to the Brazilian. 'I've been giving them a few lessons, you see. Not academic ones, practical life skills.'

'Ah.' Marcelo nodded in an approving way. 'Those are the best kind. You are a good grandfather.'

Sid seemed to sit taller. 'From now on, Marcelo and I will work together on your education.'

Marcelo put an arm around Lachie's shoulder. 'I will teach you some jiu-jitsu. You too, Caitlin, if you would like?'

Caitlin nodded, her face pink in the firelight.

'You will both learn that bigger is not always better. We know this is true, yes, *Pow-la*?' Marcelo smiled at Paula, his eyes glittering like jewels.

She couldn't help but smile back.

*

Paula heard Marcelo unzipping the tent before dawn. The sound of her father's snoring continued, despite the disturbance. The fact that Marcelo had offered to share a tent with Sid from the outset had been a pleasant surprise; Hamish never would have subjected himself to such a chore. But coming from a family of mostly male cattle ranchers, Marcelo claimed he wasn't bothered by snoring. And it reassured Paula to know that her father had a jiu-jitsu master lying next to him at night.

She didn't hear his footfall across the sandy earth, but saw his silhouette at the caravan window, adjacent to her bed.

'*Pow-la*,' he whispered.

She sat up and opened the window. The spaghetti strap on her white cotton nightdress slipped off her shoulder and she righted it immediately.

His face was inches from hers.

*I must look a sight*, she thought.

She tried to smooth her hair, but could feel it springing up at odd angles, still wild from sleep. She noticed a few stars still shining in the dull light, then checked her watch: it was just after five o'clock. Somewhere nearby, she heard another tent being unzipped. Someone going out for an early surf, no doubt.

'Good morning,' he whispered.

She grinned at him, the sea air cool on her face.

*Yes, it* is *a good morning.*

'I'll just wake up Lachie and Caitlin,' she whispered back.

As she moved to climb off the bed, he reached in through the window and caught her by the wrist. Swiftly, yet softly.

'Wait,' he said. 'Can you hear it?'

She listened. The call of a solitary seagull, the *scrape-scrape-scrape* of a surfer waxing a board, waves crashing against the sand.

'That is the sound of beauty,' Marcelo whispered, his tone reverent. He dropped her hand, then leaned closer to the window. 'So much beauty everywhere.'

She looked into his eyes. Surely he didn't mean *her*?

His exquisite lips were moving, but she could no longer hear his words. She felt herself drawn towards them.

There came a sharp creaking sound from the children's bunks and Caitlin suddenly sat up.

Paula pulled back from the window.

'Hello,' Caitlin said, rubbing her eyes. 'Are we training?'

Marcelo smiled. 'Yes, we go to the beach. I will meet you and Lachie there in five minutes.'

Caitlin leaped out of her bunk like a trapeze artist, landing on Lachie's legs in the bunk opposite.

He groaned. 'What are you doing?'

'Training time, sleepyhead,' said Caitlin, sounding excited. 'Marcelo's lessons.'

Paula looked back at the window, but Marcelo was already gone.

As the children began getting dressed behind the curtains they'd strung around their bunks for privacy, Paula lay back on her bed. Imagining, for a moment, sharing it with Marcelo. She touched a hand to her wrist, where he'd held it through the window.

Energy was coursing through her. She couldn't possibly go back to sleep now.

*Bugger it, I'll go for a run too.*

She slipped on her sports gear and followed the children to the beach, keeping a careful distance. Not wanting Marcelo to see it in her eyes, how he'd made her feel. And certainly not wanting him to think she was checking up on him, like some sort of helicopter mother.

*The mother I used to be, not so long ago.*

'I'm just going to . . .' She gestured towards the curve of sand stretching westwards.

What *was* she going to do? Walk or run or sit in the dunes and contemplate what the hell she was up to? Thousands of kilometres from her husband, flirting with a man seven years her junior?

She turned on her heel and jogged away, the cool sand tickling the soles of her feet. She'd been jogging quite a bit since leaving Melbourne—Lachie's self-appointment as Swearing Monitor had guaranteed that—but never on soft sand. The last time she'd jogged like this was before their marriage, when Hamish was still living at Brighton. Back when they'd wake up on a Saturday morning and make love, before wandering down to the beach for a coffee and an exercise session. Hamish would peel off his clothes and race up and down the sand in his bathers, but Paula had always been too self-conscious of her jiggling bits for that. Instead, she'd donned a sporty two-piece tracksuit for some slow laps of the beach.

More than seventeen years on, her bits were still jiggling—and then some. The excess weight had crept up on her, thickening her waistline, broadening her hips, padding out her bottom. Never filling out her chest, however. Surely she looked like a wide-tailed duck now, lumbering across the sand in three-quarter leggings and an oversized singlet. A squat, almost-forty-year-old mother, who'd stopped worrying about exercise years ago. A woman on first-name terms with the staff at her local bakery. Who, on a bad day, went to the fridge or pantry and stuffed her mouth full of whatever she could find: biscuits, cheese, pickles, dried apricots, last night's leftovers. Chocolate, always chocolate. Washing it down with a glass of Diet Coke, or a red wine at night. Feeling like a failure, swallowing back the tears.

A woman who'd let herself go.

If only Marcelo had seen her in her prime, years ago.

*Oh, get over yourself,* she thought. *He's not even looking.*

Just to be sure, she glanced over her shoulder.

And there they were, the three of them, watching her.

Caitlin and Lachie stood dumbstruck, as if asking themselves: *What is Mum doing? She never jogs.*

And then Marcelo, with two fists raised in the air, triumphant.

# 9

After an uncomfortable night in the hatchback, Hamish was relieved to get out of Adelaide.

Just after nine o'clock, his telephone rang. He hoped it might be Paula or one of the kids, but the caller ID said *Nick Bridge*.

He grimaced and inserted his earpiece.

'Morning, Nick.' He tried to sound laid-back.

'Hi, Hamish. Sorry for calling you on your sick bed.'

Hamish didn't reveal his true whereabouts.

'What can I do for you, Nick?'

'Gary asked me to contact you about the December convention, to see if you want to do a keynote. We know you're on leave, so if you don't think you're up for it . . .' Nick paused. 'Gary's asked me to step in.'

Delivering a keynote to hundreds of Crossroads staffers at their annual team-building event was an opportunity Hamish usually embraced, but this year, the prospect was unappealing.

'You go ahead and do it, Nick,' Hamish said.

'But won't you be better by then?' Nick sounded stunned.

'Probably.' Hamish exhaled. 'But it's your turn this year.'

There was silence for a moment.

'Well, thanks, Hamish. I really value the opportunity.'

It wasn't false gratitude.

'Good luck with it, Nick. Goodbye.'

Hamish gripped the steering wheel, marvelling at how unfazed he felt. Sure, there was some mild, passing discomfort about unleashing Nick-the-Dick more fully into Hamish's rightful role at Crossroads. But the world hadn't ended, it seemed.

In fact, he'd been *gracious.* Nick had practically said so himself.

He stuffed his telephone into the recess of the driver-side door. He'd only been on the road for thirty-six hours, but Melbourne felt like an eternity ago. His work at Crossroads was a receding priority compared to reclaiming his family.

And now he'd been gracious, a word that had dominated the speeches at his father's funeral.

*Gracious, gentlemanly, a true family man.*

Hamish's eyes stung.

I can embody those qualities too, he thought.

*I can be my father's son.*

*

For the next few days, Hamish combed every caravan park and camping spot along the eight-hundred-and-fifty-kilometre coastal route to the Nullarbor Plain. Flawless shorelines dotted with mining smelters, thriving fishing communities alongside barely functional pastoral operations, quaint churches next to graffiti-covered public toilets. Blink-and-you'll-miss-them towns attempting to market their once-significant history, trying to be something other than a service centre for the traffic on highway number one. Hamish stayed focused on spotting a cream-coloured caravan with two green stripes down its sides, towed by a black dual-cab ute.

But sometimes he found himself wondering what had caught Paula's attention along the way. Whether the kids had seen the landscape as spacious and spectacular, or dozy and derelict. He didn't dwell in any place too long, but forced himself to press on. Wanting to catch them before they crossed the border into Western Australia, where the sheer vastness of the terrain would make them much harder to find. Wherever he stopped, Hamish sought out caravan park owners and managers, asking if they'd seen his wife and children. And always, the response was negative.

Until he reached Ceduna, at the eastern end of the Nullarbor Plain, on his fourth day out of Adelaide.

He pulled into town after ten hours of driving and followed the signs to a caravan park with budget cabins.

He paid the nightly fee to a talkative woman named Linda, who'd lived in Ceduna her whole life. After she'd chewed his ear about the region's whaling history, he subjected her to his own spiel, almost as an afterthought.

Linda's eyes lit up. 'Paula, you say? With two kids?'

She thumbed the pages of her bookings register.

'Yeah, they were here a week ago. The young fella caught some choice snapper off the jetty.'

That didn't sound like Lachie at all.

'Uh, I don't think so,' said Hamish. 'My son's not a fisherman.'

'Not the *really* young fella. I meant the *other* young man, the Italian.' She looked thoughtful. 'Maybe he wasn't *that* young, it's hard for me to tell these days—*everyone* seems young. The policemen round here look like they should be delivering the newspapers.' She laughed at her own joke.

Linda seemed easily muddled; Hamish doubted she'd met his family.

'My wife is travelling with my father-in-law too,' he added, just in case.

'Oh, of *course*, Sid.' Linda looked animated. 'We *really* hit it off. Lovely fella. Cooked a mean barbie, too.'

Linda *was* talking about his family. But what did she mean about a *younger Italian man*?

'Did they say which way they were going?' asked Hamish.

Linda laughed again. 'There's only one road west, love.'

Hamish felt like slapping her. 'Of course. How long does it take to cross the Nullarbor?'

'Depends how fast you're going. Twelve hundred clicks to Norseman, across the border into Western Australia. You can do it in a day if you're keen.'

They were long gone, then.

'But Sid said he wanted to do some hunting on the Nullarbor—funny ol' bugger. And the Italian fancied some surfing at Cactus. I think they were heading there for a few days.'

'Cactus?'

'The beach south of Penong, about ninety clicks up the road. It's famous. You've never been through these parts before, have you?'

Hamish shook his head.

Linda's eyes narrowed suddenly. 'Why aren't you travelling with them, anyway?'

'I . . . uh . . .' Hamish fumbled about for an explanation. No one had asked him that before.

'This isn't a domestic, is it?' Her voice had a hard edge. 'If you're chasing the missus and kids with a court order on you, I'll call the coppers.'

Hamish cut her off. 'No, no. Nothing like that.'

Part of him wanted to explode right there, to tell Linda to shove her budget cabin up her fishwife's arse. But another part of him knew what might happen if he did. Rural Australia was different to the metropolis: everyone was connected to everyone else, and it paid to be nice to the locals.

Linda stood with her arms folded.

'Look,' he said, 'I've made some mistakes with Paula, and I want to try to get her back.'

'Well,' said Linda, her face softening. 'I like a man who can see the error of his ways. Lord knows, most of you *can't*.'

She traced her pen across a laminated map of Australia pinned to the wall behind her.

'They left here a week ago. Let's say they went to Cactus for three or four days, then took their time across the Nullarbor. Maybe stopped to do some hunting along the way, like Sid said, or a bit of sightseeing . . .' She counted on her fingers. 'I reckon they could be at Norseman tonight. So if you give it a big push tomorrow, you might catch them the day after.'

Hamish felt suddenly grateful. 'Thank you, Linda. That's really helpful.'

Linda smiled like she was his new bosom buddy. 'I can make you some bacon and eggs in the morning, if you like. There aren't too many places to stop on the Nullarbor. You'll need a good breakfast to line your stomach.'

'Thanks,' said Hamish. He wasn't really a breakfast person. 'That'd be nice.'

'I'll bring it over at six-thirty, then?'

Hamish nodded. 'I'll set my alarm.'

'Let's get you to bed,' said Linda, waving a cabin key at him.

Following her outside, Hamish could hear the monstrous roar of the Great Southern Ocean, invisible waves crashing beyond the caravan park.

He imagined his family camped out too, not so far away now. Every night that he'd slept on his own, he'd pined for Paula beside him. Along with everything else, too; their comfortable familial routine. All of the little attentions that Paula had paid to him, which he'd somehow failed to notice until they suddenly vanished.

As for the kids, his gut ached for them. Text messages were one thing, but seeing them in the flesh was quite another. He wanted to hold them again, reassure himself that they were, even now, still a part of him. Despite all his fuck-ups and frailties, known and unknown.

*Marriage is a choice*, his father had once said to him, on the day Hamish had presented Paula with a sapphire engagement ring. *Anyone can sow their wild oats, but what's much harder is keeping the respect alive in a relationship. Week after week, month after month, decade after decade. Good luck, son. I know you can do it.*

I'm capable of so much more, Hamish thought. The moonlight shone between the wooden slats of the window blinds.

*It's never too late to be a better person.*

He lay awake in his cabin long into the night.

*

Hamish ate his bacon and eggs on the balcony overlooking the Great Australian Bight. There was something about the ocean in the dawn's breaking light which brought to mind the day he'd married Paula.

The twenty-fourth of May 1995.

It had been an overcast day and the ocean had turned a mossy green behind the colourful sweep of wooden huts lining Brighton Beach. They'd planned a low-key wedding in the gardens of a boutique beachfront hotel, not far from where Hamish was flatting at the time. Almost eighteen years ago now, he realised.

*How did I get this old, this fast?*

His relatives had arrived in a mini-bus, bedecked in the family's tartan, like a Scottish football team. His mum, his dad, his brother and his young family. His grandparents, who'd flown out from Scotland, both of them bursting with pride. Old Sid standing in the garden, rare tears trailing down his stoic face. Paula's mother, Jeanette, welcoming guests with air kisses. Her sister, Jamie, straightening Paula's train, smoothing its edges and picking at tiny blemishes that Hamish couldn't even see.

And Paula herself, an apparition in exquisite ivory lace. Her skin glowing and translucent, her hair falling in soft curls down a smooth, bare back. The profound feeling of love, deeper than anything he'd felt before, as he watched her walk slowly down the petal-strewn path towards him. How he'd felt as he waited for her, like a boy who'd captured a butterfly. And when she'd finally reached him, how he'd pulled her to him and murmured in her ear.

*My love, my beautiful love.*

My almost-virgin, he'd said later, cheekily, as they'd sipped champagne on the balcony of their hotel suite, overlooking the ocean. *If it hadn't have been for Dr So-and-So, this could have been your first time.*

She'd arched an eyebrow at him.

They'd been having sex for almost a year before their wedding. Hamish knew everything about Paula's sexual history, so vanilla in contrast to his own: she'd lost her virginity in a brief relationship with a medical intern at her first hospital posting, six months prior to meeting Hamish. At the time she'd just turned twenty-one, and was newly graduated from her social work degree. Hamish, by contrast, had slept with fourteen women prior to Paula. Which wasn't a bad effort for a twenty-three-year-old, he reckoned. Not that he ever told this to Paula, and not that she ever asked.

'Well, let's pretend it *is* my first time,' she'd said.

They'd made love three times that night, with a rare urgency and heat. Overlooking sleep and food, they'd devoured each other instead. And when they'd stood on the balcony at seven o'clock the next morning, watching the sunrise turn the sand the colour of hope, he'd felt as if he finally understood the concept of *union*. Her warm, naked body pressed against his, a hotel robe draped around them, their hearts beating centimetres apart. He'd never felt more satisfied, more complete.

And every year since then, on their wedding anniversary, Paula had tried to recapture that honeymoon intensity. Buying new silk underwear for the occasion, the type Hamish liked, sheer and lacy. Sometimes she'd entice him with candlelit dinners, baths and massages, or sensual appetisers like chocolate-dipped strawberries. On their first anniversary, she'd done a striptease for him, overcoming her natural self-consciousness to gyrate like a pole dancer to 'You Can Leave Your

Hat On'. She'd been worried Hamish might laugh at her, but he hadn't. In fact, he'd been so turned on he'd dropped his load prematurely.

The next year, emboldened by her successful striptease, she'd dressed up as a hotel maid and seduced him as she went through the motions of changing the bed sheets. Now *that* had been a good year, Hamish thought. Paula in a frilly outfit, bending over and folding hospital corners, wearing nothing but silky suspenders and a pair of fishnet stockings. There sure as hell hadn't been one like it since.

Despite her best efforts on anniversaries, there was no escaping the fact that, over the years, Paula had become increasingly indifferent to sex. On the rare occasions they did it, she hardly ever reached climax. He'd quizzed her about her vanishing orgasms, which she always attributed to fatigue. But she'd been tired for *fourteen years*, he'd calculated. Ever since the third year of their marriage, when Caitlin was a baby and Paula had fallen pregnant with Lachlan. From then on, their bedroom activities became a muted imitation of once-real passion.

Hamish wasn't sure it was fixable, either. However hard they might try, he had a sneaking suspicion that monogamy and sexual satisfaction were mutually exclusive. How could having sex with the same person, year after year, be truly exciting? Longevity and titillation weren't readily reconcilable. Even pole dances and costumes didn't help after a while, because fundamentally, the landscape remained unchanged. He was still looking at the same body, feeling the same flesh, over and over again. There were simply no more surprises.

*But I do love my wife,* Hamish insisted to himself, watching a flock of gulls circle high above the ocean's swirling surface. *Without her, I'd be cactus. So why isn't that enough?*

Hamish stared out at the waves, mesmerised. The wind had picked up and the ocean's rhythmic sets had turned into rolling mountains of jade, pounding against a rocky shore.

He wasn't a religious person; he'd doubted the existence of God since his earliest years, despite his parents' simple faith. Truth be told, Hamish thought of God as a benign cultural fiction, a sort of societal fairytale used to indulge young children and comfort the dying. As plausible and potent as Santa Claus or the Easter Bunny. But sitting alone now, watching the ocean's currents stretching to the southernmost tip of the world, Hamish suddenly felt as if he was perched on the edge of infinity. Tilting towards something grander, more meaningful than his own miniscule life.

'Penny for your thoughts.' Linda was suddenly next to him, clearing the plates.

Hamish couldn't explain the inexplicable.

'Time to go,' he said. 'Thanks for breakfast, Linda.'

*

By eight o'clock, he'd passed signs to Denial Bay and Cactus Beach, and travelled past the old silver windmills of Penong, rearing up like metal dragons along sandy fence lines.

Minutes later, even these visual distractions disappeared. At best, the landscape was unremarkable and unrelenting. At worst, it was a stark, uninhabited wasteland of Mallee scrub, stretching out forever.

Hamish had heard people waxing lyrical about 'crossing the Nullarbor', but if *this* was a taste of things to come, he wasn't a convert.

By the time he reached Nundroo, he was running a little low on fuel, but it seemed too early to stop. He checked the map and calculated that he could easily make it to Yalata, the next petrol station.

He pushed on for another fifty-one tedious kilometres. Just as the fuel gauge began to flash its red warning light, Hamish spotted the Yalata roadhouse.

He veered towards it, noticing the absence of other vehicles in the car park. The whole place looked deserted, in fact.

Hamish pulled up next to the entrance and saw that most of the windows were broken. The petrol pumps were locked, and the shopfront was unlit. Inside was a vandalised mess.

*Fuck.*

He looked again at his map. There it was, the Yalata Roadhouse, with its fuel icon. No mention of the sign now plastered across the door:

*Yalata Roadhouse is temporarily closed. Travellers are advised that the nearest fuel stop is Nullarbor Roadhouse 94 kilometres to the west, and Nundroo 51 kilometres to the east.*

Hamish knew he wouldn't make it in either direction.

*Think. Think!*

He stood up out of the car and slammed the door, kicking at the car's front tyre for good measure.

The pain took him by surprise. He hopped up and down on his right foot, bellowing.

He stumbled towards the roadhouse and sank onto the steps. Then he lay back on the dirty grey tiles, cool through his t-shirt, and stretched out his injured leg.

He closed his eyes and moved his head from side to side, racking his brains.

*You're an ideas man*, his boss had once told him, presenting him with a fat sales bonus an eternity ago. Where were his ideas now?

*

'You right, fella?'

A voice pierced the darkness.

Hamish sat up. *Where am I?*

Oh yes, Yalata Roadhouse. The pumps with no fuel.

It was just after eleven o'clock, according to Doggo's watch.

*Snoozing on the steps for two bloody hours?* He cursed at himself. Wasting precious time he could have spent pursuing Paula.

'You right, fella?'

Hamish looked up at the source of the voice. An Aboriginal man stood less than a metre away, straddling a quad bike. He was wearing a faded pair of stone-wash jeans and a long-sleeved flannelette shirt. A red baseball cap covered his short brown hair, his beard was trimmed neatly against his jaw, and he wore a pair of dusty thongs. The whites of his eyes seemed yellow against his dark skin and a fly crawled across the bridge of his nose, without him even noticing it, apparently.

'Uh, yes,' said Hamish, propelling himself upright. His left leg was aching again. 'I must've fallen asleep.'

The man looked at him, then at the roadhouse. 'Farken stupid place to sleep.'

Hamish wasn't sure what to say.

'Well, I ran out of fuel.'

'Farken stupid thing to do out here.'

Hamish nodded. It *was* stupid.

The man turned the ignition on his four-wheeler. 'Get on.'

'What?'

'Get on.'

'Why?'

'Need some farken fuel, don't you? Get on then.'

Hamish checked the highway in both directions, unsure what to do. A campervan was approaching from the west; he watched it whiz past the roadhouse without even slowing.

*I'm rooted*, Hamish thought. *This guy's my best chance.* 'Where are we going?' he asked.

The man tilted his head in the direction of the highway.

Hamish hobbled over to the four-wheeler and climbed onto the seat behind the man, with some difficulty. He couldn't possibly keep his splint up off the road.

'My knee's . . .'

The man stood in his seat and lifted his shirt, removing the brown leather belt from his jeans. Without a word, he looped the belt around Hamish's splint at shin-height. Then he pulled the strap tight, wrapping its other end around his left wrist.

It was a remarkably comfortable position, with Hamish's left leg extended alongside the four-wheeler. But it also meant the man would be driving one-handed.

'Hold on, fella,' said the man.

Hamish felt for a grip behind the seat.

'Hold on to *me*.'

Hamish gingerly put his hands around the man's waist.

'Tighter, stupid.'

Hamish gripped the man hard as the quad bike jerked into gear.

*What the hell am I doing?* Hamish wondered. *I may not get out of this alive.*

They rumbled along the highway to the west, then turned right onto an unsealed road. A warning sign flashed past and Hamish craned his neck to read it: something about entering restricted territory.

Where were they going? Hamish stared at the back of the man's neck. He'd never been this close to an Aborigine. In fact, he'd never even *talked* to an Aboriginal person before. The closest contact he'd ever had was on his Sunday-morning cycles through Preston, where he'd inevitably see a few Aborigines lying drunk in the park. One morning he'd had to swerve to avoid one, a ratty-haired old man, swaying across the road and jeering at the world.

But Hamish had seen enough on television to draw his own conclusions; you didn't have to be an anthropologist to figure it out. Aboriginal communities were troubled places, full of dysfunctional families, doped-up teens and lazy parents. People who said they wanted to work, but never did. People who claimed they needed housing, but didn't respect it when the government gave it to them. People who made excuses for themselves, who let bad things happen to their children in the name of culture. People who took handouts, but no responsibility.

*Takers.*

A small township appeared. Neat white boxes for houses, a dilapidated school, a dust-bowl oval with a bunch of kids playing Aussie Rules on it. They scooted around the outskirts for another kilometre or so before the quad began to slow. Then they pulled up next to an airstrip, where a double-prop aeroplane was offloading supplies.

'Postman today,' said the man, nodding at the aeroplane. 'Flying doctor tomorra.' He unwound the belt around his left hand and slowly lowered Hamish's leg to the ground. 'Gettin' the fuel.' He headed off in the direction of the aircraft hangar.

Hamish watched as the 'postman', presumably the pilot of PY Air, unloaded several crates.

What would it be like, Hamish wondered, living somewhere where everything had to be flown in? Where the doctors arrived by aeroplane? Where if you had a time-critical health problem, you mightn't survive?

Hamish looked down at his kneecap, visible through the cut-out in the splint. There was a lot to love about the city, he decided. Hospitals within easy driving distance, doctors on call whenever you needed them. Power and sewerage systems, road grading, rubbish removal, all taken care of by local and state governments. In remote places like this, the community had to fend for itself.

Which was probably why they whinged so much, Hamish thought. And always had their hands out.

For a moment Hamish tried to calculate how much this little adventure was going to cost him. At a petrol station, he'd pay somewhere between a dollar fifty and a dollar seventy a litre for unleaded fuel. It had been one sixty-three at Nundroo, he thought ruefully. But in this case, there was sure to be a premium for trouble, and for travel. How much cash did he have in his wallet? Hamish patted his pocket.

*Shit, it's in the hatchback.*

*I've left the keys there too.*

Hamish slapped his forehead.

*My wallet's in an unlocked car, keys still in the ignition, outside a vandalised roadhouse in the middle of the desert.*

The Aboriginal man emerged from the hangar carrying a forty-litre jerry can in his arms. From the way he hauled it, straining beneath its weight, it was almost full. That'd get him much further than the next fuel stop at Nullarbor Roadhouse, Hamish knew.

'I don't need that much fuel, mate,' he called. 'I've only got to drive a hundred kilometres to the next pit stop.'

The Aboriginal man said nothing. He began strapping the can to the rack at the back of the four-wheeler.

'Did you hear me?'

The man climbed onto the quad bike.

*He's really going to sting me*, Hamish thought. *And I can't argue with him, either. Not with my keys still in the car.*

The man lifted Hamish's leg off the ground and secured it with the belt.

Then he revved the engine, and they were back on the road.

The midday sun was unbearable. There was nothing in the landscape to absorb it; not even the dull-coloured scrub offered respite. Beneath it, the sandy earth—a rich red, toffee orange or lemon-tinged white—only seemed to act as a mirror, bouncing the scorching light back up into the clear sky.

Hamish closed his eyes against it all: the light, the heat, the wind blasting his face.

Soon they were back at Yalata Roadhouse, and the man was untying his leg.

The hatchback was still there, thank God. Hamish sighed in relief to see his wallet, too, lying in full view on the dashboard.

The Aboriginal man followed his gaze. 'Farken stupid place to leave your wallet.'

Hamish nodded. 'I know. About the cost . . .'

The man unhitched the jerry can and began siphoning the petrol into the hatchback's fuel tank with a length of hose.

*Crafty bugger. Getting the fuel into the car before we talk price.*

'I don't *need* a full tank,' Hamish objected.

The man looked up from his task. 'These little lady cars don't need much fuel, eh?'

Hamish felt slighted. *You should see my ute.*

A minute later, the man hitched the empty jerry can back onto his quad bike.

'How much, mate?' Hamish asked, poised for an argument.

The man flicked a dismissive hand at Hamish, then climbed back onto the four-wheeler.

'How much?' Hamish called over the engine noise. The man suddenly snapped off the engine and stared at him, long and hard.

'What?' Hamish felt the colour rising up his neck.

The man removed his cap and smoothed his hair. He sat for a moment, looking at the landscape around them. All was silent, bar the persistent chirruping of birds in the Mallee scrub.

Finally, the man's eyes settled on Hamish again.

'I am Pitjantjatjara Anangu,' he said. 'We are desert people in the north and north-west. The Great Rainbow Serpent Wanampi shaped this land. From the red spinifex country in the north to the head of the Bight in the west.' He gestured behind Hamish. 'Wanampi created the hills, the caves and the lakes, on his way down to the ocean. You are welcome in my country.' The man gazed at the bare landscape with proprietorial pride. 'If you're in trouble, we help.'

Hamish was speechless.

The man's lips began to curl into a smile. 'Even if you're farken stupid, we help.'

Hamish began to smile too. 'Thank you.'

'No worries, mate. Whatcha doin' here?'

'I've got some . . . business to attend to,' Hamish replied.

The Aboriginal man nodded.

Hamish felt suddenly awkward. 'My name's Hamish. What's your—'

The man revved the engine of the four-wheeler like a member of a bikie gang. Then, lifting one finger at Hamish, he sped away.

Hamish watched him barrelling down the highway, until the heat haze swallowed him up.

*

Hamish left Yalata just before three-thirty.

Not long afterwards, already bored by the unchanging scenery, he checked his phone. There were several new messages, both SMS and Skype.

He clicked on the SMS tab and saw Sid's name listed. The children had been texting Hamish more regularly now, since they'd started using their grandfather's phone. Paula was still offline, however, or pretending to be.

*Dad, r u ok? How is ur leg? Cactus Beach was cool. Out of range tho, sorry. We r in Eucla now, Perth soon. Oz is massive. Some bits boring. Luv Lachie.*

Tears sprang to Hamish's eyes. A heady combination of pain, fatigue and love.

Lachie had been the best source of information about their whereabouts to date. *Little champ.*

Where was Eucla, anyway? Hamish pulled over and examined his map: just across the Western Australian border. Only three hundred kilometres west, about a three-hour drive. Not even as far as Norseman; he could surprise them by sunset.

Hamish set off with new vigour, but the drive to Eucla was slower than he hoped. For one thing, he was spooked by the road trains—some with triple trailers—careering along the highway. They dazzled him with their bulk and monstrous roaring as they thundered towards him, horns sounding and lights flashing. It was nerve-racking when they tailgated him, worse when they overtook. Pulling alongside his flimsy hatchback, with less than a metre separating them, dragging him along in their slipstream before finally speeding away.

And then, just twelve kilometres from Eucla, Hamish was forced to stop for almost thirty minutes at Border Village, where an officious-sounding woman in an ill-fitting uniform subjected his vehicle to a compulsory quarantine inspection. Combing through his car with Gestapo-like sternness, before confiscating a limp banana from his esky with a triumphant 'A-ha!'

'Forbidden fruit?' Hamish asked, smiling at her.

She didn't appreciate the wise-crack. 'You are not permitted to take that with you into Western Australia, sir. Read the sign.'

Hamish didn't bother, accelerating away as soon as he could.

He spotted the lights of Eucla around seven-thirty, glowing dull green like low-wattage Kryptonite in the desert gloom. At the town's boundary, a welcome sign declared its population to be eighty-six. Not far beyond, a billboard signposted directions to the Eucla Caravan Park.

Hamish followed them, arriving at a petrol station. Behind it stood a two-storey hotel, its windows glinting like orange eyes in the dark. Alongside the hotel, a flat area was dotted with tents, on-site vans and caravans.

This has to be it, Hamish thought. There couldn't be any other caravan parks in a one-horse town like this.

He dimmed his headlights and pulled in behind a trailer. He didn't want to give himself away to Paula or the kids. Not yet, anyway.

Several tents were erected at the front of the site, which was little more than a fenced paddock. A corrugated-iron shed—the amenities block, presumably—stood in the middle of the paddock as if dropped from the sky by a UFO. Chained to a fence post was a locked metal container painted with the words: *Honesty Box—$4 a night.*

Hamish stood up from the car, wincing; his left knee was still swollen. He fished around in his pocket for the extra-strength painkillers he carried everywhere now, and popped two quick ones, swallowing them without water. Then he limped to the trailer and looked beyond it. From this vantage point, he could see two on-site vans, a caravan he didn't recognise and then, right at the rear boundary, his ute. The green-and-cream van was parked next to it, lights on.

*They're here. And they're still up.*

He smiled, anticipating the moment of reunion. The expressions of surprise and delight on the kids' faces.

Hamish lumbered back to the car and tried to check his reflection in the side mirror. Unable to see much, he patted down his hair and pulled a mint from his pocket.

A shower could wait. He wanted to see his wife and children *now.*

He walked up the paddock towards the campers, stopping to take a leak against a tree. As he did, he looked up. There were more stars than he'd ever seen, sparkling like glitter spilt across the sky.

*Damn it's a beautiful world.*

He resumed his shuffling across the uneven ground, imagining what he'd say to them.

*Mea culpa, mea culpa, let's have a cuppa. Or even better, a beer.*

He heard them singing before he saw them.

He recognised Caitlin's voice, high and girly, above the rest of them. Lachie's voice, alien and off-key since it had started breaking. Then the warm alto of his wife, accompanying the rhythmic strumming of a guitar.

*I didn't know Old Sid played.*

And then another voice joined in, deep and velvety, causing Hamish to pause.

He hovered behind an on-site van, then sidled up to a corner and peered around it.

There they were, not five metres away, sitting around a roaring campfire. Paula, facing him, looking more attractive than he'd ever seen her. Had she lost weight? She looked healthier, for sure. And happier. The firelight reflected on her face made her look ten years younger. He watched her singing and, for a moment, felt a sinking sensation in his stomach.

*Something's changed for her.*

Old Sid sat on a tree stump nearby, rocking from side to side, thumping his hands on his knees. Lachie was next to him, roasting marshmallows on a long stick. Caitlin was perched next to Lachie, transfixed by the guitarist.

Who the fuck was *he*?

Olive-skinned, lean and short; Hamish was confident he'd tower over him. Thirty-something, maybe.

Some European pretty boy who'd latched on to *his* family. *His* daughter.

It was one thing for schoolboys to fawn over Caitlin, or to have some idiot posting bullshit on Facebook about her. But it was quite another to have a boy—no, a *man*—living in her back pocket. Watching her every move, cosying up to her whenever the opportunity presented itself. Hamish didn't have to *see* it to know that's exactly what would be happening; he understood how blokes ticked. And by the look on Caitlin's face, she wouldn't reject his attentions.

The European seemed to be singing to Caitlin.

Anger surged in Hamish's chest. How the hell had *this* happened? And why had Paula *let* it?

He leaned against the wall of the on-site van and closed his eyes, fighting a primitive urge to barge into the camp site, wrest the guitar from the foreigner and snap its neck from its body.

*It'll only make things worse*, he thought. *It'll piss off Paula even more.*

He took several deep breaths. What would Doggo do? he wondered.

After a minute, Hamish could almost hear his mate's voice in his ear.

*Wait until morning, Hamo. Everyone will be fresher, including you.*

Hamish was buggered from all the driving, and it hadn't helped his injured knee either.

He turned away and headed back to the car. Retrieving Doggo's khaki swag from the boot—this would be the first night he'd had to sleep in it—he noticed the large plastic cover Paula used to protect the hatchback when it was parked for long periods. The 'car condom', he'd always called it. After loading his small rucksack with fresh clothes and his toiletries, Hamish locked the doors and pulled the cover over the car. He wanted to surprise *them* in the morning, not the other way around.

Hamish could still hear their singalong as he rolled out the swag behind a tree. He was at least fifteen metres from their camp; no one would see him. Unless they caught sight of his leg splint, which was a dead giveaway.

Hamish shuffled towards the corrugated-iron shed in the centre of the paddock.

It wasn't much of an amenities block—just one toilet and one shower in the men's room. As he stepped inside the shower cubicle, his phone beeped. He pulled it from his pocket and clicked on the

Skype tab, which was jiggling with new instant messages. He closed the door behind him and perched on a narrow wooden bench, scanning the messages.

One was from Nick Bridge, asking him to review the speech he'd prepared for the Crossroads convention. That could wait, Hamish decided.

The rest were from Lisel17.

*R u there Hamo?*

*Skype says u r.*

*Okay, so u r 41.*

*We all make mistakes.*

*We had something special. U know that.*

*So good 4 both of us.*

*I still want u.*

*U r still so hot 4 me.*

Hamish swallowed.

Lisel had sent several messages by Skype since the accident, generic one-liners:

*How r u Hamo?*

*R u out of hospital?*

*Wanna talk?*

But he hadn't responded, determined to patch things up with Paula.

Another instant message arrived.

*Age doesn't matter Hamo. U know that.*

He closed his eyes, imagining the moment when Lisel had discovered their almost twenty-five-year age gap. That he didn't look like Nick Bridge at all. That he was, in fact, the nondescript middle-aged man standing next to Nick in the profile picture.

He opened his eyes again.

*Hamo, pls don't ice me out.*

*I miss u.*

*I miss us.*

*I miss yr hot cock inside of me.*

*I'm wet now, just thinking about you.*

*I want u back Hamo.*

In his wildest fantasies, Hamish hadn't entertained the idea that Lisel might still be interested in him.

He stood for a moment, electrified by her words. Imagining Lisel in her bedroom, touching her silky smooth pussy.

*I can't contact her*, he thought. Even as his dick began to rear, like a cobra awakened in the dark.

He stuffed his phone beneath his towel, unbuckled his shorts and let them fall to the floor. Removing his splint and the rest of his clothes, he turned on the tap. There was no warm water available.

*Good thing too.*

He tried to erase the mental image of Lisel, hot as hell in her eensy-weensy bikini.

He ducked under the water and almost yelled.

*Fucking freezing.*

His dick retracted back into itself.

He lathered up and rinsed off as quickly as possible, then brushed his teeth. When he turned off the shower, the singing had stopped outside. He'd have to be careful heading back to the swag, he thought. Shoving his phone back into a plastic bag, he deliberately conjured a mental image of Paula. The smile lines around her mouth, the dimple on her left cheek, her intelligent eyes. The pale scar above her right eyebrow, a permanent reminder of the home renovation they'd done years ago.

He *had* to give it a proper go with Paula, for the sake of everything they'd created over the past seventeen years.

And for his *own* sake, to be the son his father had believed in.

*I won't look at my phone again tonight,* Hamish resolved.

He secured his splint in its place, pulled on a t-shirt and boxers, hung the damp towel around his neck and opened the shower door.

The European pretty boy was standing right outside the cubicle, waiting his turn.

'Hi,' said Hamish, trying to sound casual.

'Hi.'

The European smiled at him, then nodded at Hamish's leg. 'What happened?'

'I had a skiing accident.'

'Where?'

Hamish's voice caught in his throat. 'Where what?'

'Where were you skiing when . . . ?' The European waved at Hamish's leg.

'Whistler.'

It was the first place that popped into Hamish's mind; one of Paula's workmates, married to a high-profile barrister, skied at Whistler annually.

'You're a long way from Whistler.'

'Yes.' Hamish felt flustered. 'Where are *you* from?'

'Brazil.'

'Oh.'

Hamish had been prepared for Italy or Spain, but knew nothing of Brazil. Except the stunning half-naked women in sequined bikinis he'd seen on television, shimmying down the street during Mardi Gras, all carefree and hair-free.

'How long are you in Australia?' Hamish asked.

'I'm not sure yet,' said the man.

'And are you . . . alone?' As if he didn't know.

'I'm travelling with friends.'

Hamish smiled in a chummy, man-to-man kind of way. 'A *girl*friend?'

The man's eyes narrowed. 'I'm taking a shower now.'

He stepped around Hamish and shut the cubicle door behind him.

Hamish stood for a moment, his heart beating faster than usual, wanting to tear the door off its hinges.

Then the realisation hit him: it didn't look good, standing in a public toilet in the middle of nowhere, asking a stranger about his relationship status.

*He might think I'm gay.*

The Brazilian turned on the shower and Hamish left the men's room, picking his way across the paddock to his swag. The caravan was in darkness. A tent erected next to the ute was presumably where old Sid slept.

*So where is the Brazilian sleeping?*

The thought enraged him.

*If he's in that caravan with Caitlin, I'll . . .*

He lowered himself into the swag and zipped up the mosquito net.

Hamish lay awake for hours, alert to every noise that emanated from the direction of the caravan.

Eventually, he couldn't keep his eyes open any longer.

*

Speckled sunlight drifted through the mosquito net.

Hamish sat up in a hurry and unzipped the swag; poking his head out into the heat of the morning. Where the hell was the caravan?

The two tents at the front of the park were still there, the vans too.

He looked at his watch. Seven-bloody-fifteen—surely they hadn't left *that* early?

An engine was idling somewhere, and it sounded a lot like his ute.

He pulled on some cargo pants and scrambled upright. Through the shrubs lining the fence, he spotted the caravan parked at the petrol station. Bikes on the rear, a surfboard and a guitar case strapped to the ute's roof racks. Hamish could see Lachie in the back, his head bowed, probably fiddling with his iPod. Paula was in the driver's seat, scanning a map; Sid was leaning over it too.

And there were the Brazilian and Caitlin, standing outside the ute, facing away from Hamish. The Brazilian's hand was pressed gently between Caitlin's shoulder blades, guiding her into the car. As he closed the door behind her, he made a low bow. Caitlin gazed at him with patent adoration. No one inside the car was privy to their interaction.

*Motherfucker.*

The Brazilian tapped Paula's window and gestured back towards the amenities block before jogging across the paddock. He didn't notice Hamish hovering next to the tree, watching him.

*You've got it coming, mate.*

He followed the Brazilian to the shed, then flattened himself against the wall outside the entrance, waiting for the Brazilian to re-emerge. He heard the toilet flush, the tap being turned on and off.

*Hold it*, Hamish told himself, *hold it . . .*

The Brazilian walked out of the men's room.

Hamish stepped in front of him and pushed him hard against the corrugated-iron wall, gripping him by the neck. He was a lightweight compared to Hamish.

'I've been watching you,' Hamish growled. 'And I know *exactly* what you're up to.'

The Brazilian raised an eyebrow.

Hamish squeezed the side of his neck tighter, digging his fingernails into the flesh. 'Got something to say for yourself?'

The Brazilian gripped Hamish's wrist with one hand. The twist was so swift, so fluid, Hamish didn't even feel it happen.

One moment he was looking at the Brazilian's face, the next he was facing the rear of the caravan park, his right arm pinned behind his back.

And then, an intense pressure around his neck. He could feel the Brazilian's breath, warm on his ear.

'Who are you?' the Brazilian whispered, slow and clear. 'Tell me your name.'

Hamish kicked furiously with his right leg, trying to knock the other man back, but he couldn't even make contact.

'Why are you following me?'

Hamish couldn't speak with an elbow rammed under his chin. He tried to prise the Brazilian's arm away with his free hand, but the crush continued, right across his carotids. He'd seen it before on *Ultimate Fight Club.*

The blue horizon began swimming before his eyes, grey spots floated in the air.

It felt as if his head was about to pop off his shoulders.

Hamish could hear himself grunting, the desperate sound of resistance.

Then he heard nothing at all.

# 10

Paula was surprised to see the enormous dunes in the distance, shining mountains of white dominating the shoreline. They simply hadn't been visible when they'd arrived at the Eucla Caravan Park the evening before, their tenth night on the road since Marcelo had joined them.

With the Brazilian still in the amenities block, Paula turned to her father. 'Everything's going okay with Marcelo, isn't it, Dad?'

It all felt utterly seamless to her.

'Sure,' he replied, looking up from the map. 'It's *all good*, don't you reckon, kids?'

Paula smiled to hear him adopt their lingo.

Lachie grunted in a blasé way from the rear, still scrolling through his playlist. Caitlin said nothing, but when Paula turned to look at her, she noticed her daughter was slightly flushed.

'Turn up the AC please, Mum?'

As Paula twisted the dial to its coldest setting, her phone beeped in the glove box. She glanced furtively at the children before retrieving it, conscious she was transgressing her own rules yet again.

It was a message from Jamie.

*Just met Doggo at your house collecting mail for Hamish. I knew he'd gone away! Doggo didn't tell me where.*

Paula wasn't surprised. For as long as she'd known Hamish, he'd never enjoyed his own company. She tried to guess where he'd go to lick his wounds; he had mates all over the eastern seaboard. Or perhaps to Mallacoota to visit his mother?

*Thanks for letting me know*, Paula typed back. *At least you don't have to look in on him now!*

As she shoved the phone back into the glove box, Marcelo returned.

'Let's go,' he said, climbing in next to Lachie and wiping a hand over his forehead. 'It's so hot already.'

'That's the Aussie desert for you, matey,' said Sid.

A minute later Paula steered their vehicle onto the highway again.

Within a kilometre, Lachie pointed at a bloodied mass of feathers on the road, surrounded by carrion birds. 'Euw, look at that eagle.'

Marcelo peered out the window. 'How can the king of birds die like that?'

'I'll tell you how,' answered Sid. 'They fly down to the road at night to feed on road kill—kangaroos and the like—then suddenly a road train comes along. They're too slow to take off because they've eaten so much and *bam*! They become road kill too.'

Paula shuddered.

'Don't get many wedgies in Glen Waverley, do we?' asked Sid jovially.

*No*, she mused, applying more pressure to the pedal. *No wedge-tailed eagles, no cold showers, no Brazilian backpackers, no fun.*

She smiled, marvelling at how her usually hectic suburban routine had been so radically transformed. At this time on a normal weekday morning, she'd be ordering the kids into their school uniforms and out the front door. But these days, her mornings were different. She no longer woke to the jarring electronic bleating of an alarm clock, but to the whimsical sounds of nature at dawn.

Most mornings, she'd creep past the sleeping forms of her children before sunrise and open the caravan door, inhaling the fresh air and admiring the sky's changing colours. No sooner had she opened the flyscreen than her father would unzip his tent and crawl out on all fours, standing up slowly, groaning as he clutched his lower back. Then he'd greet her with the same words each morning. 'Marcelo's beaten me to it again. Ready for a dingo's breakfast, Paula?'

At first, she'd sought an explanation.

'You *don't know* what a dingo's breakfast is?' he'd asked, pulling a face. 'And you call yourself an Aussie? It's a piss, a drink and a look around.'

Their own 'dingo's breakfast' always involved a ramble around the camp site in which they found themselves, along sandy tracks to the beach, up wooded trails to bush lookouts, or along the wide roads of sleepy town centres. Sometimes they'd happen upon a local bakery, a lucky find in an otherwise deserted street, and buy still-warm loaves to bring back to the camp site. It hadn't taken long for Paula's 'Weet-bix only' breakfast policy to fall by the wayside.

After their walk, they would sit together on foldaway chairs near the caravan, cradling steaming mugs of hot tea between their palms, waving away the blowflies—early risers too—and chat about the route for the coming day. Sometimes they'd watch Marcelo at a distance, doing his callisthenic routine, or reminisce about Paula's childhood; their Christmas holiday road trips, the butchery, her mother. Then her father's eyes would mist over as he talked about 'his Jeanie'.

When the conversation lulled, they would simply sit in comfortable silence, sipping their tea and listening to the sounds of the camp site awakening. Caravan doors opening, footsteps on gravel paths, showers running, bacon frying. Until Caitlin and Lachie burst out of the caravan, looking for fresh bread and jam, a stretch or a swim, eager for another day on the road.

And then Marcelo would return from his morning exercise, all glistening with sweat and gushing about some piece of Australiana. A banksia, a snake skin, a seed pod. A king tide swamping the beach, a kangaroo with a joey in her pouch, a peach-faced parrot that had eaten breadcrumbs from his palm. It was a real delight for Paula, seeing her country through the eyes of a foreigner.

Would Hamish have savoured that too?

Paula couldn't erase her husband from her mind, despite the many distractions of the road. She wondered daily how he was faring with his injury, whether he was coping by himself. Regretting what she'd done to his laptop and telephone, so violently cutting his ties with the world. Her behaviour then—it seemed to her now—had been bitter and borderline maniacal. But how could she ever have realised *that* if she hadn't embarked on this road trip?

The kids were in regular communication with Hamish, who seemed to be using a new phone. She'd received a few messages herself, the latest one being: *Paula, I'm sorry, hope you're having a nice time.*

She was still too angry to respond, but once or twice, usually after her second cider at Drinkypoos, she'd toyed with the idea of calling him—just to check if he was okay—before stopping short.

Seventeen years of marriage, she told herself, squandered with a seventeen-year-old girl.

There was no need to contact him.

'Hey, Mum!' Catie's voice jolted Paula out of her reverie.

She snapped to attention, refocusing on the highway. *How is it possible to drive so fast without really concentrating?*

'Can you switch off Lachie's music? It's my turn.'

'No it's not,' objected Lachie. 'We played yours yesterday.'

'What about *mine*?' asked Marcelo, leaning forward and passing an iPod to Sid. 'I think we need some João Gilberto and Chico Buarque. Maybe a little Marisa Monte.'

The names sounded glamorous.

'Great idea!' said Sid, plugging in the iPod.

As they drove further west to the sounds of Brazil, Paula kept catching Marcelo's eye in the rear-view mirror. It was a habit born of years of driving, but after a while, she began to feel embarrassed about it. She trained herself to look at Lachie instead, who was perched in the middle of the rear seat.

Her son didn't seem to mind being marooned between Caitlin and Marcelo. He'd become quite helpful to Paula, scanning either side of the highway like an aircraft navigator, calling out waypoints and landmarks. He was especially adept at spotting wildlife—lizards, birds and even a pack of emus running too close to the road—or the rare roadhouses that suddenly sprang out of the sandy flat like mirages. Mundrabilla, Cocklebiddy, Balladonia. Lachie announced each road stop like a tram conductor.

After hours of driving, Paula's right foot began cramping up over the accelerator, which she attributed to all the jogging she'd been doing. She'd managed six mornings in a row at Cactus Beach, a personal best for her, and her legs felt stronger for it. But her eyelids became heavier too, as they traversed mile after mile of unchanging landscape. Driving in the desert was disorienting; distances were deceiving, and landmarks appeared much closer than they were. The road seemed to curve in the heat, only to straighten again as they drove.

'Want me to take over now?' Sid asked suddenly.

'Yes, please,' she said, apologetic. 'I've hit the wall.'

She swapped positions with her father and for the remaining half-hour of their journey, Paula let her mind wander again across her primary preoccupations: her teenage children and their relationship with technology, her husband and his online infidelity and, inevitably, Marcelo. Something was transpiring between them, but she wasn't sure exactly what.

Physical attraction, yes. She was flattered by his attentions. But did they have a long-term future? She doubted it. He was only a temporary visitor to Australia; Brazil was in his blood. It oozed out of him as he described the beauty of his country, sang its songs by night, or trained her children in the art of Brazilian jiu-jitsu. He loved Brazil too much; he would never choose to make Australia his home. And even if he did, the seven-year age-gap between them was significant. One day he was sure to make a *younger* Brazilian woman exquisitely happy.

Yet in the dawn light at Cactus Beach, they'd *almost* kissed through the caravan window.

Why? she found herself wondering.

Why would a breathtaking Brazilian male want to kiss a cuddly Australian housewife?

*My husband doesn't even kiss me anymore.*

In the absence of an obvious answer, Paula found herself upending the question.

*Why not?*

*

After driving more than seven hundred kilometres from Eucla, they finally pulled into the grounds of the Norseman hotel. Beyond it lay an empty caravan park where they planned to spend the night. The broad, shaded veranda of the hotel was a welcome refuge from the merciless heat.

'I'm havin' a beer before we pitch camp, fellas, I'm parched,' said Sid, collapsing into a chair near several pot plants.

'You think *you're* thirsty,' said Caitlin, lying down on the faded cedar floorboards and closing her eyes. 'Lachie and I did fifty burpees yesterday. After the three-kilometre run.' She jerked a thumb at Marcelo, who grinned at her.

'What's a burpee?' Sid asked.

Lachie immediately lunged face-first towards the floor, thrust his legs out behind him, did a low push-up, then jumped back into a standing position.

'Wow.' Paula had never seen her son look so athletic. 'You're like a marine.'

'Good technique, Lachie.' Marcelo turned to Paula. 'Burpees are part of jiu-jitsu training. No equipment necessary and you can do them anywhere. I can teach you, if you like?' He smiled at her.

For a moment she imagined Marcelo's body pressing down against hers.

*Yes, I like.*

'I'm in,' said Sid suddenly. 'I might be an old bugger, but there's life in me yet.' He nodded at Marcelo. 'We've got a special trainer with us and time up our sleeve. Why don't we all get fit? I mean, *really* fit?'

Marcelo laughed. 'You are very interesting, Sid. Not all people your age have such—'

'Disregard for medical opinion?' Paula interjected. 'I mean, you've got to be *careful*, Dad. Dr Cassin said you shouldn't exert yourself, not with your heart murmur.'

Her father looked crestfallen.

Paula cast around the table for support, but no one said a word. Marcelo sat fiddling with a sugar sachet. Lachie leaned against the side of the veranda and shook his head almost imperceptibly. Caitlin lay rigid on the floor, her eyes fixed on the ceiling.

'I was going to say *alegria de viver*,' said Marcelo, his voice soft. 'Joy for life. You have it, Sid.'

The sugar sachet Marcelo was fingering suddenly split open and tiny white granules cascaded across the table. 'It's an unusual quality. So many people do not appreciate life, even when they still have it.' Marcelo stood up from the table. 'I think I will take a walk now.'

Paula's stomach plummeted as she watched Marcelo stride away.

'Good one, Mum.' Lachie looked at her reproachfully.

Caitlin's gaze remained focused on the wooden struts above her.

A metallic creak sounded as saloon-style doors were pushed open from within. An older woman with blonde pigtails and bright red lipstick appeared at their table.

'Hope I haven't kept ya waiting too long.' She smiled as she pulled a spiral-bound notebook from the pocket of her apron and a biro from behind her ear. 'Whaddya want?'

*Any humble pie on the menu?* Paula thought.

'I'll have a beer,' said Sid, sitting straighter in his chair. 'Not too early, is it?'

'Ya kidding, aren't ya?' The woman's laugh was deep and throaty, redolent of desert nights, hard liquor and too many cigarettes. 'Never too early for a coldie, love.'

'Alrighty, then.' Sid grinned at the woman. 'I'll have a schooner of your best. Two soda waters for the kids. You want one too, Paula?'

He looked at Paula as if there was no tension between them. It was a trait she'd always appreciated in her father: he never bore a grudge.

Paula nodded. 'Yes, thanks. We've got a friend coming back shortly too.' She gestured out into the shimmering heat.

'Is he a mad-dog Englishman?' the woman asked. 'Only the Brits go wandering around in the midday sun. And the Germans, come to think of it.'

'Brazilian,' said Caitlin.

'Oooh,' said the woman, laughing again. 'I had one of those once.' She leaned towards Paula. 'A bit ouchy on ya pink bits, eh?'

Paula was speechless. One minute they'd been ordering drinks, the next they were discussing intimate hair removal.

'He'll have a soda water too, please,' she mumbled.

'Right you are.' The waitress walked back towards the saloon, her hips swaying in too-tight jeans, before turning.

'Ya gonna stay tonight?' She pointed to a notice pinned on a nearby wall. 'Monthly karaoke night. Everyone comes from around the traps.'

'That settles it,' said Sid. 'We're going to need a powered site for our van out yonder, uh . . . ?' He leaned forward, squinting at the woman's name tag.

'Rhonda.' She pushed her chest out, as if that might help Sid's eyesight. 'The name's Rhonda.'

'Ah.' Sid smiled, eyeing her cleavage. 'I *love* the Beach Boys.'

Rhonda cackled, as if it was the first time in her life anyone had made that connection.

'Ya gonna *love* our karaoke night then,' she said, batting her eyelids.

Paula looked at her father, incredulous. He was notching up a few too many liaisons on this journey for her liking. There'd been Brenda in Lorne, Linda in Ceduna, and now Rhonda was shaping up as Ms Norseman. They all looked the same—short, big-chested, bigger smiles. Even their names were similar, like a flock of aged groupies, all swarming around her father.

She stood up from the table. 'I'll go park the caravan.'

'Choose any site ya like,' called Rhonda.

Paula stomped away towards the empty car park. She could feel her father's eyes burrowing into her back. Wondering what was wrong with her, she guessed, why she was so . . . tetchy.

*Why* am *I so tetchy?* she asked herself as she climbed behind the wheel of the ute.

As she turned the key in the ignition, hot air blasted out of the air-conditioning vents. She crumpled forward against the steering wheel, shoulders sagging, inhaling the pungent smell of overheated plastic.

*I need to talk to Jamie.*

She reached into the glove box, removed her telephone and dialled her sister's number.

It rang out.

*Of course*, Paula thought, *she's at work. Where most normal people are on a weekday.* The tears began to trickle out of the corners of Paula's eyes.

A sharp knocking near her ear made her jump.

Marcelo's face was hovering near the window. He tapped his knuckle against the glass again.

She opened it.

'Did I scare you?'

She shook her head.

They looked at each other for a moment, then he opened the door for her. 'Come,' he said softly. 'I have something to show you.'

She wanted nothing more than to follow him.

As she got out of the car, he caught her hand in his.

Their shoes slipped over the sand as they walked beyond the northern reaches of the caravan park. Moving across the desert flat, skirting around scrub and stones until they reached a large, spiny cactus, its needles shooting skywards. Marcelo pointed to an orange mound behind the plant.

'Look, *Pow-la*, an ant hill.'

Didn't they have them in his country?

She wouldn't know; he was the first Brazilian she'd ever met. Unlike Rhonda, she'd never had a wax of the same name either. Her perceptions of Brazilian males were informed exclusively by media snippets: random images of soccer players, drug dealers, tree fellers and kidnappers. Usually unkempt, overconfident and a tad sleazy. Not quietly self-assured, yet vulnerable. Or agonisingly handsome, with eyes like liquid pools. The singing surfer, the philosopher cowboy, the gentle combatant.

They squatted down together, watching the orderly lines of ants marching in and out of the ant hill.

The sun was hot on Paula's neck, she could feel the sweat inching down her chest and into the padding of her bra. Always padded bras, frequently push-up too. She envied women with natural cleavage.

Marcelo swayed a little on his haunches, then looked up into her face.

'They seem so simple, don't they?' he said. 'This small hill, very plain. But so much is going on under the surface. Not many people know it, but these structures are strong enough to survive hurricanes.'

His eyes met hers.

'You are like that, *Pow-la*. I see it. Very strong on the outside, but complicated underneath.' He took her right hand and pressed it against his chest. 'Always doing things for others, never for yourself.'

She opened her mouth, but no sound came out. She could feel the firm muscle beneath his t-shirt.

She tried to stand up.

'Don't go,' he said, pulling her back down. 'Don't you see your own beauty?' He reached out and ran the back of his hand down the side of her face. 'Beauty inside, and out.'

*Beauty?*

He began to lean forward.

*Surely he's not going to . . .*

His lips brushed hers, soft and full.

It felt as if she was falling through a cloud.

'Mum?'

Lachie's voice, right behind them. 'What are you . . . ?'

Paula scrambled up like a guilty schoolgirl.

Lachie looked between her and Marcelo.

'The drinks are ready.'

He turned on his heel and charged back towards the hotel at full speed.

'Oh, no,' Paula groaned. 'He saw that.'

Marcelo nodded.

She hesitated, torn between her overwhelming desire to lie down in the sand with Marcelo, and her urge to run after Lachie.

'I have to go,' she said.

'I know.'

She bolted after her son.

# 11

Lachie avoided Paula for the rest of the afternoon.

At first he stayed close to his grandfather, who was busy testing the dingo trap he'd been itching to use since they'd entered desert country. But when Marcelo offered to help Sid dig a pit for the trap a few kilometres from camp, Lachie declined to join them. Instead he helped his sister, who'd begun spring-cleaning the caravan.

Paula watched Catie remove the contents of the cupboards, passing items to Lachie for reorganisation. After almost a month on the road, the caravan and ute were in mild disorder—basic items were no longer in their designated places, which sometimes led to frustrating searches. Normally, Paula would have been the one leading the charge to tidy, but her standards had slipped.

*After so many years, I've lost the will for order. But Caitlin clearly takes after me.*

She wasn't sure if that was a good thing.

Paula lay on a wide, cushion-covered bench beneath the hotel's veranda, waiting for a moment when she could corner Lachie alone.

As she watched her children potter about the caravan, she reflected on how they'd adapted to their altered living conditions. Hamish was still in frequent contact with them, but they didn't seem to be fretting about his absence, or the life they'd left behind in Melbourne. Probably because they knew they were *going back*, she thought. They barely discussed the Facebook incident now, and they'd managed to stick to her 'Social Media Sunday' rule. Overall, Paula was pleased to note, they both seemed to be enjoying themselves more than she'd expected they might.

Paula began to feel drowsy, until she couldn't keep her eyes open any longer. Drifting into half-sleep, she could almost feel Marcelo's soft lips brushing hers again.

The sound of her telephone woke her.

She hunted around, locating it beneath a newspaper.

'Hi Jamie,' she said, smiling.

'Bedded the Brazilian yet?'

'Well . . .' Paula lowered her voice to a whisper. 'I almost kissed him today.'

'You *didn't*.' Jamie sounded genuinely shocked.

'But we were sprung by Lachie.'

'My God. I thought you were kidding about all of that.'

Her sister's disapproval made Paula embarrassed.

'Look, Jamie—' Paula suddenly spotted Caitlin and Lachie now, sitting at a table on the hotel's veranda, absorbed in their own activities. 'The kids are here. I've got to go, sorry.'

'Wait, Paula.' Jamie's voice was gentler. 'I'm all for fun, but please be *careful*. I don't want you to get hurt, or the kids. What's it been, ten days since you met this guy?'

'Eleven,' Paula corrected. 'Thanks, Jamie. I'll call you back.'

She stood up from the bench, slipped her phone into her pocket and strolled towards the children. The sun was sinking in the west—how long had she been napping? With her cleaning complete, Caitlin now appeared to be penning yet another letter to Amy. Lachie was reading a sci-fi novel called *Moondroids from Uranus*, avoiding Paula's gaze behind its schmaltzy cover: green aliens with spaghetti-like tentacles clambering over a derelict New York streetscape.

'It's almost sunset, kids,' Paula said. 'Maybe you should move to the caravan, Catie, or the mozzies will start biting. A letter to Amy?'

'Yep.' Catie stood up, stretched, and sauntered off.

'Lachie,' said Paula, turning in his direction, 'can we talk now, please?'

'Whatever.'

She fell in beside him. They began walking away from the camp site. The air was cooling quickly now, and the desert's silence was punctuated by the squeaking and rustling of small nocturnal creatures. As they made their way through the low-lying scrub, Paula was certain she saw something slithering away in her peripheral vision, but by the time she'd turned her head, it was gone.

Despite the stilted silence with Lachie, Paula couldn't help but feel exhilarated by the sunset. The russet earth beneath a darkening sky, the sun's yellow arc dipping lower on the horizon.

'Look at that, Lachie. The sunset looks just like the Aboriginal flag.'

She'd seen the black, yellow and red flag a thousand times before, on flagpoles and banners, but never brushed across the sky and the earth.

Lachie stopped walking and gazed out to the west.

'Hey, yeah!' he said, before quickly resuming a slightly bored expression.

'Listen, Lachie.' Paula reached for one of his hands, but he snatched it away. 'Marcelo and I, we're not . . .' She paused, not knowing how to continue.

'Look, I'm sorry, Lachie,' she tried again. 'It must have been very confusing to . . . see what you did today.'

He looked at her, incensed. 'You *kissed* Marcelo.'

'Kind of.'

She wasn't sure how she'd classify it. Yes, their lips had touched. Yes, it had felt wonderful. But the whole thing was over before it had even begun, terminated by Lachie's sudden arrival. And Marcelo had kissed *her*; she hadn't really kissed back.

*Had* she?

Lachie was watching her, a slightly disgusted expression on his face.

'It's been really difficult for me lately, Lachie,' she said. 'What with Dad and everything.'

'You didn't have to *kiss* Marcelo.'

She tried to work out what was disturbing Lachie most. The fact he'd seen her kissing at all—she and Hamish rarely displayed affection in front of the children—or the fact it was a man other than his father?

'Sometimes it happens, Lachie. Life's more complicated when you're an adult.'

'Why?' His eyes were shiny. '*Why* is it more complicated?'

*It's a reasonable question.*

Years ago, she'd been sold the fairytale of lifelong romance. Girl meets boy, they fall in love, have children and grow old together. And up until a month or so ago, Paula had believed *she* was living that fantasy with Hamish—albeit with its challenges and monotonies. For better or for worse, she'd understood their life to be about simple choices between consenting adults; the mature acceptance of certain personal trade-offs for the preservation of the family unit. That was the arrangement she'd *thought* she'd shared with Hamish, at least, until he went and jeopardised everything—their relationship, their family, the life they'd created—by fooling around online with a teenage girl.

Paula sighed. 'I don't know why it gets more complicated when you grow up, Lachie. Things aren't so black and white.'

*Mere motherhood statements. Can't I do better than that?*

Lachie glared at her.

'*My* life is complicated now,' he said. 'And it really sucks.'

She winced. *My children are now actors in this complicated drama of Hamish's making.* A bolt of anger surged through her, the fury she'd suppressed since their departure from Melbourne. The names she sometimes called Hamish in her sleep, when rage ravaged her dreams.

*Arsehole. Wanker. Philanderer. Cradle-snatcher.*

But it wasn't *all* Hamish, she had to admit.

She'd been an enabler in the whole sordid business, by settling so thoroughly into domesticity. Permitting her roles as wife and mother to alter the woman Hamish had married. Erasing almost every part of her identity pre-children, until she was almost unrecognisable, even to herself.

She'd *allowed* that to happen. Encouraged it, in fact.

Lachie scuffed at the earth with the toe of his sneaker, avoiding her gaze. 'When we get home, will we still live with Dad?'

The look on Lachie's face instantly transported her back to his early childhood. The uncertainty, the vulnerability. All those days of kissing his bruises, comforting him in new company, carrying him past barking dogs and down treacherous stairs. He looked up at her now as he had a decade ago, trusting and hopeful and utterly fragile. As if she was queen of his universe, holding the key to his life and fate.

*I* cannot *crush that trust*, she thought.

'I don't know yet, Lachie. I have to talk to your dad first. I've been too angry to talk to him properly.'

It was an unpalatable truth. She couldn't put off talking to Hamish forever. And as much as she didn't feel like it, she owed him a chance to explain himself. It was only fair, a principle they'd attempted to instil in their children from the beginning.

'Look, I'll call Dad soon. And when we get back to Melbourne, I'll sit down with him and talk about everything.' She touched Lachie's hand. 'And whatever happens, it will be okay. I promise you.'

She saw a spark of hope in his eyes.

Suddenly he threw his arms around her neck.

She buried her nose in his hair; slightly greasy, but nevertheless *him*. The Lachie smell she loved.

'And you won't kiss Marcelo again until you've talked to Dad?' He pulled away to look at her.

Was that a promise she really wanted to make?

'Lachie, I'm not sure if that's . . .'

His lips quivered. 'You always tell us to *fight fair.* But *you're* not being fair to Dad.'

Paula felt utterly conflicted.

She looked back at the caravan, where Caitlin was sitting at the table writing to Amy; their missives sometimes ran to twenty pages. Her father and Marcelo were outside having a beer now, presumably having finished digging their pit. The regular buzzing of the portable fly-zapper suspended near the caravan door was audible even at a distance.

'You're right, Lachie,' she said finally. 'I need to hear your father out.'

*Before I go kissing another man.*

'Promise?' he asked.

'Promise.'

She nodded towards the caravan. 'Let's go. Your grandfather's threatening to sing "Help Me Rhonda" at karaoke tonight. I think we need to talk him out of that.'

Lachie grinned at her.

As they walked back together, Lachie wound an arm through hers.

She'd done the right thing by the kids, she thought, as well as Hamish. Jamie would probably applaud her maturity too.

*This is what adulthood is all about.*

*

They arrived at the Norseman bar just after eight o'clock, through a parking lot now packed with two- and three-trailer road trains. Rhonda had suggested they come early, as seats filled quickly. Dozens of truckies planned a stopover in Norseman on karaoke night, apparently; it was the highlight of their monthly calendar.

A wall of smoke hit them behind the saloon doors. The national no-smoking protocols clearly hadn't reached Norseman, or weren't being enforced. The hotel pub was packed with beards, tattoos and testosterone.

Rhonda was holding court behind the bar, goading a queue of men. She waved at Paula with girlish excitement, pointing to a high round table in the corner with a handwritten sign perched on top: *Reserved for caravan park guests only.*

Paula waved back gratefully.

The table was positioned close to a makeshift stage, with five bar stools clustered around it. Paula waited until the children had sat down on either side of Marcelo, then said, 'I'll get some drinks.'

She picked her way through the crowd of truckies nursing stubbies, some chatting to clusters of local women wearing tight jeans, low-cut tops, high heels and bright lipstick. It crossed Paula's mind that perhaps they were prostitutes trucked in for the evening.

'Where has everyone come from?' she asked Rhonda, when she reached the bar.

'We've got no night-life in the desert, darl,' said Rhonda. 'So we take every chance we can get. Had a few couples meet here at karaoke, even had a wedding last year.' She grinned with pride. 'You never know, you might find someone here ya self, if you're on the market.' She filled three beer glasses with straw-coloured pilsener, and another two with soda water.

Rhonda leaned towards her. 'Are you with the Brazilian? He's attracting quite a lot of attention.' She nodded at a group of local women, all long hair and hard faces, tittering in a corner.

Paula blushed. 'No, I'm not with Marcelo.'

'Ooh, *Marcelo*. Can't wait to tell the girls he's available.'

Paula lifted the tray of drinks from the bar and turned to make her way back to their table. Suddenly she heard a familiar voice from behind the microphone.

She froze.

Her father was sashaying across the stage, belting out the Beach Boys' 'California Girls'. He gesticulated at the crowd of mostly middle-aged males with beer guts, who'd presumably spent the better part of the day behind a steering wheel. Judging by the appreciative tenor of their whooping, her father was successfully conjuring the image of southern girls, northerners and mid-west farmers' daughters.

As she nudged her way across the room, Paula watched her father in disbelief. He was crooning and swaying and revving up the audience, until most of them were singing along with him. When she reached their table, Caitlin and Lachie and Marcelo were standing too, cheering him on.

By the final chorus, Sid had removed his shirt in a mock striptease, and was rubbing it across his back as if towelling off after a shower. Or perhaps a surf, thought Paula, gawping at his theatrics. Two local women, giggling hysterically, clambered up onto the stage and began pawing at his chest.

*They* really *don't get out much*, Paula thought.

Her father was enjoying the limelight and, red-faced with the effort of it all, stood whistling the final bars of the song.

'Thank you very much,' he said, as the crowd bellowed their appreciation. Then he lifted his fists like an Olympic gold medallist and bounced off the stage.

He high-fived Marcelo, then downed half a beer on the spot.

'What was *that*, Dad?' Paula laughed, half shocked, half delighted. Her father, the desert karaoke star.

'I dunno,' he replied, grinning. 'But it was a helluva lot of fun.'

Someone began calling for an encore. A single clap quickly became a rhythmic beat, hands and voices demanding that he return to the stage.

Over the next twenty minutes, her father delivered a selection of tunes perfectly suited to his audience. Robert Palmer's 'Simply Irresistible', Marvin Gaye's 'Sexual Healing', a rousing version of Men at Work's 'Down Under'. Finally, sweating and smiling like a seasoned performer, he serenaded the audience with a rendition of Neil Diamond's 'Sweet Caroline'—accompanied by almost everyone in the bar. Paula had to admit that to hear all those truckies singing their hearts out to Neil Diamond had an incongruous charm.

'Thank you very much, gentlemen and *ladies*.' Her father waved at a gaggle of women nearby. 'Now it's time for the *real* pros to have a go.'

He bowed and stepped off the stage.

A skinny blonde took the microphone and began wiggling her hips to the opening bars of 'Heart of Glass'.

'Gramps!' Caitlin looked at Sid with admiration as he joined the table. 'Since when have you been a rock star?'

'Oh, I've spent some time behind the microphone at the odd Rotary function over the years.'

'*Singing?*' Paula pulled a face. 'I thought it was all badges and barbecues.'

'Rotarians have fun too, you know.'

She laughed.

'So, *Pow-la*, will you sing with me?'

Marcelo's words made Paula flinch. 'Ah, no,' she mumbled. 'I've got a terrible voice.'

'Go on, love,' her father urged. 'What about "Islands in the Stream"?'

*I'd need a bit more bust for Dolly Parton.*

'No, no,' Marcelo said. '"I've Had the Time of My Life".'

She smiled, remembering the year she'd first seen the classic film *Dirty Dancing*, when she was Caitlin's age. She'd watched it six times over one summer before buying the soundtrack. Sitting in her bedroom, staring at a poster of Patrick Swayze, listening to the duet over and over again until her mother threw open the door and turfed her outside.

*But Mum's dead now, and so is Patrick Swayze. And I'm* still *waiting for the time of my life.*

Paula glanced at Marcelo. From the gleam in his eyes, he had his own *Dirty Dancing* story. Probably most people did, the world over.

'Come, *Pow-la*,' he urged.

Lachie glared at her across the table.

'No, thanks,' she said.

'Why don't *you* get up there, Catie?' suggested Sid, nudging his granddaughter.

Caitlin sat straight-backed on the stool. 'No.'

'Go on, love,' he urged. 'You'll be great.'

'I really *don't* think so.'

Marcelo turned to her. 'Why not?'

She didn't reply.

The singer on the stage—a bearded man wearing a green cap pulled backwards over long hair—had just finished a loud but off-key version of 'The Pub With No Beer'.

Marcelo nodded at Caitlin. 'Now is our chance.'

He caught her by the wrist and pulled her onto the stage.

She stood away from him, looking wooden. Although Caitlin was slightly taller than Marcelo, they made a handsome couple. A stage light shone from behind, catching the edges of Caitlin's hair, making her seem almost ethereal. Marcelo looked swarthy and toned, his white t-shirt stretched tight across his chest. A woman wolf-whistled; Marcelo ignored her as he clasped the microphone.

*'Now I've . . . had . . . the time of my life . . .'*

A hush fell across the room; clearly it wasn't often that a Brazilian god visited Norseman. The women all had dreamy expressions on their faces, while the men looked intrigued or irritated.

Paula couldn't bear to watch Marcelo performing with her daughter.

'I'm turning in,' she whispered to her father. 'Lachie's tired too.' She nodded at her son. 'Come on, let's go back to the caravan.' *You, who made me promise something I shouldn't have.*

'No.' He pointed at the stage. 'I want to watch this.'

Marcelo was holding Caitlin's hands, trying to make her dance.

Paula felt like dragging Lachie out of the pub by his ear.

'Suit yourself,' she said, slinging her handbag over her shoulder.

'Paula.' Her father reached across the table and touched her hand. 'Is everything okay?'

She nodded, knowing he saw all the fury and sadness below her composed surface.

'We need to talk,' he said, his eyes gentle.

'Tomorrow, Dad. Can you watch out for Lachie and Catie tonight, please? Make sure they get back in one piece?'

'Of course.'

Marcelo and Caitlin were singing the chorus now. *Caitlin only even knows this song because of me. Because I've been playing it all her life.*

The crowd was enjoying the spectacle; some singing along, others doing their best *Dirty Dancing* moves.

Paula tucked her bar stool under the table, hating the sting of petty envy she felt toward her own daughter.

'*Pow-la*, where you are going?'

It was Marcelo's voice, mid-tune, over the PA.

She kept walking.

Marcelo missed several beats, then resumed singing.

She pushed the saloon doors open.

The night air was a cool respite from the stuffy aroma of perspiring bodies. She took several steps out onto the veranda and closed her eyes, sucking the oxygen into her nostrils.

Out and in. Out and in.

If she breathed deeply enough, she could almost stifle the sound of Marcelo and Caitlin's duet.

Almost, but not quite.

She began to walk across the crowded car park, then broke into a jog. Fleeing the music, fleeing her feelings.

Reaching the caravan, she unlocked the door and groped her way to her bed.

She could still hear Marcelo and Caitlin, and the mob egging them on.

Paula felt for her phone in her pocket.

*You were right, Jamie*, she typed. *The Brazilian's just a stupid fantasy.*

She pressed 'send'.

Now the crowd was cheering and cat-calling again.

She screwed her eyes shut.

*

Hours later, she opened them and sat up, instantly alert.

In the car park.

She'd rushed straight past it.

A yellow hatchback that looked just like hers.

She stumbled out of bed, past Caitlin and Lachie sleeping in their bunks, and opened the door of the caravan. She looked out over the moonlit car park, almost empty now.

Had she imagined it?

A dingo howled in the distance and she shivered, wondering if perhaps her father's trap had snared its first quarry.

A shadow moved. It was a silhouette she recognised.

She peered at her watch. What on earth was he doing up, at this hour?

'Marcelo?' There was something unusual about his gait.

*'Pow-la,'* he said, staggering and almost falling against the caravan. 'I need a doctor. This—' he pointed to his abdomen—'is sick, there is something wrong inside me.'

'Have you had too much to drink?'

He shook his head. 'I only had one beer.' He clutched his stomach.

'What is it?' Paula had all but forgotten her first-aid training. Marcelo groaned and doubled over.

'Oh, God.' She stepped out of the caravan and put a hand on his back, crouching down to look at his face.

'In Brazil, I had this once before,' he gasped. 'I forget the English word. Problem in my . . .'

'Intestines?' she prompted.

'No . . . an inside part.'

'Spleen? Liver? Appendix?'

He nodded vigorously, still doubled over. 'Yes. Appendix is bad.'

'Okay, that *is* serious.'

Out here in the desert, a ruptured appendix could be fatal.

She'd noticed a sign to the district hospital in Norseman earlier.

'Get in the car, Marcelo,' she said, plunging into mother mode. 'You need to see a doctor.'

'In Perth?' he asked.

'No, there's a hospital nearby. I'll wake Dad and tell him what's happened. He can stay here with the kids.'

Marcelo straightened up a little. 'I don't want to wake Sid. The pain is not that bad,' he said, in a slightly embarrassed tone. 'I think it can wait for Perth.'

'No, no.' Paula dismissed him with a wave of her hand. 'We'll get you checked, just to be safe.'

They followed the blue street signs marked with a white cross, arriving five minutes later at the district hospital on Talbot Street.

The car park was inexplicably full. The word 'Emergency' was painted above an automatic door on the small hospital building. Beyond it, she could see the waiting room was jam-packed too.

What were all these people *doing* here at two o'clock in the morning?

She'd read enough newspaper articles to know that medical resources were limited in rural and remote Australia, but she'd never witnessed it firsthand.

She helped Marcelo across the car park, through the door and up to the front desk. A young man was bent over it, shuffling through papers.

'Can I help you?' he said, in a distracted tone.

'We'd like to see a doctor, please.'

The young man looked up and smiled; he had silver braces on his teeth. 'I'm it for tonight.'

'You?' Paula was shocked; he looked barely older than Lachie. 'I thought you were . . .'

'The receptionist?' He laughed. 'She's just getting a cup of tea. We've been busy. It's always like that on karaoke night, for some reason.' He pushed a clipboard in Paula's direction. 'You can fill out these forms, please.'

He walked into the waiting room and called out 'Mr Jacobsen? William Jacobsen?'

An elderly man raised his hand and, assisted by his wife, stood up unsteadily.

'Come through,' the doctor said, gesturing to a nearby consult room, 'and thank you for your patience.'

Paula looked around at the rest of the motley crowd in the waiting room. Several men, one pressing a bloodstained rag on a gash to his forehead, another wearing fishing gear. A mother with a young child asleep on her lap, a large Indigenous family, a young man muttering to himself. An assortment of others, sick or frail.

What kind of care could Marcelo possibly receive here, tonight?

A plump woman appeared behind the desk, holding a mug. 'Hello,' she said. 'You've got the forms? Good. You might be waiting a few hours, I'm afraid, unless it's urgent.'

Paula turned to Marcelo. 'How are you feeling now?'

His face had slightly more colour to it.

'I am okay,' he said. 'Just a little pain. This place is very busy. Can we go to Perth instead?'

It was the choice Paula would make for her own children. 'But can you wait that long?' she asked doubtfully. 'It's an eight-hour drive.'

'I think so.' Marcelo appeared calmer. 'The pain comes and goes. I can lie down in the caravan on the way.'

Paula began weighing up the risk of Marcelo travelling in a caravan without a seatbelt.

'Alright,' she said, finally. 'Let's go.'

They walked out of the hospital and across the car park to the ute. 'But you can't move around in the caravan when we're driving, okay?'

Marcelo nodded, leaning against the headrest and closing his eyes. 'Thank you, *Pow-la*.' His voice was hoarse. 'This is a lot of trouble for you.'

As they drove back to the caravan park, Paula did some mental calculations. It might take a while to rouse the kids and her father at this ungodly hour, but if they packed up quickly, they could make it to a decent hospital by lunchtime.

*As long as his pain doesn't worsen*, she thought, glancing at Marcelo's slumped form.

Anxiety and tenderness coursed through her.

*I can't deny it*, she thought. *I've tried to, but I can't.*

She could push through eight hours of driving for him.

She would do virtually *anything* for him.

# 12

*This time, I'll get it right. Teach that Brazilian a lesson he'll never forget.*

Hamish drained the last of his coffee. Bitter and gritty, like warmed-up bilge water.

Some dog-ugly woman was behind the microphone, butchering 'Like a Virgin', one of Paula's favourite songs.

*Screw this,* Hamish thought.

He'd been sitting in a corner of the pub's veranda since the karaoke started. Obscured by several large, decorative cacti, seemingly a compulsory fixture for a desert pub. A continuous line of smokers moved in and out of the bar, taking their pleasure against the wooden railings. A waitress with greying pigtails had asked Hamish, more than once, if he needed anything. He'd said no, but the old girl kept popping her head around the saloon doors to check on him, until finally he'd felt compelled to order a coffee.

*Bloody rural Australians. Always in everyone else's business.*

He'd been patient for an hour, but the duet from *Dirty Dancing* was too much. That greasy Brazilian making eyes at his daughter, in public, on a stage. And no one doing anything about it. Not even Paula—she didn't give a shit, apparently—leaving in the middle of it, abandoning their children to the care of old Sid.

Hamish didn't stir as Paula walked out of the bar and stood within metres of him. She looked up at the night sky for a moment, before jogging off across the car park. He watched her arse as she moved; it was definitely smaller now.

*And I should know, I've seen that view a thousand times.*

He was on the verge of following her, when he caught the duet's climax in the bar. In a smooth dance stunt that wowed the crowd, the Brazilian lifted his daughter in the air.

He could deal with Paula later, Hamish decided. For now, he had unfinished business with the Brazilian.

It was almost eleven o'clock when they finally emerged from the pub. The Brazilian had one arm around Catie, the other around Sid, who looked a bit pissy. Lachie was bringing up the rear, like a faithful dog trotting at the Brazilian's heels.

Hamish followed at a distance as they lurched across the car park. He crouched next to the hatchback, watching as Caitlin disappeared into the caravan. Sid urinated behind a tree, then proceeded to brush his teeth in a small bucket outside the van. The Brazilian took a towel and toiletries from the tent, then walked towards the amenities block. It was exactly as Hamish anticipated; Eucla had taught him that the foreigner took showers at night. The Brazilian whistled as he walked, obviously in a good mood.

*Not for long, amigo.*

Lachie suddenly jogged after the Brazilian, calling his name. Hamish couldn't hear their conversation, but his son appeared to be doing most of the talking. The Brazilian kept shaking his head; Lachie looked pretty worked up.

*Is Lachie defending his sister?*

At one point, Lachie pulled a telephone from his pocket. The Brazilian reached for it, but Lachie ducked away.

*Touch my son and I'll kill you.*

The Brazilian held his hands up, open-palmed, and Lachie slipped the phone back into his pocket.

They talked some more before, finally, the Brazilian turned away. He continued walking, slower now, to the amenities block.

Hamish waited until he could hear the water running before sneaking across the sand. Standing a metre from the shower door, he laid a small hand towel over the plastic revolver and aimed it at the door handle.

For a moment he thought of Doggo's wife, Tina, and her crazy predilection for carrying toy guns around. When he'd left Melbourne a week earlier, he never could have imagined using Tina's weapon of choice against a Brazilian sleazebag.

His hands trembled a little as he heard the taps being turned off, a towel buffing skin, clothes being donned.

Then the click of the lock and the handle turning.

The Brazilian stopped dead.

His eyes settled on the shape in Hamish's right hand and a muscle twitched at the side of his neck.

'Come for a chat,' said Hamish, motioning towards the door. 'Keep your hands where I can see them. Don't say a word. Now walk.'

Miraculously, the Brazilian obeyed.

Hamish's heart was battering at his chest as he skirted behind the Brazilian.

'Walk to the yellow hatchback parked near the Mack truck.'

The Brazilian complied.

'This little one?'

'Shut up.' Hamish didn't need the reminder. 'Open the door. You're driving.'

Hamish climbed into the seat behind the Brazilian, and pointed the gun at his head.

'Start her up.'

They drove to the place Hamish had scoped out earlier: a deserted rest area overlooking clay salt pans about ten minutes west of Norseman. Hamish didn't think much of the view, but figured it was a prime spot for intimidation.

'Park it down there.'

The Brazilian drove to the furthest reaches of the parking area, beyond the glow of the single streetlight.

'Get out of the car and put your hands on the bonnet.'

Hamish stepped out of the car behind the Brazilian, training the gun on him. He took a small Maglite torch from his pocket and shone it in the Brazilian's eyes.

The Brazilian looked nervous, shying away from the light.

'Spread your legs, or I'll blow your fucking balls off.'

'Please, I—'

'Shut up, motherfucker.' Hamish was beginning to enjoy this. 'Pissed yourself, have you?' He shone his torch at the crotch of the Brazilian's jeans.

The Brazilian didn't reply.

Hamish took a step forward. 'That's what pussies like you *do*. Pussies that prey on little girls. It's illegal in Australia, mate. And the big girls in prison will get you for it. They'll rearrange your arsehole for you, down in maximum security.' His voice was shaking. 'So, what do you reckon I should do? Shoot you now, or call the coppers for a holiday in the big house? What do you reckon?'

The Brazilian held one hand up to shield his eyes.

'Don't move!' yelled Hamish, lifting the gun higher.

The Brazilian put both hands in the air, then suddenly turned around and sat on the car's bonnet.

'Stand up!'

The Brazilian didn't move. He seemed to be taking Hamish in; his clothes, his shoes, the towel over the gun. After a moment, he stood up from the bonnet and walked once around the hatchback, kicking idly at the back tyres.

'Freeze!'

The Brazilian shook his head.

Hamish was losing control.

'Who *are* you?' the Brazilian asked. 'Tell me now, and I won't hurt you.'

'Hey, I'm the one with the gun, mate,' Hamish spat, brandishing it under the towel. 'I don't think you're in a position to—'

A sharp pain ricocheted through his right hand.

'Fuck!' Hamish screamed, dropping his Maglite.

The revolver landed nearby, kicked clean out of his fingers. The Brazilian pounced on it, turning it over in his hands. Then he began to laugh. 'So you are not police.' He held up the plastic revolver and pretended to shoot. 'Pow! Pow!'

Hamish began to edge towards the car; his big idea had gone pear-shaped and he didn't have a Plan B.

The Brazilian moved with feline speed. 'Tell me who you are.' He leaned against the driver's door.

There was no escape.

'I'm Caitlin's father,' Hamish said defiantly. 'And I know exactly what you're up to.'

The Brazilian looked blankly at him. 'I don't understand.'

'Come on, mate,' said Hamish. 'You're a guy, I'm a guy, Caitlin's hot. I'm not going to let you just waltz in and tag my daughter.'

The Brazilian stood for a moment, then he smiled. 'You are *Pow-la*'s husband?'

'Paula, yeah.' Hamish didn't like his accent.

'And you say I am interested in Caitlin?'

Hamish rolled his eyes. 'I *know* you are, mate. I've seen you with her.'

The Brazilian nodded slowly. 'Mr . . . what is your name?'

'Hamish.'

'Ah yes, *Pow-la* mentioned it.' The Brazilian's stance was no longer defensive. He extended a hand. 'Hamish, I am Marcelo and you are mistaken.'

Hamish crossed his arms. He couldn't shake the Brazilian's hand even if he tried, his fingers were throbbing. 'Don't bullshit me, mate.'

Marcelo hesitated. 'What do you want from me?'

'I want you to leave my daughter alone and get the hell out of my family. Go back to the Brazilian hole you came from.'

'I'm afraid I can't do that.'

'Then I'll call the police,' Hamish exploded.

'I see.' Marcelo nodded, as if resolving something. 'Then I have no other option.'

The Brazilian melted away into the night.

Hamish spun around, desperately trying to locate him.

There was nowhere to hide nearby; *how* could he have just disappeared?

Then the pressure, slowly tightening around his neck.

He could smell Marcelo's body, feel him clamped against his back like a barnacle. It was a sickening sensation, just like in Eucla. He flailed about, but couldn't peel Marcelo's arm off his neck; the crush was excruciating.

Hamish knew exactly how it would end.

'I am sorry,' Marcelo whispered in Hamish's ear. 'I didn't want to do this, but you gave me no choice.'

Hamish's legs kicked about uselessly.

'I want you to know, I am not interested in Caitlin. I will not touch her.'

Marcelo's breath was hot on his neck, unbearably close.

'But I cannot say the same about your wife.'

*

When Hamish came to, Marcelo was gone.

And so was the hatchback.

But next to his head was a bottle of water and the long-sleeved sweater Marcelo had been wearing.

Hamish rolled over and spat into the dust; there was nothing he could do but wait out the night.

He lay down on the top of a concrete picnic table and looked up at the glittering orbs of The Milky Way stretched above him. Eventually, he fell into a fitful sleep.

In the coolest hour before dawn, Hamish awoke and, to his chagrin, reached for Marcelo's sweater. Then, being unable to go back to sleep for the pain in his hand, he sat and watched the sky's colours change. All was silent, save a solitary birdcall. A wallaby loped up out of nowhere and snuffled about, metres from his feet. Hamish didn't move, wondering if the animal was even aware of his presence, following it with his eyes until it crossed the highway and disappeared into the scrub.

The morning air was crisp and fresh, like the scent of a newly bathed baby. Now *that* was an aroma he hadn't smelled in a long time; Catie and Lachie, all soapy and innocent, after bathtime together. Back when the kids were still little and the months and years had stretched ahead, tantalising in their possibility. Before those cherub-like children had turned into teenagers, moodier versions of their former selves. Those preschool years now seemed so simple with the clarity of hindsight. No hormones, no Facebook, fewer fuck-ups on his part.

Hamish hung his head.

How had it come to this?

His life of merely a month earlier now felt like years ago.

Sure, he'd behaved badly online. But did he really deserve *this*? Exile in the desert, a wild-goose chase to find his family, battling a Brazilian stranger with designs on his . . .

*Wife.*

Hamish shook his head, remembering the Brazilian's final words. Claiming he was after Paula, not Caitlin. It was hardly believable, despite Paula's weight loss.

The distant sound of an engine made Hamish look up. A white mini-bus was rumbling along the highway in a westerly direction. He glanced at his watch; it was just after six o'clock.

Hamish walked to the highway's edge, waving his left arm.

The mini-bus slowed. As it neared, Hamish could make out an

intricate Indigenous dot pattern painted across its body, beneath the words *Yalata Nullarbor Tours.*

The bus pulled up alongside Hamish and the window opened automatically.

'You right, fella?'

Hamish almost wept with relief as he recognised the red cap, the stone-wash jeans, the long-sleeved flannelette shirt. The unflinching poker face.

'Thank God it's you.' He smiled at the Aboriginal man behind the wheel. 'I've just spent the night out here.'

'Farken stupid place to sleep.'

'I know, I know . . . it's a long story. Could I catch a lift to Norseman?'

The driver nodded. 'Coulda walked there. It's only ten clicks up the road. Get in.'

Hamish sat down in the nearest seat, directly behind the driver.

The door closed.

As they hummed along the highway, the driver kept looking at Hamish in his rear-view mirror.

When the township of Norseman appeared, Hamish tapped him on the shoulder.

'This is the second time you've rescued me,' he said. 'What's your name?'

'Frank.'

*Farken Frank*, Hamish thought.

'Well, thanks, Frank.'

'Just don't make a farken habit of it, mate. You on the run from the pigs or what?'

Hamish laughed. 'My wife's on the run. From me, with our kids.'

Frank shook his head. 'No good, mate. Happy wife, happy life.'

He changed down a gear as they entered Norseman's outskirts.

Outside the hotel, Hamish scanned the camp site where the caravan had been parked. There was nothing there now except an empty patch of dirt.

'Shit,' he said. 'Paula's gone already.'

How had they upped sticks so quickly? It was only six-thirty in the morning. And where the hell was the hatchback?

'I'm buggered, mate.' He raked his good hand through his hair. 'My knee's stuffed, now my hand. A Brazilian ninja's done me over twice and he's latched on to my wife, too. She's disappeared with him and the kids *again*. I've got nowhere to stay in Perth, I don't know what the fuck I'm doing.' He choked back the tears. 'I'm sorry.'

As the van's engine idled, Frank felt for something behind the sun visor.

'Here, take this.' He handed Hamish a business card.

*Frank Gamma. Owner Operator, Yalata Nullarbor Tours.*

'I'm doing a job this morning, but if you need help later, or any time, call me.' His brown eyes looked sympathetic. 'I know about chasing the missus, fella. Been there, done that.'

He took his phone from his top pocket. 'Gimme your number. I'll text you a few places to stay in Perth. Good locations, decent grub, nothing too flash.'

'Thank you.' Hamish's voice was croaky. Out here, this blackfella was his only friend.

He recited his number, watching Frank key the digits into his phone.

'Well, hooroo.' The van doors clamped shut and Frank accelerated away.

Hamish tucked the card into his pocket and walked across to the hotel, craving a shower.

*But my gear's in the car.*

He sat down in the place where he'd been the night before, on a wooden bench in a corner of the veranda.

'G'day there. Marcelo said you'd be along.'

The pigtailed waitress appeared next to him, her breath rank with cigarettes and coffee.

'You need some brekkie, love?' She placed a menu card in front of him.

Hamish suddenly realised he was ravenous.

'Yes, please. But, uh, I don't have my wallet.'

'No, stupid. I do. That was some night you boys had, eh?' She put her hands on her hips. 'Marcelo left in an awful hurry last night, poor thing. Said it was his gut, but I reckon he'd had a skinful.'

Hamish's head was reeling. 'Where did you say my wallet was?'

She nodded in the direction of the hotel. 'In the car with the rest of your stuff, out the back.'

Hamish stood up. 'Show me.'

If he left now, he might just catch them.

He followed the woman through the bar, along a dark hallway that reeked of fried sausages, then out a rear door. There it was, the hatchback, shining yellow in the morning sun.

He opened the driver's door.

'Darl, it's dead.' The woman shook her head.

Hamish turned the key in the ignition.

Nothing.

He tried again.

Zip. Zero. Zilch. Not even a sputter.

'The engine was real hot last night, Marcelo said.'

Hamish peered under the car, spotting the tell-tale ring of dampness beneath.

'Hole in the radiator,' he muttered, reaching under the chassis and pulling the offending stick free. 'Fucker.'

'Happens out here real easy, love,' the woman said. 'Especially at night. You run over a stick, or a rock flies up from the road.'

But Hamish knew it wasn't just an unfortunate accident. The Brazilian had killed it, good and proper. Tampered with it in the night, using a screwdriver or similar to pierce the radiator, making sure he couldn't be followed. If it had been any other mechanical problem, Hamish could have fixed it; a dead battery, even a snapped fan belt. But not a hole in a radiator.

'I'll ask Kev to order you a new one,' the waitress said. 'Only takes forty-eight hours for delivery from Perth.'

*Only forty-eight hours.* Hamish shook his head. He'd been shafted by the Brazilian *again*.

'You okay, love? You look a bit worse for wear. And you'll need an ice pack for that.' She lifted his right hand, all bruised and puffy. 'Fall over pissy, did you?'

He didn't reply.

She tested several of his fingers. 'Nothing's broken, but the swelling's nasty. Best to wrap 'em up.' She looked up at him. 'I'm Rhonda, by the way. What's your name?'

'Hamish.'

'Just you wait here, Hamish, I'll grab the first-aid kit. We'll get you sorted.'

Not soon enough, he thought.

*

Three days later, Hamish was back on the road to Perth, with a bandaged right hand and a new radiator.

His family had seventy-two hours on him, and they'd be ensconced in a caravan park on the coast by now. Perth was one of Australia's smallest capital cities by population, but to Hamish it might as well have been New York. He knew no one there, and had little idea where to start looking for Paula and the kids. If he was lucky, Lachie might text him and tell him their location.

Hamish kept his mobile connected to a recharger as he drove through the hamlets of Salmon Gums, Grass Patch and Scaddan. He could have taken the northern route to Perth through Kalgoorlie, but he'd had his fill of deserts and salt lakes. The southern route, while slightly longer, at least held the promise of ocean views.

Just after he passed through Gibson, a text message arrived from Frank outlining four budget options for Perth, one of which was in Cottesloe.

*Thanks mate*, Hamish typed back, hoping he wouldn't have to use any of them.

He stopped for a coffee at a roadhouse in Esperance, noticing all the other people doing the same. Some were truckies on the job, but everyone else—what the hell were *they* doing? Grey nomads with motorhomes, families with young children in kombi vans, a handful of lone travellers like him, some poring over thick Lonely Planet guides like converts reading the Bible. A German cyclist, gaunt and hairy-legged, who was having an animated disagreement with a stern-mouthed roadhouse staff member about the price of a sandwich.

'Look!' cried the German, pointing at a fluorescent yellow sign stuck to the refrigerator. 'It says two dollars special.'

'Read the fine print,' replied the attendant in a bored tone. 'That's for salad sandwiches only. You've picked ham and cheese. That's five dollars.'

The cyclist ranted in German before throwing his money onto the counter. Then he turned and flounced away, click-clacking across the tiled floor in his cleats. He was obviously hungry; he'd devoured half the sandwich before he was even out the door.

*We're all crazy*, Hamish thought, watching the German straddle his heavily laden bicycle and push off towards the road. *Every single one of us, thinking we're so damn important.*

Hamish drained the last of his coffee and, feeling a little morose, reached for his phone again.

Lachie had done the right thing by him in Eucla, maybe he would again.

He began composing a message.

*Lachie, are you still in Perth? Where are you staying?*

Just as he pressed 'send', an instant Skype message arrived.

*Hi Hamo, r u online?*

*Do u miss me?*

He zeroed in on Lisel's profile picture, as he'd often done when they'd fooled around online. He glanced around the roadhouse, as if someone might read his mind. But no one did; everyone else was engrossed in the minutiae of *their* moment. Chewing gum or sucking barley sugar, guzzling soft drinks or deep-fried food, restraining unruly kids or not even trying.

*We're all human*, Hamish thought. I'm *human.*

*Yes I miss u*, he typed back, feeling guilty as he did.

She replied instantly.

*R u ok?*

*Not really*, he thought, looking around the roadhouse at the sea of unknown faces. His own family was close by, but not close enough. He desperately needed some human contact.

*Am in Esperance*, he typed, not answering her question.

*Wow! So near 2 me. Only 700 k.*

Then, quickly, another message.

*R u coming 2 Perth, Hamo?*

He paused, nursing his right hand in his left, thinking about Paula. He'd pursued her across the desert, trying to make amends, and been rewarded with two altercations with a Brazilian. His family had been so preoccupied welcoming Marcelo into their fold, they'd almost forgotten about him. Yes, he'd fucked up. But their punishment was disproportionate to his crime.

*Yes*, he typed back to Lisel.

*OMG!* came the immediate response.

He laughed aloud.

*Where r u staying, Hamo?*

He stalled for a moment.

Another message arrived.

*We have a guest room. I can ask my mum. I can make something up. Let me think.*

A long time ago, he'd imagined flying to Perth on a business trip. Meeting Lisel in a park, maybe. Reaching out and touching that soft red hair of hers, kissing her if he was really lucky. But staying in her home? That was beyond the stuff of fantasies.

*Be careful*, he warned himself. *She lives with her parents.*

He stood up and ordered another coffee.

Suddenly he felt as nervous as hell. Good nervous, like when he was fourteen and about to kiss a girl for the first time.

Several minutes later, another Skype message appeared.

*U can be a sports teacher billet. We've had two stay at our house b4, a lady and a man. I can ask Mum 2day. Get back to u l8r.*

He reread the message, trying to envisage it.

If Lisel's mother agreed, then somehow discovered he *wasn't* a teacher, she'd call the police for sure. He quickly Googled 'age of consent in Western Australia', aware that sometimes states and territories differed on these matters.

It was sixteen years old in the west, he discovered, the same as in Victoria. Lisel was old enough to decide for herself.

His cock sprang up in his jeans like a jack-in-the-box.

Walking to the car, he wondered who would contact him first—Lachie or Lisel.

*Either way, things are looking up.*

*

Their messages arrived within the hour.

Lachie dutifully advised him that they were staying at a caravan park near Cottesloe Beach, and would be heading north in a few days.

*Have fun!* Hamish replied.

And then Lisel's Skype message.

*I faked a note from school about teacher billets. Mum said yes. U can stay 2night and tomorro. But u need to go out during the day. I said u r training Year 7 and yr name is Hamish Black.*

Hamish began typing, but another message arrived.

*What time will u get here?*

It was an eight-hour drive to Perth.

*Around six o'clock*, Hamish replied.

*Okay. I am working at Maccas til 10,* she wrote, posting a sad-looking emoticon.

Hamish couldn't imagine a girl like Lisel working at a fast-food chain.

*I will sneak into ur room after Mum is in bed.*

*All wet now just thinking about u.*

*This was meant 2 b Hamo.*

He thought for a moment, then typed another message.

*Will your dad be home?*

It took several moments before she responded.

*My dad's dead.*

*Thank God for that,* Hamish thought.

*

Munglinup, Jerramungup, Manjimup. Long blackfella names for the arse end of the world, deserted forest country. Then a swathe of suburban shit-holes at which he didn't care to stop, before suddenly, Perth's skyscrapers towering like shiny beacons in a majestic sky. Manicured gardens and bike paths. Wide streets, with enough sandstone to offer a sense of history. Beaches, white and long and sandy, close to everything. A city neither big nor busy, but still cosmopolitan.

*It's paradise,* Hamish concluded. *Totally underrated by east coasters. And Lisel lives here.*

He looked up her address and plugged it into the GPS, then swore under his breath.

He'd assumed Mandurah was a suburb of Perth; it was actually seventy kilometres south. He'd driven through it already. The return trip would take another fifty minutes.

Night had fallen by the time he finally pulled up in front of 9 James Street. The unit block was neat and Mediterranean-style, four storeys high with a wall around its perimeter and a security gate. It was perched on the edge of a man-made canal, just one in a long row of almost identical apartment blocks.

It was past eight o'clock, much later than he'd said he'd arrive, but still two hours before Lisel was due home. Perhaps he'd turn in early, pleading fatigue.

As he got out of the car, he began to feel apprehensive.

*If it's not working, I can always leave.*

At the security gate, he pressed number nine.

'Yes?' A female voice, soft and insipid.

'It's Hamish Black . . . the teacher billet.'

'Oh yes, come in.'

An electronic beeping signalled the opening of the gate.

Hamish walked into the foyer and checked the unit listing. Pressing the elevator call bell, he straightened his shoulders and waited.

Man, he needed to do a shit. It always happened when he was nervous or excited. Before his Sunday-morning cycles, before important work meetings. Before contacting Lisel by Skype.

*Lisel.* He sucked in his stomach, doubting he was good enough for her. But every part of his body was thrumming at the prospect of finally meeting her later that night.

The elevator doors opened, then closed behind him.

Level one, level two. He began to sweat. Level three. Another bell announced his arrival.

He strode out of the lift, attempting to look relaxed.

A woman was standing in the doorway of unit twelve, holding the door ajar with her foot.

'Mr Black?' Her smile was like Lisel's.

He extended his hand. 'Call me Hamish.'

'I'm Toni.' She brushed her ginger-coloured fringe out of her eyes. 'Come in.'

She would have been beautiful once, he thought. A willowy, well-proportioned body in a long figure-hugging dress. Summery green eyes, warm and friendly. But the sun hadn't been kind to her pale skin, which was smattered with freckles and moles. And when she turned to speak to him, he noticed the deep lines on her face. She had to be late forties at least, Hamish guessed, maybe even early fifties.

She made small talk as she held the door open.

*How was your flight?*

*Have you been to Mandurah before?*

*Mind the step.*

Then she showed him down a dimly lit hallway, with several closed doors on either side.

She opened the first one. 'This is Lisel's room. She's still at work.'

It was a shrine to pink and purple. A single bed was adorned with a heart-shaped cushion inscribed with the word 'LOVE'. A white French provincial bed-head, with chiffon scarves wound around its cast-iron knobs. A framed version of the photo Lisel used for her Skype profile stood on a desk, next to a computer covered with a pink dust protector.

Toni flicked off the light and shut the door again.

'That's my room,' she said, gesturing to a closed door, 'and here's the bathroom. But you can use the laundry next to your room, it has a toilet and a shower. Here's the kitchen and the lounge room.'

They walked through the living area.

'And this is the guest room.' She opened the door. 'Quietest spot in the house. When the washing machine's not on.' She laughed.

Inside, the furniture was minimal: just a bed and a desk with a computer on it. Double doors led out to a leafy balcony overlooking the garden. He noticed the folded towel, the face washer, two small canisters of shampoo and conditioner. Nice touches, typical of a mothering type. Paula would have done the same thing, he thought involuntarily.

'Thank you for having me at such short notice.'

'No trouble,' said Toni. 'We've done it before.'

*We.* In the absence of a husband, Hamish wondered how many other family members there might be.

'Is it just you and your daughter?'

'Yes. My husband passed away three years ago.'

'I'm sorry.'

'It's been tough, being alone.' Toni shrugged. 'But it's getting a little easier now.'

Suddenly Hamish began to wonder whether he shouldn't just leave before Lisel arrived home. Toni's single-parenting woes weren't something he wanted to hear right now.

'Would you like some dinner?' she asked. 'You must be hungry.'

'Ah, no, thank you.'

She waited, as if for an explanation.

'I had a meal earlier. And I've got to . . . prepare for tomorrow.'

'Where are you doing the training?' she asked. 'At school?'

He tried to recall the story he'd agreed with Lisel. 'I'm not sure. I'll check the schedule.'

'I can give you a lift to wherever you need to go.' She smiled. 'Just let me know tomorrow.'

'Thanks.'

He'd have to consult with Lisel and determine a way to decline Toni's offer.

'It's Year Nine you're training, isn't it?'

He nodded in a noncommittal way.

'Must be difficult playing soccer when you've got a sore leg and . . .' She pointed at his hand. 'What happened?'

'I hurt it boxing.'

It was the first thing that came to mind, his boxing classes in Glen Waverley. He'd sprained a finger that way before.

'And the leg?' She eyed his knee brace.

'Skiing accident,' he said. 'But it's completely healed. I'm just wearing the brace for support.'

'You're certainly very active.' She laughed. 'But then you *are* a sports teacher.' She kept smiling, until he looked away. 'Is there anything else I can do for you?'

'No, thank you,' he said. 'Goodnight, Toni.'

'Sleep well,' she said, closing the guest-room door behind her.

# 13

He'd been waiting for what felt like hours. After a shit, a shower, and a shave, his usual routine.

Forty-five minutes had passed since Lisel was supposed to arrive home. He'd peeked out into the lounge room once, to find everything in darkness. Toni's bedroom door, at the other end of the hallway, was closed. He'd heard her retire just before ten, after she'd finished the last of the dishes and watched a bit of television.

Still, they'd have to be careful not to wake her, Hamish thought. Vigilant bloody mothers—everything they did would have to be super silent.

The idea revved him up even more.

He was wearing a pair of red cotton boxers and a new grey t-shirt. Not that she'd see them up close, they couldn't even risk turning on the light. He reached beneath the bed and found the small tin of mints he'd secreted there, next to the packet of condoms.

And then, a sound.

The softest click of a door handle being turned.

A lithe silhouette appeared in the doorway for a moment, then the door closed again.

'Hamo?'

'Lisel?' He sat up in the bed. 'I'm here.'

'Shhh.'

He saw nothing, but he could sense her closer now. He could smell her, a sweet, freshly-showered fragrance of jasmine and musk.

His dick throbbed against his boxers.

'Lie down,' she whispered. 'We can't wake Mum.'

'I want to hold you . . .'

'Shhh.' A fingertip touched his lips.

He felt soft hands on his shoulders, lightly pushing him back onto the bed.

He waited, feverish with anticipation.

Suddenly she straddled him, her thighs next to his hips. She lowered her pelvis against his and began to rub herself against him. He gasped and almost creamed himself on the spot.

'Lisel . . .'

She cupped a gentle hand over his mouth. 'Shhh.'

His hands stroked the side of her thighs; she was wearing light cotton pants, pyjamas maybe. His right hand was bruised, he couldn't feel anything with it. But he sure as hell could feel her crotch rubbing against his.

She pushed his t-shirt up and over his head. He reached up to do the same, but she caught hold of his hands.

'Hold this,' she whispered, guiding his hands to the cast-iron bed-head behind him. Then, he felt fabric against his wrists, being looped around and around.

'What . . . ?'

'Just scarves,' she whispered, giggling a little.

She pulled the fabric tight, fastening his wrists to the bedhead.

He felt his cock deflate a little. Lisel was clearly more experienced than most girls her age.

She lay her chest against his and murmured in his ear, 'You are so hot, Hamo.'

His cock lurched upwards again.

He strained to kiss her, but without the use of his arms, he couldn't reach her.

'Please, Lisel. Kiss me.'

Their lips met and he tasted her for the first time; minty, like she'd just brushed her teeth. Her soft tongue flickered expertly around his, before pulling his tongue hard into her mouth.

'We don't have much time, Hamo,' she whispered. 'Fuck me now.'

He groaned aloud.

'Shhh.'

Her weight shifted and she lifted her pelvis from his. Then suddenly she moved off the bed.

The scarves around his wrists gave a little, but he left them there. He heard fabric dropping to the floor, the soft sound of Lisel removing her clothes.

Suddenly she tugged at his boxers, pulling them down his legs and off his feet.

He waited, his cock pushing up into the air, desperate to be inside her.

'The condoms are under the bed,' he whispered.

He sensed her reaching for the small packet he'd stashed there, before hearing the sound of a plastic sachet being opened. He *hated* condoms—but teenage pregnancy scared him more. Then he felt her fingers touching the head of his rod. Her lips over the top, drawing him into her mouth, deeper and deeper.

He arched his back, on the verge of orgasm.

'Lisel, I—'

She drew back immediately, leaving his dick wet and pulsing.

He waited, his heart thudding in his ears.

Then he felt the rubber ring on the tip of his cock, slowly rolling down his shaft. Gently but firmly, getting it right.

She pressed the base of his cock harder than he would have liked. His dick sagged a little with the force.

And then she was on the bed again, hovering over him, legs straddling his hips.

She waited, teasing him until he couldn't stand it any longer. Then she sank onto his cock.

He hissed aloud.

She began switching her hips back and forth.

The sweet intoxication of being inside her, finally, after fantasising about it for so long. It was building for him, faster than ever before.

'Lisel, I'm—'

She moaned aloud and thrashed her hips; he could feel her contracting around his cock.

That was enough for him.

He exploded into the condom as she collapsed on top of him, whimpering a little. They lay panting together in the darkness.

'That was amazing,' he whispered, feeling his heartbeat thumping at his temples. 'I've wanted you forever.'

He felt her tits now, against his chest. He wanted to reach up and hold them in his hands, soft and smooth.

His dick started to tingle again, even though he'd just dropped his load. She'd had that effect on him right from the beginning.

He began to work his wrists out of the scarves she'd used to tie him up. 'I want to see you,' he whispered, pulling one hand free. 'Let's switch on the light, your mum won't wake up.'

'But we're *dead* if she does,' she whispered back, rolling off the bed.

'Lisel . . .' He pulled the other hand free and sat up, groping for the bedside lamp. He could sense her moving away, but he didn't want her to go.

'Wait,' he called.

'I have to work tomorrow,' she said. He heard the sound of the door handle being turned softly.

And then she was gone.

Hamish lay in the unlit room, his eyes wide open, half shocked, half elated by what he'd just done. He stroked his chest, absently twisting the hairs that sprang from it. He could feel a slight twinge in his hip flexors; the aftermath of all that thrusting.

Damn, it felt *good*.

He mightn't have a foreign accent, but he still knew how to satisfy a woman; Lisel had practically mewed like a kitten. After the big dry with Paula—she hadn't had an orgasm for months—it was reassuring to know that the problem didn't reside with *him*.

The mental image of his wife assailed him.

*As of right now, I am an adulterer.*

*

'Did you sleep well?'

'Yes, thanks.'

Hamish looked at the bowl of granola and fruit that Toni placed in front of him. A pot of freshly brewed coffee and a small jug of milk rested on a placemat nearby.

'You certainly know how to look after your guests.' He poured himself a cup of coffee, avoiding her gaze.

'Lisel told me you're teaching Year Seven at Cottesloe today. And you don't need a lift?'

'That's right.' He glanced at Lisel's bedroom door, thankful she'd spoken to her mother. Wondering when she'd done it; he hadn't heard them talking.

As if reading his mind, Toni explained, 'she woke up early and went back to bed. She was exhausted, poor thing.'

Hamish was relieved. He realised he didn't want to see Lisel. In fact, all he wanted to do was get out.

'McDonald's is terrible, rostering kids so late on a school night,' Toni continued. 'But it's a twenty-four-hour restaurant, so there's always plenty of work. And without Lisel's dad around anymore . . .' She looked pensive. 'It's a big help with the pocket money.'

She passed a jug of orange juice to Hamish.

'So, how long have you been teaching?'

He almost choked on his granola.

'Oh, well, let's see.' He looked at the ceiling, as if mentally calculating his length of service. 'Seventeen years now. Gets away on you.'

She smiled. 'That's what happens when you enjoy something.'

'Yes, I love it,' he continued, because he felt he had to. 'Teaching's the most satisfying job on the planet. Helping young minds to flourish. I wouldn't do anything else.' He needed to deflect her attention. 'What do you do, Toni?'

'I work in child protection with the police.'

He swallowed. 'You're a police officer?'

She laughed. 'No, no, I'm an administrator. I've been seconded to the police from my job in the Department for Child Protection.'

So she was a public servant. He heaved an internal sigh of relief.

'Sounds interesting,' he lied.

Toni proffered a plate of toast. 'Well, I don't think I'd describe it as *interesting*. Reading about kids whose lives have been wrecked by domestic violence, sexual abuse, that sort of thing. It's usually all within the family, of course. Or people known to the family.'

'Of course,' said Hamish, beginning to feel uncomfortable. 'Society needs people like you, helping those poor kids.'

He directed the conversation towards more mundane topics; the weather in Perth, its tourist attractions and Toni's life story. It was far safer to keep the conversation squarely focused on her. And she wasn't entirely uninteresting, having worked in Edinburgh, Toronto and Alice Springs. She was particularly passionate about Indigenous issues; her face went a youthful pink when talking about her work in Australia's red centre.

When that topic was exhausted, her eyes met his. She smiled in a conspiratorial kind of way.

'Will you be wanting dinner tonight?' she asked. 'I'm slow-cooking a sausage hotpot.'

'No, thanks.' This was his chance to escape. 'I received a message that tomorrow's training's been cancelled,' he lied, gesturing at his mobile phone. 'So I won't have to stay another night after all.'

'Oh.' She looked disappointed. 'Why?'

He struggled to think of a reason. 'Some staffing mix-up.'

He pushed his chair back from the breakfast table. 'Thanks, Toni, I'd better be going.'

She stood up too, blocking his exit. Her hair fell across her shoulders, and her robe slipped open at the chest.

'Let's go wake Lisel up,' she said suddenly. 'I'm sure she'd love to meet you before you go.'

Hamish watched her float down the hallway in the direction of Lisel's bedroom.

'Come on,' she said, looking over her shoulder at him.

As she walked, her robe unwound itself. When she turned again, he caught sight of two long, slender legs. White as white against a short black negligee.

He forced his gaze upwards.

'What?' she asked with a small smile.

Was she *flirting* with him?

He shook his head. 'Nothing.'

She stood for a moment, her hands on her hips, looking at him with cool green eyes.

'Come on, let's wake Lisel.' She beckoned to him with one finger. 'It's time she got up.'

'Please, let her sleep,' he objected, following Toni down the hallway. 'She mightn't . . .'

'Shhh.' She turned at the doorway and smiled like they were sharing a secret. 'Let's surprise her.'

She opened the door.

Sunlight speared into the room of pink. There was no one in the single bed, but he noticed the open book on the bedside table, a half-drunk orange juice, an iPod recharging at the wall.

'Where's Lisel?' he asked.

Toni shook the bathrobe off her shoulders. 'Right here.'

Hamish stared at her.

'You don't think a seventeen-year-old could give you a ride like last night, do you?'

She walked over to the single bed and climbed atop on all fours, facing away from him. Then she flicked up her negligee, revealing two firm white buttocks and a ginger bush below.

'You need a woman of *experience* for a fuck like that.'

*Jesus.* Hamish began to back away.

'Can't handle the truth, Hamo?' Toni sprang off the bed, landing a metre from him. 'We've *both* taken liberties with it.'

He fled down the hallway, through the lounge room and into the guest room, slamming the door behind him. Panicked, he began piling things into his bag, fumbling with the zip.

He heard the door open.

She leaned against the doorframe, naked now. Speckled-egg skin, long limbs, tits like limp balloons. A too-old face on top of a sun-damaged neck.

'I'm here for the taking, Hamo. We're good together. I can set you off like a firecracker.'

Hamish swallowed, immobilised.

A loud buzzing echoed along the hallway; an impertinent, imperative sound.

Neither of them moved.

Then it buzzed again, another three times.

'Just let me get rid of that.' Toni took a bath towel from the back of the chair and wrapped it around herself.

She began walking towards the intercom in the hallway.

Hamish heard the pinging sound of the elevator's arrival in the vestibule beyond the front door.

Toni wheeled around. 'Hide,' she hissed.

He stood rooted to the spot.

'Fucking *hide*, I said.'

She slammed the guest-room door in his face.

He heard the sound of a key in the lock, and the front door opening.

'Hi, honey,' Toni cooed in a syrupy tone. 'Did you forget something?'

'My iPod.' A youthful voice.

Hamish seized his bag, threw open the door and barged across the living area and down the hallway.

He stopped at the sight of the girl in the doorway.

*Lisel.* In all her perfection.

Tall, with deer-like limbs protruding from her blue school uniform. Breasts sitting high on her chest, porcelain skin, rosebud lips. Everything he'd ever imagined, and more.

Eyes that looked right through him.

'Who's this?' she demanded of her mother.

'A friend.' Toni pushed the iPod into her daughter's hand.

'I can see that.' Lisel's tone was petulant. 'You *said* you weren't going to do this again. I'm telling Dad.'

*Dad?*

'Don't you dare.' Toni lunged at her daughter, but Lisel dodged and bolted out the front door.

Hamish rushed after her, his bag clipping Toni's legs as he passed.

'Don't go, Hamo,' Toni called.

He galloped down the stairs after Lisel.

By the time he reached her, she was already at the front gate of the unit block.

'Lisel,' he puffed, winded by the running, his left knee screaming.

He put a hand on her arm.

'Don't touch me,' she yelled. 'My mum's mentally ill, you know. She can't help what she does. But the men who come here, *you're* all the same. Thinking with your dicks, taking advantage of her.'

She picked up a fluorescent-pink skateboard that was leaning against the front fence, and threw her bag over her shoulder.

Then she took three long running strides and skated away down the road, her red hair trailing behind her.

'Hamo.'

He looked up in the direction of the voice.

Toni was leaning over the balcony, three storeys up, dangling the keys to the hatchback from her fingers.

'Keep the bloody car,' he said.

He strode away with his bag, as fast as his weak knee would carry him.

*

'Hamo, are you there?'

Hamish grunted into the phone. Grateful to God, if there was one.

'I can't hear what you're saying, mate. Where are you, Hamo?'

He could hear Doggo whispering to Tina.

*Can't keep a good man down*, Hamish was trying to say.

'What's that?' Doggo sounded anxious.

*You worry too much*, Hamish mumbled.

'Where are you, Hamo? Can you tell me slowly?'

*Pervert. Perfect. Pert. Perth.*

'Did you say Perth, mate?'

*Yesss.*

Hamish reached for the wine bottle and, finding it empty, threw it away.

Then he lay his head on the grass. The earth was pushing up against his right ear. Spiky green lines obscured his vision, but he could still see the sky. A flawless ceiling for an imperfect planet.

'Keep your phone charged and *on*, Hamo.' Doggo's voice was persistent. 'Hang on, Tina wants to say something.'

Hamish couldn't reply. The air was pressing down on him so hard, he wanted to puke.

'Hamo.' Tina's high-pitched voice. 'I'm not letting Doggo get on a plane until you tell me *exactly* where you're staying.'

*A two-storey sandstone box, the youth hostel in the city.*

'You're mumbling, Hamo.'

*Backpackers on Wellington Street.*

'Did you say a backpackers? Where?'

His tongue wouldn't wrap itself around 'Wellington'.

*A street like gumboots*, he tried to say.

He'd never been so pissed in his life.

*Pissed newts. Bum roots. Cum toots. Gumboots.*

*Yes, gumboots.*

*Only a different word for them.*

*It's a city in New Zealand too*, he wanted to say.

*Ah, bugger it, I give up.*

*Thank you Doggo, thank you Tina.*

*Thank you ball boys, thank you linesmen.*

He pushed the phone away into the jungle and closed his eyes.

*

'Who's that?' Hamish tried to sit up.

'It's Doggo, mate.'

Hamish began to cry.

Doggo's hand closed over his. 'You're in hospital now, buddy. It'll be alright.'

'Hospital?'

He couldn't keep his eyes open long enough to see Doggo, but he could still feel his friend's hand.

'What happened?'

'That was some bender you went on, mate. Gave yourself alcohol poisoning. The youth hostel found you unconscious on their nature strip on Friday night. Thought you were dead. Luckily you called me before you passed out. I got here as quick as I could.'

There was something that Hamish felt he needed to know, but his mind couldn't pinpoint it.

'How long have I been here?'

'Been two days since they found you. It's Sunday afternoon. You're on IV fluids now.'

'Where's Tina?' Hamish had a feeling he'd spoken to her recently.

'Back in Melbourne with the kids.'

'Where are *we*, Doggo?'

Doggo paused. 'Mate, this is Perth.' His tone was disbelieving. 'You're in Royal Perth Hospital.'

Suddenly it all came rushing back.

Chasing Paula and the kids across the Nullarbor Plain. Losing them in Eucla, and again in Norseman, after Marcelo did him over. Looking up Lisel in Mandurah. Wanting her more than anything. Screwing her crazy bitch mother instead.

Bile rushed into his throat.

'Mate, I'll call the nurse,' Doggo said.

The vomit sprayed out of Hamish's nose and mouth.

He couldn't stop retching.

# 14

The waiting room at Royal Perth Hospital was swarming with suffering humanity.

While Marcelo squirmed with discomfort, Paula helped fill in the required forms. Discovering along the way that his surname was Fernandes, that his birthday was on Christmas Day, that his blood type was the rarest in the world. All small pieces of information that helped her to feel closer, somehow, to Marcelo Fernandes.

When a nurse finally hurried over to see them, Paula almost hugged her. It had been nine hours since they'd left Norseman in the dead of night and, as far as she could tell, Marcelo's appendix hadn't ruptured—although they'd pulled over several times and watched him disappear into the scrub to vomit. The nurse checked his vital signs, all of which were normal. But given his obvious distress, he was triaged to high priority and taken for clinical assessment soon after.

'I'll wait here and mind your backpack,' Paula said, when a doctor called his name.

'No, no. I take the bag with me. My mother's urn is in there.'

She nodded, understanding.

'Don't wait for me.' Marcelo smiled weakly at her. 'Take the others to the campsite first. They are tired.'

There was sense in his suggestion; everyone was overwrought from the long pre-dawn journey. She really couldn't ask them to wait much longer in the hospital car park.

'Okay,' she said. 'Have you got your phone?'

Marcelo looked anxious. 'The battery is dead, I forgot to recharge.'

'No matter.' Paula tore a small piece of paper from her diary and scribbled down her number. 'Just call me on one of the public phones in the foyer, as soon as you've seen the doctor.'

She held out an envelope of money she'd withdrawn from the hospital ATM, her maximum daily limit. 'Take it.'

'What's this?'

'You're not covered by Medicare,' she explained. 'You'll have to pay. This won't be enough if you need an operation, but we'll talk more once the doctor's seen you.'

'I can call my father,' he objected. 'He can transfer money.'

'Just see the doctor first.'

She pushed the envelope into his hands.

'Thank you, *Pow-la*.' His brown eyes were grateful.

She watched the nurse escort Marcelo beyond the opaque doors.

*

Twenty-four hours passed; she assumed Marcelo must have undergone surgery.

At the forty-eight hour mark, with still no word from him, she telephoned the hospital.

'How do you spell the surname?' asked the operator.

Paula spelled it out.

The operator's fingers tapped at a keyboard. 'We have no record of a patient of that name.'

'But I was there in emergency with him,' Paula insisted. 'He had appendicitis.'

'Was he *admitted* to the hospital, ma'am?' The operator sounded irritable.

'Can you check for me?' asked Paula. 'He was definitely seen by a doctor in emergency, but I don't know if—'

The operator interrupted. 'Are you a relative, ma'am?'

'No.'

'Then I'm sorry, I can't disclose that information.'

Paula struggled not to snap. 'He's a friend from overseas, he has no family here. I'm travelling with him. Please, can you help?'

The operator exhaled. 'Ma'am, patients come in to emergency and they're seen by a doctor. They're either admitted to hospital, or they're treated for their complaint and sent home.'

'So he was sent home?'

'I'm sorry, ma'am, I can't disclose that information.'

Paula hung up.

'What's wrong?' asked Sid, setting his newspaper aside. Caitlin pulled out her earbuds and Lachie looked up from *Moondroids from Uranus*.

'Marcelo's gone.'

'Where?' asked Caitlin.

Paula's eyes began to smart. 'They've got no record of him at the hospital. Well, they do, but they won't tell me what happened because I'm not a relative.' She felt like kicking down a door. 'He was seen by a doctor, but he wasn't admitted. So we can only assume . . .' She shook her head, unable to fathom it. 'He was sent away.'

'But why didn't he call you?' Sid looked concerned. 'You gave him your number, didn't you? And he had money?'

'Yes, yes. I gave him some.' Paula frowned. 'But maybe it wasn't enough? I should have just *waited* for him at the hospital.'

She began straightening the beach towels on the makeshift washing line, fighting back tears.

What could have happened to Marcelo?

'I hope he's not in trouble,' she said, after a moment. 'I mean, he's not used to our medical system, he doesn't know anyone—'

'Maybe he just doesn't want to travel with us anymore,' Lachie interjected. 'Maybe he's *over* us.'

Her son's face was hidden behind his book again. Clearly he was still upset about what he'd seen in Norseman.

'I reckon he would've said something if that was the case, Lachie,' said Sid. 'Remember what we agreed in Adelaide? That we'd talk, if things weren't working out? And look,'—he pointed at the surfboard and guitar case still strapped to the roof racks—'he would've taken those if he'd intended to leave.'

Paula's mouth went dry.

*Surely Marcelo wouldn't have just slunk away?*

*We had a connection. I know we did.*

*And we shared the beginnings of a kiss.*

Suddenly she was struck by an awful thought; *maybe Marcelo left* because *of that kiss. Specifically her behaviour following it, her aloof body language that said*, I choose my children over you.

A sick feeling gripped her stomach and she slumped down at the card table.

Caitlin stayed perched on her chair, gazing out over Cottesloe Beach. 'Well, whatever's happened to Marcelo, he was . . . nice.'

Paula didn't trust herself to speak.

'Did you have a crush on him, Catie?' Sid asked suddenly, with a grandfatherly wink.

'No,' said Caitlin.

*She's lying*, thought Paula, avoiding her father's eyes. Hoping he wouldn't ask *her* the same question.

'I think we've *all* had a bit of a crush on him,' Sid said. 'He's a remarkable young man. It's okay to like someone, Catie.'

Caitlin blushed. 'He was nice, but . . . no. The way he was training us was cool.'

'I liked that too,' said Sid, patting his granddaughter's knee. 'Had me feeling like a whippersnapper again.'

They sat without speaking for several minutes, watching the beautiful people of Cottesloe power-walk, cycle and rollerblade their way along a postcard-perfect foreshore. In the day's deepening light, the sky looked like a giant artist's palette, streaked burnished gold, mauve and tangerine.

Colours to make you cry or sing, Paula reflected, or both.

Sid stood up and wrapped his arm around Paula's shoulders. 'What say we all go visit the hospital first thing tomorrow and see what we can find?'

Paula nodded at him, grateful.

*

'We have *no* record of admission,' repeated the woman behind the administration desk. 'And in the absence of proof of kinship, we can't release details about his consult, either.' She looked from Sid to Paula.

'Ma'am, this boy is new to Australia,' said Sid, with a polite smile. 'We're his only friends. Can you at *least* tell us what time he left the hospital? That would mean a lot to us.'

The woman sighed. 'I'm not supposed to do this.'

She clicked through several screens on her computer. 'Quarter to five pm on the day he came in. *Please* don't ask me anything else.'

'No, ma'am, and thank you.' Sid ushered Paula back towards the waiting room.

Lachie and Catie looked up from their magazines.

'Any luck?' asked Lachie.

Paula shook her head.

Back in the car, they did several aimless loops of the city.

'Mum,' said Catie, after almost thirty minutes, 'I don't think we're going to find Marcelo this way.'

'And I'm hungry,' said Lachie.

'You're cooking lunch, mate,' Sid reminded him. 'And watch that whiney tone.' He turned to Paula. 'We probably should head back to Cottesloe and think up a new plan.'

Paula nodded. 'Lachie might be right. Maybe Marcelo just didn't want to keep travelling with us.'

'Maybe,' said Sid, veering into a U-turn bay. 'Or maybe something's happened that none of us expected, something we couldn't have dreamed up if we tried. Life's like that sometimes.'

They drove back to Cottesloe in silence.

*

Four days later, after visits to all the major backpacker hostels and several tourist information centres, Paula decided it was time to move on.

'We've done our best to find him,' she said, gazing out at another Cottesloe sunset. 'That's all we can do, really.'

'I reckon, Mum,' agreed Lachie.

'He'll be fine,' Caitlin added.

She looked between her children, resenting how willing they seemed to let Marcelo go.

'I wish *I* could be so sure.'

Sid squeezed her hand. 'Look, it's disappointing to lose Marcelo. But we started out as the Awesome Foursome, right? And you know, we don't have to stop our training, either.' He stooped and picked up a pair of Lachie's sneakers, taking one in each hand and pitching them at the children, chuckling at their shrieks.

'We'll get back to Gramps's life lessons tomorrow,' he said. 'Next lesson is "Valuing our Bodies". We'll begin with a beach run along Cottesloe. You lot can jog, I'll shuffle. Then the young 'uns can teach me a thing or two about push-ups and burps.'

'Burp*ees*,' said Caitlin.

Paula felt fatigued already. 'Isn't it time for Drinkypoos, Dad?'

'But we're swearing off alcohol for the next four weeks, love. It's all part of valuing our bodies.'

Paula gaped at him. 'You're kidding, aren't you?'

'Nope.' Sid opened his esky and turned it upside down, shaking out the last of the ice for emphasis. 'We're all out of grog anyway. No soft drink for the kids, either. Even the diet variety is full of chemicals. Their insides must've been brown and frothy back at Apollo Bay.' He reached out and pinched Caitlin, who squealed.

Then he turned to Paula. 'Nothing naughty in our bodies for the next month, until we get to Darwin. Marcelo started this lesson, but *I'm* going to finish it.'

*

Over the next few weeks, Paula dropped a dress size. Sid's 'valuing our bodies' lesson prescribed a stringent daily exercise routine, plotted against their itinerary.

She'd already lost some weight en route to Perth, largely due to the change in routine. Back home in Melbourne, she'd often found herself comfort eating when she was bored or alone. She hadn't recognised the habit, until the road trip forced her to stop. Helped, of course, by the presence of Marcelo from Adelaide onwards; having a handsome Brazilian nearby conveniently curbed her appetite. Then, after Marcelo's inexplicable disappearance in Perth, she didn't feel much like eating at all.

'We'll be fit and fabulous for Christmas Day in Darwin,' Sid kept intoning, whenever one of the children complained about their new regimen. Paula didn't object; in fact, this was one life lesson she was happy to embrace. Apart from the obvious physical benefits of Gramps's Boot Camp, as Lachie now called it, their strict timetable of fitness-related activities helped keep her mind off Marcelo.

Their days began with stints on their bicycles, taking turns at cycling in front of the ute for ten, fifteen, even twenty kilometres. It slowed down their journey, but better enabled them to appreciate the gifts of the Western Australian coastline. Long, white beaches, unpatrolled and unpopulated, with bottlenose dolphins frolicking in blue breaks. Ancient shells littering the sand, exquisite stars and spirals and fans catching the sunlight in pearly contours. Charcoal-coloured stromatolites in warm, shallow waters, strange fossil-like formations bearing silent witness to prehistoric life on earth. At times Paula felt like a time traveller, lobbed back to an epoch when Australia was inhabited only by its Indigenous people, before nature's gifts were colonised by burgeoning populations and modern tourism.

Most lunchtimes, they pulled off the highway wherever they found themselves, by the beach or in a tiny township. The modest contents of their sandwiches—and the freshness of the bread—varied according to local supply chains. On arrival anywhere, the children made a beeline for the general store to scavenge among unappetising displays of overripe fruit and wilted vegetables. Sometimes they discovered an unexpected treasure—a firm tomato, an unbruised avocado, or fish freshly caught from the Indian Ocean—and carried it back to the caravan like pirate's bounty. But on days when supplies were scarce, they settled for sandwiches of tinned tuna and limp celery.

After lunch, Lachie laid out their beach towels under the caravan's awning, and led them through a floor routine. This was the jiu-jitsu warm-up that Marcelo had taught them at Cactus Beach: twenty burpees, thirty sit-ups, twenty push-ups and a walk along a balance beam. They improvised with whatever they could find; sometimes a low fence, an empty feed trough, or simply a line drawn in the sandy earth.

As days became weeks, Paula found herself using parts of her body long dormant—her deep abdominals, triceps, quadriceps. And she found herself constantly thirsty; the heat of a mid-December day in Western Australia was punishing. Paula often felt so drained after their midday exercise session, she was forced to have a siesta, much to the mirth of Caitlin and Lachie. But she was also becoming stronger. Paula could feel it in her legs, comparing them to her first day on the road: that putrid unisex toilet she'd squatted over in Geelong, her thighs begging for mercy.

*No mercy* was her mantra now.

In the soft light of late afternoons, in the place of Drinkypoos, they would go for a swim or a run—or sometimes both. After dinner, they gathered around a campfire and, in the absence of their Brazilian music-maker, Lachie took up Marcelo's guitar. Lachie had only ever really managed to fumble a few chords, but with the recent inspiration of Marcelo and long afternoons of practice, he mastered several ABBA tunes, 'The House of the Rising Sun' and a simplified version of the Caetano Veloso song that Marcelo had sung nightly.

*Each of us knows the pain and the delight of being who we are.*

As they sang the same songs over and over, Paula gazed up at the cosmic vista above them, frosted diamonds studding a velvety sky.

Sometimes, usually at Sid's prompting, they danced on the sandy earth, moving and weaving and collapsing into helpless laughter. Cackling themselves stupid *without* the benefit of alcohol, Paula was surprised to note. Hours of self-generated entertainment, without an iPad, tablet or laptop to be found.

Their former life in Glen Waverley, the orderly schedule of school and work and weekend timetables, seemed thoroughly alien now.

*When did I stop dancing and singing?* Paula sometimes wondered, on nights such as these.

When did I start just *surviving*?

# 15

The good thing about Doggo was he didn't say jack shit.

They sat together in a café overlooking the Swan River, watching the eclectic folk of Fremantle—a tide of dreadlocked, bare-footed odd-balls—amble past.

'Hungry as hell,' said Hamish.

In hospital, he hadn't eaten much; rehydration was the priority.

'Maaate,' said Doggo. 'I could eat a horse and chase the jockey.'

They dived into their bacon and eggs, a level of comfort between them born of almost three decades of friendship. It was the type of amiable silence Hamish had once imagined might develop in a long-term marriage to the right woman. Complete mutual understanding, no words necessary; Doggo passed Hamish the tomato sauce before he even asked. Only breaking their peace when some nice piece of arse wandered by.

Not that arse held much interest for Hamish now.

Arse was what had gotten him into this whole God-awful mess.

They'd spent five days in Fremantle, holed up in some arty-farty bed-and-breakfast place that Tina had booked online. It did the job, allowing Hamish to recover from the hospitalisation. They'd played poker, read the newspaper, gone out for long walks and hot meals.

And slowly, he'd told Doggo everything. How he'd set out from Melbourne determined to find his family, just wanting his life back. How he'd discovered a foreign bloke in their party, and his increasing concern for Caitlin. The altercations with the Brazilian and the stupid plan he'd hatched to bully him out of Norseman. Its dismal failure and how, with his pride wounded and feeling lonely, he'd started Skyping with Lisel again. How in a moment of weakness he'd followed his dick to Mandurah, falling prey to some sick whore who used her daughter's photo to bait suckers like him. The swamping guilt he now felt for betraying his wife's trust, for *real* this time.

Doggo said all the right things.

*Maaate.*

*You couldn't have known, eh?*

*Could've happened to me.*

*Could've happened to anyone.*

But Doggo's consolations wouldn't last; he was due to fly back to Melbourne in just two days, having taken a whole week off work. It was more than Tina had wanted, and more than Hamish could expect. But the prospect of being by himself again made Hamish's guts twist.

Lifting the coffee mug to his lips, his eyes began to sting.

Doggo noticed, of course.

He put a hand on Hamish's shoulder. 'We've got a strategy, right? You're going to get yourself up to Darwin, meet Paula there, and tell her everything. And I mean *everything.* You're going to spend some time with the kids, then you're going to go home. The sooner you're back in Melbourne, the better.'

Hamish nodded.

'Where did Lachie say they are, again?'

Hamish checked his mobile.

Lachie and Catie had sent several messages from Cottesloe, but Hamish had been too preoccupied in Mandurah to respond. Now they were making their way up the Western Australian coast, heading for the Top End.

'Somewhere north of Carnarvon. Wherever the hell that is.'

'Give 'em a week or two and they'll be in Darwin. You've got to get up there too, buddy. Keep in touch with the kids and stay off the bloody grog.'

Hamish knew he was right.

'Let's book the flight now,' said Doggo, reaching for his telephone.

'Nah, mate. I've got a better idea.'

Hamish showed Doggo a message he'd received from Farken Frank a few days earlier.

*Attention Customers & Friends of Yalata Nullarbor Tours. We have a small tour bus departing Perth–Darwin this week and can offer reduced fares for passengers wishing to travel between 7 and 18 December. Beat the Xmas price hike!*

Doggo rolled his eyes.

'Just catch a flight, for God's sake,' he urged. 'It'll be much quicker, mate.'

'I don't care how long it takes.'

'Just spend the money, Terry Tightarse.'

'It's not about the money, Doggo.'

'Well, what *is* it about, then?'

It was the first time that Hamish had detected a note of impatience in Doggo's voice.

The prospect of spending a lonely week in Darwin waiting for his family was more than unpalatable; Hamish feared he wouldn't be able to stay off the grog. Not all by himself.

He dialled the number on the card.

Frank answered within three rings.

'It's Hamish here. The one you . . . yeah. Look, about that fare you're advertising to Darwin . . . *Five hundred*? Where's the discount in that?'

Doggo was shaking his head and drawing a finger across his throat.

'Seven o'clock tomorrow? Roger that. Pick up from Freo, hang on.'

Hamish read out the address.

'Righto, mate. What's that?' Hamish pursed his lips. 'Alright, five hundred *plus* shared fuel. Shit, man.'

He put down the phone.

'You just got shafted, didn't you?' said Doggo.

Hamish shrugged. 'Yeah, but I owe the guy already.'

*

Hamish threw his bag into the mini-bus and passed Frank an envelope containing ten fifty-dollar notes.

'I'll count 'em,' said Frank, pressing his finger under the seal.

Hamish turned to Doggo, who was standing awkwardly on the kerb.

'Maaate.' Doggo pulled him into a tight hug.

It surprised Hamish, but he didn't shrink from it.

Not until Frank coughed from the driver's seat.

Hamish grasped Doggo's hand and shook it, hard, trying to transmit everything he felt about his friend through the firmness of his grip.

'Thanks for coming over.' Hamish's voice was shaky. 'And say thanks to Tina, too, for putting up with me again.'

'She'd do anything for you, mate. She loves you.' Doggo's eyes flickered a little. 'We all do. See you in Melbourne soon, okay? And *not* bloody anywhere else. I'm not comin' to get you out of the shit somewhere else, mate. Don't go shaggin' another sandgroper.'

Hamish laughed and clapped Doggo on the shoulder. Then he climbed onto the mini-bus, sitting down in the seat immediately behind Frank.

'You got the whole bus to y'self, mate,' said Frank, gesturing at the empty seats behind him. 'It's just you and me to Darwin.'

'Yeah? Well, it's easier to talk from here.'

The doors whipped shut and Frank shifted the bus into gear.

Hamish waved at Doggo until he was out of sight.

After several minutes, Frank spoke again. 'Don't like farken talkin' anyway.'

'What's that?'

'You said you wanna talk. Well, I don't like farken talkin'.'

'Okay.' Hamish said. 'Not much of a tour guide then, are you?'

Frank's mouth, reflected in the rear-view mirror, curled upwards.

Hamish watched the galleries, cafés and antique shops rushing past his window. Paula would've been in her element in Freo, he thought, with all those trendy trinkets for her dustless shelves.

'Which way are we going?' Hamish asked.

'You're payin' me to take you, right?' said Frank. 'So leave it to me.'

Hamish did just that, closing his eyes north of Perth.

*

It was a hot, fitful sleep, plagued by disturbing dreams. Aberrant images of Caitlin and Lachie, Paula and Sid floated like ghosts through the recesses of his mind. Pale-faced, solemn, trying to say something that he couldn't quite discern. And others, too. His dead mother-in-law standing in a car park, holding a rifle. His own mother, sitting in the nursing home in Mallacoota, looking up from a book as if she didn't quite recognise him. His father walking through the door of his childhood home, scooping him up and tossing him into the air. And Hamish, a child again, shrieking with joy. Then, suddenly, the pockmarked face of Lisel—or was it Toni?—pressed up against the front door, her mouth a ragged maw, her eyes blood-shot and unseeing. His father striding to the door and slamming it in her face.

A thumping sound jolted Hamish from sleep. Frank's unblinking eyes were trained on the road ahead, his back erect and unmoving.

'Hit a galah,' he said. 'Farken stupid birds.'

A single pink feather fluttered across the windscreen.

Lulled by the rhythm of the bus rattling along the highway, Hamish closed his eyes again. It was as if everything that had happened in recent months, the unravelling of his ordinary life, suddenly caught up with him. Freed of the need to drive, and still weak from the alcohol poisoning, Hamish abandoned himself to sleep.

It was well after dark when they pulled into Newman, a mining town surrounded by sandy plains of red desert. Frank had managed to cover twelve hundred kilometres from Fremantle in just one day's driving.

They found a pub with basic guest rooms upstairs for travellers and, hungry for a counter meal, walked straight into the bar below.

A pack of miners in high-visibility shirts milled about, playing pool, watching football on gigantic plasma screens and downing beers.

'G'day,' said Hamish, nodding at a small group as he waited at the bar.

A young blond miner scrutinised Hamish, then Frank. His eyes narrowed. 'Where're you blokes from?'

'Melbourne,' said Hamish. 'Frank's from the Nullarbor.'

He gestured to the bartender, trying to attract his attention. The cranky old geezer wouldn't even acknowledge his presence.

'Frankie, eh?' The man folded his arms across his chest and smiled; Hamish noticed then that one of his teeth was gold-plated. 'You boys an item, then?'

Hamish doubted he'd heard him correctly. 'Pardon?'

The blond man nudged a mate in the ribs with his elbow.

'Pardon?' he mimicked Hamish, with an accent reminiscent of Prince Charles. 'We don't have queers in Newman. No ebony-and-ivory action here, ain't that right, Boner?'

A large bearded man wearing a pair of wraparound sunglasses turned towards Hamish. Tattoos covered every exposed section of Boner's skin, except for his face.

'No fuckin' faggots in Newman,' he growled.

The pub turned quiet; the entire room of miners was watching them.

'But we're just here for a meal,' said Hamish, squeaking a little. 'I'm not a pillow-biter.'

Hamish didn't mind homos, as long as they steered clear of him. But out here in the Great Sandy Desert, being gay was clearly a crime.

Frank suddenly appeared at his side.

'That's *not* what you said last night, honey,' Frank purred, laying his arm across Hamish's shoulders. He puckered his lips, leaning forward to kiss Hamish.

His response was reflexive, jerking his head back and knocking Frank sideways.

Frank fell hard, arse up on the wooden floor, collecting two bar stools on his way. The collision was loud, and probably painful.

But Frank looked up at Hamish and began to laugh.

'Farken stupid idiot,' said Frank, shaking his head at Hamish. 'Can't you take a farken joke?'

The miners looked between them, a little uncertainly now.

Frank stood up and dusted off the seat of his pants. Then he turned and rolled his eyes at Boner. 'Farken citysiders. All wound up, aren't they? Tight as a Taiwanese cunt.'

Hamish's mouth dropped open.

Boner roared with laughter. 'Too right, mate.' He clapped Frank on the back. 'Take 'emselves too fuckin' seriously.'

The other miners exploded in convulsive laughter, taking their leader's cue.

Hamish laughed too, as if Frank was his best buddy. As if they poofter-bashed for fun together on the weekend. Then he turned back to the bartender, hiding his relief.

That was almost a lynching, he thought. Until farken Frank intervened, defusing the situation like a munitions expert in landmine country.

The bartender was polishing glasses at the other end of the bar, still ignoring Hamish's entreaties. Must be stone deaf, Hamish thought. Frank, who was now jesting with the miners, called out, 'Get me a

Diet Coke, will ya, Hamish?' He looked around the group. 'Poofters don't drink beer.'

The laughter erupted again.

They spent the next few hours playing pool with the miners, many of them glorified truck drivers on six-figure salaries. Permanent itinerants, flying in and out of Newman every week or ten days, returning to the major centres of Broome, Port Hedland, Perth or Darwin to take their pleasure with wives or whores.

Hard-working, hard-drinking, rough-talking frontier men.

For Hamish, who had always considered himself a bloke's bloke, the night couldn't end soon enough.

*

The next day's drive was lurching and uncomfortable for Hamish, who was nursing a nasty hangover, despite the fact that he'd only drunk one schooner. The recent alcohol poisoning had obviously played havoc with his liver; as soon as Hamish pressed a beer to his lips, he'd felt queasy. He'd drained the glass anyway, mostly because he didn't want to attract the miners' attention again. But that one beer now caused him to groan with every bump on the road. Frank, by contrast, embarked on the fourteen-hundred-kilometre drive to Fitzroy Crossing without complaint.

They stopped once to refuel and drink bland coffee.

'Fuck,' moaned Hamish, as they stood watching the rain stream off the roadhouse roof. 'I feel like shit, man.'

'We're driving a farken long way today, fourteen hours or so. You should've stuck to the Diet Coke last night like me,' said Frank.

'You been to Newman before?'

'Nah.'

Frank reached out and caught some rainwater in his empty styrofoam cup, then lifted it to his lips.

'So how'd you know what to say to those miners last night?' Hamish grimaced, reliving the fear. 'I mean, they thought you and me were . . .'

'Yeah, I know.' Frank rocked his hips back and forth, with a roguish grin. 'I meet fellas like that every day on the Nullarbor. They've got egos bigger than their dicks, mate. Always thinkin' city fellas know nothin' about the bush. I just confirmed their opinions for 'em. Told 'em what they wanted to hear, y'know?'

It was a principle Hamish understood perfectly. He'd used it professionally and personally for years; listening earnestly, like he really cared. Nodding solemnly, before telling his family or staffers whatever they wanted to hear. It stopped the wife nagging, the kids whining, the employees grumbling. Got them off his case long enough to develop a backup plan.

Hamish nodded. 'Yeah, well. How you managed those miners was pretty bloody cluey, mate.'

*Had a few assumptions of my own, before I met this clever bugger.*

'Let's go,' said Frank, glancing at his wristwatch. 'We don't want to be gettin' to Fitzroy Crossing too late.'

Hamish followed him to the van, rather reluctantly. He wanted to linger and watch the tropical downpour. And to talk some more, too.

*

Arriving in Fitzroy Crossing later that night, Hamish suddenly understood Frank's urgency.

The atmosphere was oppressive; an uneasy silence broken only by the distant murmuring of dissatisfied voices. Drunken bodies were splayed under trees, behind bushes, across public benches. Hamish opened a window in the mini-bus and tried not to be caught staring. On one side of the road, young men played cards next to a small campfire, bickering as they gambled. Nearby, a toddler—who should have been in bed hours ago, Hamish thought—played in an abandoned car, perilously close to broken glass. Further along, a teenager shrieked at her barefoot son, slapping his hand away from her handbag. She looked up at Hamish, her eyes hostile, as the mini-bus passed.

*If it's like this on the street, what are their homes like?*

Hamish vaguely recalled a current affairs program he'd watched from the comfort of his suburban lounge room. Something about an alcohol ban yielding positive results in Fitzroy Crossing, reducing domestic violence and other crimes in the area.

But the ban had since been lifted, and the scourge of alcohol had returned.

Hamish had done his fair share of travelling, but he'd never seen anything like it. He tried to imagine a similar spectacle in Glen Waverley: drunk and disorderly adults with their innocent, wide-eyed charges. If it happened there, the police would be called, support services galvanised. Back in Melbourne, playgrounds were closed at the suggestion of a faulty swing; a child with unusual bruising would be interrogated by its carers; potentially dangerous toys were whisked off shelves faster than you could say 'eye gouge'. Yet you could get away with anything here, it seemed, a world away from the eastern seaboard.

Hamish felt sick again.

'Frank, I think I'm going to . . .'

They turned into the driveway of a tired-looking motel.

Before Frank had even parked the bus, Hamish plunged out the door and fell onto his hands and knees. He vomited, heaving three or four times on the asphalt.

Frank crouched down next to him, proffering a bottle of water.

'That's some hangover you got y'self, fella. Lasted all day.'

Hamish took a sip of water, swilled it around his mouth and spat it out. He peered down the driveway at the shadowy figures beyond. The invisible people of Fitzroy Crossing.

Frank followed his gaze. 'It's not all bad, mate,' he said. 'Some punters reckon this place is Australia's best-kept secret. In a good way.'

'You're kidding.'

Frank shook his head. 'I'll take you to the river in the morning, it's the lifeblood of this place. You'll see a different side of Fitzroy Crossing down there. Community programs for families, improving things a bit. Nothing's ever all bad, fella. Or all good, for that matter. Sometimes people just need a bit of confidence to forgive 'emselves and start over.'

Frank's words felt personal, somehow. Hamish placed a hand over his chest, physically struck by the fragility of it all. Suddenly aware that life was too precious, children too vulnerable and relationships too important, to screw it up so badly, almost deliberately.

*His* life, *his* children.

*His* relationship.

In Fitzroy Crossing, many people didn't stand a chance from the beginning, Hamish thought. Little boys clutching at the hands of their disengaged mothers. Little girls who didn't make it to adolescence before some arsehole molested them. If they ever had a decent crack at life, it was in spite of their circumstances.

But Hamish hadn't ever had to struggle like that, he now realised. Sure, he'd worked hard in life, bloody hard. But almost everything he'd ever wanted had been delivered to him on a platter. Including a decent childhood, a good education and the nurturing given to him by his conservative and committed parents. All of it had set him up for his future life: the life which he was now slowly annihilating, for reasons he couldn't understand.

Hamish wiped his mouth with the edge of his t-shirt. 'I'm swearing off the alcohol, Frank,' he said quietly.

'Did that myself seven years ago. Drunk Diet Coke ever since,' Frank said.

Hamish sat back on his heels. 'Why'd you do it?'

Frank removed his cap. 'Used to drink, since I was eleven. Everyone thinks it's okay, right? Then one night, I almost killed the missus. Hurt her real bad.' He lifted his shirt and pointed to three long white scars under his ribcage. 'Some of the old fellas took me to country and taught me a lesson. Never touched the grog again.'

'Fuck, mate.' Hamish had heard of payback in some tribal cultures, spearings and the like. Would Sid happily take a spear to him for what he'd done to Paula? He guessed so.

*And I'd deserve it. After Lisel and Toni, the fights with the Brazilian, a whole collection of cock-ups.*

He craved the simplicity of settling scores like that; confessing his errors, submitting to retribution, earning a clean slate again.

But as it was, he wasn't sure that Paula would ever forgive his misdemeanours; and if she did, she almost certainly wouldn't forget them. It was a hell of a lot more complex the whitefella way.

Looking at Frank for a few strange seconds, Hamish felt as if he was standing before a mirror. Staring into the eyes of a flawed man, trying to make sense of his life, striving to do better.

Maybe that *was* good enough.

Hamish lifted his face to the night sky. A single desert star hovered above them, its pale light poking through the rain clouds gathering above.

*I'm going to remember this moment forever. This is how change begins.*

# 16

The further north of Perth they travelled, the more warped Paula's sense of time became; a day in the northern reaches of Western Australia felt like a week.

Travelling anywhere took much longer, its population centres were smaller, its landscape starker. Shops closed early, and only stocked the barest of essentials—bread was white, milk was full cream, fresh produce scarce and exorbitantly priced. But the flora and fauna were dazzling in their diversity. There were animals, or evidence of them, everywhere: Jurassic-looking lizards, emus and camels by day, dingos and even brumbies nosing around the caravan at night. And the people were different, too. Always friendly and courteous, but with an iron edge; like frontier pilgrims, shaped by the austerity of their surroundings.

For the first time in her life, Paula allowed her daily rhythms to be dictated exclusively by her body's needs. She stopped checking her watch to determine when to eat or sleep. Instead, she exercised until she was spent, rested when she was tired, ate only when her stomach grumbled. By the time they reached Broome, loose fabric flapped where her flesh had previously been. She'd lost at least eight kilos, she guessed; not quite all of the excess weight, but enough to make her feel much healthier.

Her father, too, looked the fittest he'd ever been, like a competitor in the Masters Games. The children were tanned and surprisingly compliant; Caitlin was always a willing participant, while Lachie, who sometimes complained of aches and pains, usually finished with a satisfied smile. The lure of technology had waned entirely; the iPods and telephones stayed in the glove box—and not *only* because of the patchy network coverage in remote Western Australia.

While the physical fatigue from their training was pleasant enough, it soon affected their non-fitness activities. Paula found it hard to stay awake at night, even for their rousing family campfires. Sid began dozing in the car, sometimes before midday. And they both started forgetting things: Paula left her only pair of swimmers strung over a gum tree near the Roebuck roadhouse, while Sid left Marcelo's guitar case propped up against the Derby jetty one evening. Thankfully the guitar itself wasn't inside; Lachie had carried it back to the caravan, strumming as he walked.

The last time Paula could remember being so physically fatigued, she'd been a child herself. Swinging off trees and monkey bars, playing chasings and Red Rover and Bulldog in the playground, whooping and plunging into deep pools from diving boards, holding her breath until she felt her lungs might burst. Relishing the physicality of childhood; unconscious of how her body looked, just *using* it for its purpose.

It was decades since she'd enjoyed that kind of relationship with her physical self, and she resolved never to slip back into old habits. This was one relationship worth preserving forever.

*

Her telephone beeped after midnight; she always kept it by her side after dark.

Judging by the nocturnal sounds all around, it was still long before dawn. She groped for the phone, brought it close to her face. There were three new messages.

The first was from *ID withheld*, sent some six hours earlier.

*Mrs McInnes, I have tried calling but can't get through. Please contact me for an update on the Facebook incident. Regards, Derrick Nelson.*

For Paula, Burwood Secondary College, the Facebook scandal, all of it now seemed utterly peripheral. The offending post had been offline for weeks, the student body had been counselled about cyber-bullying and demeaning content. Since leaving Perth, Catie and Lachie had stopped talking about it altogether, and this seemed a reasonable litmus test of any ongoing impact. Hamish's initial response had been spot-on, Paula decided; they were barrelling towards Christmas, and almost everyone had lost interest in it.

Everyone except Mr Nelson, it seemed.

*Sorry, we've been out of range*, she typed back. *I'll call from Darwin in a few days.*

The second message was from Jamie.

*Are you okay? Pls confirm when you get this? A bit worried about you.*

Paula had been meaning to call Jamie for weeks, ever since their arrival in Perth. But something had always stopped her; mostly the shame she felt for articulating to Jamie her feelings for Marcelo. She dreaded telling her sister about the vanishing Brazilian; one day he'd been there and trying to kiss her, the next day he was gone.

*Hi J*, she typed. *We're all okay, in remote WA. Network patchy. Will call you from Darwin soon.*

She pressed 'send' and, less than a minute later, received a reply: *Thank God! Missing you xx.*

Paula turned her attention to the third message, from another *ID withheld*.

*Paula, sorry no contact 4 so long. Can I meet you for dinner in Darwin?*

Her heart skipped a beat.

Marcelo, finally.

*Are you okay?* she typed.

*Yes*, came the response. *Jetty Restaurant Darwin wharf next Thursday night @ 8? Great oysters there . . .*

Paula flushed with pleasure, remembering their afternoon on the jetty at Denial Bay, the unspoken sexual tension between them as they'd devoured a dozen oysters together.

So Marcelo was in Darwin; the timing was perfect. They were camped at Timber Creek, just over the Northern Territory border, and were due to arrive in Darwin by Wednesday.

*Yes*, she replied, blocking the mental image of Jamie's disbelieving face. *Will look forward to it!*

She resisted the urge to ask more questions: there would be time enough for that on Thursday.

And maybe, just maybe, they'd finish that kiss.

*

It took all of her courage to walk into the beauty salon on Daly Street in Darwin's central business district.

They'd pitched camp in a caravan park in Malak on Tuesday morning, a full day earlier than predicted. Not long after, with the children and her father engaged in a lengthy game of Monopoly, she'd caught a bus into the CBD and wandered around. She needed a new outfit for her dinner with Marcelo, as all of her existing clothes were shapeless and unflattering. When she glimpsed the words *Bare Beauty* imprinted across a shop window, she'd crossed the road and pushed open the glass door before she could reconsider.

'Can I help you?' asked a pretty young woman with heavy blue eyeliner and a warm smile.

'I, uh . . .' Paula looked around, to see if there was any one else within earshot. 'I'd like to have a Brazilian wax, please.'

It was entirely out of character. She'd practically bludgeoned Hamish with her objections when he'd suggested she try one, years ago. But here in the sultry tropical north of Australia, poised to meet a Latin American heartthrob for dinner, the idea felt far less confronting. In fact, it was downright intriguing.

The woman checked her appointments. 'Sure, I have forty minutes before my next client. Come on through.'

Paula followed her down a short hallway painted in pastel pink. At the first door on the left, the woman stopped.

'I'm Sienna,' she said, opening the door for Paula. 'Just take everything off and pop this on.' She brandished a small plastic square and placed it on the bed. 'It's a disposable G-string, I'll be back in a moment.' Sienna glided out of the room.

Paula looked around the windowless cubicle, plastered with glossy advertisements spruiking the benefits of Resalyne, a wrinkle reducer, and Kelpamax, a line of seaweed-based skincare. A pot of wax, thick and sticky like honeycomb, stood on a bench nearby. Paula wondered if there was enough in the pot; she hadn't had a wax of any description for almost two months. Her bikini line was now postively Biblical.

Paula took off her shorts, then her sensible beige underpants. She concealed the latter in a neat pile beneath the bed, sensing that a girl like Sienna wouldn't be caught dead in grandma undies like those.

She picked up the small sachet on the bed and attempted to open it. It was so well-sealed, she struggled to break the plastic.

'Ready?' asked Sienna, sailing into the room again.

'Oh.' Paula blushed a deep red, standing bare-bottomed in front of a woman she'd just met. 'I'm having a bit of trouble.'

Sienna relieved her of the sachet and expertly tore it open.

'There,' she said, shaking out a voluminous G-string made of synthetic white netting. She passed it to Paula, who couldn't tell where her legs were supposed to go.

Once she'd worked that out, she attempted to step into it without bending over too much.

She couldn't scramble onto the beautician's table quickly enough.

'Okay,' said Sienna, prising Paula's knees apart and splaying them sideways. 'Have you had a Brazilian before? Oooh.'

'What?' Paula had never felt so self-conscious in her life.

'It's been a while since you've had a wax?'

Paula died a thousand deaths. 'Yes, well, I've been . . . travelling.'

*Seven weeks on the road will do that to you.*

'It might be a bit painful removing all that,' said Sienna. 'Just so you know, we recommend waxing every three to four weeks, so it doesn't get too dense.'

*It's a bikini line, not the Bois du Boulogne.*

Sienna moved the G-string to the right. Paula didn't have to look down to confirm that her vulva was exposed; she could just *tell.*

'So,' said Sienna brightly, dipping an oversized paddle-pop stick into the pot of wax. 'What are you doing for Christmas?'

Paula blinked: she'd almost forgotten about it. Usually she arranged everything months in advance, but this year she'd been too preoccupied. Besides, it didn't really *feel* like Christmas. Away from their home in Melbourne, travelling through the outback in wet season. No Christmas tree, no stockings, no department-store windows with snowy displays. No Hamish.

'We'll be here in Darwin,' said Paula. 'But I haven't organised anything yet.' She winced at the sensation of warm wax being smeared perilously close to her privates.

'Is it too hot?' Sienna asked, concerned.

Without waiting for an answer, she bent forward and began to blow on the wax.

*This is just too weird.*

In her mind, Paula began reciting the elements of the periodic table.

*Hydrogen, helium, lithium, beryllium . . .*

It was a technique she'd used since high school to distract herself from uncomfortable things like pap smears, blood tests, or standing naked in front of her dermatologist at her annual mole check.

She'd only just passed carbon and nitrogen, when Sienna suddenly tore off the wax.

'Fuuuck!' Paula's eyes flew open at the sound of her own voice. 'Oh, I'm so sorry.'

'That's okay.' Sienna's face was neutral. 'You've never done this before, have you?'

Paula exhaled. 'No.'

'Well, it's not very pleasant. But I've done thousands of them and you'll be done in no time.'

Paula folded her hands—now damp with perspiration—in front of her chest. 'You've really done thousands?'

Sienna nodded. 'They're very popular. My oldest client is seventy-three. Reckons it spices up her sex life.'

Paula didn't know whether to be impressed or shocked. She knew several of her friends had Brazilians, even Jamie had tried it once. But she'd counselled Paula against it: *Unless you want to look like a plucked Christmas turkey.*

'The hardest clients to wax are the blokes.'

'*Men* do this?' Paula couldn't imagine why.

'Yes, I get a lot of cyclists. Must feel nice under their lycra.' Sienna giggled. 'There are some really blokey ones too. With, like, gorilla fur.' She reached for some talcum powder. 'It can get pretty ugly trying to wax their taints.'

'Their taints?' Paula lay mortified as Sienna powdered her nether regions.

'Yeah, you know: 'taint their bum, 'taint their penis. The bit in between, the perineum.'

'Oh.' Paula nodded, as if she discussed the topic regularly.

Hamish was a cyclist, but she couldn't imagine him having his 'taint' waxed.

Sienna suddenly ripped out another tuft of hair.

Paula managed to repress the shriek, but only just; her eyes began to water.

*What the hell was I thinking? I'm too old for this.*

'Do Brazilian men like Brazilians?' Paula asked, half croaking.

Sienna smeared more hot wax onto her. 'Oh, I think *all* men like Brazilians, honey. People are saying that the Brazilian is dead, you know, and that the rough muff is making a comeback. But I'm not so sure.'

*The rough muff?*

'I've been working in beauty for eleven,' said Sienna, 'and it's all about trends, you know? False eyelashes, acrylic nails, Brazilian waxes, the crack-back-and-sack wax . . .'

Paula didn't dare ask.

'All these trends come and go, like the seasons.'

*There's a season for everything,* Paula thought, gritting her teeth. The honeymoon period. Early-childhood blues. Primary-school consolidation. The monotony of family routines. Teenage upheaval. Mid-life crisis. Running away from it all.

*What next?* Paula wondered.

'Are you doing this for someone special?' asked Sienna.

Paula frowned at the personal question. Then she looked down at Sienna's bowed head and figured she'd earned the right to ask.

'It's more for *me*, really.' Paula said. 'I just wanted to see what it feels like, before I turn forty.'

'Uh-huh.' Sienna had heard it all before, it seemed. And probably seen it all, too.

'I guess you've met a lot of people, with your job?' Paula asked, searching for more distraction from the discomfort.

'Uh-huh.' Sienna ripped away two more strips of wax but, for some reason, these didn't hurt as much.

*Perhaps I'm going numb.*

'Yeah, it's funny. Lots of women are worried about what they're like down there, you know?' Sienna looked up from her work. 'I get lots of ladies asking me, "Do I look normal to you?" and it's funny, I'm not like a *doctor* or anything.'

Paula nodded, desperate to ask the same question.

'And there are lots of blokes out there who want their wife to look a certain way. From watching porn, I guess, everything all neat and tucked up.' Sienna rolled her eyes. 'I mean, what a *hide*.'

Paula had seen those sorts of vulvas before, in a stash of pornographic magazines she'd found when cleaning the top of Hamish's wardrobe. She'd sat for twenty minutes on the edge of their bed, leafing her way through airbrushed images of hairless twenty-somethings with full breasts, intimate piercings and half-closed eyes. And symmetrical, petal-like labia, undamaged by childbirth or gravity.

Paula hadn't mentioned her discovery to Hamish, because the magazines had dated back to his late teens. Predating *her*, even. But the images sometimes haunted her when they made love; did Hamish actually want a woman who looked like that? So on the one occasion he'd suggested a Brazilian, she'd completely overreacted.

'It's not as if men's bits are very attractive, are they? Hairy and dotty and dangly.' Sienna laughed again, smearing wax in the vicinity of Paula's anus.

Paula had to stop herself from diving off the bed. 'Do you wax around the . . . ?'

'Uh-huh.'

Sienna ripped the wax away.

Paula screeched.

'Okay, not long now,' Sienna chirped. 'Almost done. Just tidying up your landing strip.'

'My what?' Paula raised her head and looked down.

Sienna was now tweezing around a thin vertical line of hair she'd left where a triangular thicket had once been. Angry red dots surrounded it.

*There's that plucked turkey.*

'Your husband's going to *love* you for this,' Sienna cooed, after a moment. 'That's if you're . . .' She glanced at Paula's left hand, looking for a wedding band.

*My husband wouldn't believe me if I told him.*

'All finished,' said Sienna. 'You can get dressed now.'

She disappeared out the door.

Paula swung her legs off the bed and let them dangle there for a moment, noticing the altered sensation. Bare skin on smooth vinyl, where hair had previously protected. It felt cool, nude and slightly bruised.

And, she had to admit, just a little sexy.

She stood up and looked at herself in the full-length mirror, twisting her hips left and right.

*I'm almost forty and, bugger it, I* am *sexy.*

She slipped her underpants back on, noticing how bare it felt.

Then she smiled to herself.

Having practically wept with the pain of having her pubic hair removed, one thing was for certain. She was going to *enjoy* this Brazilian.

# 17

'I need to take a piss, Frank.'

Frank rolled his eyes at Hamish in the rear-view mirror. 'Again?'

'Yep.'

'It's all that farken water you're drinkin', mate.'

Hamish nodded, feeling virtuous.

He'd refilled his water bottle three times already. Normally, his morning consisted of several coffees and not much else, but today, for the second day in a row, he'd drunk close to two litres of water before breakfast. Collecting it straight from the creek where they'd camped for the night. It had been energising for Hamish, stuck in the middle of nowhere with a blackfella whose bush skills put his to shame.

Hamish looked out the window of the mini-bus. It was only nine o'clock, but menacing clouds hung low in the sky. It would bucket down soon.

He leaned forward and tapped Frank on the shoulder. 'C'mon mate, I need to go.'

Frank slowed the bus, pulling over in the red gravel shoulder at the highway's edge.

They were somewhere north of Kununurra, about seven hundred kilometres from Darwin.

Hamish walked around the back of the bus to take a leak. When he'd finished, Frank pointed at a craggy escarpment in the distance.

'Look at that, mate,' he called. 'Barramundi dreaming.'

Hamish squinted at the rocky outline, khaki green against the grey sky. After a while, he began to see it. A natural formation that suggested the shape of a fish, shimmering purple along the spine. Shiny silver flecks in the rock layer, a hint of scales. He'd heard Aboriginal stories before; about the rainbow serpent, the Willy-Willy man, the Dreamtime. But he'd never seen them reflected in the landscape.

He looked over at Frank, who was smiling like it was Christmas morning.

'Why barramundi?' he asked. 'We're a long way from the sea.'

'In monsoon they're everywhere, mate. Rivers and estuaries.'

Hamish wasn't an angler; he'd always thought barramundi was an ocean fish.

Frank waved a hand at the land around them. 'This was all sea once anyway, back in the Dreaming. You can still find shells in the dirt sometimes.'

Hamish had found a few shells like that in his backyard in suburban Melbourne.

'Our bodies are from the sea, too,' Frank added. 'Split us open, we're all just salt and water inside. That's what blood is, you know. Everyone bleeds the same.'

They stood in silence.

'Come on, fella,' said Frank finally.

As they headed back to the vehicle, Hamish noticed a sign not far from where they were parked. Weather-worn, wooden, hardly detectable on the side of the road: St John of the Gorge.

It was staked beside an overgrown wallaby trail that meandered in the direction of a broken-down barbed-wire fence.

'I'm going down there,' Hamish said, nodding at the sign.

'Why?' Frank looked wary.

'Need to take a shit.'

It was an honest answer. But there was something more, too. Something about the mystical landscape, the soothing silence, the enigmatic sign, the wallaby trail disappearing into the scrub; it all made him feel like an eight-year-old again. Excited and intrepid, like a colonial explorer. And whenever he felt that ball of nervous possibility in his gut, he felt compelled to walk towards it. And, inevitably, he needed to take a shit, too.

Frank made a grumbling sound. 'I'll wait here.'

Hamish tramped through the long grass at the side of the road until he reached the fence. Scaling a pile of rocks at a post, he jumped down with a thud on the other side. And it wasn't too hard on his knee, Hamish realised. *I'm back.* He turned for a moment, flicked one thumb up at Frank, then kept following the wallaby trail.

He had to crouch several times to avoid low-hanging branches; the sweat collected across the small of his back as he scrambled along. The sun emerged from behind the clouds, and began beating down on his bare head.

*Bloody crazy weather of the north. I should've brought my hat.*

He suddenly thought of Paula, who never forgot such things. *But she's not here. Might never be again.*

His eyes stung.

The earth sloped downwards, and the trail became harder to detect. The undergrowth was still damp, with morning dew that brushed his sneakers and ankles. His shorts were soon covered in small furry pods, sticky with a sap-like substance. As the pressure on his bowels intensified, he emerged into a small clearing.

A wooden shack stood next to a boab tree. It was clearly uninhabited, but Hamish checked anyway: it was empty inside except for leaf litter strewn across the floor and a large bark mat in the corner. A simple cross, fashioned from sticks, hung from a nail in the doorframe. A sharp white tooth was bound to the centre of the cross by a thin strip of leather.

Hamish inspected the tooth; it looked canine, like a dingo incisor.

A ring of stones at the door suggested a campfire hearth, next to several large flat rocks.

*Who lived here once, and when? A religious hermit?*

Hamish's stomach clenched with anticipation. He really needed to take that shit.

Striding away from the hut, he looked for the right spot, straying further down the slope. Not more than five metres on, the earth suddenly fell away into a long, narrow cleft.

He edged towards it, then peered over.

The cleft turned into a rock wall of sandstone and quartz, leading down to a green gully. At the bottom, a slow-moving river wound its way between two sandy banks. A waterhole had formed at one edge of the gully, where rocks had created a natural dam. Sunlight speared down onto the pool's surface from the cleft above, creating flashes of emerald and lime.

*The kids would love it here.*

He began climbing down, finding one foothold, then another. Not far below was a wide rock ledge; he dropped onto it with a grunt. Beyond that, it was an easy scramble down to the riverbank.

The air was cooler here and his gut churned with the beauty of it all.

The urge to shit was overwhelming.

He dropped his pants and had barely crouched before the faeces spurted out.

'Crap.' He looked down at his calves, spattered with brown.

Something was wrong with his stomach, he decided. Northern Territory Belly, or was he detoxing, after all these years? With no alcohol or coffee for the past few days, perhaps his system was shitting itself, literally.

He stood up and kicked off his pants and boxers, then lifted his t-shirt over his head and threw it onto the ground.

He looked at the waterhole. Then, without testing for depth, he took a running dive.

*Paula would've killed me for that.*

But it was as deep as it looked, he couldn't even touch the bottom.

He swam out into the middle and trod water. Then he reached down and began brushing the backs of his calves, cleaning the shit off.

When he was confident it was all gone, he floated on his back, gazing up at the cavern walls. Rocky swirls like whipped cream and folds of chocolate, tiny green shoots poking out of impossibly inhospitable places. Life triumphing, despite the conditions. *That's what life does*, Hamish thought. *Whoever you are, whatever you've done, life doesn't judge you. It just keeps going.*

As river water filled his ears, Hamish listened to his own heartbeat, feeling its calming thud within his chest. Dappled sunshine drifted through the cleft above, golden shards of light touching the deep green.

*I'm truly alive here.*

His leg brushed some river debris.

And then he heard a voice. Muffled, from beneath the waterline.

He lifted his head to see Frank scrambling down the rock wall.

*What's* he *doing here?* Hamish wondered, mildly irritated by the intrusion. He raised a leisurely hand in Frank's direction.

'Get the fark out! SALTY!' Frank's eyes bulged with fear. 'SWIM!'

Hamish's stomach somersaulted. And then, as if in slow motion, he began to swim.

Freestyle, feeling like he was hauling himself through quicksand.

The water was rushing into his eyes and nose and lungs. He swallowed some and spluttered, then swallowed some more. The coughing plunged him under the water.

He felt something brush his leg again and he lost sight of the bank.

He tried to find a point of focus. Where was Frank?

Suddenly, something gripped his calf.

*This is it.*

A moment later he was face down on the sand.

Frank was standing over him, thumping him between the shoulderblades. 'Get up! Farken *move*!'

Frank yanked him upright and they fled the riverbank.

Reaching the rock wall, Hamish tried to find a foothold but slipped.

Frank half pushed, half lifted him up the side.

They only stopped climbing once they reached the safety of the wide rock ledge, more than half way up.

Hamish flopped down on his back, wheezing.

Frank crouched next to him, dripping wet, peering at the gully below.

'Look.'

Hamish sat up.

A saltwater crocodile now lurked in the shallows, its beady eyes and spiny tail poking above the waterline.

'Jesus Christ.'

'St John of the Gorge,' corrected Frank, still panting. 'The croc hunters give 'em holy names up here, if they're hard to catch. Sign of respect.'

'I didn't know.'

How *could* he have known?

Watching the crocodile, Hamish contemplated how close he'd come to certain death. He'd seen a Discovery Channel documentary about salties once; how they flipped you over and over in a death roll, before stuffing you in an underwater cavern, coming back to bite chunks off you.

Hamish shuddered. 'Frank, I—'

'Shut up.'

Frank was shaking.

'Of all the farken stupid things you've ever done, and you've done more than your fair share in the time I've known you, that farken takes the cake, fella. What the fark were you thinkin'?'

'I didn't know there were crocs in—'

'It's a farken *billabong* and we're in the farken *Northern Territory*, fella.' Frank shook his head in disgust. 'And didn't you *see* the farken croc hunters' hut?'

Suddenly the crucifix with the tooth made sense.

'I thought it was a dingo tooth . . .'

'Dingo tooth, your naked arse.'

Hamish felt suddenly self-conscious; he'd left his clothes on the riverbank.

'Farken skinny-dippin' in a croc-infested billabong.' Frank stood up. 'Yer farken lucky that croc didn't snap off yer dick and have it for breakfast. Now for the love of God, come back to the van and put some farken clothes on.'

Hamish looked up at Frank, already scaling the rock wall with the agility of a spider.

'Frank, I . . .' Gratitude flooded through him. 'I owe you one. I mean, more than one. And I'm sorry.'

'You should be, fella. You're about as useful as a one-legged man in an arse-kickin' contest.'

Hamish couldn't help but laugh.

He laughed and laughed, until he almost wet himself.

Then Frank started laughing too. Leaning against the rock wall, heaving and cackling and clutching his stomach.

'C'mon,' said Frank, finally, drawing breath. 'Ya dumb fuck.'

Stark naked and shoeless, Hamish followed him up the rock face.

*

They arrived at Darwin's outskirts by sunset.

'Where're you staying, fella?' Frank idled the bus outside a derelict community hall.

'There's a backpackers. Let me just look it up.' Hamish reached for his mobile in the pocket of the fresh trousers he'd donned after his close encounter with St John of the Gorge.

Frank cleared his throat. 'Some of my mob lives out at Brinkin, not too far away. Be staying there a week or so myself, doing a few jobs up here. It's grog-free. You'd be welcome too.'

Looking at Frank, Hamish realised he wasn't joking.

'Mate, thanks.' Hamish's heart felt light enough to fly right out of his chest. 'That's really generous, but I don't want to be any trouble . . .'

'Trouble?' Frank sniggered. 'Trouble's haulin' your bare arse out of a billabong, fella.'

They pulled out onto the road again.

Twenty minutes later, they parked in the driveway of a nondescript cement house in Darwin's north. A wide veranda encircled it and five wooden steps led down to a neat yard and vegetable patch. Beyond the backyard, parkland stretched out onto wide coastal flats.

Frank sounded the horn.

Dogs barked from a shed nearby, and a baby cried from a house across the road. But all else was quiet; they waited to see if anyone would emerge.

'Get comfortable, fella,' said Frank. 'They're not home.'

Hamish checked his watch.

'Don't start with *that*,' said Frank. 'Get used to waitin', mate, it's the farken tropics. You know what they say about the Northern Territory?'

Hamish shook his head.

'That "NT" is short for Not Today, Not Tomorrow. Not Tuesday, Not Thursday.' Frank laughed. 'Hang on, here's good news.'

A white four-wheel drive carrying far too many people pulled into the driveway behind them.

'Hey!' Frank climbed out of the van and greeted them all. Kissing some of the women, shaking hands with the men, lifting the children into the air. They all seemed to be talking at once in their own language.

'Everyone, this is Hamish.' Frank waved a hand in his direction. 'He's a mate.'

The words made Hamish's eyes watery.

*Out of all of this, I've made a friend.*

He hung back a moment, not knowing what to do. Not wanting to stuff it up somehow, wreck a friendship before it had really begun.

Should he shake hands with everyone?

Two children ran forward and grabbed his hands, forcing him to drop his bag. Wavy hair, inquisitive eyes and spectacular white smiles.

'*Namura, namura!*' they shouted, tugging him in the direction of the backyard.

A woman smiled and spoke to Frank.

Frank turned to Hamish. 'The kids have found some oysters down at Dripstone Beach. They want to show you.'

'Uh, okay.' Hamish let himself be led away by the children.

'I'll take your stuff inside,' called Frank. 'Ever shucked oysters straight from the sea, fella?'

Hamish shook his head, grinning.

Then he followed the children as they danced and skipped over a well-worn path to the beach. Every now and then they stopped to point out something of interest—a flower, a bird, lizard tracks in the sand—using words he'd never heard before. When he attempted to repeat them, they fell about laughing, presumably at his accent.

In the hazy light of a Darwin sunset, holding hands with two children with whom he shared neither language nor history, Hamish felt the happiest he'd been in a long time.

# 18

Paula checked her reflection in the mirror and, for the first time in years, didn't critique it. Her skin was sun-kissed, her limbs looked longer, her stomach flatter. Sure, her breasts were still disproportionately small, but there was something about her that was radically different. She looked healthy. Blooming, her father said.

The long blue dress she'd bought at Casuarina Mall was particularly flattering for her figure; a billowy, strappy number that showed off her toned arms and shoulders. When paired with cork wedges, she looked taller. Her hair had grown a little, and tonight she'd taken care to style it in feminine waves that floated at her neck.

*Didn't even need travel curlers.*

She'd dabbed a musky scent on her pulse points and contemplated not wearing any underpants. But her mother's voice had triumphed from the grave: *What happens if there's a big gust of wind? Or you have an accident and go to hospital? What will the doctors think?*

Paula settled instead on a new pair of silk knickers. For years she'd been buying black lace for Hamish's benefit, but this time she chose fire-engine red, feeling positively dangerous as she slipped into them.

'My word,' said her father, as she walked from the amenities block just before seven-thirty. 'Someone's going to be impressed.'

She *almost* told him she was meeting Marcelo.

'Where are you off to, Mum?' Caitlin looked at her mother with admiration. 'You look amazing.'

'Oh, out to dinner with an old friend from university,' she lied. For tonight, at least, Paula wanted Marcelo all to herself.

'Have a good time,' said Lachie, peering over the top of his book.

She made her way to the front gate of the caravan park and waited for the taxi.

*

The restaurant was perched at the far reaches of the old timber wharf overlooking Darwin Harbour. Paula stood at the doorway, fidgeting with her hair, feeling deliciously nervous.

She walked in and scanned the room for Marcelo.

A figure stood up from a table in the far corner.

She stopped in her tracks, immobilised, as he walked towards her.

Before she could move he was at her side, bending down and kissing her cheek.

'You're beautiful, Paula McInnes.'

She stared up into Hamish's face.

'You're like a different woman.'

The message she'd received from *ID withheld* hadn't been from Marcelo at all. Somehow, she'd unwittingly agreed to have dinner with her husband.

The disappointment was crushing.

'Are you alright?' Hamish asked, taking her elbow and guiding her towards the table.

Flustered, she told the truth.

'I don't really want to be here, Hamish.'

And it was about time for more truth, she decided.

Hamish pulled out a chair for her all the same.

'Look, I know you're still angry with me, and I deserve it. What I did was *wrong*, Paula, I know that now.' He looked at her with pleading eyes. 'But please, sit down and let's have a drink. It's taken me forever to find you.'

His apology was disarming; Hamish was usually so convinced of his righteousness.

'Alright,' she said finally. '*One* drink.'

He took a seat opposite her.

A waiter appeared with a bottle of champagne and a crystal flute.

'Madame.' He moved to pour the sparkling liquid into the glass.

'No thanks.' It was just like Hamish to order *for* her. 'I'm off alcohol at the moment.'

'You're kidding?' Hamish beamed. 'So am I.'

He waved the waiter away, before calling him back. 'Just make it two sparkling waters, please.'

They sat in silence, looking at each other. With anyone else, she might have felt awkward. Hamish appeared to be noticing all the small changes in her. And he liked what he saw, evidently.

For his part, Hamish looked gaunter, with more signs of stress around the eyes. His skin was peeling in patches across his neck, evidence of a recent sunburn. But his knee appeared to have healed well, since she hadn't seen any sign of a limp.

'What are you doing here?' she asked.

He grinned. 'What do you think?'

'A business trip?'

The waiter reappeared with their drinks.

Hamish raised his glass at her. She didn't reciprocate.

'I followed you, Paula,' he said. 'It's taken me a month to catch up with you on the road.'

'What, in the hatchback?'

'Yes, it's a long story. I got as far as Perth, but it broke down and I had to leave it there.' He laughed. 'A mate of mine drove me from Perth to Darwin.'

'Which mate?' She couldn't recall any friends of Hamish's living in Western Australia.

'His name's Frank, a bloke I met on the Nullarbor. Got me out of some tight corners. He's a tour guide, drives for a living. I've been staying with him up here, at his family's place. He's an Aborigine.'

She looked at him, wondering whether to castigate him for using the term *Aborigine*. For years she'd explained just how offensive it was to some Indigenous Australians; a fact that had been drilled into her during her social work degree.

It was difficult to imagine Hamish driving the length of Australia with an Aboriginal for company, then staying in his house. For as long as she could remember, Hamish had been ambivalent about 'blackfellas', as he sometimes called them in private. Singing their praises when it came to sport: *That blackfella can really kick a footy around*. But quick to criticise them for laziness and neglect in almost every other domain. Yet here he was describing his first ever Aboriginal *friend*, which was more than Paula could claim in her own life.

So *he* had changed too, on some level.

Hamish looked up at her, his eyes moist.

'I've missed you and the kids so much. I wanted to say . . .' He reached across the table for her hand.

She pulled it back into her lap.

'I was an arsehole. What I did was so wrong. It's been really hard without you and the kids. I'll never *ever* take you for granted again.' His lips trembled. 'Will you come home to me, Paula?'

She stared at him.

The reality was, she hadn't decided that yet.

She'd imagined having an answer by the time she crossed the Victorian border. Darwin was way too early for a resolution.

And sitting across from Hamish now, her uncertainty wasn't dissipating. She didn't feel angry, she didn't feel disappointed; she simply didn't feel much at all. A curious, flat, emptiness was spreading across her chest.

'I . . . I don't know.' She searched for the right words. 'A lot has changed for me. I don't want to slip back into old habits.'

He looked at her appreciatively. 'You've obviously changed your eating habits. You look *fantastic*.'

She dismissed his approval; *those* weren't the sort of habits she'd meant at all.

'What do I have to do?' he asked suddenly. 'How can I make things better, Paula?'

Suddenly she felt as if she were at a job interview, but she hadn't researched the question.

'It's not about specific things, really.'

'Go on,' he said, leaning forward.

She began to feel irritated. Hamish was bulldozing her into a discussion she wasn't ready to have.

Paula shook her head.

'Please tell me,' he persisted. 'I'm ready to hear it.'

'What am I supposed to say, Hamish?' she blurted. 'That your breath smells in the morning and you *always* kiss me before you've brushed your teeth? Now *that's* easily fixed.' It had been a daily irritant for seventeen years.

Hamish sat back in his chair, looking slightly winded.

'That you leave cups all over the lounge room, sports socks on the floor, and you *never* change the toilet roll? That sometimes I feel like I have *three* children. Does *that* help?'

She knew she sounded unhinged.

'Alright, Paula.' Hamish lowered his voice. 'This is all a bit *trivial*, isn't it?'

'Well, you badgered me into it,' she snapped. 'You're not even ready to have the *real* conversation we need to have.'

'What do you mean?' He looked defensive.

'We're murdering our marriage, that's what I mean. We've stopped doing *everything* that ever meant anything to us as a couple. It's like we're roommates who *never* have sex.'

His eyes narrowed. 'You're always too tired.'

'Probably because I'm flat out running after *our* kids,' she retorted.

'Oh, and *I've* got it easy at work?' Hamish looked put out. 'You've *always* resented me for working full-time.'

'And *you've* always expected a gold medal for it.' She was getting worked up now. 'Along with a bloody pipe and a throne at the end of each day.'

'I *do* earn the money.'

'Most of it,' she corrected. 'I work part-time too, remember. *And* I run the household, look after the kids, cook the meals . . .'

He snorted. 'If you can call it cooking.'

'But who *else* is going to do it, Hamish?' Her voice was shrill. 'Who else is lining up for all that domestic drudgery?'

'I pull my weight on the weekends.'

A young couple at an adjacent table looked askance in their direction.

*It's all ahead of you*, she felt like calling out to them. *Enjoy your bliss now, people, because it's downhill from here.*

Paula took a deep breath. 'You're right, Hamish. Arguing about housework *is* petty, but our relationship hasn't been working for a while. What you did with that girl online was just the last straw.'

'We've got two beautiful kids, Paula,' he countered. 'We've had a good marriage . . .'

'You think? I'm not so sure now.'

Hamish looked at her in astonishment.

'When we first met, we made love *all the time*,' she said. 'Now I can't even *remember* when we last did it.'

'But *you're* always exhausted,' he insisted.

Paula deliberated a moment before speaking.

'Can you remember that conversation we had years ago, when Lachie was three months old? We were making love and—'

'Paula . . .'

She ignored him. 'You stopped in the middle of lovemaking and asked me a question. Can you remember what you asked, Hamish?'

He looked embarrassed. 'This isn't helpful, Paula.'

She glared at him. 'You asked me, "Can't you just *tighten up?*" That's what you said.'

'It was years ago,' he said. 'And I told you I was sorry.'

She nodded. 'But I've remembered that question *every single time* we've made love. I've spent *years* wondering if I was "tight enough" for you—or if you'd really rather be with someone else, like one of the girls in that porn stash of yours.'

Hamish gawped at her.

'Your online affair just *proved to me* that I wasn't enough for you, Hamish. I'm not sure I can trust you again. I doubt I'm what you want, anyway, if I ever *was*.'

His eyes were glassy. 'You *are* what I want. You always have been. You still are.'

'I think you just like the *idea* of me,' she retorted. 'You've got the great career and the kids, so you need a compliant wife.'

'That's *not* true, Paula.'

They sat looking at each other.

Finally, Hamish spoke again.

'That thing I said . . .' He reddened. 'It was the stupidest thing ever, Paula. You'd just had a baby. I didn't think it would . . .'

'Stay with me forever?' She glowered at him. 'Well, it *did*. No wonder I'm *tired* all the time. It's a horrible thing to be worried about, Hamish, because there's not much I can do about it. A bit like penis size.'

Hamish looked like he'd just been hit with a bat. 'Isn't mine . . . big enough for you?'

He was almost whispering.

She sighed. 'I don't really *know*, Hamish. I haven't had much to compare you with.'

They fell into silence again, avoiding each other's gaze.

Eventually, Hamish looked up at her. 'Have you finished?'

Paula shrugged. 'Probably not. I'm still angry.' She stood up from the table. 'But for tonight, yes.'

He looked subdued. 'I'm so sorry I've hurt you, Paula.'

For the first time that evening, his voice sounded *real*. Disheartened and uncertain, like *she'd* been feeling for months.

Paula sat back down.

'I can't guarantee anything in the future, Hamish,' she said, looking out at the harbour. Noticing for the first time the boats, like fairy lights, floating out at sea.

He nodded, as if he understood. 'I'd like to see the kids before I fly home on Sunday. For Christmas, you know.'

'Of course.' The sadness pressed down on her chest. 'They've missed you.'

'It's been nice getting their texts. Sounds like they've been having an amazing time. More than once I've . . .' Hamish rubbed a hand across his eyes. 'I've remembered the trip we wanted to do together.'

'Our adventure scrapbook.' Her hands were shaking as she drained her glass. 'Well, I'm doing it.'

Hamish looked broken. 'If you need anything on your way back home, let me know. You've still got the number for my new phone?'

Paula nodded, suddenly recalling what had happened to the old one; she'd flushed it down the loo. 'I've behaved badly too,' she said, looking at her hands. 'I'm not perfect by any means. This is something I never, *ever* wanted for us. I don't know how we got here, really.'

'We can reverse the damage,' said Hamish quietly. 'I know we can.'

She looked into her husband's eyes, seeing vulnerability there for the first time.

'I'm sorry, Hamish,' she said. 'But I need more time.'

Paula stood again to go.

'Call me anytime,' he repeated. 'For anything.'

She walked out of the restaurant and into a taxi.

*

She heard the beeping of text messages before she was ready to get up.

Her family had been awake for hours, cooking breakfast and moving about the camp site. But after her unexpected meeting with Hamish the night before, she'd slept like she'd been drugged. Even as light poured in through the caravan window, she remained suspended in strange dreams that she just couldn't shake.

'Mum.' The sound of Lachie's voice penetrated her sleep. 'You've got a few messages here.' He pushed the phone into her hand. 'How was your night?'

She raised herself up on one elbow. 'What do you mean?'

'With . . . your friend.'

By the expression on his face, she suddenly knew.

'Lachie, have you been talking to your father?'

He looked guilty.

'It's okay,' she said. 'You're allowed to.'

'I called him this morning with Gramps's phone,' he said quickly. 'Dad didn't call *me,* I promise.'

'Then you know I saw him last night.'

'Who?' asked Caitlin, stepping into the caravan.

Lachie turned to his sister. 'Dad. He's in Darwin.'

'Where?' Caitlin's voice became squeaky with excitement. 'Can we see him?'

Paula nodded. 'He goes home on Sunday.'

'Mum met him last night,' said Lachie, turning back to Paula.

'So *that's* why you were all dressed up.' Caitlin grinned.

Paula felt the weight of their teenage expectations, of Mum and Dad and happy families.

'Yes, I talked to your dad,' she said evenly. 'And we agreed to talk again when we all get home.'

Lachie prompted, 'And?'

'And I'm afraid that's it for now, Lachie.'

He just stood there, gutted.

It was understandable, of course. Thirteen-year-old boys wanted their worlds to operate in simple, predictable ways.

'I want to go and see him now,' said Lachie suddenly. 'Are you coming, Catie?'

His sister nodded.

Lachie stalked out of the caravan without so much as looking at Paula.

Caitlin turned to her. 'Don't worry about Lachie,' she said. 'I love you, Mum.'

The declaration caught Paula by surprise. 'Thank you, Catie.' She watched her daughter climb out of the caravan too.

Paula's phone vibrated in her hand and she saw she had five new messages. Did she even want to read them?

She clicked on the inbox.

*Paula, thanks for meeting me. Trust me, we can rebuild from here. Hamo.*

Then another.

*Please give me the chance to show you how much I've changed. Hamo.*

The third was from Jamie.

*Why the radio silence? Are you in Darwin?*

Paula could just picture Jamie's alarm at the news that Hamish had followed her there.

She scanned the fourth message, from *ID withheld*.

*Mrs McInnes, please contact me as soon as possible. Derrick Nelson.*

She'd completely forgotten to call him, again.

Then, the final message.

*Paula, this is Marcelo. I lost your number in Perth, I only just found it. I am in Darwin. Where are you?*

Her heart began galloping in her chest.

She stared at the message for a minute longer.

*I'm in Darwin too.*

The response was immediate.

*I was hoping for that. I am staying near George Brown Botanic Gardens. Can we meet today*?

It was almost midday. She'd slept the morning away, without even a hangover to blame. And now the kids had gone to see their father.

*Yes, 3 o'clock*, she typed. *Where?*

*At the water fountain on Gardens Road.*

She smiled. *OK*.

Paula bounded out of bed and down the caravan steps. She greeted her father, who was poring over the *Northern Territory News*, with a lavish kiss.

Predictability and simplicity were for thirteen-year-olds.

# 19

She took a cold shower at the amenities block, then rubbed sweet coconut oil all over her body. Its heady, tropical smell reminded her of hibiscus flowers and lost summers, years ago at Brighton. She didn't bother with much make-up, just a brush of bronzer and a dab of lip gloss. Anything else would streak down her face in the steamy heat.

Just before three o'clock, Paula followed the GPS to a leafy district about two kilometres north of the central business district. As she parked the ute on Gardens Road, the heavens suddenly opened; she was forced to sit in the car, waiting out the downpour. Ten minutes later, she finally emerged into lighter, mist-like rain.

*Why didn't I bring an umbrella in monsoon season? And* why *didn't I wear a bra?*

It had seemed like a natural choice as she'd changed into her dress, the same one she'd worn the evening before, but now she was getting nervous. Wishing she'd followed her usual routine, worn a little more make-up, packed a raincoat. Everything was damp; her skin, her clothes, her feet. Her hair would be wild, too; she reached up and tried to pat it into place. As she did, she spotted the water fountain beyond the wrought-iron gates of the garden.

Marcelo stepped out from behind the gate. He held his leather jacket over his head, but was still soaked through. He'd obviously been waiting *in* the downpour.

'We are wet,' he called, grinning at her.

'Yes.' She laughed, walking towards him.

He moved forward to hug her.

'I missed you, *Pow-la*.'

She pulled away from him. 'What happened, Marcelo? Why didn't you call me?'

'I am so sorry,' he groaned. 'I lost your number at the hospital. The doctor gave me some tablets and told me to go home, but I couldn't find the piece of paper you'd given me. I pulled apart my backpack and it wasn't there.'

'What was wrong with you?' Paula asked.

'Food poisoning.' Marcelo looked embarrassed. 'Not my appendix.'

The Norseman pub's counter meals weren't the freshest, as Paula recalled.

Marcelo shook his head. 'I didn't know where you were staying, so I caught a taxi to the nearest caravan park. I remembered you saying that was the plan but I couldn't remember *where*.'

Paula sighed. 'I probably didn't tell you.'

'Then I went to another caravan park, then another. Then I thought, this is stupid. There are too many caravan parks in Perth, I won't find them here. But if I keep going, maybe I will see them on the road? So I hitchhiked north, stopping in bigger towns like Geraldton, Port Hedland and Broome. I waited four or five days in each place, looking out for you, but I didn't find you. When I got to Darwin this morning,

I came straight here to scatter my mother's ashes.' His eyes were shiny. 'And you know what? Suddenly, your number was there again, stuck under the urn's metal casing. It just fell out, like a gift from *her*.'

She saw the pain and joy inscribed across his face.

'Oh . . . Marcelo.' She wrapped her arms around his waist.

They stood in the rain, their arms entwined, her ear pressed against his chest.

Suddenly he lifted her up off the ground.

She squealed as her thongs slipped off her feet.

He buried his face in her neck, sending goosebumps down her arms.

Slowly, he let her slip down the front of his body, until her feet touched the ground again.

His eyes found hers, vivid and searching. Then he bent forward and, gently, kissed her.

She let herself melt against him.

'Come,' he said suddenly, smiling at her through the rain. 'Or we will drown.'

He took her hand and they ran along a path into the gardens. Past bedraggled floral displays, a deserted playground and a barbecue area, and on through a small administration precinct. A dilapidated tin-clad café stood next to a plant display centre, neither of which looked occupied. An Aboriginal man in a green ranger's uniform emerged from the display centre as they ran past.

'How 'bout this rain, eh?' he called. 'Where're you goin'?'

Marcelo only waved and pulled Paula along faster.

She was panting by the time they reached the signs to a track marked *Rainforest Loop*.

'Best place to take shelter from the weather is in a rainforest,' said Marcelo. 'My country has the best ones.'

He pointed to a narrow wooden bridge straddling a stream. They crossed it, then continued along a boardwalk that led into dense, green foliage. Broad leaves arched above them, dripping in the wet.

To Paula's surprise, Marcelo stepped off the boardwalk. They began to pick their way over lichen-covered rocks and around the buttresses of sprawling trees draped in lianas.

'Where are we going?'

Marcelo held a finger to his lips. 'I know a secret place.'

They walked further, until her dress was sopping at the hem and her perfect coral-coloured toenails were covered in mud.

'Marcelo, I . . .'

'We're here,' he said, motioning to an enormous, gnarled fig tree.

She tried to compose herself; wiping the beads of sweat from her upper lip and wringing out the hem of her dress.

'Look,' he said. 'This tree is very old.'

He lay his leather jacket on a low branch and took several steps towards the bulky trunk. Then he crouched down and disappeared into a cavity at its base.

'Where did you go?'

'I'm inside.'

'Oh, shit.' She slipped a little over the leaf litter, then dropped onto her knees and crawled—first on her hands, then down on her stomach—into the tree. The front of her dress was muddy now, but she didn't care. She was so pent up, she'd follow him anywhere.

It was dark inside, except for some speckled light filtering through the cracks in the trunk.

She stood up. 'Marcelo?'

Her voice sounded strangely high-pitched. Nervous. For almost all of her adult life, her sexual experiences had been exclusively with

Hamish. Whatever else she knew, she'd pieced together from her brief relationship with her first boyfriend and Hollywood films.

Paula's eyes began to adjust to the dimness.

'I'm right here.'

Marcelo had managed to move behind her.

Suddenly she felt his hands around her waist and he drew her to him, pressing his face into her neck.

She smiled, then almost laughed aloud.

*I'm standing inside a fig tree, with a Brazilian . . . and a Brazilian.*

His hands moved over her stomach then cupped her breasts, and his mouth closed over her earlobe.

She arched against him.

His hands roved over her neck and shoulders, then down her arms. His fingers brushed her nipples through the thin fabric of her damp dress, making her shiver.

He moved a hand to her leg, inching up her dress until he found the soft flesh of her inner thigh. His other hand fondled her breast, his lips nuzzling at her neck. She hooked her arm behind his head, running her fingers through his thick hair.

He slid the strap of her dress off one shoulder, and then the other, peeling the dress down to her waist. She moved her hips, letting it fall to the ground, then kicked it away.

'You are perfect, *Pow-la*,' he whispered.

She pushed back against the hardness beneath his jeans, making him groan.

'*Pow-la . . .*'

His fingers moved across her stomach, tracing the curve of her waist and her bottom, then gripping the points of her hips.

He pushed his erection against her, harder now, before turning her around and kissing her fervently.

The sweet delirium of his taste, his smell, his tongue probing hers.

Their bodies writhed together, pelvis to pelvis, weaving and tilting.

She moved her hands under his t-shirt, touching his smooth torso. Daring to caress what she'd only ever secretly admired.

As she lifted his t-shirt higher, he pulled it up and over his head.

Even in the shadows, she could make out the muscular outline of his shoulders.

She heard him unzip his jeans.

Then he was moving one leg between hers, pressing against her, kissing her deeper still.

Her hands roamed to his trunks, pushing them down off his hips.

She sensed him stepping out of them and reached for his cock, moving her hand up and down its shaft to the silken head.

He kissed her hungrily now, his fingers working their way beneath her knickers. Light feathery strokes against skin still tender from waxing, exploring the moist warmth between her legs.

He murmured something in his own language, then wrenched her knickers off.

'Marcelo,' she moaned.

'You are such a *woman*.'

She pressed her naked body against his, guiding his penis between her thighs.

Suddenly he lifted her off her feet and pushed her against the tree.

His fingers glided across her collarbone and breasts, drawing a soft line to her navel, then downwards in long, languorous swirls. He took her nipple in his mouth, fondling the other with his finger.

A moment later, she felt his breath against her stomach. His lips played across her skin, teasing her, tasting her, lower and lower.

And then he was kneeling before her, his lips and tongue and hands pleasuring her, until her breaths became ragged.

As her ecstasy began to build, he stood up and gripped her hips between his hands, lifting her leg over the crook of his arm.

She'd never wanted anything so much in her life.

His teasing was almost unbearable as he came close to pushing inside her.

Then he seized her hips and pulled her onto him.

He paused for a moment and she whimpered, unable to stop herself from grinding against him.

Then he began moving inside her, and the intense, rhythmic pressure was overwhelming.

'*Pow-la*.'

He grunted with each thrust, a raw, primitive sound.

Her moans matched his as he plunged in and out of her, pushing her closer and closer.

The sweat slid off their frenzied bodies.

For a moment she floated on a dark cusp, feeling nothing but Marcelo.

Her climax exploded as he erupted into her.

Wave upon wave of pleasure, their bodies heaving and twitching. A sticky, sweaty annihilation.

The world was reduced to the sounds of their breathing.

*

Eventually they found her knickers, but they couldn't locate her dress. How could it have *disappeared* inside a tree?

They looked harder, scrabbling around until she found it; trampled underfoot.

'Oh, no . . .' she groaned, feeling how muddy it was. She couldn't tell the back from the front, either.

'I'll have to put it on outside,' she said, leaving Marcelo hunting for his own underwear.

Paula dropped to the ground and exited the tree the way she'd entered. Inching backwards out of the hole at the trunk's base, she felt light drops of rain on her bare legs and back.

Then she stood up and, feeling a little self-conscious, turned around.

'G'day.'

The Aboriginal ranger they'd passed earlier stood no more than two metres away.

Her hands flew up to her chest.

'You know sex in a public place is illegal?' His eyes were mocking. 'Although I don't know if inside a tree is classified as public, exactly.'

Marcelo practically burst out of the base of the tree. Wearing nothing but a pair of trunks, now streaked with dirt, and holding the rest of his clothes.

He stood between Paula and the ranger.

'Have you been outside listening the whole time?' Marcelo demanded.

'No, I just saw your leather jacket hanging there a minute ago.' The ranger pointed at the branch on which Marcelo had left it.

Paula tried to put on her dress, mud and all, but it was difficult to do, with an audience.

'Well, what do you want then?'

The ranger seemed to take umbrage at Marcelo's tone. 'I was just sayin' to your girlfriend, *mate*, that you both put on quite a show. And I'm within my rights to call the police about it.'

Marcelo passed Paula his leather jacket and jeans.

She grabbed them gratefully, forcing her feet into the legs of his wet jeans. They were a better option than her dress right now.

'Got your clothes all dirty with the gymnastics, did you?' the ranger asked, his eyes still dancing. 'Serves you right.' Then he reached for the walkie-talkie clipped to his belt.

'Please,' said Marcelo, taking a step forward. 'I'm sorry. Don't call the police. We were just having a bit of fun.'

'Ever heard of a bedroom?' the ranger asked.

Paula grimaced, mortified, as the man looked her up and down.

'Get going, you two.' He jerked a thumb in the direction of the path. 'Get outta here, before I change my mind.'

They scrambled off into the rainforest, like guilty adolescents: Marcelo in his muddy trunks, carrying his t-shirt and sneakers; Paula swimming in Marcelo's jeans and leather jacket, slipping about in her thongs.

By the time they reached the gate, they were both laughing.

They bolted to the ute through the rain, heavier now, and lunged into the front seats.

'That was close,' said Paula, still giggling.

*The best sex I've ever had and I could've ended up in court for it.*

'We should leave,' said Marcelo, his bare chest heaving. 'In case he *does* change his mind.'

Paula started the engine, pleased she'd had the presence of mind to hide the key under the tyre. Otherwise she might have lost *that* in the fig tree too.

As they moved out onto the road, Marcelo slipped his wet t-shirt over his chest and pulled on his sneakers.

'There,' he said. 'Much better.'

They looked at each other—damp and dishevelled, smiling like besotted teenagers—and burst into laughter again.

# 20

They drove with no particular destination in mind.

After a while, Paula glanced at Marcelo.

He was gazing out the window—a little broodily, she thought.

'Marcelo, are you okay?' she ventured.

'Yes, yes.'

'Where are you staying?'

'In a backpackers.'

'Do you want to get your things and come back to the caravan park?' It seemed like a natural suggestion.

'Sure.'

His response didn't seem all that enthusiastic.

Her inner critic began to berate her.

*You didn't turn him on enough.*

*You weren't hot enough.*

*You weren't tight enough.*

'Marcelo,' she blurted, 'did I do something wrong back there?'

She focused on the wide, flat street in front of her, gripping the steering wheel too hard.

'No,' he said. 'Of course not.'

She wanted to know more; to understand *how* good it had been for him. Her own experience had been cataclysmic.

'I got a Brazilian,' she faltered.

'I noticed.'

'I thought you might like it.'

She felt his hand on her thigh.

'*Pow-la*, you're a sexy woman,' he said. 'You're beautiful natural.'

Paula wasn't sure what to make of this, having spent her adult life trying to badger her body into submission; waxing, tinting, streaking, exfoliating, moisturising, fake tanning. An endless treadmill of treatments designed to *combat* the natural.

'You are perfect, *Pow-la*,' he said. 'I'm the one who's . . .'

He suddenly pointed at a junction ahead. 'This is the turn-off. Right here, please.'

She veered into Acacia Avenue and immediately spotted the hostel several hundred metres along. They pulled up outside a deserted tyre yard and a dilapidated-looking office block.

'I won't be long,' said Marcelo.

'Okay.' She smiled at him.

He opened his door and then, as if changing his mind, closed it again.

Leaning across the front seat, he cupped a hand under her chin. 'You are *perfect*, *Pow-la*. Trust me.'

Then he pressed his mouth against hers, moving his hand beneath the damp leather jacket, tracing a line from her collarbone to her nipple.

Suddenly she was breathless again.

'I have been swimming, I think?' he said, pointing to his still wet trunks.

She giggled as he climbed out of the car.

She watched him stride up the path to the hostel, quite a sight in his trunks and t-shirt.

The man who'd inadvertently helped her tackle Hamish's question—*Isn't my penis big enough?*

*Now* she knew the answer.

Paula shifted in her seat, noticing some tender spots. Something lumpy was pressing against her buttock, too. She reached into the back pocket of Marcelo's jeans and removed the offending item: his leather wallet.

Flipping it open, she caught sight of the large lettering of his driver's licence: *Republica Fedarativa Do Brasil.* She removed the card to look at the photo: Marcelo looked good even in a mug shot. She squinted at the name underneath.

*Gabriel Gustavo Pereira.*

Everything contracted to those three words.

Not Marcelo Fernandes, born on 25 December 1980, blood type AB negative.

Someone named Gabriel, with entirely different personal details.

Paula struggled to breathe. *Who is this man?*

The man to whom she'd just abandoned herself. Her charismatic, multi-talented travelling companion.

She felt her stomach heave, like she might be about to vomit.

*Who have I just made love to?*

Without any protection, she suddenly thought.

*Oh, God.*

She needed to get out of the car, now.

But as she opened the door, she saw him walking towards her in a fresh change of clothes.

She froze, her hand gripping the door handle.

He tapped at the window.

'Please, pass me my wallet? I have to pay.'

She passed it to him, her hands trembling, then watched him walk back up the path.

*Leave now*, she thought. *Just close the window and go.*

But he was back a minute later, throwing his backpack into the ute and climbing in next to her.

He moved across to kiss her.

She pressed herself against the door.

'Who are you?' she asked. 'Who are you *really*?'

His face was expressionless.

'I saw your driver's licence.'

His jaw tightened. 'Okay. *Pow-la*, let's drive. I will tell you.'

*

They stopped at a children's playground less than a kilometre away. It was drenched and deserted, as everything in Darwin seemed to be. They sat on the swingset, their feet trailing across the paperbark chips below.

'I've made some mistakes in life, *Pow-la*,' Marcelo began. 'But this is the biggest.'

She looked out at the flat suburban wasteland. Darwin in monsoon season, a town in tears.

'My name *is* Marcelo,' he insisted.

She desperately hoped it was true.

'For many years, I wanted to come to Australia, but it took me a long time to save up the money. When I had enough, I told my family my plan. They wanted to help me, of course. We don't have much, but my father gave me some of his savings for the visa. My younger brother Pietro helped me get a passport, my big brother Lucas booked the flight. The night before I left, we had a family *churrasco.* Not like your barbecues—a real one.' He smiled. 'Even the big cattle boss came. And Lucas came from the *favela,* to say goodbye. We sang songs, remembered my mother, we got drunk.'

She waited.

'When I woke up the next morning, the sun was already high. My brother Lucas told me, you were too drunk last night, *idiota*, you are late. Here is your luggage, I will drive you to the airport.'

He shook his head. 'It was all so rushed. I said goodbye to my family and we drove to Porto Alegre. I almost missed the flight to Sao Paulo. I checked in my backpack, my guitar, my surfboard, but I kept my mother's urn in my carry-on bag. When I got on the aeroplane, I was so nervous, I had to use the white bag . . . what is that called?'

'The travel-sickness bag.' Paula noticed that Marcelo's almost-perfect command of English seemed to slip the more upset he became.

'In Sao Paulo, I transferred to the international flight. There was a stopover in London and then Hong Kong, so I had time to read my guidebook. The map showed that Adelaide is very far from Darwin. I couldn't believe that Lucas had booked me on that flight.'

He shook his head.

'I collected my luggage in Adelaide and went through customs. The lady there opened my carry-on and said, "What is inside the cylinder?" I told her about my mother's ashes and showed her the document from the Brazilian authorities. She said, "I'll check with my supervisor." When she came back, a man was with her. He looked at the papers and after a while, he let me go.'

Marcelo gazed across the empty playground.

'I was standing at the taxi rank when a man came up to me and said in Portuguese, "Are you Marcelo?" He told me he was Lucas's friend and could give me a lift to the city. I was surprised, because Lucas never mentioned this. But that is my brother, very spontaneous.'

Paula didn't like the sound of this.

'We drove twenty minutes to a house somewhere and the man said, "Come inside." He wasn't smiling anymore, and he took my luggage with him.'

Paula grimaced. 'You didn't follow him, did you?'

'I wanted my stuff back. But inside the house, the man pulled out a pistol.' Marcelo raked his fingers through his hair. 'He took everything out of my backpack and stripped it open with a knife. Inside the lining were bags of white powder.'

'Drugs?' Paula gasped. 'What did you do?'

'Nothing.' Marcelo looked stricken. 'What *could* I do? The man weighed the bags. Then he gave me a new backpack and told me to leave. Lucas has paid his debt, he said.'

Marcelo bowed his head. 'Lucas *used* me for his business in the *favela*. I was his courier to Australia.'

Paula flinched. 'What happened next?'

'The man pushed me out the door. He gave me my guitar and surfboard and said, "Keep walking." And he told me what would happen if I ever talked.'

Marcelo exhaled. 'I walked fast for thirty minutes, maybe more, and then I got *angry*. I telephoned Lucas straight away and asked, "Why did you do this to me? I am your *brother*." Lucas told me that he had no choice; if I didn't deliver the *coca* to Australia, they would've killed him. And maybe come for our father too.'

'*Who* would've killed him?' Paula's mind was spinning.

'The *favela* boss in Porto Alegre, the drug king.' Marcelo's mouth twisted. 'He is an evil man. He took my brother into his business when Lucas was a teenager, when he first left for the city. Within six months, he had Lucas delivering and selling *coca*. My mother tried to get Lucas back, but she died trying.'

His eyes filled with tears.

'Lucas set me up. I was lucky to get through the airport. Maybe it was a miracle of God, they were only interested in the urn.' Marcelo crossed a hand over his chest.

'What did you do?' Paula asked.

'I was in shock, walking the streets. After a while, I came to a club, there was a party, many old people wearing hats. It looked like a safe place. So I went in and ordered a drink and then . . . I met Caitlin. And you.'

Paula shook her head in disbelief. 'You mean the Walkerville RSL? On Melbourne Cup day?'

He nodded.

'But that means you *lied* to me about how long you'd been in Adelaide. You said you'd been there three days, when we first met.' She studied his face. 'Now you say you arrived that same day.'

'I am sorry, *Pow-la*, I couldn't be honest with you straight away. I didn't know you. But when we talked later at the barbecue, I felt like I could trust you. After we began travelling together, I got worried the police were following us. I even hurt your husband, thinking he was police.'

'You met *Hamish*?' She was dumbfounded by this revelation. 'Where?'

'On the Nullarbor, in two places. He was persistent. He thought I liked *Caitlin*.' Marcelo looked heavenward.

Paula was having trouble processing all of this information.

'In Norseman I discovered he was your husband, not a police officer,' continued Marcelo, 'so I decided to tell *you*. But that same night, I fell sick and we drove to Perth and I lost your number and . . . well, you know the rest.'

'I don't actually,' said Paula. 'We looked for you in Perth, Marcelo. We stayed longer in Cottesloe, wondering if you might turn up. I was really worried.'

'I am sorry,' said Marcelo. 'It took three days for my stomach to get better, then Lucas called me. Something went wrong in Adelaide after the drop-off, his contact there was being watched by police. Lucas told me to disappear quickly, to fly back to Brazil using a new ID, just in case the police linked me to the drop-off.'

Marcelo shook his head. 'I panicked. Where could I get a new ID? But Lucas gave me a contact in Perth so I went to see him, and he made me this.' He pulled out his wallet and showed her the driver's licence she'd seen earlier.

'He's making a new passport too, but that takes three weeks. It's a more complicated job, I had to pay a thousand dollars upfront. He's going to call when it's done.' Marcelo sighed. 'So, while I wait for his call, I hitchhiked to Darwin to put my mother to rest.' He crossed his hand over his chest again. 'And to find you.'

She frowned. 'This person in Perth, can you trust him?'

'He is my only chance. Lucas said it is too dangerous to use my real papers now. The police could be following me already.'

'But couldn't you just go to the police and tell them everything?' she asked. 'About Lucas, I mean, that you were his unwitting courier. You're the victim here, Marcelo.'

He shook his head. 'I can't do that to my brother. I am angry with him, but he is still blood.'

She couldn't repress her frustration. 'So you'd rather be caught trying to leave Australia using a fake passport than report your brother to the police for using you as a drug mule?'

Marcelo opened his palms, as if surrendering. 'Family is everything. If Caitlin or Lachlan were in trouble like this, would *you* call the police?'

Paula knew, she wouldn't.

She sighed. 'We're in a mess, Marcelo.'

There wasn't really a 'we', she knew. They were two individuals from completely different worlds, thrown together by a random set of circumstances. There was little past to anchor them, no future to anticipate. And yet they'd shared a rare connection in the present; one of vulnerability and tenderness, laughter and physical attraction. Sensations and emotions of which Paula's life had been devoid for too long.

He reached for her hand.

'All I wanted was to come to Australia to put my mother to rest. I didn't know I would become a courier for my brother.' His eyes met hers. 'Or that I would fall for you, *Pow-la*.'

He pulled the chains of the swingset together, until they were face to face.

'I'm ashamed,' he said. 'For involving you and your family in this. You don't deserve it. You are a good person.'

It struck Paula that no one had ever said that to her. And yet, that was what she'd tried so hard to be, all her life. A good daughter, sister, wife and mother.

'What do we do now?' she asked.

'Kiss,' he said. 'It will come to us.'

He leaned forward and gently pressed his lips against hers.

*

They arrived back at the camp site just after seven o'clock.

As the ute drew closer, Paula spotted her children and her father, with a bucket and sponges, washing the caravan. Wet season in the Northern Territory hadn't been kind; the van's gleaming cream exterior had turned a muddy brown. Caitlin had been agitating to wash it for the past week, but Paula had been unable to summon the energy.

They'd obviously had dinner, too, judging by the dishes propped up on the drying rack. Thanks to their grandfather's 'life lessons', the children had become almost entirely independent when it came to meals: shopping, cooking and cleaning up after themselves. It was a turnaround which she could only attribute to this trip.

The three of them looked up as she parked alongside the caravan.

'Hi,' she said, smiling as she hopped out. 'Look who's here.'

Caitlin gasped as Marcelo stepped out of the passenger door.

'Is that Mar—?' Her face dropped. She looked Paula up and down. 'Where are your clothes, Mum?'

Amid Marcelo's revelations in the playground, Paula had forgotten she was wearing his clothes.

Caitlin looked between her mother and Marcelo. 'Are you two . . . ?'

'Yes,' Marcelo responded, his tone even.

Paula whirled about, pulling a face at Marcelo. They hadn't discussed talking to the kids about *them*.

Caitlin looked horrified. She turned to her brother. 'Lachie, let's go home with Dad. Gramps, can you please take us back to where Dad's staying?'

Sid looked at Paula for direction.

'Catie, I know this is a lot to take in . . .' she started.

'I'm sick of surprises,' her daughter spat. 'I want to go home.'

'Me too,' said Lachie. 'We've had enough of *your* trip, Mum. We're going back to Melbourne with Dad.'

'Did your father suggest that?'

Lachie shook his head. 'It's *our* choice, Mum. There are too many rules on this trip that *you* don't follow. *You* get to do whatever you want.'

'Yeah,' added Caitlin, her tone indignant. 'You chuck out my Playboy nightie because you think it's too sexy, but what are *you* wearing, Mum? You look like a dirty ho.'

Paula felt crushed to the core.

'Let them go.' Marcelo's voice, soft in Paula's ear. 'Let them go with their dad, if they want to.'

She turned back to her children.

'Don't you even want to stay for Christmas?' She choked on the words.

'We'd spoil the romantic atmosphere,' Caitlin sneered.

'Kids,' she begged. 'Please don't do anything rash.'

'What, like you?' Lachie's tone was caustic. 'You've always said honesty is the best policy, Mum. But you've broken *your* promise.'

She averted her gaze. Wearing Marcelo's clothes, she really didn't have a leg to stand on.

'Alright,' said Paula. 'It's your decision. Gramps can take you over tomorrow.'

'Now,' said Caitlin quietly. 'We want to go *now*.'

'Okay, if that's what you want,' said Paula.

Sid looked worried. 'You sure?'

Paula nodded. 'I'll call Hamish. But I can't watch them go.'

She strode to the ute and took her telephone from the glove box. 'If you need anything, kids, just call.' She couldn't bring herself to say goodbye. Without another word, she fled the camp site.

*

When Sid returned from dropping off the children, he was gloomy and withdrawn. Marcelo attempted to cheer them up by cooking a Brazilian-style barbecue, but neither Paula nor Sid were remotely in the mood.

Then, when Marcelo tried to seduce her in the caravan just before midnight, she brushed off his overtures. He said he understood, murmuring words of consolation.

*How quickly things change*, she thought. *Here I am, in a position to live out the very fantasy I've harboured since Adelaide—just me and Marcelo, alone in the caravan—and yet, I can't think about anything except the kids.*

They were safe with Hamish, she knew, and soon would be back in their family home in Glen Waverley. But it felt so *wrong* to be separated from them after spending two months in such close proximity.

She lay motionless next to Marcelo, until his steady breathing told her he was asleep. The silence was punctuated by his phone vibrating irregularly, but Marcelo didn't stir.

She watched his face as he slept, a face of beauty and symmetry, for which she'd fallen, harder than she'd imagined possible.

*But I don't really know this man at all. And I* never *should have let my children go.*

Paula rolled away from Marcelo and sat up at the window, pushing the curtains aside. The caravan park was bathed in silver moonlight.

She'd made an error of judgment, but there was still time to fix it.

Tomorrow, she decided, she would set things right with Catie and Lachie. Apologise for everything and ask them not to return to Melbourne with their father. They mightn't be dissuaded, but she had to try.

With the comfort of resolution, she lay back down next to Marcelo and, eventually, fell asleep.

*

'*Pow-la.*'

She sat up. He was as beautiful as ever in the morning light. His lips, soft and full, begged to be kissed. But first she had to tell him what she'd resolved.

'Marcelo, I—'

'I'm sorry to wake you, *Pow-la*. I need your help.' He pushed his phone into her hand. 'This message came in from Perth last night.'

*Flight QR901 to São Paolo transit Doha, exit Perth 1230 Mon. Collect passport 0900 at airport.*

'How am I going to get to Perth by Monday?' Marcelo's face was ashen.

It was just before eight o'clock on Friday morning.

'You'll have to fly,' she said. 'There's no other way. It's four thousand kilometres.'

'I can't,' he objected. 'It's too risky. I *have* to fly back to Brazil, but Lucas told me to stay out of airports and go by road.'

His hands were shaking as he reread the message. 'Please, can you drive me, *Pow-la*?'

'I'm sorry, Marcelo. I can't do that.'

His face fell.

It was too far to travel in three days, and besides, she'd already determined her course of action. She couldn't abandon her children, not even to their father. And Monday was Christmas Eve.

'Please.' His forehead was beaded with sweat. 'Help me, *Pow-la*.'

Looking into his eyes, she knew she couldn't abandon Marcelo, either. She thought for a minute, then said, 'I think I might know someone who can help. He's a tour guide in Darwin. Maybe we can pay him to take you back to Perth.'

'But I have no money, *Pow-la*,' said Marcelo.

'I do.'

He gripped her hand. 'Can we trust him?'

'He's looked after Hamish before,' she said.

Paula found her phone and began composing a message to her husband.

*

Hamish's friend Frank was on the verge of leaving Darwin, when she called.

'Farken crazy tryin' to get to Perth that quickly,' he said. 'I'll have to drive all night, in the farken silly season too. It'll cost you.'

And so Paula raided the caravan freezer again, counting out one thousand dollars before driving on to an address in Brinkin.

Fifteen minutes later, they found themselves standing on a dusty kerb next to a colourfully painted mini-bus.

Frank emerged from a white cement house surrounded by an orderly yard.

'G'day,' he said, extending his hand to all three.

'Where's Hamish?' asked Paula, looking down the drive for signs of her children.

'Took 'em out to the airport already,' said Frank. 'They're waitlisted on an earlier flight.'

'Oh.' Paula felt like she'd been kicked in the stomach. Hamish hadn't mentioned that when he'd sent her Frank's number.

She'd planned on talking to the kids again in the clear light of day, persuading them to resume their trip with her, especially now that Marcelo was leaving.

Tears blurred her vision.

Frank fixed his gaze on Marcelo.

'Who are *you*?'

'This is my . . . friend, Marcelo,' explained Paula. 'He needs to get to Perth quickly.' She fished around in her handbag and found the white envelope stuffed with notes. 'Here's the payment.'

Frank nodded, looking Marcelo up and down.

'Ever heard of aeroplanes, fella?'

'I get very plane sick.' Marcelo grimaced. 'I go by land wherever I can.'

Convincing, Paula thought.

'You'd better not vomit in my bus, fella,' Frank said, taking the envelope from Paula. 'I'll count this inside.'

He turned back to Marcelo. 'Get ready to go, Michaelo, I'll be back in a minute.'

Paula didn't highlight his mispronunciation.

She watched as Marcelo unstrapped his surfboard from the roof racks and took his backpack from the ute.

'Don't forget your guitar,' she called. 'Lachie's left it on the back seat.'

*Ever the mother*, she thought.

'Keep it,' said Marcelo. 'Without the case, it will damage easily. It already has dents.'

'Oh.' She reddened, remembering how they'd accidentally left the case in Derby. 'Sorry about that.'

'It's no matter,' said Marcelo, taking a step towards her. 'Lachie is learning now. He can have the guitar.'

'He'll be thrilled,' she said. 'That's really kind. Now here's something for you.'

Reaching into her handbag, she passed him an envelope. 'This is in case you run into any trouble. If you don't spend it, just take it home.'

She remembered his family didn't have much money.

'Thank you, *Pow-la*,' he said. 'You are so kind.'

'Okay, we *both* are.'

They laughed, then stood looking at each other.

How could either of them make sense of what had happened between them in the last thirty-six hours—or over the past month, for that matter?

Sid sauntered away, pretending to be interested in a tropical orchid growing in the garden.

'*Pow-la*.' Marcelo took her face in his hands. 'You have been so good to me. My mother would be grateful.' He pointed to his heart, where the tattooed *Lili* lay beneath his t-shirt. 'Take this.' He passed her his leather jacket, still damp from their previous afternoon in the Botanic Gardens. 'I will come to Melbourne and get it back from you some day.'

'I'm afraid of losing you,' she whispered.

It was true. She was afraid of what she'd think about now, without Marcelo as a delightful distraction. Afraid of the decisions she'd have to make, sooner than she wanted to, about Hamish and their life together. Afraid of never again experiencing the sexual chemistry she'd shared with him, unsurpassed by anything she'd ever known before. Afraid of having nothing new and spontaneous and joyful in her life to celebrate anymore.

He shook his head. 'You are not losing Marcelo, *Pow-la*. You have found yourself.'

His lips brushed hers.

'Time to go,' Frank called.

She reluctantly moved away from Marcelo.

He walked over to Sid, shook his hand and said something that made him laugh, before pulling him into a hug. Sid looked weepy, which made Paula more so.

'Don't know what you see in him.'

It was Frank's voice, low in her ear.

Paula turned. 'Pardon?'

'Hamish might be farken stupid sometimes, but he's got heart. This guy, Martino . . .'

'Marcelo,' she corrected.

'Whatever. Wouldn't trust him as far as I can throw him.'

'Well,' she said, irritated, 'you can't be a very good judge of character then, can you?'

Frank said nothing. He climbed aboard the mini-bus and took his place behind the wheel.

'Sit up the back, Mario,' he ordered.

Marcelo took a seat in the back row, then turned and looked through the rear window at Paula. He mouthed her name, put two fingers to his lips, and pressed them over his heart.

She smiled through her tears.

With a one-finger salute in their direction, Frank pulled away from the kerb.

Paula stood watching the mini-bus, her father's comforting arm around her, until it disappeared from view.

# 21

They drove in silence, retracing the route to the caravan park.

*What are we going to do*, Paula wondered, *now that our group is devoid of children and Brazilian lovers?*

'Are you okay, Pokey?'

Paula smiled; her father hadn't used that nickname in years.

'I don't know, Dad,' she said. 'Everything we've seen and done on this trip, then meeting Marcelo, it's been . . .' *The time of my life*, she realised suddenly. *I've just gone and had it.*

'It's been amazing, Dad. But it's unsustainable.'

The road trip had been steadily whittling away at Paula's ten-thousand-dollar lump sum. Her three-month budget calculation had allowed a modest sum for contingencies, but no nasty surprises; certainly not a one-thousand-dollar Darwin-to-Perth carriage fee for Marcelo. Not to mention the additional money she'd given him for the hospital.

'I think we're just going to have to go straight home, taking the shortest route,' she said, defeated. 'I'm sorry, Dad.'

It seemed like such a shame, having come this far. But without her children or Marcelo, and with just over a thousand dollars in the freezer now, she didn't have much choice.

'He was worth it, Paula. A very nice young man.' Her father paused. 'But maybe we should go to the airport first and see if we can catch the kids before they fly out?'

She smiled at him. 'Great idea.'

Her father reached forward and turned on the CD player. 'Let's play some of Lachie's awful music on the way, eh? About shovels and rakes and all that nonsense.'

She laughed.

As her father fumbled with the iPod connection, her mobile rang.

She immediately recognised the number: Mr Nelson, principal of Burwood Secondary College.

'Sorry, Dad, I need to take this, I've been putting it off,' she said, pulling over on the side of the highway. 'Let's swap and you drive?' They exchanged places as she answered the call.

'Mrs McInnes, I'm relieved to get through,' said Mr Nelson.

'Hello,' she said, feeling her jaw clench. The principal's voice epitomised everything she *hadn't* missed about Melbourne.

'Some new information has come to light in our Facebook investigation. Is now a good time?'

'Sure,' she said, as Sid nosed the ute back onto the highway.

'Facebook investigated the account that created the offensive post,' he said. 'It took them a while to do the IP tracing, and they only got back to us ten days ago. I've been trying to contact you ever since.'

'I see.' She refrained from apologising; she'd been more than distracted these past few weeks.

'Facebook discovered that the James Addams account was created then accessed from just two IP addresses.' Mr Nelson paused. 'One was a computer in your home, the other in Amy Robertson's.'

'I don't understand.'

'I'm sorry, Mrs McInnes, but it seems that Caitlin and Amy created the Blow Queens post themselves.'

'What?' she gasped.

'Our school counsellor, Mrs Papadopolous, spoke to Amy last week. She's admitted to everything.'

'Oh my God.' Paula closed her eyes.

'I know this must be hard to hear.' Mr Nelson sounded conciliatory. 'But school's finished for the year and we've decided, under the circumstances, not to reveal this to the wider school community. We think it will only make the situation worse.'

'But why?' Paula asked weakly. '*Why* would they do that?'

Mr Nelson cleared his throat.

'Amy and your daughter are . . . having a romantic relationship. Apparently a Year Eleven boy spotted them together after soccer training and threatened to tweet something about them. So they decided to pre-empt him by creating a false Facebook account under the name of James Addams. Then they created the image of the phallus and posted it to Charlotte Kennedy's Facebook page. She's one of the most popular girls in the school, so it went viral quickly. The whole thing was designed to distract the boy who'd seen them and publicly disprove his suspicions.'

Paula shook her head.

'But . . . Caitlin could have just *talked* to me,' she said. 'She knows that. We could have worked it out.' Tears pricked her eyes. 'I am so sorry.'

How had her relationship with her daughter devolved to this? Paula had convinced herself they communicated honestly and openly, but this proved otherwise. At her most vulnerable moment, instead of turning to her parents, Caitlin had hatched a foolish plan with Amy that only led to deeper trouble.

'As I said, I don't intend to share this with anyone. Only the school counsellor, Mrs Papadopolous, is aware of what's happened. No one was hurt, the post is offline now.' The principal sounded as if he was trying to justify the decision to himself.

'But when you get back to Melbourne,' he continued, 'we'd like to have a joint family meeting with Amy and her parents, as well as Caitlin and your husband. It's all very unfortunate. We do understand, on some level, *why* the girls did it, but they went too far. They need some more counselling, and we're going to have to manage the fact that they are . . . well, they *think* they are . . .'

'Lesbians.'

Paula couldn't imagine the moment she'd be forced to deliver this news to Hamish.

'Talk to Caitlin first, then contact me when you're home,' continued Mr Nelson, his tone sympathetic. 'I'm sorry, Mrs McInnes.'

'Thank you,' she whispered, ending the call.

She hung her head and cried.

'Paula?'

Her father looked at her, clearly worried.

'Oh, Dad, this is *awful.*'

'What's happened?'

She covered her face with her hands.

'Do you want me to pull over?'

'No,' she said, from behind her hands. 'Let's just get to the airport as quickly as possible.'

She *had* to see her children before they caught a flight home, to tell her daughter what she desperately needed to know.

*No matter what you do, no matter who you are, I love you.*

*

'The flight's closed.'

The Qantas clerk at the desk outside Gate 11 shook his head.

'But my children are on that plane . . .' Paula clamped a hand over her mouth to stop the sobs bursting out.

'But there's nothing I can *do*, ma'am,' the man objected. 'They've closed the doors, I'm sorry.'

*You're* not *sorry*, she wanted to yell.

'It's okay, Pokey.' Her father pulled her to him.

She could feel him nodding at the Qantas staffer over the top of her head, as if to reassure him too.

'We can leave Darwin today,' he said. 'Collect the caravan, head straight down the Stuart Highway. Be back in Melbourne in five days, tops.'

'But it's Christmas in *three*.' She was hiccupping against his chest, in great gasping sobs.

Her father stroked her hair. 'It's not the end of the world. We've survived two months on the road, we can manage another few days. We can make it fun, our last hurrah. Christmas in the bush, just the two of us.'

The prospect made her cry even harder.

She loved her father—more deeply than ever, having shared this road trip with him—but she couldn't contemplate Christmas without her children.

As she bawled into her father's shirt, Paula suddenly understood how Hamish must have felt. Waiting for news from his family as they travelled around Australia without him.

*Isolated. Lonely. Bereft.*

The guilt was crushing.

She didn't want to punish Hamish anymore.

The Qantas clerk coughed. 'Excuse me, ma'am.'

Paula raised her head from her father's chest.

'Have you considered a stand-by for tonight's flight? It's the red-eye special, there are always no-shows.' The man tapped away at his keyboard. 'It's showing full, but if you're prepared to wait at the airport until tonight, something's sure to come up.'

He placed a box of tissues on the counter.

Paula took one, checking the man's name tag.

'Thank you, Roland.' She blew her nose several times. 'What do you think, Dad?'

'What about Hillary?' her father asked. 'And Clinton?'

Roland looked thoroughly confused.

'Maybe that's a job for Frank,' said Paula. 'I'll take Hillary to collect our bags now and catch a cab back here. I can pay the caravan park for every day Hillary and Clinton sit there. I'll ask Frank to come and collect them the next time he's up in Darwin.'

'You reckon?' Her father looked anxious. 'What about the cost?'

Paula shrugged. 'I'm sure Hamish will be happy to cover it—especially if it means we're all home by Christmas.'

'Alright.' Sid didn't sound confident.

They stood together at the floor-to-ceiling plate glass window, watching the Boeing 767 now pushing back from the terminal, poised to transport Hamish, Caitlin and Lachlan back to their family home in the south.

The Qantas clerk hailed them again. 'I've just put a good word in for you with guest services. Let's see if I can get you bumped up the queue.'

*

Just after midnight, they found themselves in seats 45B and 45C, adjacent to the rear toilet. But for all Paula cared, they could've been strapped to the aeroplane's wing. Immediately before take-off, she texted her sister.

*We're coming home tonight! QF 417 arrives 6.30am.*

Jamie's response arrived just as a flight attendant told Paula to switch off her mobile phone.

*I'll collect u at the airport. Can't wait to c u again. U just made my Xmas!*

It was the emotional balm Paula needed.

She leaned back, squeezed her father's hand, and closed her eyes for take-off. Listening to the thrumming of the engine on ascent, feeling the slight yawing of the aircraft, floating comfortably in the night.

*This is the right thing,* she thought. *We're going home.*

Her father slipped his hand out from under hers. She opened her eyes to see him scrolling through the in-flight entertainment listing, utterly comfortable with tablet technology. She smiled, remembering his Melbourne Cup win at Walkerville RSL in Adelaide. Placing a few token bets using an iPhone app, then changing Barry and Shirl's life.

The entire trip had been life-changing.

Walkerville, the Melbourne Cup, Marcelo. It had all begun only two months back, triggered by a trio of life events that Paula could never have anticipated; the 'Blow Queens' Facebook post, Hamish's bicycle accident and hospitalisation, her chance discovery of his online liaisons. Her wild rage that prompted a spontaneous around-Australia caravanning journey. The unexpected gifts of the road: precious moments with her father, quality time with her children, a breathtaking foreign lover.

A chance, at almost forty, to do things differently; to lose weight, get fit, shift diehard habits. To hold off on the beers and have a Brazilian wax instead. And then, to reflect on more subterranean truths: her daughter's emergent sexuality, her own passion reawakened, the malaise affecting her marriage. And the *real* Marcelo revealed: not a benign Brazilian backpacker, but an unsuspecting drug mule for his wayward brother.

*Will Marcelo make it out of Australia safely?*

No news was good news, she hoped.

Paula closed her eyes once more.

*

'Ladies and gentleman, shortly we will be landing at Tullamarine airport.'

Paula craned her neck to see the pastoral patchwork below, glowing pale yellow in the sunrise.

'I've missed Melbourne,' she murmured.

'Me too,' said her father. 'But give us a week and we'll be wishing we were on the road again. It's the human condition.'

*The 'grass is always greener' syndrome,* she thought, *poisoning the present. Everyone striving for something* better; *a better job, a better body, a better partner. Rarely cherishing what they already have.*

Paula thought of Hamish. *The husband I have.*

She glanced at her father, who looked thoroughly spent. 'What's wrong, Dad?'

'I just wish we could've finished the trip the way we started it, Paula. With the kids, in Hillary and Clinton. You reckon Frank will bring them back for us?'

'First week of January, he's got it sorted.' She patted his hand. 'Frank's got a transporting mate who can do it on the cheap for us, a semi-trailer backload to Melbourne. He'll deliver Hillary and Clinton right to our door. Then you can move straight back in to Clinton.'

He shook his head. 'I think I'll go back to Greenleaves.'

'Nonsense, Dad, you're staying with us.'

'No, Paula.' He sounded determined. 'For starters, I don't *want* to see the inside of Clinton ever again.'

She laughed.

'And you and Hamish need some time alone, without me hanging around. If you're going to make things right.'

She leaned back against the headrest.

'I'm not sure I *can* make things right with Hamish, Dad. I can't trust him.'

*Or myself,* she thought, thinking of Marcelo.

Sid clipped his tray-table into the upright position. 'But we all do things out of character every now and then, Paula. Hamish did, with that girl on the internet. You did with Marcelo. It's equal again between you two now, isn't it?'

She doubted it ever *had* been equal.

'*You* never do anything out of character, Dad.'

'Not true, my girl. What about all those ladies on the trip, eh? Huey, Dewey and Louie.'

She smiled, remembering them: Brenda, Linda and Rhonda.

Her father looked pensive for a moment. 'They were all larrikin versions of your mother, come to think of it. I spent the trip looking for her replica.'

The *Fasten seatbelts* sign flashed above their heads.

'You really loved her, Dad?' Paula asked.

His eyes grew wistful. 'More than infinity,' he said. 'Even though *she* was a benevolent dictator too.'

Paula didn't like the inference. 'Too?'

'Well, you *do* run a tight ship, Paula. But if Hamish knows what's good for him, he'll start appreciating it.'

Paula pulled the strap of her seatbelt tighter around her waist for landing.

She wasn't so sure she wanted to run a ship anymore, let alone a tight one. So many things had changed for her, subtly and radically. She didn't think she could make love to Hamish again, or at least not for a very long time. But she didn't relish the prospect of being a single parent, either; the solitude, the hard slog, the financial difficulties. That alone was incentive enough to try to work things out. And then there were Catie and Lachie. Both of them old enough to recognise life's complexity, yet young enough to hanker after a fairy-tale ending for their parents.

Her father studied her face. 'I've got something for you, Paula.'

He shifted in his seat and removed his wallet from his back pocket, checking through the compartments until he found what he was looking for.

As the aeroplane touched down on the tarmac, their bodies lurched forward.

He pushed a small white square of paper into her hand, but she couldn't hear his words above the roaring of the reverse thrust.

She unfolded the paper and read the message.

*Paula, look in the caravan freezer. Dad x*

She blinked. 'What, where we keep the cash?'

He nodded. 'I stored it there for safekeeping. I was going to surprise you at Christmas. You can take a look when Clinton gets back to Melbourne. Something for a rainy day, just in case things don't work out with Hamish.'

'I cleared the money out of the freezer yesterday. Nothing else was in there.'

'But you probably didn't feel *right* up the back, did you?'

She shook her head, mystified. 'What's in there?'

Sid smiled. 'Proof that *everyone* does things out of character, once in a while.'

*

'Paula! Dad!' Jamie rushed across the Arrivals hall, her arms outstretched. 'My God! You look *incredible.* What on earth have you two been *doing* up north? Why are you back early? And where are the kids?'

'They're home already with Hamish.' Paula laughed, hugging her sister. 'Long story.'

'It'll take *at least* three beers,' said Sid.

'But you're wearing a flippy dress, Paula!' Jamie looked amazed. 'That's got to be a first.'

Paula glanced down at her summery Darwin attire; a strapless red frock with white polka-dots. She pulled a black cardigan over her shoulders. 'Is that more Melbourne now?'

Jamie grinned. 'Well, I can't *wait* to hear your stories. Let's get you home.'

She stooped to help with their bags.

They chatted all the way, with Paula doing her best to fill her sister in on everything that had transpired on the trip. When she reached the part involving Marcelo, Sid suddenly plugged in his iPhone and did his best impression of Lachie, humming and tapping his knees.

As Jamie drove them back through the streets of Glen Waverley, Paula took in all the landmarks—the medical centre, the shopping plaza, the public school—with a sense of both relief and unease. The landscape of her former life, in all its blessed and tedious familiarity.

*Will I ever adjust to normal life again?*

As they parked outside the house, the curtains in the lounge room billowed.

A moment later, Catie and Lachie came bounding down the front steps. Lachie, wearing his mother's apron, smelled of bacon. Catie, still in her nightie—one they'd never had to argue about—looked like she'd just woken up.

The children launched themselves at Paula as if it had been forty-eight days since they'd last seen her, not forty-eight hours.

She pulled them to her, smiling at Hamish over their heads.

'Welcome back,' said Hamish, his voice a little husky. 'Hello, Sid.' He reached out to shake his father-in-law's hand, then nodded at Jamie. 'Thanks for picking them up. I would've done it myself if I'd *known* about it.'

'No trouble,' said Jamie brightly, as Hamish lifted the bags from the boot. 'I won't stay.'

Paula extricated herself from the children and bent down to embrace her sister through the car window.

'Thanks, Jamie,' she whispered, casting a brief glance in Hamish's direction. 'We need to debrief more.'

'When you're ready.' Jamie beamed at her. 'It's *so* good to have you back. And you've done a *brilliant* job of looking after Dad.'

Jamie waved at the group. 'See you Tuesday, everyone. Christmas dinner at mine, anytime from noon.' She winked at Paula. 'I figured you mightn't be up to the cooking.' She beeped her horn and accelerated away.

Paula turned back to her family.

'Come on up—Lachie's just made a chorizo omelette for breakfast,' said Hamish. He smiled at Paula. 'How'd you manage to teach him *that*?'

'Oh, he must take after you, Hamish,' said Paula, catching Caitlin's eye. 'My cooking still *sucks*.'

'Paula.' Sid turned to her with mock sternness. 'If you *ever* say that again, you'll do five hundred metres up the front.'

'And fifty burpees,' added Lachie.

The children laughed.

Hamish looked from one to another.

'A joke from the road,' Paula explained.

'Oh.' He looked momentarily put-out, then began lugging the bags up the stairs. Sid followed after Hamish, relieving him of one.

Paula put her arms around Lachie and Catie.

'It's good to be home,' she said. 'Got any of that omelette left?'

*

After breakfast, they moved out onto the back veranda for a cup of tea.

Hamish nodded at the grassy square where the caravan usually stood. 'Frank reckons he'll deliver it just after New Year. In the meantime, we'll make Sid a camp bed in the lounge room. I'll sleep in my swag in the backyard.'

'No, Hamish,' Sid objected.

Hamish held up a hand. 'It's the least I can do.'

He didn't look at Paula, but she was grateful; Hamish obviously recognised that they couldn't just resume their ordinary positions in the marital bed.

'Let's go, Lachie,' he said. 'You can show me where to set up my swag. You've got more experience than I have now. We'll need to put a tarp over it, I reckon.'

'I'll help too,' Sid volunteered.

The three of them headed down the back stairs.

Paula watched them go, then turned to her daughter. 'Come and have a chat in the lounge room.'

Catie followed her inside.

Paula sat on the sofa. 'Come,' she said, patting her lap.

'What?'

'Give me a hug,' said Paula. 'I've missed you.'

Catie looked a little wary, then lowered herself onto her mother's lap.

They sat in silence for a while, their arms wrapped around each other.

As Caitlin relaxed, Paula rocked her back and forth.

'This is what I used to do when you were a baby,' she said. 'You can't remember it, but can you imagine it?'

Catie smiled as Paula began to sing a lullaby, once her failsafe for putting her to sleep.

*'Golden slumbers kiss your eyes,*
*Smiles awake you when you rise,*
*Sleep, pretty Caitlin, do not cry,*

*And I will sing a lullaby.'*

After a moment, Paula took her daughter's hand. 'I had a phone call from Mr Nelson,' she said gently. 'I know you created the Facebook post.'

Caitlin's eyes widened.

'Why didn't you tell me about Amy?' Paula asked. 'We could have *talked* about what the boy at school saw, we could have planned a way to deal with it. But you went and did something false and risky and just plain . . . stupid.'

Caitlin nodded through tears. 'I know it was stupid.'

'How long have you and Amy been . . . ?' Paula didn't quite know how to phrase it. Were Catie and Amy in a full-blown relationship, or just involved in one of those passionate platonic crushes so common with teenage girls?

'I don't really want to talk about it, Mum.' Catie hung her head.

Paula nodded, trying to be reasonable. 'Okay, but we'll have to soon. Whatever's going on . . . I'm not angry. I'm just disappointed by how you've handled it. Thankfully Mr Nelson has decided to keep it quiet, or you mightn't be going back to Burwood Secondary College next year. Honestly, Catie, I expected more from you.'

Caitlin looked dejected. 'I didn't think you'd want to know about me and Amy.' Her tone was wounded. 'I didn't think you'd be able to handle it. I mean, you get worked up about a *nightie*. And I knew *Dad* definitely wouldn't like it.'

*That his little angel was a lesbian? She's dead right.*

'Well, I'm sorry,' said Paula, taking her daughter's face in her hands. 'When you're ready to talk more about it, I'm ready to listen. Whatever's going on for you, Catie, I *always* want to know. Sometimes it might take me a while to process it, but you've got to trust me: *nothing* will make me not love you. And honesty is *always* the best policy.'

Caitlin looked at her mother, doubtfully. 'But *you're* not always honest. You were doing stuff with Marcelo that we didn't know about.'

'Yes, but I wasn't trying to mislead you.' Paula closed her eyes, feeling embarrassed. 'I've probably not been the best role model to you lately, have I?' She opened her eyes again and looked directly at her daughter. 'Turns out *I'm* human too. Everyone is in this family. We've *all* made mistakes, in one form or another. But we can forgive each other, can't we?'

Caitlin nodded, her eyes glistening.

'And we're going to have to pick the right time to tell Dad about you and Amy,' Paula said. 'After Christmas, at least.'

'He'll go ballistic,' whispered Catie.

'Probably.' Paula pressed her forehead against her daughter's. 'But all I want is for you to be happy, Catie, whoever you love.'

Caitlin smiled at her. 'Me too. For you, I mean, Mum.'

Paula blinked, a little startled by this insight.

They sat like that, their foreheads pressed together, until the men of their family returned to the room.

*

On the first Friday afternoon of the New Year, Paula returned home from work to find everyone at their usual posts.

*Assume the position*, she thought. Sid was gardening, Lachie was playing on his new games console, Caitlin was listening to her iPod and Hamish was busy behind his laptop.

Their trip around Australia now felt like a surreal blip on the otherwise blank radar of her existence. Reinstated as queen of her suburban life, Paula had slipped back into the routines of work and school holidays again, as though none of it had ever really happened.

*Except that it did happen*, she often thought, as she hung the washing or made the beds. *And I've got the pubic stubble to prove it.*

'How was your day?' Hamish asked, standing up to greet her. He'd been utterly attentive since her return.

'Alright,' she said, placing her handbag on the kitchen bench. Her part-time job as a social worker at Bella Vista had been waiting for her, just as she'd hoped. They'd been unable to fill her position, even temporarily; few people were interested in award-wage work at an aged-care facility.

'One of the residents is dying,' she said, her voice flat. 'He'll probably pass away tonight with some extra morphine.'

A feverish finale to eighty-seven years of love and pain, aspiration and boredom, triumph and failure. *The inexorable end that awaits us all, sooner or later.*

'Can I get you a drink?' Hamish asked, in a consoling tone.

'Thanks.'

He began fixing her a lime and soda, their new drink of choice at home.

'Want to go for a run after this?' he asked. 'You look stressed.'

He was trying so hard to prioritise her needs. Still sleeping in his swag under a tarpaulin in the backyard, cooking the evening meals whenever the children didn't, even trying to bond with Sid in the garden.

She watched him crack the ice cubes out of the tray.

*So I don't feel anything yet. But Hamish* is *my husband of seventeen years. And his affair was online; mine was real.*

The children had obviously told their father what they'd seen in Darwin—their mother wearing Marcelo's clothes—but, quite uncharacteristically, Hamish hadn't raised the matter with her.

*Bygones are bygones*, he'd said to Paula on her first night back at home. *We've both made our fair share of mistakes.* He'd obviously been reading the stash of personal-psychology books now piled under the coffee table. Perhaps they'd helped him grapple, too, with Paula's revelation about Caitlin's sexuality. Instead of reacting in the way Paula feared he might—shock, rage, or stony silence—Hamish had simply sat alone for several minutes, before nodding with acquiescence. Then he'd quietly initiated another father–daughter chat with Caitlin. *Only this time I'm leaving my judgments at the door*, he'd said to Paula with a wry smile. *I don't want to push her out onto her bike, ever again.*

It was this, more than anything else, which finally persuaded Paula that Hamish's own process of self-discovery—the lessons he'd learned as he'd pursued them around Australia—might lead to lasting change. While Paula herself was still finding it difficult to talk with Caitlin about her sexuality, Hamish had handled it elegantly.

*She* really *had to give Hamish credit,* Paula thought.

*He* did *deserve a second chance.*

# 22

'Look who's here, Mum!'

Lachie and Catie ran to the lounge-room window and peered at a semi-trailer parked outside, bearing the words 'Top End Transporters'.

'Ah!' said Sid from the sofa, sounding genuinely pleased. 'Our old friends, Hillary and Clinton.'

'But *you're* not sleeping in Clinton, Sid,' said Hamish. 'That's my job for the next few weeks. You can stay in the lounge room. I'll upgrade from swag to caravan.'

'Only if it's not too much trouble.' Sid looked between Paula and Hamish. 'I can go back to Greenleaves.'

'No way,' said Hamish, clapping a hand on Sid's shoulder. 'It'll be my pleasure.'

Paula wondered whether it really *was* such a sacrifice for Hamish. The lounge room was less comfortable than the caravan, and certainly less private. And was it a good idea for Hamish to camp overnight in Clinton? All alone, except for his laptop?

*Bygones are bygones*, she told herself.

Hamish joined the children at the window. 'Hang on, who's that?' He began to smile. 'Well, I'll be buggered.'

He strode to the front door and opened it. 'Frank!' he called, beaming. 'What are *you* doing here? Talk about personal service. Tell the driver to bring 'em up into the back yard, mate.'

Paula watched as the driver expertly manoeuvred the ute and caravan off the semi-trailer and up their steep driveway, with Frank's assistance.

'Hey, Mum, remember your jackknife on the first day?' Lachie taunted.

Paula poked her tongue out at him.

'You *didn't*?' Hamish repressed a smirk. 'Okay, I won't say a word. I'll go get Frank.'

He disappeared down the front stairs.

A few minutes later, they returned.

'Frank, meet the kids,' said Hamish. 'Catie and Lachie.'

They waved at him.

'You know everyone else?'

'G'day,' said Frank, removing his cap and nodding around the room.

'What brings you to Melbourne?' Paula asked. 'Would you like a drink?'

'No, thanks. Just doin' my job, ma'am.'

He seemed different, Paula thought.

Frank reached into the blue backpack he was carrying. 'I've got something for you.'

He pulled out a white envelope and placed it on the dining-room table. 'There's the one-and-a-half grand I owe you.'

Everyone stared at the envelope.

'What do you mean?' Hamish asked.

'You two paid me a couple of times. Hamish out of Freo, Paula in Darwin.'

'But you *earned* that, mate,' said Hamish. 'And there's another grand here for this job too.' Hamish opened his wallet.

Frank shook his head. 'Give it to the driver out the front. I've been working on another job of my own. A bit like trying to trap a pack of dingos. Watch the seven o'clock news.' He zipped up his bag. 'I'll be back in touch. We're going to be seeing a bit more of each other.'

Frank pulled his cap back onto his head and walked towards the rear stairs.

Hamish followed him. 'What are you talking about, mate?'

Frank turned. 'Just watch tonight's news.' Then he walked back to Paula and lowered his voice so that no one could hear. 'And *you* should check out the freezer in the caravan.'

Frank strode past Hamish and down the stairs.

'Which channel?' Lachie called after him.

'Any one you like,' came the reply.

Paula watched through the lounge-room window as Frank jogged down the driveway, then climbed into a navy Commodore parked outside their house. She couldn't see the driver behind the car's tinted windows. The car drove off.

Hamish looked around the room. 'Does anyone know what the hell that was about?'

No one said a word.

'I guess we'll just have to wait for the news,' said Caitlin, slightly breathless. 'It's on in fifteen minutes.'

They sat, the five of them, mute and unmoving on the sofa.

It was the second item of the evening, after a story on Melbourne's planned Olympic bid for 2024. Behind the newsreader, an image of

Marcelo appeared; Paula read the caption, open-mouthed. *Record drug haul.*

The newsreader's eyes followed the autocue.

*'A single phone call from an anonymous source in Adelaide provided an important breakthrough in a joint police investigation that netted one of Australia's largest-recorded cocaine seizures—two hundred and fifty kilograms, worth an estimated two hundred million dollars.*

*'The deputy commissioner of the Australian Federal Police told a news conference today that 'Operation Dingo' had been conducting surveillance into trans-Nullarbor narcotics movements across three states and territories for more than six months. But it was a simple tip-off from a concerned member of the public that ultimately led to the arrest of a seventeen-member international drug syndicate.'*

The camera cut to a news conference, where three uniformed officers sat in front of a pack of reporters. The central figure, identified as the deputy commissioner, leaned into his microphone.

*'A Belgian backpacker identified a suspicious individual at an Adelaide budget hostel in November and contacted police. That individual was tracked across several sites of interest along the Nullarbor Plain trucking route, and ultimately led police to an alleged ringleader. One phone call allowed us to unravel a syndicate that will be stopped forever.'*

The newsreader appeared again.

*'On Wednesday, police searched four properties in Adelaide, Perth and Darwin, arresting and charging eleven people with possessing a commercial quantity of drugs. A precursor to the heist was the arrest on 24 December of two people alleged to be among the group's ringleaders. The pair were apprehended at Perth International Airport attempting to board a flight for Brazil.'*

An image appeared on the screen: two mug shots. One of Marcelo, the other of an olive-skinned young woman, beautiful despite her scowl.

*'Thirty-three-year-old Australian Mark Ferris, of Bowden in Adelaide's northern suburbs, and his Brazilian-born wife Liliana, thirty, are among seventeen people accused of operating the international syndicate.'*

The camera cut to footage of the pair being escorted from a sandstone courthouse and into a waiting police car. Marcelo, wearing aviator sunglasses, held a protective arm around Liliana's shoulders while extending the other towards the camera.

'*No comment, you bastards,*' he called, as they were jostled by the media.

His accent was broad and unmistakably Australian.

The newsreader appeared again. '*Mr and Mrs Ferris were the subject of fraud allegations aired last year on ABC TV's* Four Corners *program, but they have never been charged. Police investigations continue.*'

The background image shifted to the next item, *China slow-down inevitable*, as the newsreader refocused on her autocue.

Paula sat frozen.

No one else stirred.

Marcelo Fernandes.

Mark Ferris.

An Australian, not a Brazilian.

A drug smuggler, not a drug mule.

With his *wife*, Liliana.

Paula recalled the word 'Lili' tattooed on Marcelo's chest.

*Mark Ferris. A thirty-three-year-old fraudster from Adelaide.*

The humiliation of it all.

*How naive have I been?*

Falling for every stock-standard Brazilian stereotype he'd ever conjured; the hip-swivelling, horse-riding, lady-charming sex god—with a Brazilian wife to help him perfect his act.

She'd *wanted* to be convinced by Marcelo Fernandes.

She'd *needed* to be.

'You alright?' Sid whispered, taking a handkerchief from his pocket and passing it to her.

She buried her face in it, even though she wasn't crying. She wanted to hide from the world.

Hamish stood up and began pacing the room.

'Farken Frank's a . . . *pig*. A bloody undercover copper. I *knew* he was cleverer than your average blackfella.'

'Oh, *Dad*.' Caitlin and Lachie chorused.

'And . . . my God,' Hamish continued. 'They said a *Belgian backpacker in Adelaide* tipped off police. That was stinky bloody Sasha! He called the coppers on *me*, that strange bastard. He said he would, and he bloody did!' His eyes were saucer-like. 'Then *I* must've led the pigs to Mark Ferris, without even meaning to. Yalata Roadhouse, Eucla, Norseman, Darwin.'

Paula could hear Hamish blathering, but she wasn't paying attention.

*I had unprotected sex with a conman.*

The words revolved in her head.

*Unprotected sex. Conman.*

'I never picked he was Aussie,' she heard Lachie murmur to his sister. 'Did *you*?'

His conspiratorial tone made Paula look up. 'What?' Her children appeared decidedly cagey. 'Did you two *know* about any of this?'

Lachie looked alarmed. 'Well, we didn't know he was Australian, Mum. But, uh . . . Catie found some drugs in the caravan at Norseman.'

He glanced at his sister in an apologetic way. 'Honesty's the best policy, sis.'

Paula turned to Caitlin. 'Is this true?'

Her daughter nodded. 'It was when I cleaned out the caravan in Norseman. Remember?'

'Where was I?' asked Sid, looking utterly confused.

'Setting a dingo trap with Marcelo—I mean *Mark*,' replied Lachie. 'And Mum was asleep.'

'*Asleep?*' Hamish shot a reproachful look at Paula. 'So, Catie found some drugs. What happened next, son?'

Lachie shrugged. 'Well, we waited a few hours, until the end of the karaoke. Mum was already asleep . . .'

Hamish glared at Paula again.

'I went to talk to Marcelo and Catie hid in the caravan with Mum's phone,' Lachie continued. 'I told him that we knew about his stash and he should leave within a day. And that if he didn't agree, Catie was watching and would call the police right away.'

Hamish nodded with a satisfied look that said, *Atta boy!*

'You threatened *him*?' Paula waved feebly at the television, remembering the size of the drug haul. Marcelo-Mark was leading a *syndicate.*

Caitlin and Lachie looked at each other.

'We didn't want you to get hurt, Mum,' explained Lachie. 'We just wanted him to go quietly. We could see you really liked him.'

Hamish made a harrumphing sound.

'But what drugs did you find, Caitlin?' Paula asked, weak at the very thought.

'Cocaine I guess.' Caitlin didn't seem too perturbed. 'I tried to move his surfboard bag under the junk seat when I was cleaning. It was way too heavy.'

The junk seat was the storage area under the cushion-covered seat in the kitchenette. Initially a place for storing Monopoly, chess and other family games, it had soon become a repository for infrequently used items like the bicycle pump and the car jack. Lifting up its heavy wooden lid was such a chore, no one ever bothered to do it. Marcelo had brought his surfboard with him on the trip, but after their first surfing safari at Cactus Beach, he'd simply strapped the board to the ute's roof racks and stored its cover under the junk seat.

*Junk* seat indeed, Paula thought.

'I guess Mark didn't count on Caitlin's cleaning fetish.' Lachie sniggered.

Paula could well remember the children cleaning out the caravan at Norseman, after Lachie discovered her almost kissing Marcelo. She'd been trying to find a way to talk to her son, but he'd avoided her all afternoon. When her father and Marcelo had gone off to set a dingo trap, Paula had dozed off. While she was sleeping, Caitlin had obviously found more than she bargained for.

'I can't *believe* you confronted him,' Paula said.

Lachie looked pleased with himself. 'But he left, didn't he? Put on a big show about his appendix. But *we* knew what he was up to.' He smiled at Catie. 'Trying to get to Perth fast. Took his backpack full of drugs and just disappeared.'

She suddenly remembered how Marcelo had lain in the caravan all the way to Perth, supposedly in terrible pain. He'd obviously retrieved the surfboard bag and transferred its contents to his backpack. Which, on reflection, *had* seemed rather heavy as she'd helped him drag it across the hospital car park.

'But I don't understand why you didn't *say* anything.' Paula looked at her father, appealing for his support. 'Why didn't you just *tell* me or

Gramps? My God, this is becoming a *theme* in your behaviour, Caitlin. I could have reported Marcelo . . . *Mark* . . . to the police in Perth.'

And *not* made love to him in Darwin, she thought.

'But if we'd done that—' Caitlin chewed her lip—'*you* would've called off the trip and sent us back to school. We were having heaps of fun—and you looked *amazing*, Mum. You were so different. It was like we had the *real* you back.'

'Mark went quickly,' added Lachie. 'We had no idea he'd turn up again in Darwin.' He looked thoughtful. 'When he did, we got rid of him as soon as we could, by . . . you know, heading home with Dad.' Lachie shot a slightly guilty look in the direction of his father. 'We just *knew* you'd follow us, Mum.'

Paula couldn't believe what she was hearing. That her children had kept crucial information from her, about a potentially dangerous criminal in their midst, on the basis of *her* emotional fragility? Then, on Marcelo's unexpected return, they'd rescued her from his clutches by deftly playing her emotions and departing with their father? Here she was, thinking *she* was running the trip, when in fact they'd been managing *her*. They'd been manipulating *both* of them, Hamish and Paula, like marionettes.

'Yeah, why *did* Mark come back?' mused Lachie, as if he and Caitlin were the only ones in the room.

'I thought he liked Mum,' said Caitlin. 'But he actually had a wife. That's so *gross*.'

Paula's face was aflame; she could feel herself heating up, recalling how she and Marcelo had made love in the Botanic Gardens. If she'd known he'd had a wife—a beautiful Brazilian one, at that—she would have made different choices. If she'd realised he was Mark Ferris, an

Aussie fraudster from Bowden, she *never* would have wound up in the position she had.

*Would she?*

Hamish stared at Paula, his mouth working quietly, making her squirm.

'Well,' he said finally. 'This is all too much information for a boofhead like me. I need some time to think.' He walked to the kitchen and picked up his phone. 'It's Friday-night beers and Doggo's waiting. See you later.'

The front door slammed behind him.

Paula hung her head, unable to look at anyone.

After several moments' silence, Sid patted her shoulder. 'Steady on, Paula. We'll find out more soon enough. Why don't you come and have a glass of wine with me? Just one. It'll do you good.' He stood up from the sofa with some difficulty. 'I, for one, am completely bamboozled.'

Paula followed him, as if on autopilot. Then, suddenly, she turned towards the lounge room. 'Hey, kids—want to come and have Drinkypoos with us, like old times?'

Her children looked at her as if she was deranged.

'*Teen Survivor*'s on now,' said Lachie, changing the channel with the remote.

Paula felt relieved, somehow, that they were still behaving in *slightly* predictable ways.

In the kitchen, she pulled up a stool next to her father. 'Why didn't *you* say something to me, Dad?'

'Well, I didn't *know*. I thought he was a fine young man. A bit rough around the edges, maybe, but still a Brazilian gentleman.'

Paula nodded. 'He was. I mean, he wasn't Brazilian. But *some* of it had to be true. I mean, he *could* surf.'

She remembered watching Marcelo emerge, slick and shining, from the ocean.

'And he was good at jiu-jitsu,' added Sid. 'And guitar.'

Paula nodded. 'He had loads of charisma.'

'Too right.' Sid grinned. 'Remember his duet with Caitlin in Norseman? That *Dirty Dancing* song? The locals had never seen anything like it.'

Paula also recalled how jealous she'd felt watching her daughter on stage with Marcelo. Her infatuation had been all-consuming, defeating her better judgment. But her children had uncovered the truth, in part. Certainly more than *she* had.

She took the only wine she had in the house—a bottle of red for cooking—from the kitchen bench and poured two glasses. She hadn't consumed any alcohol since swearing off it in Perth, not even at Christmas and New Year. But this series of revelations was enough to push anyone off the wagon, she decided.

'I wish Jamie was here,' said Paula, thinking about her sister in Coffs Harbour, staying with Rick's family for the rest of the summer. Had Jamie seen the nightly news too?

Sid took a long draught of wine, then suddenly snorted over his glass. Red liquid sprayed out of his nose and across the bench as he doubled over with laughter.

'Fools, that's what we've been. Prize-winning turkeys, plucked and roasted.'

'The police won't think it's funny, Dad. We're going to have to tell them *everything,* you know, or they might think we're accomplices or something.'

Sid shook his head. 'Frank must've worked out *weeks* ago that we're clean as a whistle. You need to have intent to be an accomplice, or be taking a cut of the action. We were all just bystanders, you know, taken for a ride.'

*In my case literally.*

'But what about Lachie and Catie?' she protested. 'I mean, they *knew* about the drugs. But they didn't say anything, to protect me from my own emotions. Honestly.'

*How have I so completely misjudged my children? When did I stop seeing them for what they truly are? They are agents, in their lives and mine. Making decisions that have affected the whole family.*

The stark realisation of their independence rammed through her.

'But they're still just *kids*, Paula.' Her father topped up her glass. 'And I think that matters in a court of law.'

'I hope so,' she said, drawing a deep mouthful. 'Because they've made some pretty far-reaching choices on behalf of all of us.'

*And I've made some really stupid ones*, she thought. *Even stupider than Hamish.*

*I'm the one who needs to be tested for STDs.*

She bowed her head.

Her father stood up from the bench. 'It'll be alright, Paula, I can feel it in my waters.' He gave her an encouraging squeeze. 'Now let's chop the carrots, eh? It's our turn to do dinner tonight.'

The realities of life remained, even amid the drama.

*

The counsellor at the sexual health clinic, a bearded hipster named Terence, explained about the HIV window period.

'It can be anywhere from nine days to six months,' he said, passing her an information booklet. 'It just depends on your body and the

HIV test that's used. The point being, you can be infected with HIV for a while and you *won't* test positive.'

Paula blanched. 'You mean, I have to wait six months for a test?'

'No, not that long.' Terence checked his notes. 'In light of your recent infection risk, we'll do a physical and get some bloods done to investigate things like chlamydia, the hepatitis family, syphilis. Your unprotected intercourse was how long ago?'

'Just over two weeks.'

'Then we could do the HIV test in three months.'

Paula nodded, her eyes brimming.

What the *hell* had she done?

Taken her life in her hands, for temporary physical pleasure. Earning herself the longest three months of her life.

Terence said kindly, 'I know how you feel—the waiting game is *awful.* But there's just no point testing for HIV now.' He removed a consent form from a folder. 'Here, read this and sign it. Then we'll get the other blood work done.'

She scanned the document, unable to focus on the words swimming before her eyes.

She marked the page with a biro.

'Any questions?' Terence asked.

'My husband . . .' Paula's voice broke.

*Doesn't even know what I've done.*

The counsellor nodded, his expression sympathetic. 'You need to assume the worst and avoid sexual relations until you've had the results of the HIV test. You may well be infectious.'

Terence opened a drawer and removed a brochure, placing it on the table in front of her: *Talking to your partner about your HIV status.*

'It's a difficult conversation,' he said. 'But you've got to have it.'

His pager beeped from his belt.

'I'll take you across to pathology now. As soon as the results are in, I'll call you. It usually takes one or two weeks. Here's my business card, if you need to talk in the meantime.'

Paula looked at the shiny blue rectangle.

*Terence D. Abbott. Senior Counsellor, Melbourne Sexual Health Clinic*

When they reached the door, Terence turned. 'I know it's not much help, Mrs McInnes, but there are plenty of people going through *exactly* what you're going through right now.'

Paula doubted that somehow.

*

A fortnight later, as she was preparing dinner, Paula's mobile rang.

It was the clinic.

She darted down the hallway and into her bedroom, closing the door behind her.

'Mrs McInnes, it's Terence Abbott here.'

She couldn't even greet him properly.

'The final blood results are in and it's good news. You're all clear.'

'Oh, thank God.' The air rushed out of her lungs.

'You still have to do the HIV test,' he continued. 'But in the absence of any other infection, it's looking much less likely now. You can call me in a month or so to make the booking.'

'Thank you so much, Terence,' she said, ending the call.

She stood for a moment, shell-shocked, before walking slowly back to the kitchen.

'What, Paula?' asked her father, looking up from the casserole he was stirring on the stove.

Her telephone rang again.

'Hang on, Dad,' she said, lifting the phone to her ear. 'Terence?'

A young male voice asked, 'Is that Paula McInnes?'

'Yes.'

'Inspector Andrew Holmes here, WA Police. Do you have a moment?'

She hesitated, then said, 'Go ahead.'

'Earlier today one of our officers at Mandurah apprehended an unlicensed seventeen-year-old woman driving a yellow Toyota Echo registered in your husband's name. We tried calling the mobile attached to the registration, but the number's inactive. Your name was listed as a nominated operator.'

*Her* hatchback?

Hadn't Hamish said it had broken down in Perth and couldn't be fixed?

'We assumed it was stolen, particularly as the young lady in question comes from a . . . complex background,' the officer continued. 'But she says your husband gave it to her, so we're calling to check her story.'

Paula tried to make sense of it.

'The young lady's name is Lisel Fogarty. Do you know her?'

*Lisel.*

Paula's mouth dropped open. 'Uh, yes . . . we do.'

'Did either you or your husband give her the car to keep?'

Her hands were trembling. 'We were travelling through WA in December. The car was old . . .'

'Did you *give* her the car?' The officer sounded like he had pressing business elsewhere.

Paula exhaled. 'Yes, my husband did.'

'Okay. Well, Lisel was caught driving it without any parental supervision, and the vehicle registration should have been transferred by now.' He sounded irritable. 'But I'll take that up with her mother. At least we know it's not stolen.' The officer thanked Paula and hung up.

Paula stood staring at her telephone.

'Everything okay?' asked Sid.

'Not really, Dad.' She steadied herself against the island bench. 'But it will be.'

*

Hamish knocked three times, then poked his head around their bedroom door. He'd been sleeping in the backyard for well over a month now—first in a swag, then in the caravan—and she'd just started considering letting him back in the house.

'I'm sorry,' he said. 'Did I wake you?'

'No,' she said, pulling her bathrobe tightly across her chest.

He had that bleary look she despised; the one he got after three or four Friday-night beers with Doggo. Or five or six.

'Want to come out on the veranda for a cuppa?' he asked.

She shook her head.

'Come on . . .' He stepped into the bedroom.

'No.' She held up the flat of her hand, like she used to when their children were toddlers.

'What?' he asked. 'It's just a cup of a tea.'

'Hamish, it's not happening. Not now, not ever.'

'What do you mean?' He searched her face. 'We've been alright these past few weeks, haven't we? Things are almost back on track.'

'No they're not.' She waved her mobile phone at him. 'I heard from the Western Australian police earlier tonight. They found Lisel driving our hatchback.'

Hamish's mouth opened and closed, then opened again.

'You weren't *ever* going to tell me that you met Lisel in Perth, were you?'

Hamish closed his eyes. 'Look, it was her *mother* I met, not Lisel. It's a long, ugly story that I—I'm ashamed of. And I really didn't think you needed to hear it.'

She nodded. 'Just like I didn't think *you* needed to hear about *my* indiscretions, which at the very least I limited to a grown man. Do you think that's an environment of trust for our relationship?'

He stood silent for a moment. 'Did you and Mark Ferris actually . . .'

She watched him watching her, wanting to know so badly.

'Yes, we did. Only once.' Her heart was battering at her chest. 'But I'll remember it for the rest of my life.'

Hamish's nostrils flared, like he'd just been punched in the stomach.

'We shouldn't be here, Hamish,' she continued. 'It's only because of what happened in Darwin that we are. It was Christmas, the kids came home with you, we almost fell back into our old life.' She looked around their bedroom, then back at Hamish. 'But it's over.'

'I've been trying really hard.'

'I'm not denying that.'

They stood looking at each other.

'I'm not going anywhere,' he said suddenly. 'This is my home too.'

'Then *I* will,' she said. '*I'll* stay in the caravan. You can stay in our bedroom. Tomorrow, I'll call a solicitor. We can settle things amicably and move on. We should have done it years ago.'

'You're not serious, are you?'

'Deadly.'

His eyes narrowed. 'You'll regret this, Paula. I'll make sure you don't get a cent more than you deserve.'

*Showing your true colours now.*

'And I'd pay good money *not* to have to live with you, Hamish.'

She walked to the bedroom door, then turned. 'We've got two great kids, Hamish. You said that in Darwin. If nothing else, let's not make it really nasty, for their sakes. We can tell them tomorrow, or some other time when we've both cooled down a bit.' She saw a glint of recognition in his eyes.

She shut the door behind her and crept out into the lounge room, past the sleeping form of her father. The two kids were already in bed, or so it seemed.

*They're in their bedrooms and quiet*, Paula corrected herself, *which may not equate to sleep. I'm never going to assume anything about those two again.*

She stole down the stairs and out into the backyard. Then she opened the caravan door for the first time in a month.

*This is it. I'm cutting my losses and starting again at almost forty.*

Fear flooded through her.

She climbed into the caravan and looked around.

*The last night I was in here, Marcelo was too.*

*Mark*, she corrected herself.

Everything looked the same as it always had. Although Farken Frank and his forensic team had presumably combed through it; whatever her father had put in the freezer, Frank knew about it too.

She'd been meaning to check it for weeks, but Hamish's presence in the caravan had given her a good reason to avoid it.

She crouched down and opened the fridge, flipping up the small silver door to the freezer. Seeing nothing, she felt inside, reaching back as far as she could.

Her fingers closed around something taped to the rear wall. She pulled it free. A small white envelope, with a note scrawled across it.

*Paula,*

*Winnings from my one-dollar bet on the Melbourne Cup first four.*

*I did a dummy run with a buck of my own before placing Shirl's bet.*

*Split it with your sister.*

*Love, Dad. xx*

Carefully, she opened the envelope.

The reverse side of a bank cheque, with words penned neatly in her father's hand: *Please pay Paula McInnes.*

His signature, followed by his full name printed in capitals below.

She turned over the cheque.

For the amount of $969,406.60.

# 23

Winter was Paula's favourite time of year in Melbourne. The season of hot pies and Aussie Rules, morning frosts and Sunday afternoon movies, Ugg boots and flannelette pyjamas.

And this particular winter, it was her season of second chances.

In April, she'd been declared HIV negative.

It was a moment of liberation so transcendent, she'd floated above the earth for days afterwards. Unbothered by trivialities, grateful beyond words.

By July, the papers confirming her separation from Hamish were finalised and lodged.

Come August, with the police investigations almost over, she was poised to cash her father's Melbourne Cup winnings.

The post-arrest investigations had spanned six months from February, with the police grilling Paula about every minute detail of Mark Ferris's movements during the time he'd travelled with them. All members of the family, even Jamie, had been subjected to multiple interviews with numerous officers, mostly individually, but sometimes as a group. For Paula, one of the most uncomfortable sessions had involved recounting to three stern-faced detectives, including Farken Frank—whose real title was Detective Senior Sergeant Frances Reid—exactly what she'd done with Mark Ferris in the Darwin Botanic Gardens.

On the final day of questioning, Frank and Paula sat in the interview room across a bare wooden table. At least two police officers had been present at every other interview, but this time, Frank was doing most of the talking. Finally explaining to Paula how Mark Ferris had gone about targeting her family.

'Mark Ferris is an experienced conman who went to Walkerville RSL on Melbourne Cup Day last year to scope out the mob of susceptible seniors there,' said Frank. 'It's one of the oldest tricks in the book, Mrs McInnes. Whenever there's a vulnerable bunch of people drinking together on a public holiday like Anzac Day, Australia Day or Melbourne Cup, it's a recipe for success for cons like Ferris.'

'Ferris saw you and your party arrive, noticing three elderly people in your group—Sid, Barry and Shirl—and the conspicuous absence of a father figure. He decided to target Caitlin, the teenage girl of the party, as an entrée to meeting you. He rightly recognised you to be the family decision-maker.'

Frank removed his cap and placed it on the table.

'Ferris's reconnaissance was going nowhere in particular until Barry and Shirl had a lucky windfall, care of your Dad's online bet. This alone made Ferris push for an invitation to the barbecue at the Gillespie's home later that night. There Ferris learned about your family's travel plans, along a route that broadly coincided with some of his own pressing business. He was well aware of the existing police surveillance operation along the Nullarbor, so he did everything he could to get invited along with you.'

'But why?' asked Paula. 'Why didn't he just hitchhike or hire a car?'

'Travelling with a family made him less conspicuous than if he'd travelled alone, and less susceptible to random stops,' Frank explained. 'It gave him the opportunity to do a series of pick-ups and drop-offs in network locations, and come and go from your party as he pleased. He did several weeks' work in Perth, for example, before rejoining you in Darwin. And he was able to get some pocket money from you, Mrs McInnes.'

She winced, remembering the money she'd given Marcelo in Perth and Darwin—without him even having to ask for it.

*How didn't I see it?* she wondered, disgusted with herself.

'Don't feel too bad,' Frank said, intuiting her response. 'Ferris has been a person of interest to police for years. He's an expert at getting people to part with their cash with tear-jerker tales of dead mothers, sick grandmothers, needy sisters. He's been stranded before, lost, terminally ill; one time he told someone he was a returned serviceman with post-traumatic stress disorder from the Gulf War. The bloke's brazen; we discovered that even Barry and Shirl gave him a thousand dollars on the night Ferris stayed in their home. For an animal rescue centre in Brazil, he told them.'

*Brazen, not a Brazilian.*

Paula felt foolish all over again.

'You're not the first to believe Ferris's stories, but we certainly hope you're the last. We just didn't have enough evidence to nab him before now. We needed Hamish for that.' Frank chuckled appreciatively.

'But how did Hamish lead you to Mark Ferris?' It was something

Hamish hadn't stopped skiting about, but Paula couldn't quite piece it together.

'Well, an initial intelligence report was filed on your husband in Adelaide,' Frank replied. 'Police there interviewed a Belgian backpacker and a youth hostel staffer, who described Hamish's erratic behaviour, his argumentative demeanour and a suspiciously heavy bag.'

Frank refilled Paula's glass of water, before helping himself.

'After leaving Adelaide, Hamish managed to drift further onto our police radar by being spotted asleep on the steps of an abandoned roadhouse at Yalata,' he continued. 'We ran a quick background check on the licence plates of the car he was driving and a few other cross-checks, like ringing his workplace. We found out he was supposed to be at home in Glen Waverley on sick leave—which really got us going.' Frank smiled. 'I've been based at Yalata with Operation Dingo for the past year, so I was the one dispatched to learn more about Hamish. He seemed pretty harmless to me, but I kept track of him for a few days. It was a throwaway reference he made to a "Brazilian ninja"—travelling with *you*, Mrs McInnes—that sparked my interest. With a bit more digging, we found a photo of this individual—taken by a waitress at the Norseman bar during a karaoke event—and matched it to a file image of Mark Ferris. At that point, headquarters deployed further undercover resources.'

He shrugged. 'Problem was, that very day Mark Ferris disappeared in Perth. This left us with nothing much except the "friendship" I'd cultivated with Hamish. So we started monitoring activity to and from your husband's mobile, to help us locate your family and Ferris, but quickly became aware that Hamish had been hospitalised in Perth with alcohol poisoning.'

'*What*?' said Paula. 'My God.'

This was news to her; Hamish hadn't revealed this at their dinner in Darwin, nor any time since.

*Just another thing he was never going to tell me.*

'From the tenor of his conversations with his friend Trevor Dogger, we guessed he'd try to fly to Darwin in pursuit of you,' continued Frank. 'But if he did that, I would have lost my connection with Hamish, and he was our only link to your family and, therefore, Ferris.'

Frank folded his hands behind his head and leaned back, stretching. 'In an operation like this one, Mrs McInnes, the key element is the capacity of the undercover officer to gain the confidence of the target. That's a difficult trick to pull off once, and almost impossible twice. We got lucky the first time with Hamish at Yalata. If I'd let him fly to Darwin, we would've been forced to introduce a new undercover officer there—and we probably wouldn't have gotten *that* lucky a second time. Do you follow me?'

Paula nodded, feeling chuffed to be receiving such a detailed briefing.

'We had to distract Hamish from flying and try to convince him to hire *me* to drive him to Darwin,' Frank continued. 'So we sent him a fake "broadcast message" from Yalata Nullarbor Tours, offering discount bus fares to Darwin, hoping like buggery he'd take the bait.' Frank laughed. 'Lucky for everyone, he did. I spent five days driving him up there, then stayed with him almost ten days in Darwin. Sure enough, Ferris popped up again in the company of your family. Hamish was the first to alert us.'

Paula cocked her head.

'So you knew exactly who Mark Ferris was, when I asked you to drive him back to Perth?'

'Yes ma'am.' Frank nodded. 'And so did the officer who followed you and Ferris into the Darwin Botanic Gardens, posing as a ranger.'

Paula's mouth dropped open. 'That ranger was a policeman too?'

'One of our Territorian colleagues. We were monitoring Ferris's phone activity by then, and we knew he'd made a plan to meet you in the Botanic Gardens. We couldn't leave you alone with him, without some means of back-up.'

Paula couldn't quite believe it: she'd had unprotected sex with a conman, but had been covered in other ways.

'We were planning to nab Ferris in Darwin,' continued Frank, 'but then we got wind of the fact he was going to try to leave the country with his wife, Liliana, another person of interest in Operation Dingo. So we waited to get them both at Perth airport instead.'

*Liliana.*

Paula had smarted about it for months, turning scarlet whenever she thought of that heady afternoon. Calling herself names in the shower, when driving the car, before falling asleep at night.

*Ignoramus. Pathetic. Idiota.*

Frank drained his glass of water. 'Any other questions? This is our last interview, so now's the time to ask.'

Paula nodded. 'I've been thinking about his family. Was *any* of what he told me real?'

She'd lain awake countless nights, remembering the heart-rending tale of Marcelo's mother, murdered in the *favela*, his wayward brother Lucas, his grieving father and younger brother languishing on the farm.

Frank twirled a pen between his fingertips.

'Look, it's hard to distinguish truth from fiction with players like Ferris. He probably drew on some of his past—that's why he's so convincing. What we *do* know is that he grew up on a run-down property on Adelaide's fringes, the middle kid in a family of three boys. His mother was a heroin addict who died young, when Ferris was eight. His dad was a no-hoper, really. Unemployed, lived on welfare, roughed up the kids after a few drinks.'

Paula winced.

'*Don't* feel sorry for Ferris,' Frank cautioned. 'We've all got complex backgrounds. But most of us don't go around rorting people, do we?'

He closed his file, preparing to conclude.

'I . . . I do have one last question,' Paula ventured, suddenly nervous.

'Fire away.'

With her stomach roiling, she finally asked what she'd been desperate to know for months. 'Why do you think Mark Ferris had *sex* with me?'

Frank looked at her evenly. 'Well, it wasn't necessary to the success of his delivery schedule, that's for sure. My colleagues and I haven't really seen this before, Mrs McInnes, which leads me to conclude that only *you* can answer that question. Presumably he fancied you.'

Paula closed her eyes for a moment, relief flooding through her.

And then, suddenly, she began to cry, with the sheer release of knowing that not *everything* had been an illusion.

'I'm sorry, Sergeant,' she said, fumbling in her handbag for a tissue.

'Call me Frank.'

He stood up and passed her a neatly pressed handkerchief from the top pocket of his shirt.

'It's been dreadful,' she said, wiping her eyes with it. 'Not just the investigations, but the separation from Hamish.'

Frank nodded sympathetically. 'Been through it myself.'

She'd ceased all contact with Hamish in February and commenced negotiations through lawyers. Seventeen years of marriage, reduced to a clinical barrage of emails beginning with the words '*Acting on behalf of my client . . .*'

It sickened Paula to the core. Communicating with her husband through a third party. Fighting for fifty per cent of their shared assets. Able to access her children for only *half* of the week. Spending a good portion of the other half dwelling on how *she'd* contributed to the demise of their marriage by so willingly losing herself in the role of mother, to the detriment of their relationship. By normalising that process as *just something you do*, a natural extension of parental commitment.

She'd tried to look after herself in the months since the separation; exercising regularly, eating well, eschewing alcohol. Leaning on her sister Jamie for support whenever she felt particularly down, in the days and weeks when she simply couldn't feel *anything*. And sometimes, when the feelings flooded out, weeping on her sister's shoulder, grieving for the life she'd lost with Hamish. Regretting all the petty omissions and overt lies that had gradually eroded the respect in their marriage and, ultimately, led to senseless infidelities.

'Did you and Hamish try counselling?' Frank prompted.

'For a couple of months, when we first separated. It helped me recognise my role in the whole sordid mess. It wasn't just big, bad Hamish, you know?' She smiled weakly. 'But after six counselling sessions, I realised I couldn't take him back. Hamish lied to me shamelessly, only telling the truth when he was caught out. He had an online affair for almost a year with a woman he believed to be seventeen years old, then slept with someone he thought was her at the very time he was supposedly trying to win me back.'

Paula shook her head. 'Hamish has always been a man of

contradictions, but I couldn't accept *that.* He kept telling me he'd changed, but I couldn't see it. It's actually very hard to change, isn't it?'

Frank nodded. 'My wife and I couldn't manage it.'

Paula waited for him to elaborate, but when he didn't, she said, 'As soon as Hamish worked out I wasn't going to try again, he got *really* angry.' She sensed that Frank probably already knew this. 'He basically shut down the counselling and we went straight into mediation, trying to get our financial settlement sorted. It took us three months to agree on terms, and it's not over yet.'

She looked at Frank. 'I guess I imagined that separation would be a new beginning, but even when the divorce comes through, I'll *never* be free of Hamish. We have to see each other every week, dropping off the kids. It's painful *every* time.'

She closed her eyes again, fighting back tears.

'It takes a few years,' said Frank, in a consoling tone. 'But it *does* get better. At first you're angry, then you move towards acceptance. And then, believe it or not, one day you get to indifference. That's when you can see your former spouse in the company of a new partner and not even *care.*'

'Well, I'm not there yet,' she said. 'The kids are coping better than I am.'

Caitlin and Lachie seemed to be adapting well to their new visitation schedule; staying with Paula four nights a week, then with Hamish for three, plus alternating weekends. At first, Paula feared they might push back, seeing their father alone in his rented two-bedroom apartment in Springvale. But they'd been excited about sleeping in bunks again, and after their first few visits with Hamish, they seemed quite resigned to the split.

'You know what Lachie said when he came back from visiting Hamish the first time? "Don't freak out, Mum. We know why it's happened. Some people just can't be happy together." So now I'm getting relationship advice from my teenage son.'

Frank laughed. 'Children have more insight than we think. They're more resilient, too. They'll survive, Paula. And so will *you*.'

Paula had concluded that almost *everything* was survivable. Sexual emancipation, then patent mortification at the hands of an Australian conman and drug smuggler. A lengthy police investigation. Separation from her husband, counselling and mediation. And now, only now, the beginnings of a subtle reversion to normal life. Something far less dramatic, something more ordinary, and the relief and grief that accompanied that transition.

She'd survived it all.

Frank smiled at her again. 'I'm afraid it's time to wrap up.'

'I know,' she said, standing up from the interview table. 'Thank you, Frank, it's been good to talk. I guess we won't be meeting each other again.'

'Not in a policing context, I hope.' He opened the door for her. 'But you never know when our paths might cross. Stranger things have happened.'

'They certainly have.' She laughed wryly.

He held out his hand to shake hers. 'It's been a pleasure, Paula.'

'For me too,' she said. 'Goodbye, Frank.'

*

On the morning the bank cleared her cheque for almost a million dollars, she sent a text to her sister.

*Come to mine tonight for a little celebration @ 7.30?*

Jamie responded instantly. *I'll be there. What are we celebrating?*

*Second chances*, Paula texted back.

Later, they gathered in her lounge room: Paula, Jamie, their father, Caitlin and Lachlan. It was nothing unusual, just an ordinary Friday evening in the winter school holidays, exactly the same type of gathering they'd convened weekly since her separation from Hamish. Jamie had been so supportive, popping around every few days with a casserole or some other home-cooked meal that Paula couldn't be bothered preparing herself.

'Jamie!' Sid greeted his daughter with a kiss. 'Come and have a drink!' He disappeared into the kitchen.

Jamie watched him go, then whispered to Paula, 'What's up with him?'

Paula pretended to be mystified, knowing full well that Sid was anticipating the moment when Jamie discovered she was almost half a million dollars richer.

Paula felt a lump in her throat as she remembered how their father had staunchly rebuffed her attempts to give the cheque back to him.

'The money's for you and Jamie,' he'd insisted. 'I would've got two cheques, but I wanted to hold almost a million bucks in my hand. But don't cash it until the divorce is through, I don't want you splitting it with Hamish.'

Paula had followed her father's advice, but chosen not to reveal her solicitor's. Namely, his opinion that Hamish's legal team would probably mount an argument that Sid's windfall had existed *prior* to the divorce settlement, and therefore claim an entitlement for Hamish.

Her father didn't need to know that, Paula had resolved. Not yet, anyway.

'How are you guys?' asked Jamie, noticing her niece and nephew on the sofa. She stooped to kiss them.

'Er, good,' said Lachlan, dodging the kiss.

'Hi Aunty Jamie,' said Caitlin, standing up. 'It's the season finale of *Teen Survivor* tonight, sorry.'

'I know, no time for Aunty Jamie. Off you go then. I'll bring your cousins around on Saturday though, okay?'

The children nodded, then headed to the TV room.

Watching them leave, Paula's chest tightened. *Good on you, kids,* she wanted to call out.

*Troopers, the pair of you.*

*I love you more than infinity.*

Jamie sidled up to Paula.

'Are you okay? You sad about Hamish?'

'No. Well, sort of. It's just the usual.' Paula smiled. 'I've got something to show you, Jamie.'

Their father returned from the kitchen holding a bottle of champagne and three crystal flutes, the best she had. He poured Jamie a glass, filled his own, then waved the bottle at Paula.

'Surely you'll have one tonight, Pokey?'

With the exception of the night they'd watched Marcelo on the nightly news, Paula had avoided alcohol entirely and felt all the better for it. Her father, however, had resumed his 'medicinal' consumption, as he termed it.

'Okay,' she said. 'As long as it's just one.'

She watched her father fill her glass, then raise his own. 'To you, Jamie!'

He beamed and touched his glass against hers.

'Hang on, this isn't about me,' said Jamie, puzzled. 'We're celebrating Paula's new start, aren't we?'

Paula smiled. 'We are. And this is part of it.'

She reached into her handbag and removed a white envelope, then passed it to her sister.

'Over the years we've had a bit of . . . *tension* about money.'

Jamie looked taken aback. 'Well, I—'

'No more of that,' Paula interjected. 'Just open it.'

'What is it?'

'Ask Dad,' replied Paula. '*He* earned it. I got exactly the same amount.'

Jamie tore open the envelope and stared at the cheque. 'Is this a joke?'

Paula shook her head.

'It's not . . .' Jamie's face was ashen. '*Drug* money, is it?'

Sid chuckled. 'Almost as bad,' he said. 'The devil gambling. Remember what your mother used to say? Money can't buy happiness, but it sure takes the edge off.'

Paula laughed, remembering more of her mother's words:

*Better to be unhappy in a Mercedes-Benz than unhappy on a bus.*

To which Paula had always responded, I'd rather be *happy.*

Her father smiled at Jamie. 'Hopefully *that* will take the edge off.'

'Almost five hundred thousand dollars?' Jamie squeaked, stunned.

Then suddenly she launched herself at them. They hugged and laughed together, until the tears came, streaking down their faces even as they laughed some more.

Finally Jamie stepped back and, still holding their hands, said, 'Rick won't believe it. How did you win so *much*?'

'I finally put a few bucks on the Melbourne Cup,' said Sid. 'There were seven pre-race favourites, I didn't back *any* of them—and not one of them ended up in the first four, either. Turns out my magic formula works.' He laughed. 'Took me a few weeks to calm down enough to collect the cheque. They kept calling me on my mobile. Most people would've collected the money real quick, but we were on the road, so I had to wait until Perth.'

'Then it's really *your* money, Dad,' objected Jamie.

Sid groaned. 'Your sister said exactly the same thing. Listen up, girls. I'm on my way to eighty now. I've lived my three score years and ten. I don't need much money, I just want to have you two nearby, with your families. I'm happy in the caravan out the back.'

He smiled mischeviously. 'Well, there is *one* thing I'd like.'

Paula and Jamie exchanged a look.

'I'd *really* like to finish our trip, Paula.' Sid swallowed more champagne. 'I mean, we bypassed Queensland and New South Wales.' He looked at Jamie. 'Why don't we *all* go on a road trip next summer holidays, heading north? You can bring the kids and Rick, Jamie. Give yourselves a long overdue break, eh?' His eyes were shiny with excitement. 'And Catie can bring that friend of hers, Amy. They sure kept Australia Post busy last summer. And maybe I'll finally get to trap that bloody dingo, too. They've got them on Fraser Island, you know, dozens of them.' He shook his head. 'I never got to check that trap at Norseman . . .'

'They're a *protected species* at Fraser, Dad,' Jamie said, looking alarmed. 'But, sure, it's a deal . . . as long as we don't pick up any backpackers along the way.' She nudged Paula with her elbow.

Paula smiled, remembering the gigantic fig tree on a rainy wet-season afternoon in Darwin. The sweltering heat, the lush tropical beauty, the indescribable physical intensity. In those seventeen minutes of pleasure, she'd recovered the sexual confidence rocked by seventeen years of marriage to Hamish. In fact, Paula had finally conceded that Mark Ferris's parting words to her in Darwin had been spot on. That saying goodbye to Marcelo—or, at least, her fantasy of him—ultimately mattered far less than everything else she'd claimed for herself on that journey.

'No backpackers,' she agreed, blushing a little.

Jamie winked. 'Hey, I saw Mark Ferris on TV. He's *drop-dead gorgeous.* Believe me, I understand *why* it happened. Would've done the same myself, given the opportunity.'

They laughed together. The kind of laughter only sisters could share, born of decades of mutual understanding.

Her sister, her confidante and conspirator. Her best friend still.

'Cheers to that,' said Paula, clinking her glass against Jamie's. 'And to Dad's outrageous fortune. At least *something* good came out of Walkerville.'

Having watched several divorced friends struggling financially, with no fortuitous windfall to assist them, Paula knew how lucky she was. While she'd never be free of financial challenges, her father's gift would be a huge help.

'What are you going to *do* with all that money?' asked Jamie, in hushed tones, as if it was a secret.

'Pay off most of my new mortgage,' said Paula. 'And retrain as a midwife.'

It was the first time she'd articulated the idea out loud. 'I've had enough of endings in aged care. I need some new beginnings again.'

'Good for you,' said Jamie. 'You've been toying with that for years.'

Paula nodded. 'And I'd love to do some more travel.' She pointed to the scrapbook on the coffee table, its brown cover torn in several places now, sporting a faded photograph of Hamish and Paula in their first year of marriage.

Jamie bent down to read the title, handwritten by a much younger Paula.

*Our Adventure Scrapbook.*

Paula's eyes began to smart. 'It's a big world out there. So many places to go, things to see. It was *never* going to happen with Hamish.'

'Oh, Paula.' Jamie pulled her sister into a hug. '*I'll* come with you. Rick and I will be able to pay off our mortgage now, so *I* can be your travel buddy for some of it. Rick's a bit of a homebody, and the kids are old enough to cope by themselves. We could do girls' stuff . . . but overseas.'

Paula stared at her sister, surprised and delighted.

'Count me in too,' added Sid, putting an arm around each of his daughters. 'Never been abroad in my life, but I'd *love* to see a grizzly bear.'

'Oh, for goodness' sake,' said Jamie. 'Just stick to dingos for now, Dad.'

Sid chuckled and raised his glass again. 'Let's have a little toast, eh? To endings and beginnings. Let's end our trip Downunder properly this summer, then we'll see what beginnings we can dream up around the globe. The world awaits us, girls.'

They touched their glasses together one more time.

*Beginnings and endings*, Paula thought, *false starts and surprise finishes.*

There had been so many over the past ten months. Some of them had come crashing into her life, like meteors from outer space; others had been cultivated, self-inflicted even, over many years.

And yet all of them now seemed connected by a curious synergy barrelling inevitably towards this moment, in which she found herself standing in the kitchen with her father and her sister, relishing the present and planning for the future. Her children in the next room, masters of their own universe, raucously debating the carefully constructed stories of 'reality' TV.

In everyday life, Paula knew, the issues were more complex, the stakes much higher. Her future would never be the glossy stuff of escapist fantasies, a neat set of challenges easily resolved by the season's end.

It would be solid and real, painful and delightful, sometimes unpredictable but always worth the struggle.

And for the first time ever, she felt confident that she wouldn't just slip back into survival mode, treading water against the currents of her existence.

It might take time, Paula knew, but she'd *never* just survive, ever again.

She'd thrive.

# Acknowledgements

My heartfelt thanks to the extremely talented team at Allen & Unwin, in particular Jane Palfreyman, Siobhán Cantrill, Ali Lavau, Christa Munns, Ann Lennox, Andy Palmer, Marie Slocombe and Amy Milne.

A huge thank you to the lovely friends in my life who read early drafts of this work: Kim Healey, Jodie Thomson, Sarah Barrett, Rachael McLennan, Michelle Taylor, Debba Reed, Natasha Brain, Ellen Fanning, Tati Guedes, Louise Rosenthal, Tegan Molony, Ewa Wojkowska, Sarah Bramwell, Gaile Pearce, Amanda Thomas—thank you for your incredible gift of time, energy and insights, all of which helped me to craft a better novel.

For their technical and editorial feedback, I am especially grateful to Dr Connie Diakos and Senior Sergeant Danny Russell of Tasmania Police, who went way beyond the call of duty or friendship. Huge thanks and love. And speaking of love, special honours are due to Professor Ibu Dokter Jan Lingard, who deserves post-nominals for her efforts. Amazing stuff, Booster.

Thanks to Colin Healey, Simone Eley and Robbie Smyth, for specific geographic feedback; to Jack Manning Bancroft and Dr Ben Scambary, for their Indigenous-related input; to the late Sidney H. Smith, and the late Charles Keogh, both of whom helped inspire the character of Sid; to Jason Dick for his valuable time and expertise; to Don Norris, whose cheery demeanour always makes technology seem much more interesting; and to Suzanne Kent, for being who she is.

Thanks also to Beverley and Richard Higgins, for their strategic child-minding and unceasing generosity, as well as to Cate Campbell, Margaret Bale and their families, for their ongoing support.

Virginia Lloyd, my agent and friend, once again offered careful reading, perspective and support at every stage of the process.

To my mother, Lesley, you continue to inspire me, even from afar. And to my sisters, Amanda and Melissa, and their families—I am so grateful for your presence in my life and useful feedback. Thanks to the Jack and Jones families, too, for their helpful barracking (and not too much heckling).

Finally, I thank Stuart, my husband, for his love and support—editorial, material and emotional.

And to my children—Oliver, Skye and Luke—you keep me focused. I love you more than infinity.

## Praise for *The Mothers' Group*

'Fresh and compelling . . . The prose is sharp, the characterisation even sharper . . . Higgins looks at the difficult moment of becoming parents with an unflinching but powerful humanity . . . A top-shelf novel about contemporary Australian life.'

*The Weekend Australian*

'. . . an enthralling read. Be prepared to burn the midnight oil, as it is impossible to put down.'

*Sunday Herald Sun*

'. . . a compelling insight into the modern family . . . it's hard to put down because it's just so real . . . I almost felt part of the group, getting to know them and sharing their inner thoughts, feeling their pain, frustration and confusion.'

*WriteNoteReviews.com*

'An insightful and sensitively written novel that will resonate with many new (and less new) parents.'

*The Age*

'I'm completely blown away . . . Make yourself comfortable before you start reading this book because you won't be putting it down . . . *The Mothers' Group* is the kind of book that stays with you long after you've read the final pages. Buy it, share it, and fall in love with it like I did.'

*The Bub Hub*

'. . . a compelling insight into the modern family . . . Honest and perceptive . . . the kind of book that will make the reader forget that dinner needs to be cooked. It's hard to put down because it's just so real . . . I almost felt part of the group, getting to know them and sharing their inner thoughts, feeling their pain, frustration and confusion. For mothers of all ages, all experiences—read this . . . It's a book I will read again and I'm looking forward to reading more from Higgins.'

*WriteNoteReviews.com*

'. . . this is a story that immediately rings true when it comes to real-life motherhood . . . This book grabbed me immediately because I've been there . . . I've felt the pain and the joy and shared the experiences with my own eclectic group of first-time mums . . . I felt like I was on the same level as the character—sharing in their world. Then before you even realise it you get pulled into the storyline and you can't put it down. *Brilliant.*'

*The Truth About Mummy*

'I never just stop and read. But this book had me hook, line and sinker . . . I loved it . . . It is funny, sad, thought-provoking and has fantastic twists in the plot that make you keep on reading.'

*Woog's World*

'Six mothers brought together by their babies and almost driven apart by unforeseen developments and events. I joined their group for two days and got the inside scoop on all the stuff we don't always talk about as mothers. Taboo subjects, controversial debates, differences of opinion. I could not put the book down and mourned the loss of my new-found friends when I turned to the last page . . . This is a book that any mother can relate to, whether she has a mothers' group or not.'

*Crash Test Mummy*

'. . . an engrossing story which slowly reveals each character's multi-layered background before leading to an incident that shatters them all.'

*The Weekend West*

'*The Mothers' Group* provides enough "aha" moments of recognition to make even the most sleep-deprived mum smile. And I should know: I read it while juggling my three-month-old daughter.'

*Australian Bookseller & Publisher*

'. . . an impressive fiction debut . . . An insightful portrayal of first-time parenthood, relationships and friendships, this novel makes for compelling reading.'

*Book'd Out*

'This heartfelt debut novel explores how challenging and bewildering motherhood can be . . . and how much empathy, reassurance and wisdom can be found in the shared experience of a support group.'

*Better Homes and Gardens*

'A fascinating insight into modern motherhood.'

*Weekend Gold Coast Bulletin*

'There is so much to love in this first novel . . . it is sensitively and incisively written. It is the perfect bookclub choice for new mothers—full of issues that will ring very true for them.'

*Manly Daily*

'. . . an unflinching and compelling portrait of the modern family.'

*Burnie Advocate*